Four Walls and A Leaky Roof

Brenda Meisels

ISBN: 149129891X
ISBN 13: 9781491298916

Four Walls And A Leaky Roof

⌒⊙

Brenda Meisels is a retired social worker-psychotherapist. Her first novel Family at Booknook, a story of a single mother's love and her feisty daughter's determination, was published in 2009. She lives with her husband in Ann Arbor, Michigan.

FourWallsAndaLeakyRoof.blogspot.com

Acknowledgements

T hank you to authors Susan Scott Morales and Margaret Fuchs Singer, whose ideas, editing, and patience were instrumental in my completing this work. Another group of skilled writers—Rachel Nelson, Clare Cross, and Diane Kimble—were supportive, offered advice, and were attentive to details. I am indebted to these five talented women.

Sharon Feldman and Sally Brush, social workers informed about abuse, read early chapters and rendered thought-provoking comments. Sally Seymour recommended that I write in the first person, which helped me find my characters' voices. Ellen Toronto shared information on publishing. Diane Neal's thorough reading of the manuscript nudged me to dig deeper.

My accessible and encouraging editor, Susan Malone, insisted that "Tulip" be rewritten in the third person. She was right.

Kudos to my husband, Murray Meisels, for accepting Tulip and her brood into our home for the past four years.

In my personal and professional experience, I have been awed by the ability of abused women to pick up the pieces, fasten them together, and make something, albeit imperfect, of their lives. Their struggles and victories inspired me to write this story. Thank you.

This story is for survivors of abuse—those who have repaired their lives, those who continue to struggle, and those who may not yet acknowledge their abuse. You know who you are.

1

"**B**itch!" Marshall's boot slammed into Tulip's ankle. He grabbed the collar of her shirt and hurled her toward the wall.

She pictured her head as a giant yellow egg splattered on the paint. Instead he opened the closet door and tossed her in. The lock clicked. She had landed on his hunting coat, which smelled strong and wild like the squirrels he shot, his sweater greasy with spit and snot. Shivering, she squirmed into the foul coat and wrapped the sweater around her bare feet. His shotgun—the one he had threatened her with yesterday—pressed against her back, the barrel round and hard. She checked the chamber. One. Her finger connected with the trigger. In his coat, holding *his* loaded shotgun, she was the hunter. Tulip laughed out loud.

Marshall banged on the wall. "Shut up, bitch, or I'll beat the shit out of you."

"Try it!" She eased herself up.

Her son Tucker cried out, "No, Daddy!" *Whap!* A howl.

Tulip's hand went to the scar on her forehead. She cocked the gun. When he opened the door—if he opened the door—she'd be ready. There were other guns in the house. They could have a shootout. With her luck she'd be the one riddled with holes, her blood staining the carpet she'd just cleaned. Or, if she did kill him, they'd be hauling her sorry ass off to jail and her kids would be orphans. She stood there at the ready, her shaking hands gripping the shotgun.

Marshall banged on the door. "Whore!" A chair crashed against the dresser. "Damn." The bed creaked. Panting. A foot smacked against the sole of a boot, then another. The bed groaned in relief. The door opened, banged shut. Footsteps faded.

"I have to pee," she pleaded, almost a whisper.

The house was quiet, tomb-like. She had lost track of time. She had to pee. Had Marshall gone to work?

"Hunter! Ernest! Tucker!" she called. No answer. Too scared. She pulled one of Marshall's shirts off the hanger and squished it under her head. She had to think, make a plan, but her eyes betrayed her.

In her dream pee filled the room. She pushed on the door. It did not budge. She yanked. She banged. Marshall, in cowboy boots and a ten-gallon hat, waved two six-shooters at her. The face changed to her brother Calvin's. Instead of bullets, bits of bloody meat shot out, striking her face with a force so strong her legs buckled. She gasped and breathed in rotten roast. Calvin unzipped his fly and pulled out a bottle of Old Milwaukee.

Footsteps. Tulip's eyes flew open. A single ray of light shone under the door. The lock turned. She clicked off the gun's safety and steadied it.

The door flew open. "D-d-don't shoot!" Tucker's eyes were huge with fear, blood dried on his swollen lip.

She gulped for air. "You need a haircut, Tucker." That's what she said. Not "Are you OK?" Or "Thanks for unlocking the door." But "You need a haircut."

"D-D-Dad's gone to work. H-He said not to let you out. But I g-g-got the key out of the drawer. D-don't be mad at me."

She patted his head. "Daddies shouldn't lock mommies up. You did a good thing." Although Tucker was ten, he needed the simplest things explained. He couldn't read, and his classmates called him "retard."

Her pants damp, she slithered out into the destruction. Her hidden romance novel was dismembered, its parts strewn about the living room. Her favorite lamp, the one similar to a kerosene lantern, had been smashed against the wall, the metal dented and the globe in sharp confetti pieces. Tulip stood on Marshall's sweater and slid across the floor, gathering bits of broken glass in its folds.

Wear it now, Marshall.

Tulip scooted her way into Ernest's room. "Ernest!" she cried.

Saucer eyes peeked out from under the bed. Whimpering, he crawled to her and grabbed her leg.

Two safe, one to go.

She smoothed Ernest's dark hair "Hey, eight-year-olds don't cry." She peeled his arms from her.

Reaching for her legs, he dogged her to Hunter's room.

Tulip tried Hunter's door. Blocked. "Open your door." No answer. "Hunter!" Tulip's heart pounded. She turned to Ernest. "Did Dad go after Hunter?"

Ernest's blue eyes were blank.

Tulip banged on the door. "Hunter, Hunter, open the damned door!"

The bed creaked. Feet thudded on the floor, then steps and scraping. Pulling back the chair that braced the knob, she opened the door. A Batwoman comic lay open on Hunter's pink spread. Hunter sat on the bed, her green cat eyes narrowed. At nine, she already acted like her dad. Tulip wanted to smack her.

Ernest sighed. "Nah, he wouldn't do anything to her. He never bothers her."

Tulip had to get her children out. But she was wobbly-weak and not thinking straight. She had tried to leave before. She could run, but without friends or money, she might as well stay put. But this time she had a plan. She could lie down and die or get up and try. She had a window of time while Marshall was at work. The kids must be starving, but no one seemed to have had the stomach for the untouched roast. Hunter opened a box of saltines. Tulip resurrected the day-old doughnuts buried behind the towels in the cupboard. The coffee pot still lukewarm, she poured herself the dregs. For a moment she pretended that he'd left it for her. She cackled. Sure, he'd leave her mud. She bit into the glazed raised doughnut, her favorite. Rock hard.

Tucker stuffed a doughnut in his mouth, hunks falling onto the floor.

"You're making a mess, Tucker!" The irony of the situation struck her and she hiccupped with laughter. Eyes huge with fear, Tucker hid his mouth with his hand.

Hunter took a huge bite of doughnut, grimaced, and flung it. It thudded onto a daisy plate. She laughed, hysterical.

Ernest's eyes questioned his mother. Like she should have all the answers. Tulip opened her arms and he crawled into them, his heart thudding against her chest.

"We'll go to D's," she said. She did not want to be beholden to D, to anyone. But D had urged Tulip to come, had said she should before Marshall killed her. Just for a night, a week at most. Give her time to think.

With Ernest's arms around Tulip's neck and his legs around her waist, she searched for the phone. She found its disconnected cord snaking across the floor. She squared her shoulders. "Humph. Guess we'll just surprise her."

Marshall's brand-new 1968 Ford Thunderbird sat in the drive. Ford got their payments ahead of schedule, but getting grocery money out of Marshall was like shaking the last dribble of milk out of the bottle when you needed a full cup.

The family made do with macaroni and cheese. Marshall drove his pickup to work with the key to the Thunderbird in his pocket. Cramming the kids in that car and tearing out of the drive would have felt good. But a long time had passed since Tulip had been allowed to drive, and on this frigid night they might end up wrapped around a tree. Better to walk before Marshall showed up soused. No more black eyes or broken ribs. She had to get the kids out or use the gun. She wasn't certain she could pull the trigger. If she did, she'd have to kill him.

The thought of dragging three kids out in the middle of a winter night made her heart race. D had warned her about the Fleszar murder, nineteen-year-old girl found all chopped up. Some deranged sex pervert on the prowl, she'd said. But that was last summer. No one would be out on this night. It should have been snowing. Instead, sharp ice pelted their heads and dampened their paper sacks. Each carried two, one for clothes and a toothbrush, and one for whatever else they wanted. Tucker's bunny Mr. Knight lopped over the side of his bag, stuffing oozing from of his head.

D's house was a half-mile away. The kids did not complain about the walk or the weather. After a while the pain in Tulip's chest eased. Was the cold, damp air helping? No, it was getting out of that house, which was burning with rage, the air so filled with anger and fear that it ate up all the oxygen. Down the block they trudged, a platoon of soldiers in training heading toward no-man's-land. Marshall wasn't due home for hours but she imagined him skidding around the corner, horn honking, kids scattering, the pickup bouncing over the curb and running her down. She must calm down. There were no cars on the street and porch lights could guide them.

Then, although it was winter, hail and rain unloaded on them. Tucker screamed. Ernest whimpered. But tough little Hunter put her head down and just kept walking.

"Put the bags under your coats!" Tulip hollered through the wind.

Tucker struggled to unbutton his coat. Tulip squished a sack between her legs to free a hand to help. The sopped paper gave way. Underpants, bras, and tampons fell into a puddle. Tucker jerked. Mr. Knight toppled into the inky water. Tucker yelped—a wolf pup, howling into the wind. Even after Tulip rescued Mr. Knight, Tucker would not, could not stop. She stooped and groped in the mud for her underclothes. Hail beat down on them. "Just a few more blocks," she said. "We can make it."

An engine roared. Tires splashed and squealed to a stop. Glaring headlights blinded her. A door sprang open. A dark shadow towered over her. The biggest, blackest shoes she'd ever seen plunked down on a muddle of tampons, huge white worms sucking up water.

"What are you doing out on a night like this?"

Tulip's gaze followed the shoes up until they connected with a badge. Shit—a cop. Better than Marshall, better than the murderer. But hell, he could be the pervert. "Didn't know there was a law against walking."

"Get in." The voice was gravelly.

He waved the kids into the back of the patrol car, bent down, and picked up toothpaste and soap. When he moved his giant foot, Tulip grabbed her personals.

"Where you taking us?"

"Where do you want to go?"

So he wasn't hauling her sorry ass to jail. "D's. Delilah Snyder, 286 River Street." Tulip's voice sounded like cracked glass. She crawled in, she and her children soaking the law's seats.

The cop guided the car onto the road and spoke with authority. "Well, what happened?"

Another man challenging her. She bristled. "Nothing unusual. I always pack up in the middle of the night, haul my kids out of bed, stroll to D's. I especially prefer stormy nights...what the hell do you think happened?"

He smiled, a small mouth stretched over big white teeth. "There's been a fight—husband? Drinking? Hit you?"

She had said too much. He'd be calling the welfare.

The sleet and hail had stopped. Tulip stared straight ahead, watching the wipers brush the last drops of water from the window.

"You could file charges."

The last thing she needed was the law messing in her business. She shook her head.

"I could talk to him. Sometimes that helps."

"No! We're leaving!" She bit her lip until she tasted salty blood.

"What are your plans?"

"Stay with D. Work."

"Where?"

"Joe's. Waitress." She was trembling with cold, maybe fear, and she sure as hell didn't want no cop pressuring her or thinking on taking her kids.

The car pulled into Delilah's drive. Tulip sprang for the door.

"Wait." He handed her his card. "Ken Gordon. If you need help, call."

If Tulip were truly honest, another reason they'd left was Hunter, her feisty one, the one her husband left alone. Or Tulip hoped he left alone. Tulip's beat-up mom couldn't save her, but Tulip sure as hell wasn't going to let what happened to her happen to her daughter.

That day, right out of bed, Marshall started drinking. By supper, an empty six-pack of Old Milwaukee sat on the kitchen counter. She'd made a pot roast, which gave her the willies. It reminded her of what she had to forget, horror-picture memories that popped up when she least expected them. But grocery money was dear and chuck was cheap. She'd cooked it at 250 degrees, four hours. Falling apart it was. But Marshall was ornery-mean. "Tough," he muttered, and flung that roast. It flew across the table, landing smack-dab on Tulip's plate, grease stinging her face. Tulip, who hated roast, now had a whole platter. She couldn't stop her laugh. Marshall slammed his fists on the table. The kids scattered. Tulip hightailed it to the bedroom and locked the door, feeling a bit smug that she'd outrun him. She would wait until after he'd gone to work, when it was safe to come out.

She lay down on the bed and was far away, dreaming, when she heard Hunter cry, "No! No! Out! Out!"

She met Marshall coming out of Hunter's room.

Now she rang the doorbell once, twice; the third time she kept her finger on it. Thunder roared. The sky opened.

Ernest whimpered. "She's not here."

Finally, shuffling footsteps. The bolt sprang back. D cracked the door, flung it open. Her bulk filled the doorway. Eyes swollen from sleep, she gaped at Tulip. "What? What the hell happened to you?"

D had told Tulip for months to leave Marshall. Now Tulip was there with three drowned rats needing to come in out of the cold, and D was standing there in her fuzzy brown robe, a bear blocking the entrance.

"Did you mean it?" Tulip asked.

"What?"

"That we could stay with you?"

D rubbed sleep from her eyes, opened then closed her mouth.

"You don't act too pleased to see us."

"Hell, what do you expect, pulling up in a police car in the middle of the night? A forty-gun salute? Get in here." D reached for Tucker, pulled him in, and stripped off his drenched jacket. "Get out of those clothes before you catch your death of dampness." Her jowly face broke into a smile. "You kids want some cocoa?"

In no time the kids were sitting in their PJs at the kitchen table, eating toast and drinking cocoa. D put them to sleep in the spare room, boys in the bed, Hunter on the floor. Tulip didn't like her being in the same room with the boys, but at least she wasn't in the same bed.

Built after World War II, D's two-bedroom house was no-frills: kitchen, living room, and bathroom. She offered to share her bed, but Tulip took the couch. Wrapping herself in a feather quilt, she lay shivering and thinking, thinking how shitty her life was. In the morning, Marshall would be after her. She was scared—scared to stay, scared to go.

When Marshall had shoved her in the closet, she knew they had to leave or he'd kill her, which would've been a relief. You don't feel pain when you're dead. Some mothers kill themselves; a few even take their kids with them. Mothers drive their cars into a lake or turn the gas on. Murder. Maybe in some cases that was their only choice. Tulip didn't know and she wasn't judging. She just knew she had to get the kids out of there. Marshall had to have someone to beat on. If it wasn't her, it'd be Tucker. He'd leave a toy out or, heaven forbid, mess his pants. Although he was ten, he did that sometimes when frightened. He was slow and you couldn't blame him. She'd have left with Tucker when he was a baby, but Marshall got her pregnant again and then again.

So there she was with three little ones and a husband with an iron fist. Ernest had been a tiny baby and cried a lot. When she couldn't get him to stop, Marshall's crazy eye would start to twitch, and no matter the weather, she would bundle up those kids and get them out of there. Once, when Ernest was a toddler, he fell and hit his head on the coffee table. Blood gushing, he cried and cried. She could not stop the bleeding or the crying. And she couldn't get him out of house before Marshall raised his hand. No matter how bad he was hurt, Ernest never cried in front of Marshall again. When Marshall commanded, Ernest knew to come running with beer or chips. Marshall'd pat him on the head hard, as if he were a dog. But when Crazy Eye danced, Ernest knew to be invisible. That's what you do when you're at war with an enemy so powerful that a twitch of a hand could send you sailing. At that time, in Vietnam, Americans were spraying Agent Orange, poisoning plants, animals, even people. But the Vietcong, hiding underground, would crawl out—kill, and disappear. Tulip's house was like that, with Marshall poisoning the air. She and the kids tried to burrow, but there were no tunnels, no escape.

In 1968, Tulip was twenty-seven going on forty. When she looked in the mirror, she saw a scrawny, redheaded, baggy-eyed ghost of a woman—her mom. Like her third-grade daughter, Tulip used to have some feisty. She had picked the name Hunter—better to hunt than to be hunted. With Hunter for a name, her daughter would learn to stick up for herself. True to her name, Hunter did not creep around the house and took guff off no one. She knew to clear out when Marshall was home. Her hurt came out in anger. With hands tightfisted in her pockets, she took the war to school.

Marshall had it in for Tucker, who didn't have enough smarts to stay out of his dad's way. Tucker was big and gangly, with reddish hair always in his eyes. He loved to crawl in bed with his books and look at the pictures, sort of tucked in. Ernest was earnest. It fitted him. He was one serious, worried little kid. Marshall had named the boys, but Tulip named the girl. She got the name on the birth certificate before Marshall got to the hospital. But shock, shock—Marshall liked the name. First time she'd done anything right.

Maybe if Tulip had spoken up when she was twelve, they'd have taken her away and life would have been different. When she got pregnant at sixteen, it was not her fault. In 1957, abortions were illegal and single mothers were considered trash. There wasn't anything a girl could do but get married or give up the baby. Maybe Tulip should have asked for help. But when there is no help, why bother?

Sun peeping through the living room window woke her—a good omen. The earthy smell of fresh perked coffee was almost too much goodness. She wiggled her toes and stretched. Stiff and sore, but safe. D's robe lay on the couch. Slipping it on, she headed to the kitchen.

D, ready for work, sat at the table drinking coffee. She looked up from the Ypsilanti paper. "What happened to your lip?"

Tulip touched it. "Guess I bit it when the cop picked us up."

D chuckled. "You are something else. If no one was bothering you, you'd stub your toes. ….. Robe's too big for you."

"Maybe I'll grow into it."

"Could use a little meat on your bones. Maybe if you're away from that shithead you can gain some weight."

Tulip was skinny. When she'd started working, things got real bad at home. Marshall couldn't control her when she worked. He took her paycheck, but he didn't know how much she made in tips. She hungered for the lightness she found at the diner, visiting with the customers, getting to know D. She tried not to let on, but Marshall knew. He was nasty-mean about little things: his burger medium, not rare, running out of beer, Mr. Knight in the hallway. Tulip was in overdrive keeping the house spic and span and the meals the way he liked them. When they ate, she was on hyper alert. When she tried to swallow, her throat clamped shut. At work D made malts that Tulip forced down and then upchucked in the girls' room. She'd have worried she was pregnant but her periods were regular.

For the first time in months, Tulip was starving. "What's for breakfast?"

"How about I whip up some scrambled eggs and bacon?"

A horn blared. Tires squealed. A pickup roared over the curb onto the soaked lawn.

Marshall banged on the door. "Come out, bitch! I know you're in there. If you don't come out, you'll wish you had!"

D flung open the door. Her muscular arms on either side of the door jamb, she glared down at Marshall. "Jackass, get off my porch before I call the cops." She grabbed the phone from the hall table and shook it at him.

"Nah, Delilah." He tossed his cigarette onto the porch and ground it in with his boot. "You got my wife and kids in there. She's got a big mess to clean up at home."

Tulip stood behind D. Just like him, passing it off as nothing, acting like everything was her fault. She shouted from the safety of D's back, "You get out of here!"

"Why, you little slut! Hiding behind Fatso. Get your butt out here."

"*You* get out!" D's voice was a wave crashing against rocks. "I'm calling the cops." She dialed.

"Son of a bitch." Crazy Eye danced. Marshal's fist smashed against the door window. Glass flew. Crazy Eye bored through Tulip. "Bitch!" Holding his bloody hand, he whirled and stumbled down the steps.

Tulip didn't feel much like eating and D said she'd grab something at work. After she left, Tulip pried the kids out of bed. They were tired and grumpy, and there were slim pickings in the cereal department, one small box of Wheaties.

"I'm not eating that yucky stuff," Hunter declared.

"You'll damn well eat it or go without."

Tulip sent them off with a warning. "If you see your dad, don't go with him. Don't even talk to him. D will be here when you come back from school. Do what she says and don't give her any guff."

In the kitchen Tulip picked up the bowls, Hunter's untouched. Stubborn! But maybe Hunter was too nervous to eat. If Tulip was scared—and she was—the kids must be terrified. It was her responsibility to be strong and protect them. She hung her clothes, three hangers, in the coat closet. In the bathroom she found dirty underwear tossed in the tub, toothpaste in the sink and on the counter. Tucker. She picked up the shorts and sponged white yuck from the counter. Trashing D's bathroom was not good. Brushing her teeth, she glimpsed herself in the mirror: cloudy blue eyes, pale face, zits circling tight chapped lips, Marshall's complimentary scar peeking out from a wild woman's hair. Another picture memory that she would not be able to erase. She tapped the mirror. "Is there a person in there?"

She squeezed into her sleazy polyester black uniform, inhaled, and tugged the zipper up. It was the one "perk" Joe provided—size four, too small. "You look good," he'd said. *Letcher.*

Cautiously she picked her way up the icy sidewalk on River Street, left on Michigan Avenue, and a block to Joe's Diner. If Marshall pulled up, there was no way she could run. Seeing Joe's flashing neon sign was a relief. A short in the wiring caused it to flash on and off. D had told Joe that it was a fire hazard, but Joe just laughed and let it do its thing.

Tulip opened the door and felt a rush of warm air. The long, narrow diner was busy enough for three waitresses, but Joe managed with two. He'd gotten booths from a couple of restaurants going out of business. One wall sported patched red-vinyl booths, a couple with broken springs. Black-padded leather booths lined the opposite wall. Usually D and she alternated sides. People headed for the black comfy side first, and on slow days the diner looked a bit tipsy, like the *Titanic* ready to capsize. On those days they took turns picking up tables. When it was really slow, they mopped the black-and-white checkerboard floor. This was a bitch, as fluorescent lights beamed down, showing all the scuffs on the squares.

With no time to think, Tulip was on autopilot, going through the motions. Thankfully Marshall did not grace the diner with his presence. At quitting time Tulip checked the street for any sign of the Thunderbird or pickup. As a kid she had been mad at her mom for not leaving her dad, but her mom didn't have a job or a safe place to go. Tulip had both and she was still shaking in her boots.

D's cottage shone white and clean. The small lot was surrounded by a winter-bare privacy hedge, with tufts of dead grass trapped in its branches. It was a more welcome sight than Marshall's newer roomy ranch.

Tucker flung open the door. "Sh-sh-she hit me, M-Mom. Hunter hit me!"

Hunter was curled on the sofa, stuffing her face with popcorn and watching Road Runner dynamite Wile E. Coyote. A trail of kernels led from the kitchen to the living room. She shrugged. "He made a mess, spilled his juice."

Tulip sighed. "Think you're Gretel leaving a trail in the woods? Pick it up, Hunter."

Hunter screwed up her face. "He did it. Why do I always have to do everything?"

"Where's D?"

"Headache. Went to bed."

Dog tired, Tulip needed to lie down, but the couch was occupied. She went to the kitchen for a cup of coffee, sat down, and laid her head on the table.

As she was drifting off, Tucker tugged at her skirt. "W-w-what's for dinner, Mom?"

"Dinner?" She hadn't given it a thought and didn't know if D had anything for the kids to eat.

D breezed in and grinned at Tucker. "Hungry?" She went to the fridge and pulled out a package. "Burgers. We're having burgers."

"C-c-can we have F-French fries too?"

"If I have some in the freezer."

"I thought you had a headache. Kids bother you?" Tulip asked.

"Here they are, Tucker. Fries for you!" D turned to Tulip. "That time of the month. You look worse off than me. I'll brew us some coffee and fry burgers."

"I gotta get our stuff out of that house. Marshall will change the locks."

D touched Tulip's shoulder. "We will. But right now we're having supper."

After dark, when Marshall would be at work, they headed toward home. "We're going on a treasure hunt," Tulip said.

The house was dark, the pickup gone. "Listen up," Tulip said. "We're going in for clothes and your favorite toys. You can't take much, 'cause there's no room at D's. We won't be coming back. So no complaining if you forget something."

Silent as thieves in the night, they tiptoed up the walk. Tulip stuck the key in the lock. The door squeaked open. "Get cracking," Tulip said.

Ernest gasped. Marshall was slumped in a chair, feet propped on the coffee table, snoring. Tulip went limp.

D clamped her hand on Tulip's shoulder and whispered, "He's dead to the world. If he wakes up, I'll handle him." She glared at Tulip. "You have every right to be here!"

Broken picture frames were strewn about the room, furniture overturned, lampshades stomped. Tulip breathed deeply and blew out her mouth. She forced her body to straighten. D handed the kids garbage bags and shooed them to their rooms. In Tulip's bedroom her clothing was shredded on the floor, a huge butcher knife on the bed.

D squeezed Tulip's arm. "That bastard," she whispered. Then she laughed, a frightening loud laugh, and pointed to the closet, where jeans and shirts, clothes Tulip desperately needed, were still hanging. Tulip stifled a giggle. *Just like Marshall not to finish the job.* She grabbed clothes, her pillow, and cosmetics, flung them in the bag, and fled the room.

Tucker stood in his bedroom holding the empty bag. Tulip swatted him on the butt. "Get your underwear. I'll get your jeans and shirts." He nodded but did not budge. Tulip gathered his clothes and propelled him out of the room. In the hall she nearly collided with D, whose arms were filled with stuffed toys.

"We got what we can," D said, motioning to Ernest and Hunter, both dragging overflowing garbage bags. "Let's blow this hole."

Tulip lingered in the living room for one last look. The photo album was open on the coffee table, Marshall's foot right smack-dab on top of her face— the picture of her pregnant with Tucker, taken early in their marriage, when she still had hope. He'd been looking at *that* picture? She crossed the room and whipped it away. Marshall's foot flopped to the floor. His eyes flew open.

D grabbed Tulip's hand. They raced to the car.

2

Tulip and D worked the noon shift. They'd been slammed, an hour of running their feet off. By two the place was empty and the owner Joe was off to the bank.

D sat on the stool behind the register, a cigarette dangling from her mouth, shoes off, massaging her bunion. Taking a deep drag, she blew a perfect smoke ring. "Old folks. I'm sick of 'em, dollars glued to their wallets. Herman's the worst. Who ever heard of sharing a $2.99 lunch? He didn't leave a tip, not a dime."

Tulip gave the table an extra swish. She liked the way the diner looked when it was empty, the floor swept, and tables clean. It gave her a sense of order, like everything was under control. "It's the end of the month. Social Security's gone."

D grimaced. "Herman's as fat as a hog ready for butcher and just as tight as an old-maid school teacher. Mary's skinny as a Barbie doll. Next time I'm going to put his meal on a saucer and give her the plate."

The door jerked open. Marshall swayed in the entryway, Crazy Eye dancing. His brackish hair hung in oily clumps, his shirt half out. The wide leather belt, darkened with age and blood from deer butchering, hung unbuckled at his waist.

Her soapy dishrag splattering on the table, Tulip shielded herself with the bucket of water.

Boots thudding on the floor, Marshall stomped toward her. "Honey," he said, his voice syrupy.

Tulip shuddered. "You got the divorce papers!" His face next to hers, Tulip breathed in smoke and alcohol.

Marshall gripped her arm. "You can't divorce me!" He shook her, soapy water sloshing over her shoes.

Perhaps it was the safety of the restaurant, a public place with D behind the counter. Or maybe all those years of being beat down. A pressure rose up from her feet. She felt taller, stronger. She jerked away. "I'm *not* coming back. You're *not* using me for a punching bag no more!"

"Bitch!" He lunged.

Tulip flung the filthy water, hitting him full in the face. He sputtered, fell back, and grabbed for his belt. Tulip's gaze locked onto the belt, and she crumpled against a table.

"Stop!" Waving a menu, D flew across the room.

Belt clutched in his hand, Marshall faced D. His voice flinty, "She threw water on me."

D snickered. "About time you cleaned up."

Marshall was a little snot but wiry and strong. He had been picked on as a kid and maybe that was why he was so mean. But D was bigger and broader. The oversized menu was not a particularly effective weapon, but D had a black belt in karate, could break a board with her hand.

Marshall whipped the belt at her. As though it were a game and it was her turn, D caught it. "Come any closer and I'll be the one using the belt. Tulip, call the police!"

As Tulip picked up the phone, Joe swung the door open. Blood drained from Marshall's weathered face. "Didn't do nothing. Just came to talk to my wife, no law against that." Crazy eye twitching, he nodded to Tulip. "I'll catch you later." Brushing past Joe, he lurched out the door.

Tulip gulped air. "I'm in for it now."

"Don't be such a scaredy-cat. He's chickenshit. And he won't be hitting you with this anymore." With a throaty laugh, D waved the belt in the air and hurled it into the trash.

Joe stuck his fingers in his belt loop. "What the hell is going on?"

Tulip shivered cold, then hot. The belt, the way it sliced through the air, its sharp bite, took center stage in too many nightmares. Although her body was there, her mind had taken leave. The remainder of the day she snuck glances at the belt lying dormant in the wastebasket. At the end of her shift, she took the basket to the incinerator, dumped it, and lit a match. Flames shot up. She stared at the fire until the belt ignited, writhed, curled, and finally died in the blaze.

The lunch crowd had cleared. The tables needed bussing and the floor mopped. D was in a snit. "Joe doesn't pay us enough to do this crap work.

That's 'cause we're women. You think a male waiter would bus tables and mop the floor? I'd rather work construction, drive heavy equipment. But even if they hired me, they wouldn't pay *me* a man's wage." She waved her beefy arm. " I read that women make 60 percent of what men make."

Tulip motioned toward the door. "You're grouchy. Go out back and get some air. I'll take care of those coffee-drinking, pie-eating cops."

D was what they called a bra-burning women's libber. When she got tired or her back hurt, she'd go off about the evils of men. Not that Tulip disagreed. D would do good in construction. Tulip could see her in jeans and a flannel shirt, ramming around on a backhoe. Tulip wiped the tables and filled ketchup bottles. She smiled at the new picture in her head, one she wanted to keep—D unbelting Marshall. Although he'd called and threatened to take the kids, he'd not been around in a month. This was the third time Tulip had left him, but the first that she'd had help. And hope. Sometimes there was even space in her worries to hear a tune in her head—Patsy Cline, Roy Clark. She loved Johnny Cash's new song, "Folsom Prison Blues." She felt like she'd been let out of prison. Henson Cargill's "Skip a Rope," about a couple fighting, divorcing, and hurting their children, stuck in her head. But her kids were a hell of a lot better off without their dad.

They were cramped at D's, two bitches in a crate with three pups. Hunter complained about sharing a bedroom with her brothers. Every night Tulip heard the same thing: "Why do I have to sleep on the floor?"

"'Cause I said!" Tulip did not know how to explain it, but there was no way she could have Hunter sleep with one of her brothers.

D hollered—a lot. "Turn down that damn TV! Close the door! Were you born in a barn?" But she never hit them. After yelling, she'd turn around and bake cinnamon rolls. She was like her rolls, crusty on the outside but marshmallow soft inside. If Tulip swatted Hunter, D set her straight. "Corporal punishment just makes her angry," she said.

Tulip felt bad about losing control. She was wound too tight. But at night when they watched TV and popped corn, Tulip felt almost safe. In spite of her complaints, D said the little family could stay as long as they needed. Tulip didn't pay rent, but she bought groceries and helped with utilities. She was saving for a car, maybe a pickup. The idea of her, a little redhead, scooting around in a rusty pickup suited her just fine. When she had enough money, they'd rent a place of their own. Maybe she could get something close to Joe's and walk to work, but she'd need transportation for groceries. She couldn't borrow D's car forever.

Tulip did not notice the door opening or hear footsteps behind her. Fingers gripped her shoulder. Nails dug into her arm. Pin-sharp whiskers pierced her cheek. The ketchup bottle she was holding dropped to the floor, its contents flowing blood-red.

Marshall's words were slow and slurred. "I *gotta* talk to you, Tulip."

She opened her mouth to scream but nothing came out. Her eyes closed. Her mind clouded.

"I don't think the lady wants to be bothered."

Tulip's eyes struggled open. Humongous black shoes came into focus. She followed them up—legs, chest, face—to the policeman's cap. He towered over her scruffy husband. In slow motion the policeman grabbed Marshall by the collar and propelled him toward the door, Marshall's cowboy boots skipping across the floor. Belatedly she screamed.

Big Shoes took her by the arm and led her to a chair. His lips moved. "It's OK. He's gone. Calm down."

She burst into hysterical laughter. "You're Big Shoes!"

"I'm what?"

"Big Shoes—you gave us a ride." She hiccupped.

"Ken Gordon." He smiled a big-toothed smile in a face too small for the rest of him. It wasn't that she didn't like the way he looked; he just wasn't put together quite right. He was tall and gangly, with oversized feet and a head that belonged on a kid. When God made him, he must have been running low on proper-sized parts.

"Thanks," was all she could say.

"You're welcome."

As Big Shoes left, he saluted. "I'll stop by tomorrow."

That night as she lay on the couch, a full moon cast the shadow of the standup lamp onto the wall. It looked like Marshall lurking in the corner. Or maybe Calvin. She pulled the quilt tight around her neck. When Marshall attacked her, her mind played tricks on her, making her think he was her brother.

A shadow flitted across the window. Marshall? Calvin? But Calvin was in prison. She felt for the lamp switch. Light flooded the room. *Dumb-shit.* If it was Marshall, he could see her plain as day. *Thump, thump, thump.* The bastard was banging on the house. She turned off the lamp and crept to the window. Branches of the maple whipped in the wind, thudded against the house.

She was twelve. Dad had finally taken Mom north to see the fall colors, as she'd been begging him to. Later she told Tulip that he'd left her in the cabin and gone hunting. He killed two deer, one illegal. He was good with a gun. In spite of being told in no uncertain terms that Tulip was to cook her brother Calvin's supper, she was determined to enjoy her freedom. She left a note, took her babysitting money, and went to the movie *Singin' in the Rain*. It felt good standing up for herself, not like Mom with Dad. After the movie she decided that Calvin could make his own supper. Besides, there wasn't time to cook a roast. She stopped for a shake and burger.

As she neared home the temperature dropped; the wind was ferocious. Dead leaves gusted through the deserted street and piled onto the sagging porch. The door was ajar. Calvin lay on the couch, beer dribbling from the Budweiser can still in his hand, his belt curled snakelike on his bare, skinny chest. The skull tattoo on his beer-holding hand glared at her. *Passed out—good. You can't scare me, you shit-faced drunk.* She tiptoed toward her room.

He reared up. "Slut! Slut! Where's my supper!" He lunged. Skull fingers dug into her arm.

The memory—the belt explained it. When Marshall had attacked her in broad daylight, even with D there, Tulip wasn't. She was that scared-shitless kid she'd tried to bury. *Don't think about it. Rain, rain go away, come again some other day.* Shivering, she crawled into bed and covered her head.

Just before quitting time, Big Shoes sauntered into Joe's, slipped into a booth, and ordered black coffee. He tilted his cap with the shiny emblem back on his head and looked at her with brown eyes too kind for a policeman. "How're you doing?"

"Fine." Tulip gave him her fake, bubbly smile that she wore like a dress. She didn't tell him that she'd crawled into bed, pulled the covers over her head, and lay there shaking.

"Glad to hear it."

"What do you want?"

"To talk."

"Can't, I've got to get home."

"I'll give you a lift."

"In the patrol car?"

"Why not?"

"Isn't it supposed to be for business?"

He smiled, lips stretching across his narrow face. "What makes you think it's not work? You'd be in my protection."

"Protection? You can't even find that pervert who murdered the Fleszar girl way last summer. And how do I know you're not the guy?"

His lips formed a straight angry line. "Geez, woman. What a slam."

Oops, she'd better not piss off the police department. "Sorry, no offense. I'd just rather walk." She poured his coffee, picked up her purse from behind the counter, and was out the door.

She knew damn well what he wanted. And she was not putting out.

3

⤜⤏

D and Tulip sprawled on the couch in their pajamas watching *The Lucy Show*, eating the last of the popcorn, biting down on the nutty kernels seeing who could make the loudest crunch. Although it was getting on toward spring, the air was mighty cold. Tulip was snug in D's fuzzy brown robe. Wearing it felt like trading clothes in high school, but not a fair trade; there was nothing of hers that D could get into. Perhaps it was more like dressing up in a big sister's clothing, except D didn't mind and a big sister would.

"*I Love Lucy* was a better show," Tulip declared. "I miss Desi. He's too big for his britches and I like how Lucy shows him up."

"They're divorced. Can't be in the same show."

"Why not? They argued all the time anyway."

"Silly thing." D touched Tulip's face.

The caress felt good, but forbidden. Tulip sat up straighter. "They say he's a womanizer."

D put her arm around Tulip, pulled her closer, and stroked her arm through the soft robe. Tulip made a purring sound, a kitten being petted. D lifted her chin, gazed into her eyes, tenderly kissed her.

A light burst in Tulip's head. She leapt off the couch. "What the hell are you doing?"

"You don't know?" D folded her arms, covering her saggy breasts. With her hair cropped and combed back, in her baggy Michigan sweatshirt, she could have been a man.

"You're...gay?"

"Come off it, Tulip. You knew."

"You asshole!" Tulip started out of the room.

"Sit down, Tulip!" D's voice was calm but firm. "Where are you going? To the kitchen, bathroom, my room?"

Tulip sat. Flabbergasted. She'd never thought about D in that way. At least she didn't think she had. D was sort of sexless. Men did not find her attractive, and she never fixed up. "How long have *you* known?" Tulip asked.

D laughed, a strained, caught laugh. "Since I was a kid. I've always liked girls."

"You did? You do?"

"Tulip, your head's buried in the sand. Someone has to whop you on the butt to get you to notice." D shrugged. "But don't feel too bad. I'm not sure my folks know."

As though to protect herself, Tulip crossed her arms. "You're sure you're gay?"

"Hell, do you think I have a choice? It's tough keeping it secret."

"Does Joe know?"

"Huh! It's something Joe doesn't want to know. He doesn't much like me, but I'm a damn good waitress. He needs me. Look, I misunderstood. I won't bother you again." D rose stiffly. Head up, she walked to her bedroom. "Good night." The door clicked.

"Tulip, you stupid ass! When God passed out ways to get yourself kicked in the gut, you stepped to the front of the line. I'm living with a gay—a homosexual—a lesbian." The words felt alien on Tulip's tongue. She had been living with D for three months and hadn't known.

With fumbling hands, Tulip made up the couch. She punched the pillow. What had she gotten herself into? She had never thought much about homosexuals. Her dad and Calvin bad-mouthed them, called men faggots and women dykes. She'd known a girlish boy at school, squeaky voiced with teacup gestures. The jocks teased him, beat him up. She had pitied him. He couldn't help how he was. Bernie, a girl in high school, specialized in jeans and cowboy boots. When they made her wear a dress, she had still worn boots, her dress brushing across their engraved leather tops. This drove the home-ec teacher up the wall, but she never told Bernie not to wear boots. No one dared give her a hard time. Tulip had admired her.

D was nearly six feet, broad shouldered, big boned, with saggy boobs, and a jowly face. Ugly. That's why Tulip thought D didn't have boyfriends. Tulip should have known. But what the hell! D was the salt of the earth, her best friend—only friend. She was family. Not like Tulip's family, but a caring kind. When D held her—touched her—for an instant, Tulip had liked it! She had never felt that way with Marshall, not even in the early times when he was trying to be decent. What did this mean about her?

Tulip's head pounded. Dummy, dummy, dummy. You are so fucked up. She rolled up in the quilt and closed her eyes. She told herself what she always did: *Think about it later.*

D left for work before Tulip dragged herself off the couch. D's bed was unmade, a first. At work, D kept to her section, Tulip to hers. Tulip had two hundred bucks to her name, no furniture, no dishes. It reminded her of being stuck with Marshall, not knowing what was going to happen.

For the next week the two avoided each other. D went out most evenings, creeping in after Tulip was in bed. Tulip pulled the coffee table tight against the couch and tried to put D out of her mind. The night D did not come home, Tulip woke wondering where she was. Tulip had read in the paper that another EMU student was missing. A psycho was on the prowl, targeting women in their area. If he went after D, he'd get more than he bargained for. Still, Tulip could not get back to sleep.

The next morning, urging her kids off to school, Tulip was one cranky mom. Coming out of the bathroom, she smelled coffee. Screwing up her courage, she marched to the kitchen. Some things could not be talked about, but this had to be settled, even if it ended with her and the kids in the street. "Where the hell were you last night?" she demanded.

D poured her a cup of coffee, then plopped a piece of bread in the toaster. "Want some?"

"I thought that guy might've killed you."

D's voice dripped with sarcasm. "*You* concerned about *me*? Why, I didn't think you cared."

This was not the conversation Tulip intended to have. She looked D in the eye. "Do you want me and the kids to get out?"

D glared. Her hands slapped her broad hips. Tulip's mind blurred.

"No, but if you keep acting like I might attack you at any moment, I don't want you here. If you can get over your homophobia, you and the kids can stay as long as you need to."

D came back into focus. "Why? Why do you want us to stay?"

D sighed. She spoke as though Tulip was as retarded as Tucker. "Listen to me. Hear me. When I said you could come, I was not attracted to you. Hell, you were a twit. You needed my help. I let you stay because we're friends. My feelings just grew. I thought you had feelings for me. I wish it had never happened, that we could go back the way we were. I'm not like a man. You don't have to put out. You're skittish as a deer. When I come in the living room, you run to the kitchen. When I'm in the kitchen, you run to the living room. And"—a smile spread across her broad face—"this house isn't that big."

D was right. Tulip was frightened. She sat, picked up the steaming cup, and held it in both hands. "What'd you mean about my head being in the sand?"

"You've been too preoccupied with your own problems to notice me. Remember Christina, who used to come to Joe's?"

"You mean you and Christina...?"

"Yes, me and Christina! It was good. And she wasn't married like that cop who's after you."

"You're saying I got something going with a cop?"

D smiled her know-it-all smile. "I'm saying you're thinking about it."

"I got nothing going with that cop. But you're gay and you didn't tell me!"

"It's something not talked about. Do you think Joe would keep me on if he knew?"

Tulip shook her head. "You're sure he doesn't know?"

"He senses it. But as long as it's not said, he can overlook it. Joe hates homos. You've heard him talk about stringing them up. If it were acknowledged, he'd find a way to get rid of me."

"So you took us in so we could be a cozy little family?"

"No, bubblehead! You were in a tight spot. Think I wanted three hooligans and your sorry ass stinking up my house?"

Ready to have at her, Tulip gulped in air—something was burning! Flames shot from the toaster. Tulip raced to unplug it. D whipped a dishcloth over the top.

Tulip shook her finger at D. "It's your sorry-ass toaster that's stinking up this house!"

D tossed her head back and roared with laughter. She snatched up the toaster, opened the door, and hurled it into the yard. It bounced upright, charred toast popping into the air. She swished smoke out the open door, then tossed Tulip the loaf of Wonder Bread. "Guess this is it."

"Where's the butter?" asked Tulip.

"Out."

Tucker must have stuck a fork in the toaster. Tulip hoped that D wouldn't think of that. Although Tulip bought groceries and helped with utilities, she and the kids *were* sorry-ass housemates. Tulip slathered jam on the bread and handed D a piece. "I'm sorry."

D nodded. They sat in silence, eating soft bread and jam. Smoke lingered in the room—not a bad smell, almost warm. Tulip could see the toaster out the window, the burnt toast on dead grass. A lone blackbird lighted, pecked the toast, and flew away.

D cared about her, about the children. Tulip had to work this out. D had to understand why she was so skittish. Tulip cleared her throat. "Something happened to me when I was a kid. Something I've never told anyone. A secret, like your being gay. Something I'd be blamed for. But it wasn't my fault. Like your being gay isn't your fault."

D's face opened. She was expecting Tulip to explain. Tulip wanted to, but it was disgusting, shameful! Tulip sprang from her chair. "Got to do the laundry. Later, I'll tell you later." She rushed from the room, leaving D with her brow furrowed in puzzlement. Tulip couldn't talk about it, at least not yet. But for the moment, they had made up.

Tulip lay on the couch, with D's Lawrence Welk music waltzing in her ears while D put the kids to bed. In spite of Hunter's protests, D was reading Tucker's favorite, *The Cat in the Hat*, her voice gleeful as the cat destroyed the house. "I can hold up the cup and the milk and the cake! I can hold up these books! And the fish on a rake!" After she finished, Tulip strained to hear their whispered murmurs. When the little family had first moved in, D started reading the children bedtime stories. Tulip had been bound together with worry and was relieved to have a moment to herself. Now, when she was more able, her children asked for D. If Ernest needed help with a button, or Hunter's hair was tangled, or Tucker needed a hug, it was D they went to. Tulip tried not to be jealous. She understood the children being drawn to D's mothering, the warmth and safety of being cushioned between her pillowy breasts.

When near her friend, Tulip felt a certain longing. She tried not to stand too close or brush against her, which wasn't easy, wedged in that house. Tulip dressed and undressed in the bathroom, still blocked the couch with the coffee table when she slept. D didn't seem to notice. After the kids were in bed, she often went out, and stayed late. Tulip's children loved D, and apparently someone else cared for her too. Tulip began to see D in a different way—not unattractive but solid and muscular, her movements purposeful. She was a good person, slow to smile, but when she did her dark eyes sparkled as though she had a secret Tulip could never know. Tulip remembered the caress, the brushing lips. Yes, she had liked it. She cared for D, and that scared the Billy-hell out of her.

"That's it. No more," D called from the hall. She strode in, eased herself into the chair, and picked up the *Ypsilanti Press*. Tucker called for a glass of water.

Tulip hollered, "You'll pee the bed!"

"I-I'm thirsty," he whined.

"Don't start, Tucker! Go to sleep!"

D hoisted herself out of the chair. "He needs some attention. I'll take him a tiny drink."

Tulip opened her mouth to set her straight.

"He hasn't wet the bed for weeks." D tossed Tulip the paper and headed toward the bedroom.

D came back snapping her fingers and doing a shuffle. "He wanted me to kiss Mr. Knight good night." She sank back into the chair, her sturdy legs on the hassock.

"D, we got to talk. You must be getting sick of us."

"Yeah, Tulip, I'm sick of those kids, but I'm *really* sick of Mr. Knight."

Tulip laughed. "That's why you sewed his ear back...?

D waited.

"It's OK that we aren't...that we don't...?"

D put the paper down. "It's sort of like family. Three kids, a ding-a-ling mom, and"—she patted her chest—"a good aunt. We're packed in here like Joe's Grill on a busy morning. Eggs, hash browns, and bacon all scrambled together. But it works."

"So we're scrambled eggs."

D laughed. "I like scrambled eggs."

"And it's OK that you and me don't...that we aren't...?"

"Lovers?" That slow, know-it-all smile crossed D's broad face. She rose from her chair and took Tulip's hand in her strong, rough one. "Yes, Tulip."

Tulip felt the comforting warmth of D's hand, nothing more.

"With that crazy soon-to-be ex, you're a hell of a lot safer here than in a fleabag apartment."

"He's all wrapped up with a new girlfriend. I'm off his radar."

"So's the child support. But I guess you could get welfare. "

"I ain't going on the county."

D picked up the paper and moved back to her chair. "So if you stay here a while, you'll be able to save some bucks and get a car."

"What about summer? School's almost out. Last summer, when I was married, I didn't work. A babysitter would eat up my tips."

"Oh, well, aren't there some free programs for kids? And we could adjust our schedules."

"You would?"

"I kinda like your hooligans. Besides, they mind me better than you."

Ouch! D looked at her as though she expected her to say something, perhaps be grateful. "Generous offer," Tulip mumbled.

D nodded and went back to her paper.

4

Holding an oversized umbrella, gussied up in heels and a pink sundress, D's realtor friend Kathy swept into Joe's. "The weatherman's got it wrong. Summer should be hot and dry, not a monsoon." She tossed the *Ypsilanti Press* on the table. "They found her. Stabbed, raped."

"Who? what?" Tulip asked.

"Schell, Joan, the Eastern Michigan student, the one who went missing last week. It must be the same guy that hacked up that girl last summer."

D picked up the paper. "Let me at him!"

Kathy laughed. "You'll never meet up with him. He's after cute coeds."

"Duh." D turned on her heel and went to wait on a customer.

D had lost weight, wasn't so jowly. She said she wasn't trying to skinny down, that it was keeping up with the kids. Tulip knew it was because of D's crush on Kathy but didn't understand why. Kathy wasn't pretty; she had short, straight blonde hair and looked like a gangly boy. On Tuesdays after her sales meeting, she stopped at Joe's. D hung around her booth, coffeepot in hand. Regulars would raise their cups, motion, call out even. While D made a fool of herself, Tulip did double duty.

Still, she cared about D, even liked Kathy. Tulip didn't begrudge them their relationship. It was just that she was so lonely.

But her kids were doing good. With Tulip, D, and the summer recreation program providing twenty-four-seven childcare, she didn't have to worry about the pervert killer stalking them. Her kids took swimming lessons, and on rainy days the counselors taught crafts. Tucker learned that yellow and blue made green, painted stick figures, trees, clouds, and a bright yellow sun. D bought magnets for the kids to decorate, and used them to hang their schedules on the refrigerator. She raved about the lopsided ashtray that Ernest made for her. Yes, the summer of sixty-eight was a good one.

That cop Ken—Bigfoot, she'd settled on for a nickname—ran in, shaking water from his cap.

"You're flooding the place," Tulip said.

His grin nearly covered his narrow face. "Coffee, black. And how about one of those cinnamon rolls?"

"You don't want one of those. Day old."

"Then have a cup of coffee with me."

"Nope, I'm going home and having coffee, with one of D's homemade cinnamon rolls."

"Sit down. Keep me company."

"Not supposed to."

"We'll say I was getting evidence."

"Why can't you get him?"

"The murderer? We're trying. Believe me, we're trying. Sit down." He patted the seat.

Joe was off to the bank and Tulip didn't see any harm in sitting with Big Foot. She scooted in. "Well, what do you know?"

"Not much. We think it's the same guy. Both girls from EMU, molested, stabbed, bodies moved."

"What about that Mixer girl, been missing since March?"

"I'm not on the case, Tulip. And if I were I couldn't tell you." He shrugged. "So what about D's rolls?"

"D bakes all kinds of things—cakes, pies, bread—but her cinnamon rolls are the best. No frosting, just melt-in-your-mouth goodness." Tulip pointed to the day-old rolls drowning in white goo. "Put these to shame."

He sat there real easy, slim hands around the cup, smoothing it up and down as if it had a wrinkle, his nails clipped and clean. His voice was low, musical—seductive might be the word. "Has that ex-husband been bothering you?"

Tulip snorted. "Not paying child support, hasn't even asked to see the kids."

"Maybe he doesn't want another run-in with the law."

Just like a man, all about him.

"When do you get off?" he asked.

Tulip looked at her watch. Off the clock.

Bigfoot pointed to the window. The sky was night dark, a roaring waterfall pounded the street. "You can't walk home in this."

"Just three blocks."

"I'll give you a lift."

"Isn't that against the rules?" Tulip's eyes locked on his. "How do I know you ain't him?"

"Who?"

"The pervert murderer."

Bigfoot slammed the cup he'd been loving up on the table and stood. "Dirty dig, Tulip. Do you want a ride or not?"

Water blanketed the restaurant window. Leaving Bigfoot's buck on the table for Sally, the evening waitress, Tulip took off her apron and retrieved her purse. Throwing newspapers over their heads, they raced through buckets of water to the patrol car.

Tulip pointed to the no-parking sign. "Nice to be a cop."

"Has its perks." He opened the door for Tulip, started the car, and turned on the wipers. Rivers of water sloshed across the window. "Reminds me of the night I took you and your children to D's. You were something else—drenched, trying to act like you weren't on the run."

"I thought you might try and take my kids!"

"Didn't give it a thought." He reached across the seat and patted her knee. "I wasn't sure you'd get in the car."

"I was scared. And your size-twenty shoes were squishing my belongings."

"If I remember, they were pretty intimate belongings." He drove past D's house and pulled up to the curb.

"You missed the house."

"You inviting me in for one of D's famous rolls?"

Tulip couldn't pretend that she didn't know what he was after. Marshall had always taken what he wanted. She knew about rape. She didn't plan on giving in to Bigfoot, but he seemed so kind, and she felt so empty. Maybe they could just talk. D and the kids wouldn't be home for at least an hour. Hell, what did she have to lose?

They raced through the rain to the house, where Tulip fumbled for the key. Inside, she grabbed a towel and tossed it to him. Instead of drying himself, he used it to pat her face, hair, and arms so gently that she felt her eyes tear. His eyes seeking hers, he briskly dried his curly hair. At the kitchen table, legs outstretched, he watched while she made a pot of coffee. She dished up a fluffy roll and shoved it toward him. He tore off a piece, but instead of eating it, he held it to her lips. Her breath caught. She bit into sticky cinnamon dough. He kissed her—a tender kiss, his tongue finding hers. Together they tasted the sweetness.

He cupped her head in his hands. "You know that I'm married?"

She pulled away. "I got eyes. I see your wedding ring. And I ain't having an affair with a married man."

"Does that mean we can't be friends?"

"Depends on what kind of friends."

He kissed the scar on her forehead, then her eyes, nose, cheeks, and finally her lips. He caressed her, his body warm and welcoming. Her face on his chest, she molded into him.

"I want you, Tulip."

She shoved him, hard. "What makes you think I would?"

He laughed and jerked her to him, his arms imprisoning her. She slapped him.

He grabbed her hand. "What was that about?"

"Idiot. I'm not going to bed with you."

"Tulip, I'm not going to hurt you!"

"Men hurt women! And I'm sure not stupid enough to get involved with a married, gun-slinging cop." She gulped for air. "Go!"

"I didn't mean—"

She pointed toward the door.

He picked up his cap. "I'll see you at the restaurant."

She leaned into the counter and watched him run to the patrol car, his huge feet making waves in the puddles. She had ordered him out, and he had gone.

She giggled. If Marshall got wind of her messing around with a cop, he'd have the law to deal with. She touched her cheek where Bigfoot, Ken, had kissed her. Her fingers eased their way up to the scar, a warning of what could happen. But his touch had been soft, inviting, awakening feelings she did not know she had. After all, he had helped her—delivered her and the kids to D's on a freezing night. Still, she was not beholden to him. It was she who'd had the courage to leave, made a plan, got a job. She was the one who had D keep half her tips when she was still with Marshall.

As she peeled off her uniform, she glimpsed herself in the mirror. The zits around her mouth had cleared. Her skin was pale against her freckles, but she had a determined look. She had stood up to a man, a cop even. This was a picture she *would* hang onto.

5

～っ

Six blocks from D's house at 265 Hamilton, a dark sedan slowed past a sun-lit yellow cottage with a garden of orange, rust, and sunshine marigolds, a rainbow of petunias adorning the window boxes. The car inched its way by the next house, which was abandoned, then a two-story brick. At the corner it turned. The sedan appeared again and parked in front of the sidewalk leading to the front door of the cottage.

As though entering the theater for a performance, two men slid out of the car and started up the walk, in step and abreast. It seemed to Grace watching from her window that a blood-red carpet might be appropriate. She did not so much as glance at her husband, Kirby, who was drinking his lemonade and vodka too quickly, quenching his thirst from the insufferable August heat. After their son had left home, they had begun having cocktail hour. Her husband said it would relax her. But it had not, and, in what felt like an act of defiance, she often left the alcohol out of her drink. Not this night. She had been fretful all day. She had misplaced the car keys, left water running in the sink; her hand and fingers had not connected properly to a cup, which shattered on the patio brick. Now she carefully placed her glass on the oak coffee table, removed her well-worn denim apron, and folded it. She rose and walked to the door, open-ing it before the bell rang.

Mutt and Jeff in full dress blues were more boys than men—too young. The tall one spoke. "Mrs. O'Shay? May we come in?"

"I had a feeling…," she said.

Her husband, now by her side, motioned the men into the living room. Grace focused on the dark uniforms. Her son was the height of the tall young man, about six feet, but stockier. Or at least he had been before he left for basic training. They sat, she and her husband on the couch, he reaching for her hand, the young men across the room in overstuffed chairs. Silent words circled the room. Empty. Flesh and bones held in place by her husband's firm grip. The short, baby-faced one's lips opened and closed. Pictures flashed: her toddler splashing in the bath; her long-legged preschooler gleefully pedaling his trike down the block; her teenager leaning against the kitchen counter wolfing warm chocolate chip cookies.

The messengers rose in unison. Startled from her stupor, Grace stumbled to her feet. Supported by her husband, she followed them to the door. The tall, rigid one turned and saluted.

She heard her voice. "This must be hard for you."

Stiff-legged, as though they had stepped on the brake and were disciplining themselves not to sprint away, they walked to the sedan.

It was not until the next day that she asked, "How?"

The doorbell rang again and again. Grace buried her head under the pillow. She felt her husband's side of the bed. Cold. She tried to open her crusted-shut eyes, sealed by grief. She wetted her fingers and eased one open. The hands of the clock were at ten. Did she remember Kirby getting up? Mornings were her only sleep since Rickey. After a night of wrestling with visions of her son wounded and bleeding and her inability to get to him, her mind just gave up. Head throbbing, she fell back onto the pillow. Light streamed through the partially open blind and settled on the dusty dresser. She moaned, rubbed her aching head, and stretched her wire-tight legs. Yesterday's housedress lay crumpled by the bed, her sandals in line before it, a person dissolved in clothing. With a perverse pleasure she kicked the dress and walked to the bathroom, her gait uneven.

Pulling a comb through snarled, graying hair, she noted the stranger in the mirror, a once-plump woman now with sagging skin and hollowed eyes. She had every intention of going down to the kitchen and making coffee but instead found herself in her son's room. She sank into his bed, pulling the edges of the spread around her. A mummy shrouded in plaid. She touched a square to her nose and breathed deeply, the dust irritating her nostrils. Not a trace of her boy. Marilyn Monroe, lips puckered, gazed down at the space where Grace's son should have lain. "He's dead too," she said. Trophies lined the shelves; a bat leaned against the wall. In the corner was a basket containing a baseball, basketball, and football. She remembered heated arguments with the boy and his father. "Not football! It's dangerous! You could be paralyzed!" But that game had not killed him. She should have chosen her battles, saved her strength for the big one.

Rays of sun intruded, beamed through the aluminum slats of the blinds. She imagined herself yanking the cord, the clatter of metal shutting out the world. But sitting up and walking two feet to the window seemed more than she could do. She rolled the spread more tightly around her. "Not a mummy," she said. "A caterpillar in a cocoon. When I wake, oh! that I were a butterfly."

There it was again, ring, ring, ringing, then pounding on the door, an insistent rhythmic cadence. The kitchen door squeaked open. Heels clicked on the linoleum, then muted as they came up the stairs.

"Grace? Grace, where are you?" A musical voice, one note away from bursting into song.

The bereaved woman covered her head. She would not make pretty with her neighbor. Footsteps went into the master bedroom, followed by a pause. "Grace?" Prudence Goodwin tiptoed into Rickey's room and stood uncertainly, her high heels digging into the carpet. She placed a flowered casserole on the side table. "Grace?" She raised the corner of the spread. "Still in your nightgown?"

Grace covered her head, willed her neighbor away. "Sleeping."

"Dinner. I brought you dinner."

Grace rose to order the bothersome neighbor out of her house, but the words caught in her throat. She had never demanded that anyone leave her home. Instead she muttered, "Too early."

Prudence shook her head in indignation, her sprayed, bleached hair remaining in place. "It's almost five. Your husband will be home soon. Get up. Bathe. Fix yourself. I'll set the table."

"It can't be five." Grace's gaze flitted about the room and settled on the clock. She must be going crazy.

"You haven't been in bed all day, have you?"

"No." She should have been ashamed for lying. But nothing seemed to matter.

"I'll make coffee," Prudence said.

Later Grace watched her friend stroll down the walk, past the dilapidated, vacant house and into her home, where the trim on the brick was in need of paint. Grace had a fleeting thought of asking Kirby to bring it to Prudence son Dennis's attention. Kirby might help; her husband liked that sort of work. She snorted. What was she thinking? Kirby could barely get himself to the hardware store and back. He and she were no longer capable of taking care of themselves, let alone helping Prudence. Two years ago, when Dr. Goodwin had been killed, Grace was the one to bring casseroles. When the Goodwins' mower quit, Kirby loaned Dennis his. Now it was the O'Shays' grass that was too long and thirsting for water.

It was nearly six when her husband crept into the house, his lateness giving her time to shower and make the bed. She hoped that he would think that she'd been up and functioning, but dirty dishes on the counter betrayed her. She considered telling him that she had made the meatloaf but thought he wouldn't believe that she would make such inferior food. But then the way she had been the past weeks, perhaps he would.

The table was ready: meatloaf, green beans, and bread. Grace sat facing the door.

Her husband pushed his dark hair from his forehead, then rubbed his hands together. He came to her, kissed her cheek. "I'm sorry to be late. I should have called." He sat at the table, picked up his napkin. "Meatloaf?"

She snickered. "Don't get too excited. Prudence."

He touched her hand. "She means well."

"Puts on airs! Striped seersucker slacks and high-heeled sandals—she was dressed for dinner, not an errand of mercy." Grace forked a bite, smelled it, and shook her head.

Kirby took a bite and grimaced. "It's dry. Perhaps a little ketchup would help." He went to the cupboard.

Grace picked at the gray mass with her fork. "Too much bread, and in hunks. No eggs." She slung her fork across the table. "She's ruined my recipe!"

Her husband's jaw tightened. Slowly, as though with great effort, he bent and picked up the fork. "The beans are fine and we can have peanut butter and jelly."

"I taught her how to make it." Her voice rose. "Can't she get anything right?"

Her husband placed his hand over hers. "This is not about Prudence."

Grace flung his hand. "You! *You* sent him away!"

Her husband's eyes clouded, his shoulders slumped. His voice barely audible, he said, "He wanted to serve his country, to protect us."

"War is not a football game where there are rules and players abide by them."

"He wanted to go."

"*You* should have stopped him."

6

Tulip kissed the top of Ernest's head. When she bent toward Tucker, he threw his arms around her and squeezed. She laughed. "Not so hard, Tucker." At ten, Tucker was too old to kiss and hug on. Tulip ruffled his hair. "Have a good day."

Watching her kids skip down the walk, Tulip felt prideful. After two months of school, their clothes still looked good—no holes, no patches. True, some were from Salvation Army, but they had each picked out an outfit at K-Mart. She'd made the trip special, stopping at the Dairy Queen after. Someday they could shop at Penney's and go out for lunch.

On this gorgeous fall day, leaves were aflame and the sun warm, perfect for walking in the woods. Tulip slipped into her jeans, rummaged through the stuffed drawer for an unstained T-shirt, and found a crumpled but clean one that D had given her. With a dab of lipstick and her curly hair brushed into submission, she gazed into the mirror. Her freckles seemed less vivid, her bangs hid her scar. She didn't look bad.

One last look, then she grabbed the K-Mart sack, tossed in toothbrush, panties, and socks. And waited. And then she waited some more.

Three honks and she was out the door. She had expected a new car, at least an Impala, but Ken was driving a mud-splattered, beat-up Ford station wagon. He reached over and opened the passenger door.

At the sight of him, Tulip's stomach flip-flopped. "I thought you weren't coming."

"Sorry. I overslept."

She had been awake for hours, and he had overslept. Miffed, she plopped back on the stained seat, picked up a McDonald's wrapper, and tossed it in the back. "You live in here?"

"Kids."

"Seems like you could have cleaned the car out."

"I worked overtime. And Elena left me with a bunch of projects to do while she and the kids are at her parents."

"Maybe you should have stayed home and done 'em."

He reached across the seat and rubbed her neck. "Trying to pick a fight?"

Maybe she was. Her dad had never been on time. Only what mattered to him was important. When she was eight, Ernest's age, he had promised to put up a tire swing in the humongous tree in their front yard. Imagining swinging, swinging up to the clouds, she checked the tree each day for one whole summer. The swing never appeared. At least Ken had kept his word. He came—late, but he came. He stopped by Joe's every work day, ordered coffee, and left a dollar tip. When he took her home, they made out like high school kids, but she hadn't let him do it. She had been excited about this date—tromping through the woods, going to a café, having someone wait on *her*, and sleeping at the Holiday Inn. She had pictured them cruising down the road, her body nestled against his. Instead she was sitting stick-straight and couldn't keep her gaze off the dusty dash or the muddy floor. She picked up a pacifier and twisted it in her fingers. Was Ken's toddler missing it?

She felt guilty. That was it. Determined not to let it ruin her day, she stretched her legs and eased her head back onto the seat. When they were away from Ypsilanti's prying eyes, Ken reached over and pulled her close. She laid her hand on his leg and snuggled into his lean chest. On the empty road he took curves at fifty-five, her stomach doing flip-flops.

Ken broke the silence. "There just aren't any clues to those murders."

"What...? You're thinking about dead women?"

"They think it might be the same guy, a student. Don't go walking around EMU."

He sure knew how to ruin a mood. They had one day together and he was scaring her about a murderer. To her credit, she kept her mouth shut. She studied the fields, bare and brown, some with bales of hay. Ken took Highway 12 through Saline and then Clinton, where he stopped at a red light in front of the towering Clintonian Inn. Left on 59, right on 50, past more farms until they arrived at Hidden Lake Gardens.

They passed the botanical building with its outside garden of fall mums and a few straggly summer flowers. A narrow road wove through thick woods, a circus of color, gold and red accenting evergreen. Ken stopped the car at a pond, grass deep green around its slopping edges, sun glistening on inky water. A couple of gorgeous swans swam toward them, white on black, long necks arched inquiringly.

"We're here, babe." Ken reached for a bag of bread on the backseat.

"You're going to feed the swans?"

"Always do. In the spring, when their babies are small, the papa's ferocious. He'll chase you if you get too close." He laughed. "You should have seen Timmy run."

You pick me up in a filthy car filled with family reminders, Tulip thought. You're thinking about a murder and then you talk about your kid.

Ken whipped out a piece of bread and hurled it into the water. A swan swam over, bit it, then dropped it. The bigger swan scooped it up.

"Greedy male." *Like all males*. Tulip broke a slice into pieces and flung them toward the swans. The couple swam closer. They straightened their curved necks, scooped up the bread, then gracefully floated away.

Ken took Tulip's hand. On the path leaves crunched under their feet. A hawk swooped down, scattering chirping birds. A squirrel scampered up a tree. At a break in the woods, a leaf-covered meadow opened up. Laughing, Ken ran into it, flinging leaves and piling them. "Like the birds," he said. "Let's make a nest!"

Tulip giggled. "No way."

He jumped up, caught her by the waist, and wrestled her into the leaves. He kissed her face, her lips. His tongue found hers. "Please," he moaned.

"It's too public."

He stroked her hair. "You mean all the birds and animals?"

"Somebody might come along. Besides, we're going to a motel."

"OK. But you don't know what you're missing." He took her hand. "First we'll have a late lunch at the Grasshopper in Adrian, my favorite Mexican restaurant. Do you like Mexican?"

"Never ate it."

"Never?"

"Joe's and McDonald's."

"Well, you're in for a treat."

Midafternoon and the Grasshopper was still busy, the bar smoky, the booths as broken-down as Joe's. The floor needed a sweep and a scrub. "This is a favorite?"

"Wait till you taste the food." Ken slid into booth near the bar.

"Let's eat in the other room, where it's not so smoky."

"No different." He patted the seat next to him.

Tulip sat on the other side.

The waitress brought a basket of hot tortilla chips and a syrup pitcher of red sauce. "Salsa, hot," Ken said, as he poured it on a pile of chips. He leered at the waitress. "What's your name, sweetheart?"

Sweetheart's brows shot up. "Amy."

Ken winked. "Nice name, Amy. Margaritas."

"Two? Or you want a pitcher? They're on special."

He licked his lips. "By all means."

Amy looked questioningly at Tulip, then hurried away.

"What's in it?" Tulip asked.

"You've never had a margarita? Tequila. You'll like it." He grabbed a handful of chips, the sauce spilling through his fingers and onto the basket.

Tulip wiped his hand with a napkin. "Pig! You stop flirting with that waitress. She's a single mom working her ass off. She doesn't think you're cool."

"What makes you think she's a single mom?"

"You're wearing a wedding ring. You think a woman working in a bar wouldn't wear hers? She's got a fussy baby, needs sleep. Did you see the circles around her eyes?" Tulip scooped sauce onto a warm chip. "Not bad. Not too spicy."

Amy sat a frosted pitcher on the table. "Ready to order?"

Ken looked at her hand, her face, and nodded. He poured drinks and took a swig.

Tulip sipped hers. "Yuck! It's sour and salty."

Amy spoke. "I'm not fond of them either. Can give you a nasty headache." She grinned. "I like your T-shirt."

"Huh?"

"Yeah! 'Woman Power!'"

"Oh." Tulip felt the front of her shirt.

Ken snickered, drained his glass, and wiped his hand across his mouth. "Sweetheart, I'll have the deluxe plate with lots of rice and beans."

Tulip pointed to her glass and shook her head. "I need a Coke." She ordered a combination plate: enchilada, burrito, taco. She could have rice and beans any day. Amy hurried away.

"I was right, wasn't I? She's a single mom, trying to earn a living, ogled and called sweetheart by every drunk who comes in."

Ken poured another glass and took a swig. "You're leaving a lot for me to drink, babe."

"Waste of money to order a pitcher."

He chortled. "I'm a cop. I'm loaded."

"You're getting that way."

Ken stuffed himself with chips and guzzled margaritas Reaching across the table, he curled a wisp of Tulip's red hair around his sticky finger. "Pretty." He hiccupped.

Tulip slapped his hand. Amy stood at the bar studying hem. *She knew.* Tulip whispered through gritted teeth, "Why are you acting like this?"

"Like what?"

"Like, like…" She couldn't think of words to describe him—a redneck, a drunk?

"Loosen up, Tulip." He took another drink, smacked his lips.

"Drowning in drink! You are disgusting."

"Are you saying that I have a drinking problem?"

"Do you?"

Amy brought two steaming platters. Tulip blew on a forkful of burrito and cautiously tasted it. She took a huge bite and another. "Good!" She speared a forkful of Ken's rice and beans. "Wow! Better than D's!"

Sated, Tulip set down her fork. She'd had her face in her plate, wolfing food. She was every bit as disgusting as Ken. But she was *not* getting plastered.

Ken swiped his sticky chin and tossed the soggy napkin in his plate. "Ready to check in, sweetheart?"

At that moment, checking in was the last thing she wanted. "There's a bookstore across the street, Booknook. See the sign? Let's stop there, get the kids a book."

"Soon as I finish my drink."

She scooted his glass away. "You're drunk, Ken."

"No way, babe." He grabbed his glass, gulped the remainder, and motioned to Amy. "Hey, pretty lady, we're ready for the check."

Ken groped for his billfold and then stared dumbly at it. Tulip took it and paid the bill, leaving Amy a 50 percent tip. Waitressing was a shit job, but at least Tulip didn't have to deal with drunks.

Ken flopped his arm over Tulip's shoulder and teetered out of the restaurant.

"Give me the key." Tulip's words were a snarl.

She opened the passenger door. Ken crawled in, his head lopping against the seat. Tulip started the car, slammed it into drive, and headed home.

When she reached D's, Ken was still passed out. She drove the car to the next block, turned off the engine, and locked the doors. She wasn't explaining a drunk sleeping it off in front of her house.

Walking home, she heard footsteps behind her. Glancing back, she glimpsed a strapping younger man. She walked faster. He matched her steps—gaining. It was daylight. It couldn't be the murderer. Could it? She ran. Reaching the house she threw open the door, stumbled in, and locked it. Panting, she peered out the window. No one there.

That night she dreamed she was being chased down a dark alley. She ran faster and faster. Claws grabbed her shoulder, threw her to the ground. She woke, her heart thumping. So that's how she felt about Ken. The date had been a rerun of her life. She was disgusted with him for treating her like a piece of meat, but more so with herself for getting in that situation. She deserved better.

As Tulip left for work the following day, a patrol car pulled into the drive. Ken stepped out holding a huge, potted orange chrysanthemum. "Peace offering."

"Think I want your damn mum?"

"Sorry, Tulip. I drank too much."

An apology! And no one had ever brought her flowers. When Marshall hit her the first time, he had said he was sorry and that he wouldn't do it again. Ken did not promise that he wouldn't drink. Promises that you couldn't fulfill were worthless. Tulip's dad was a drunk, Calvin too. When they drank, no one was safe. However, Ken was not a mean drunk and Tulip liked him. D had a girlfriend. Why couldn't Ken be her friend? She wasn't going to risk any overnights, but an hour or two? No one need know.

When the house was empty, Ken picked Tulip up from work, a stolen hour. Once, when D was home, they had sex in the patrol car. Risky business. That day Tulip had an orgasm, her first ever. She could see the headlines: "On-Duty Married Policeman Caught with Pants Down."

7

$\sim$

What a difference a year made. No, a year and a half. Who would have thought Tulip would be tooling down the street in her own red pickup? Old Ruby was rusty, but she ran and she was paid for. Tulip cranked down the pickup window and felt the warm spring breeze on her cheeks. This was a day to celebrate. After all their hard work in school, the kids deserved a treat. She would pick them up and buy a quart of Dairy Queen to share at the park.

Tulip and D shared responsibilities. D cooked yummy food—goulash, fried chicken, and pot roast with potatoes, onions, and carrots. Tulip cleaned. It seemed fair. D, a walking advertisement for karate, tried to convince her to join. With a killer on the loose and Marshall for an ex-husband, D thought Tulip needed to know how to defend herself.

For once, Tulip was not concerned. Marshall was still busy with his girl-friend and only called when he was stinking drunk. "I'll get you, bitch!" he screamed into the phone. Tulip had learned to button her lip, hang up, and take the phone off the hook. Marshall knew not to come around. He wouldn't want to rile D, and he might have gotten wind of the cop in Tulip's life.

Still, Tulip looked over her shoulder. But she was not alone. With a killer on the loose, every young woman in Ypsilanti and Ann Arbor was frightened. Seven girls had been killed, mostly college students. For once, being poor and uneducated was a point in Tulip's favor. After the killer carved up a girl, sixteen, and in April a thirteen-year-old, Tulip told Hunter not to go to town by herself, always to walk with her brothers.

In the driveway Tulip blasted the horn. Tucker trundled out barefoot. "Go get your shoes. We're going to the park."

"I-I-I'm watching R-Road Runner."

"Tell D. Get your brother and sister. We're getting ice cream."

Tucker hightailed it inside. Tulip flipped on the radio. Wynn Stewart's mellow voice rang out: "It's such a pretty world today. Look at the sunshine…" Humming along, she leaned back and rested her eyes.

Ernest and Tucker ran out, Tucker's shoestrings flopping.

"Tucker, tie your shoes. Ernest, go get Hunter!"

Ernest shrugged. "Not here."

"What?"

"I think she went home with a friend."

"Who?"

"Didn't say."

"Shit…I suppose she told D. We'll just go without her."

At the Dairy Queen, Tucker begged for a hot fudge sundae. Tulip shook her head. "Too much, but you can have a cone."

At Riverside Park, trees were in bud, leaves popping overnight. Looking for fish, the boys walked along the riverbank, tossing sticks in the clear water. Contented, Tulip lay down on a picnic table and soaked up the sun. When they arrived home, supper was ready. Hamburgers and French fries, Hunter's favorite.

"Where's Hunter?" Tulip asked.

D shrugged.

"She didn't tell you? Ernest, do you know where she went?"

Tucker spoke up. "I-I saw her with a girl in a ponytail. Th-they got in a black car."

The pervert killer? No, Hunter wouldn't get in a car with a stranger. "You don't know who she went with?"

They shook their heads.

"She got in a car? How many times have I told you kids not to get in cars with someone you don't know?"

"Maybe she knew him," Ernest said.

Tulip's voice rose. "Him? Him? She got in a car with a him?"

Tucker nodded. "Y-yeah, and a girl."

D touched Tulip's back. "Parents pick their kids up after school."

"I don't know it was a parent. I just know there's a murderer on the loose and my little girl is out there with some strange man!"

"Settle down, think. Who are her friends?" D asked.

"I don't know."

"No, I guess you wouldn't. I'm the one who's here after school. Sometimes a little girl with a ponytail—Mary, I think—walks home from school with her. She comes in for a treat. A nice girl, shy."

"So what's her last name?"

"I don't know."

"You don't know!"

D's dark eyes flashed. "Don't you be blaming me! You didn't even know that Hunter had a friend."

"You're the one who's here after school!"

"I'm not her mother!"

The door banged open. Hunter ran in, red-cheeked and breathless. "I had the best time! We went to the woods behind Mary's house—lots of birds and squirrels. There's a creek and I saw a beaver dam!"

Tulip gripped her arm. "Hunter, don't you ever go off and not tell me where you're going!"

Hunter wrenched away. "You weren't here. You're never here!"

"Go to your room, Hunter!"

"What about supper?"

D clamped her hand on Tulip's shoulder. "Perhaps we should talk about this." Making her voice soft, she turned to Hunter. "It's good that you have a friend—Mary's her name?"

Hunter nodded.

"But we need to know where you are. Your mom was worried something might have happened to you. I don't mean to scare you, but remember the coed-killer?"

Hunter's eyes got big. "But I'm not in college."

"No, but we want to make sure you're safe. Your mom and I love you. Next time, you ask."

Hunter nodded again.

D looked at Tulip and spoke firmly. "Now let's eat before the fries get cold."

Tulip was pissed, pissed at Hunter and at D for interfering. "There's a bad man out there. You are not to leave this house without one of your brothers and you are *all* to stay away from EMU. Do you understand?"

They nodded.

"C-can we eat now?" Tucker asked.

Chairs scraping linoleum like chalk across a blackboard, they sat. No one spoke. The squishing of the ketchup bottle and clinking of forks jangled in Tulip's brain.

After, Hunter did dishes by herself with no complaints. Later Tulip heard D in the kitchen talking to her. "You said her last name was Franklin? Now, when you go to school tomorrow, you give her our phone number and ask for hers. Then if you're at her house, we can call."

When Tulip shut her eyes that night, she saw Hunter lying dead in a pool of blood. D, eyes flashing, shook her finger at Tulip. She deserved that and worse. D had remained calm and caring while Tulip had just been screaming scared. Thank God she hadn't slapped Hunter.

In July the police caught the pervert, John Norman Collins, a senior at Eastern studying elementary education. The paper reported he was a personable, helpful young man. So he had not worn his craziness on the outside like Marshall with his crazy eye, or Calvin, who was just plain evil. Tulip guessed bad guys came in all shapes and sizes, with many disguises. That monster could have been her daughter's teacher.

With the killer in prison and Marshall occupied elsewhere, Tulip had only black echo-memories haunting her. The kids were getting bigger and were tripping over each other in D's small house. At eleven, Tucker was taller than Tulip. Hunter was small for ten, but her mouth took up a lot of space. Skinny Ernest was shooting up.

D was a great housemate and Tulip's best friend, her only friend. She had learned much from D. Now Tulip knew to look directly at the children when she spoke to them, to touch Tucker when she needed his attention. So many little tricks. Tulip was grateful, but she needed to be in charge of her children. She had squirreled away money for a security deposit, first and last month's rent. With Old Ruby, her ten-year-old Ford pickup, they were ready to roll. But what if one of the kids got sick, if she couldn't pay the heat? And worse, what if Marshall lost his girlfriend and came after her?

8

⤳

Kathy sprang from the booth. "D, Tulip, I did it! I did it! I got the house. Bought it for taxes. It's old. Needs paint but has lots of potential. Good location, great family home. I'm going to flip it. My first investment." Kathy had been sitting in the booth, swinging her foot, drumming the table, waiting impatiently for Joe to go to the bank.

"'Atta girl," said D. "You tell us about it over coffee."

"Flip it?" Tulip asked, imagining a giant spatula flipping a house on its roof.

Kathy smiled. "Sell it—sell it cheap, but make a profit."

D poured the coffee. "Tulip! You could buy it!"

"Me? No one would give me credit."

"Kathy could. You could buy it on a land contract."

"Huh?"

Kathy explained. A land contract was like renting, with monthly payments. When the house was paid for, it was yours. But if you missed a payment, you could be out in the cold. The old woman who owned the house had died years ago. It was empty and in bad shape. Cheap. Kathy was divorced and knew how hard it was to get credit. A land contract with a monthly check would do her just fine.

Tulip had ideas as to why Kathy would give her so much credit. D and Tulip had a rule that there wouldn't be any goings-on in the house when the kids were home. D wanted more privacy with Kathy. They seemed good for each other, never had screaming fights like Tulip's folks or Marshall and her. The two laughed a lot, often at things that didn't strike Tulip as funny. They were affectionate, not all lovey-dovey, but a touch on the hand or a peck on the cheek. Tulip was getting used to them as a couple, could even picture them cuddled up in bed.

Tulip was alone when she first saw the house. It reminded her of a very old woman, gray, with dead skin peeling from her body. Thinning hair, bleached by the sun and uprooted by the wind, covered her head. Dirt cataracts filmed her eyes. The house stood bewildered in the midst of broken beer bottles, pop cans, and milk cartons—the neighborhood dump.

The newer homes on either side highlighted the old one's shabbiness: a yellow two-story with sparkling windows and petunia ruffles hanging from window boxes. Marigolds filling the berm and lining the walk—a friendly house. The other, a rough, dark brick with a spindly tree in front, heavy drapes blocking the sun.

Tulip felt as out of place as the old house must feel. She breathed deeply. "You worked for this, saved for this. Get your butt in there." Clutching the flashlight that Kathy had instructed her to take, she marched up the walk and onto the porch. Avoiding the splintered wood in front of the door, she took the tail of her shirt and tried the filthy black knob. The door groaned open. She entered. The door slammed shut. The house was dark and damp and smelled like piss. Her foot crunched something. She flipped on the flashlight and kicked the turd or whatever the hell it was out of the way. She beamed the light on the ceiling and followed a crack snaking down to the floor. As she walked toward the straight-up staircase, boards squeaked. She jiggled the banister. It held. "You don't scare me. You've been alone too long. You're grouchy. Old Grouchy, that's what I'll call you."

Caw, caw, caw. She whirled and started for the door. The screeching came from outside. Narrow streaks of light shone through the grime of the living room window. She cleaned a section with her sleeve. *Caw, caw.* A crow on a branch mocked her.

She gave him the finger. "You're not scaring me. I'm buying this house!"

Caw, caw.

Waving her arms, she ran from the house. "Get out of my tree, you ugly bird! Get out!" *Caw!* He flew. She clasped her hand to her mouth and suppressed a giggle. What would the neighbors think, her screaming in the front yard?

The partially opened drape in the brick house closed.

Tulip wrote the check for five hundred dollars—her entire savings—and signed on the dotted line. That night she dreamed she was huddled in a corner of the freezing house. The roof was gone. A crow lit on the rafter and cawed. Wind howled. Snow blew through the rooms and out broken windows. Marshall clattered through the door and aimed his gun. "It's time, Tulip."

Weeds were knee deep. Sun spotlighted crooked shutters, peeling paint. Hunter looked up at the broken attic window. "Geez, Mom, it looks like a haunted house."

They had spent the morning packing Old Ruby. Hot and tired, Tulip did not want to deal with one of Hunter's snits. She made her voice cheerful. "You've seen it before. You said it was cool. It's ours! A coat of paint will do wonders. And you'll have your own room." She ruffled Hunter's curly hair.

Tucker stepped on the rotten porch board. Tulip yanked him away. "Tucker, you've got to stay off this part of the porch. It's broken. You'll fall through! You have to walk around." He tapped it again. She slapped him on the butt.

Hunter threw open the door and raced upstairs with Ernest hot on her heels. Tucker panted after them.

"I call this one." Hunter pointed to the largest bedroom.

Tulip shook her head. "I told you the boys have to share. You get the small one."

"They always get the good stuff. Mine doesn't even have a closet!"

"Hey!" Ernest hollered. "The bathtub's got paws, and it looks like a cooler's hanging on the wall."

Tulip walked into the bathroom. "Water tank."

"Weird."

"Yep." She flushed the toilet. "It works."

August was humid, too hot to be moving. Tulip was thankful they didn't have much furniture—two pickup loads and a trip to the Salvation Army. D and she did most of the heavy lifting. Ernest carried boxes and Hunter ran back and forth with the lighter stuff. Kathy worked in the kitchen.

Carrying boxes too awkward and heavy for him, Tucker tried to help. Holding a box by its flaps, huffing and puffing, he lugged melamine dishes up the stairs. A flap ripped. Cups clattered down the steps.

Tulip grabbed him by the shirt. "Tucker, what in the hell are you doing taking dishes upstairs?"

Tucker threw his arms in the air, ran outside, and planted himself on the curb, where he picked his nose. Not a sight the neighbors should see.

Most everything was in, the beds upstairs. It would take days to sort the junk out. Tulip went to the kitchen and turned on the light, a bare bulb hanging from the ceiling. One wall had floor-to-ceiling cupboards. The top cupboards sat on top of wider, counter-high ones, with just a foot of counter space. Who the hell could mix up a cake on a twelve-inch ledge? The opposite wall was lined with a sink, gas stove, and an ancient refrigerator. The freezer, a small box inside the fridge, would make soup of ice cream. Tulip sighed. They'd just have to make do.

D huffed in carrying a box and plunked it on the floor. She wiped her face with her T-shirt. "It's the last one. Kathy and I have to go."

"You're not staying for supper?"

"Got to get cleaned up. We're going to the Ark to see Joan Baez." D eyed the litter in the kitchen. "You'll figure it out."

"Sure, thanks. You were both a big help. Couldn't have done it without you."

Kathy nodded and held the door open.

D opened her arms. "I'll miss you."

"Me too. See you at work."

"Take care." D hugged Tucker. "Now, you come on over any time."

Hand in hand, D and Kathy dashed to the car.

They couldn't get away fast enough. Abandoned. Tulip felt abandoned. Ridiculous. She had just moved into her own home. But everywhere she looked there were boxes and she had no idea where to begin. She cleared a chair and slumped into it.

"M-M-Mom, I'm hungry," Tucker whimpered.

"We all are. Hunter, get the peanut butter."

Hunter found it in a bag on top of squashed bread. While she and Ernest made sandwiches, Tulip threw sheets on the beds. Hunter had a single bed they'd picked up off a curb. The boys' Salvation Army mattress was on the floor, not so far for Tucker to fall. Ernest didn't like to sleep alone and woke at the slightest noise.

Sitting on boxes, the kids gobbled sandwiches. Shortly, with peanut butter gluing Old Grouchy's grime to hands and faces, they flopped into bed.

Tulip closed the bread and screwed the lid on the jar.

Upstairs, mice had made a nest in the claw-foot bathtub. Tulip found a dustpan to scrape out the droppings and scrubbed it with Comet. The water was tepid and she worried that the heater might conk out. Too tired to wash, she lounged in the tub, imagining the dirt floating off her body. She dunked her head, dumped shampoo on her hair—a lick and a promise. *B-r-ring.* So the doorbell worked. She slid down into the tub, the water washing over her face. *B-r-ring.* She willed the ringing to stop. *B-r-r-ring, b-r-r-ring.*

Ernest rapped on the door. "Mom, Mom, are you in there?"

"Yeah, Ernest. Go back to bed."

"Someone's here!"

"I know."

"Aren't you going to answer?"

"Yeah, yeah. Get back to bed." She wrapped a flimsy towel around her and crept downstairs. *God, let it not be Marshall.* She peeked through the tiny window in the door. A tall, shapely woman dressed in a suit held something in front of her. A book? Selling something at night? They didn't even let you get settled before they came at you. Tulip stood back out of the way and Ernest, who'd followed, cracked the door, the safety chain still in place.

The woman peeked around the door at Ernest. "Hello, I hope it's not too late. I saw the lights were still on and thought you might enjoy some fresh-baked brownies." Her voice sang. "I'm Prudence Goodwin. May I speak with your mother?"

Ernest turned and looked at Tulip. So the woman knew she was there. "I'm not decent… I mean I'm not dressed. I was in the tub."

"Oh, I'm so sorry, I didn't know. I live next door in the brick house." She pointed to the creepy house. "I saw you moving in. I brought you dessert." She handed the dish to Ernest.

It was a little late for dessert. That woman had been peeking out her draped window all day. She wouldn't come out in the light, and now there she was— Vampire Woman! "Thanks." Tulip pulled the towel tighter.

"You're welcome." The woman stepped back.

"Look out for the board!"

C-r-r-r-ack! The board splintered. The woman shrieked.

"Shit!" Tulip flew out the door. The woman's ankle was caught in splintered wood. She squealed and waved her arms.

Tulip bent to help. As though the towel were a life preserver, the woman grabbed on.

Tulip yanked on the towel. *R-r-r-rip.* She yelled at Ernest, "Find something sharp!" She covered her breasts with her dinky piece of towel. Ernest ran back with a metal spatula. Tulip pried at the boards.

The woman howled. "My ankle! You're hurting me!"

"Calm down. I'll have you out in a minute. You have to help me." Tulip talked to her like she would one of the kids—better, even. She might have screamed at them. "I don't want to hurt you."

The wood, rotten-wet, gave way. Moaning, the woman lifted her foot. Tulip grabbed the bigger piece of towel and held it in front of her.

Then she saw him—this guy, a teenager, standing at the bottom of the stairs, rocking with silent laughter.

She crossed her arms to cover her breasts. "Who the hell are you?"

He smirked. Even in the dim light, she could tell he was good looking, the kind of boy who had only wanted one thing from her in high school. She wanted to slap that smirk right off his face.

"Sorry. I'm Dennis Goodwin. Prudence is my mom." If he hadn't been trying to stop laughing, his voice might have been apologetic. He took the stairs two at a time and knelt over his mother. As a doctor would do, he examined her ankle, moving it back and forth. He patted her shoulder. "Looks OK."

She whimpered. "I think it's broken."

"No, Mom." He smiled at Tulip, white teeth gleaming in the dark. *Vampire mother, vampire son.* "I think the porch got the worst of it." He put his arm around his mother and helped her up. "Come on. Let's go soak your ankle."

Leaning on him, she limped down the stairs. "Are you sure it's not broken?"

"No, Mom. You can move it. You're walking on it."

"I knew that house should be condemned," she muttered.

Up yours! To Tulip's credit, she didn't say it out loud.

With the son supporting his mother, they walked toward home. He turned. "Sorry about all this. I'll drop by tomorrow and fix the porch."

Strange kid. Looked like he was sixteen but acted all grown up. Tulip flung soapy hair out of her stinging eyes and hurried into the house. Ernest was at the kitchen counter digging into the brownies, his fingers shit brown. "Just one, then get upstairs."

Tulip rinsed her hair and collapsed into bed. The house creaked. Mice scurried in the walls. Darkness filled nooks and crannies with unknown dangers. She missed D and the cocoon of her home. *Marshall! What if Marshall comes?* She crawled out of bed, got the hammer off the dresser, and put it under her pillow.

Wham—wham—wham! What the hell—the middle of the night! Someone was beating on Tulip's door. *Marshall!* She gripped the hammer and hightailed it downstairs.

Light crept through streaked living room windows. The kids were watching fuzzy cartoons in their PJs and eating dry Cheerios.

"There's a guy on the porch," Hunter said, spewing cereal.

Tulip waved her hammer. "Chew with your mouth closed."

Hunter clicked her tongue and pointed at Tucker sitting in a sea of crumbs.

The vampire's son was kneeling on the porch, battering nails into a thick sheet of plywood. He swung his hammer to the rhythm of a rock song playing softly on a radio he'd plugged into *her* electricity. Midnight-black hair curled around pointy ears. Sweat glistened on his skinny back.

"What the hell are you doing?"

He turned, his smile a toothpaste advertisement. With his delicate face and turned-up nose, he'd have made a pretty girl. "Sorry, I didn't know you were sleeping." He pointed to her hammer. "Did you come to help?"

How much had he seen last night? Tulip pulled her pajama top shut tight and spewed questions. "Do you always say you're sorry? What are you doing here so early?"

As if she were stupid or hard of hearing, he sat back on his haunches and talked real slow. "No to the first question. Only when I embarrass naked ladies—or when I wake them. Otherwise I find it hard to apologize. It's been known to get me into trouble." He stood up and brushed dust from his jeans. "It's after ten, sleepy lady. I fixed your porch. You won't have any more neighbors dropping in."

Tulip couldn't keep herself from laughing. "How's your mom's ankle?"

"Her ankle's fine. A slight sprain, a few scratches." He shook his head. "But her pride is irreparable."

His eyes were amazing—sparkling onyx. The sun felt warm and welcoming. A dove cooed. "Are you old enough to drink coffee?"

He laughed, a dimple forming at the corner of his mouth.

"It'll just take a minute. I'll get dressed."

"I rather liked the towel, but your pajamas are nice too." He leaned over and gave a nail one last bang.

Still in her T-shirt and panties, Hunter came to the door. She made a blow-fish face, flattening her nose and lips on the screen, then stepped onto the porch. "Aren't you done yet?"

"Get some clothes on, Hunter."

The strange guy tugged on his T-shirt, tossed the hammer in his toolbox, and unplugged his radio. "Got to go." He skipped down the steps and hurried toward his house. Tulip had thought he was coming in for coffee. Just as well. What was she doing flirting with a kid?

Tulip put one foot on the plywood, then another. She stomped on it. Hunter giggled and jumped on. Laughing, they held hands and jumped up and down, Hunter's red hair bouncing off her shoulders, glistening in the sunlight.

"I guess it'll hold." Tulip shook her finger. "But I don't want you playing jump rope out here."

"I don't have a jump rope." Hunter ran into the house, slamming the screen.

Hunter didn't have a jump rope? A country song popped into Tulip's head: "Skip a rope, skip a rope…now ain't it kinda funny what the children say…Daddy hates Mommy, and Mommy hates Dad…" The words were true. Children were overlooked, suffered even, when parents fought. She had to pay more attention to her children, and she could afford a jump rope.

Tulip studied the plywood, a Band-Aid covering a gaping wound. The sun had turned sizzling, sucking up all the air. Across the lawn the busybody vampire peeked out her window.

Tulip walked into the house, already warm. Every bone in her body ached. Boxes were helter-skelter around the living room. Dishes, pots, and utensils covered the narrow kitchen counter. The kids were lined up on the couch watching a blurry Superman save the city. Tulip flipped off the TV. "Put your bowls in the sink. Get dressed and organize your rooms." Surprisingly, they did not gripe.

A moment later Hunter called from the kitchen, "Mom, there's a box in the sink."

When she had lived with D, Tulip had been on a mission. She worked long hours and saved her tips. She was exhausted, often short with the kids. Sneaking off with Bigfoot cut down on family time. Now that they had a home, this was going to change. She would spend more time with the kids. She imagined popping corn on a winter's night. She could read *James and the Giant Peach*, the bedtime story D had read to the kids. They loved the magic, the idea of an adventure inside a peach. Tucker had roared with laughter when the peach crushed the two evil aunts. Listening from the living room, Tulip had felt left out. Now they could be a regular family, with Tulip doing the reading.

If there were no crisis, she could manage the payments, even buy some paint. If Marshall stayed out of their lives and paid child support, she would be sitting pretty. But she wasn't going to bother him about money, didn't want to be on his radar screen. He was the father of these kids. Well, two of them. He made ten times more money than she did, drove new cars, and lived like there was no tomorrow. All the while his kids were wearing holey pants and worn-out sneakers and eating beans. It wasn't fair. But if she went after child support, he'd be after her. She would have to double-bolt the doors. Then he'd probably come in through a window, or worse, a kid would open the door. She was on her own.

Tulip would make this house their home. D said houses had feelings, that they needed love, that they could feel neglected and unwanted. Old Grouchy had been misused, abused, and abandoned. Tulip hoped that TLC and a face-lift would give her new life. Her walls were stained, plaster cracked, but Tulip would learn to repair them. In the meantime, Murphy's Oil Soap and hot water would do wonders. She would start in the kitchen, the heart of a home. She would paint it yellow, her favorite, and someday she'd paint the beat-up pine cupboards. When she could afford it, she'd replace D's card table with a nice used used one, maybe red..

Tulip had avoided the basement, the dirty bottom, where she feared killer rats had set up housekeeping. Now, with the flashlight's waning beam, she picked her way down steep, narrow stairs into the Michigan cellar, musty, cave-like, with a brick-hard dirt floor. A giant octopus of a furnace, arms outstretched, seemed to support the kitchen above. Her gaze followed the rough cement blocks to the rafters, where knob and tube wiring dangled from the beams. Uh-oh! There were only two outlets in the kitchen. She hadn't thought about extension cords and blown fuses.

The door to the coal bin stood open. She peeked into the forbidding darkness, then shut the door. Dirt shelves around the outer edges of the basement were filled with water-stained cardboard boxes—discards of the old woman's life. Flowerpots, dishes, an iron skillet. Objects Tulip couldn't make out in the dim light and didn't want to touch. A rusty bedstead, scooter, and trike leaned against the wall. The old woman was once young, had had children.

A dinky water heater stood in the corner. There would be no lingering in the shower. A rusty stream trickled down the tank and onto the floor. Tulip felt the tank—barely warm. The date said it was from 1950—nearly twenty years ago. It had died of old age. She found the valve, shut it off, and marched upstairs.

9

The ancient window air conditioner clanked and groaned, attempting to cool the hot, humid kitchen. Grace knew better than to cook on this sweltering day—and a huge pot of chicken noodle soup? She tasted the soup, added a bit of salt, and tried it again. For months food had repulsed her. Excess weight that she had worked so hard to lose over the years had melted away, leaving her weak and flabby. Then, inexplicably, she found food comforting. Today of all days she needed comfort. She closed her eyes and breathed deeply, taking in the rich, fatty aroma. She knew Rickey was not there, but she saw him clearly: shaggy dark hair, bowl cupped in his huge hand, slurping noodles, giving her a wink and his lopsided smile. "It's good, Mom." She wiped a tear with her apron, a gift from Rickey. He'd made it in summer camp when he was eight, stenciled it with the words I LOVE MOM. He had said it was a girly thing to do, but his grin belied his words.

Although it had been a year to the day, his death still felt fresh, piercing. She had marked this first anniversary by making Rickey's favorite soup. After the kitchen was in order, she intended to look at his baby album, which she'd laid out on the coffee table. Hands trembling, she ladled soup into individual pint jars to freeze for Kirby's lunches. The first container overflowed. She imagined it exploding in the freezer, lifeless noodles strewn over packages of steak and ground beef.

Through the kitchen window, Grace watched the new neighbor children playing in their overgrown, littered backyard: a pudgy, awkward boy; a skinny dark-haired boy; and a loudmouthed, redheaded girl. The weeping willow provided an enticing, shaded play area. But last fall, on a sunny day when the tree was bare, broken glass had glistened on the ground. Those children might get hurt. If she had the energy, she should take some soup over and tell the mother about the danger. Prudence was appalled by the woman and her "brats" moving in next door, but Grace was pleased that someone was there. The house had deteriorated. With paint peeling, spirea engulfing the front porch, and weeds growing like cancer, that mother had her work cut out for her.

In a dreamlike state, Grace watched the children play. The bigger boy had commandeered a rolling pin and some large kitchen spoons and was scooping dirt into a rusty coffee can. He mixed it with water, spread it on a board, and rolled it out like dough. His hair, red like his sister's, fell over his eyes, and every now and then he brushed it aside and wiped his nose on a dirty sleeve.

The wiry boy called from the kitchen, "Tucker, Tucker, Tucker, time to eat." When Tucker wouldn't budge, the boy brought him a sandwich and a glass of something—milk, Grace hoped. Tucker stuffed the sandwich into his mouth and it was gone in seconds. He gulped his drink and then poured the last of it into the mud pie.

Standing by the kitchen window, Grace ate a bowl of soup. Tucker was engrossed in an Indian war dance; ferocious, guttural war whoops spurring him on as he threatened an unseen enemy with the rolling pin. He bent toward the earth, rose to the sun. Faster and faster he careened. The roller whipped through the air. The younger boy screamed and clamped a hand to his forehead.

Grace dropped the bowl and dashed out across the yard. The little guy held his head, blood trickling through his fingers. She ripped off her apron and pressed it over the gash above his eye. Blood seeped through the fabric.

The clumsy one clutched the remaining handle of the rolling pin. "I-I-I d-d-didn't mean to." He waved the impotent handle in violent arcs. "It f-flew." Demonstrating how the rolling pin had taken flight, he tossed it into the air

The little girl's eyes were icy. "You dumbass," she muttered.

"Your mom, get your mom," Grace commanded.

"At work," the girl replied.

"At work?" What was the mother thinking, leaving children alone in a strange house? "Get a towel! We're going to the hospital."

"With you?" the girl asked.

"He needs a doctor, stitches."

The girl shook her head.

Stubborn brat. "He needs medical attention!"

The redhead planted her feet. "We don't know you."

Grace tamped down her irritation, panic even. At least the mother had told the little girl not to go off with strangers. Grace spoke gently. "I'm your neighbor, Mrs. O'Shay. We'll call your mom from the hospital. I'm sure she would want you to go with me."

The redhead looked at her blood-spattered brother and nodded.

Grace returned her nod. "Go get a towel to hold over the cut."

While Grace backed the Buick out of the garage, the girl held a none-too-clean towel over her brother's forehead. Grace headed toward the ER. Although the wounded boy was now able to hold the towel in place, red oozed onto his shirt, pants, and finally onto the seat. Grace hoped she could get the stain out before her husband saw it. In the backseat, the girl sat ramrod straight and Trucker sniffled.

When the receptionist at Beyer's Hospital saw the boy, she called a nurse, who rushed him to a patient room. The receptionist pulled out a form. "Name?"

"I don't know. It just happened. I mean they just moved in. I saw it happen."

The cursing girl spoke up. "Ernest Burns. Our mom works at Joe's Diner." She recited the phone number.

The receptionist nodded, picked up the phone, and dialed. "Busy." After several attempts, she looked at the girl. "Perhaps you can answer the questions."

Hunter—that was her name—told the receptionist that Ernest was nine. She didn't know his birthdate but said his birthday was on Halloween.

The receptionist smiled. "I can figure it out."

Hunter knew the street, Hamilton. Grace helped with the house number. Knowing that it would frighten the mother to come home to an empty house, Grace asked the receptionist to keep ringing the diner. Then again, it would serve the mother right to find her children missing.

Two hours and four stitches later, Ernest sported a bandage above his left eye. Tucker had given up trying to understand the flight of the rolling pin. When Grace delivered them home, they were licking hospital Tootsie Pops in the backseat. She parked behind the mother's pickup.

The wild-eyed mother, strands of sunset hair escaping her ponytail, ran out of the house. "What the hell's going on?"

So she was the one who'd taught her daughter to swear! Grace checked herself. She could understand why the woman was a bit out of control. Grace had not thought to write a note and had been unable to reach her by phone. She must have been terrified when she came home and found her children had disappeared.

Ernest rushed into his mother's arms.

"What happened?" she demanded.

The children looked toward Grace, maybe afraid they were in trouble. Slowly, in great detail, Grace explained the accident.

The woman's bravado evaporated. "Oh. You live next door? You took him to the emergency room."

"This is a bit of a shock, but I assure you Ernest has a bit of a cut, stiches, but he's fine. Not the ideal way to meet, but I have been meaning to get over and introduce myself. I'm Grace O'Shay."

Tulip nodded. As though someone might be eavesdropping, she lowered her voice almost to a whisper. "I couldn't get a sitter. There's just a week before school... Thanks."

"I'm glad I could help. Welcome to the neighborhood." Grace extended her hand.

The woman rubbed her hand on the "Joe's" apron and extended it, limp and perspiring. "Tulip, Tulip Burns."

Something about the situation sent shivers down Grace's spine. "I've got to get back." She hurried across the lawn but paused at her door and gazed at the little family. She admired the wiry, stoic Ernest, the way he had not cried on the way to the hospital. She felt a pierce: Rickey. He reminded her of Rickey when he was little. Desperate for any reminder, she guessed. Ernest was shy, her son gregarious. And, she *never* left him unattended at Ernest's age.

The house had cooled some. Exhausted, she longed to lie on the couch, but the soup needed tending. She had forgotten to tell the mother about the glass. Three children, too young to be left alone. The mother knew it wasn't safe. Who knew what that retarded boy might do? She could have gotten a teenager to sit—better than nothing. Perhaps she should call protective services... but the accident could have happened regardless. You could be vigilant, but you couldn't protect children from everything.

As Grace passed the coffee table, she closed the album.

10

Grace was not snoopy like Prudence. But she couldn't help watching those children out the window. They'd come home from school, Hunter bounding along in the lead, a Tigers baseball cap clamped on her unruly hair. Ernest next, carefully stepping over cracks, pigeon-toed Tucker stumbling behind. Every so often he would stop and poke in the grass, perhaps looking for bugs. Hunter hollered for him to hurry. When they reached home they did not play outside. Had the mother told them to stay inside? How did they fill the hour they spent alone?

One day Tucker came out on his porch and sat with his head in his hands. Grace conjectured that his bratty sister had spoken sharply, maybe hit him. Grace's multicolored cat Tabby sauntered past the boy's house and onto her porch, where she began to clean herself. The boy went inside his house and returned shortly. He crept over and plopped his round bottom onto Grace's step. Holding a piece of cheese he bellowed, "K-k-kitty, k-kitty, kitty!" Tabby ran under the porch. Defeated, Tucker slumped against the post and ate the cheese. After a while the cat crept out and rubbed against his Husky jeans. Tucker held out his cheese-covered fingers and Tabby licked them. The boy giggled. Grace sensed the moist gravelly tongue tickling Tucker's skin. He grabbed the cat and ruffled her fur so that it stood on end. Tabby wriggled from his grasp and leapt off the porch.

Grace opened the door. "Having trouble?"

"Sh-sh-she don't like me!"

"Yes, she does. You have to know how to treat her. Have you ever had a kitten?"

"D-d-daddy don't like 'em!"

How could this little boy know how to be tender when he was pushed and pulled, told to hurry, and constantly criticized for doing the wrong thing? Grace gently stroked the boy's hair the way Tabby liked to be petted. "Let me show you how to make friends with the kitty." She called Tab and coaxed her into her lap. As she took Tucker's sweaty hand and laid it on Tabby's back, she remembered her son. *Rickey, Rickey, be nice to the kitty. Let Mommy show you how kittens like to be touched.*

Grace's hand on Tucker's, they stroked the cat. "Pet the way the fur grows. Be very careful. Kittens are delicate. They don't have strong bones like you."

The boy smoothed the fur from head to tail. Tabby arched her back and pressed against his hand. Grace took his fingers and tickled Tabby under her chin. "If she really likes you, she'll let you do this."

Tucker's hazel eyes shone. "Her m-m-motor's humming."

Grace eased the purring cat onto Tucker's lap and left them on the porch. When she reappeared with milk and a plate of Kirby's favorite chocolate chip cookies, Ernest and Hunter were there.

"W-we don't g-got these g-good c-c-cookies!" Tucker exclaimed. Hunter mumbled thanks and Ernest rewarded Grace with a shy smile. They gulped milk and devoured cookies.

"How's school?" Grace asked. The children looked at her blankly. She asked Hunter, "Do you like your teacher?" A slight nod. Not one thing she asked elicited more than a yes or a no. Their whirling dervish mother must not talk to them much.

Grace poured the last of the sauce over the lasagna—two pans, one to eat and one to freeze. She wiped a tear with her apron, went to the bathroom for a Kleenex, and blew hard, extra hard. This was the first lasagna she had made since Rickey. Kirby loved it, raved about it. Their son had not. "Too much red stuff," he'd said. She seldom made it, and when she did, Rickey pushed it around his plate, eating little. Why was she depriving Kirby? Was she punishing him? After all these months of him tolerating her accusations, her turning away, she owed him.

Glancing out the window, Grace noted Tulip and her ex squaring off on Tulip's porch. He took a step and towered over her. She held her spot. He grabbed her shoulders, shook her. Grace tore off her apron and started for the door. *Mind your business. What do you think you can do?* Marshall jumped off the porch and peeled out in his car, scattering gravel. With the fluffy yellow dice dangling from the mirror, he could have been a sitcom juvenile delinquent. As he rounded the corner, Tulip gave him the finger. Grace laughed. Tulip was elbows and knees with rough edges, but she loved those kids. Grace could only imagine what her life was like with that bully. What could Grace have done, with just an apron in her hand? Wave it at him? That man was dangerous, and those children were alone after school!

When the pans came out of the oven, a succulent tomato-basil aroma filled the kitchen. Those hungry-eyed children would love the cheesy red sauce. Prudence had welcomed Tulip to the neighborhood with brownies, probably out of a box. Grace could do better. Besides, she and Kirby shouldn't be eating so much rich food. She wrapped a tray in a towel and walked across Tulip's weedy lawn and onto her porch.

Tucker swung open the door, nearly colliding with her. "O-o-oh!" He reached for the pan.

Grace jerked it away. "Hot!"

"Hot," he echoed, jumping back.

With Tucker tracking her, Grace entered the kitchen. Tulip stood stone-faced by a sink full of dirty dishes. Bits of last night's macaroni and cheese languished on mismatched plates. A No-Brand macaroni box had toppled from the overflowing trash can. An open box of Cheerios sat on the table.

Grace cleared a space on the counter and set the pan down. "I brought you something for supper."

Tulip nodded. Freckles melded together on her flushed face. When she spoke, her tone was flat, resigned. "He was here. He knows school lets out before I get home."

"I saw."

"Tucker let him in."

Tucker lifted the edge of the foil from the dish and took a big whiff. "H-h-he had candy, Mom!"

Tulip shook her finger. "I don't *ever* want you to let him in! Now get out of that food and go play."

The boy puckered his lips and slouched out of the kitchen. As he passed Grace, she patted his shoulder.

Tulip gestured toward the pot. "Want some coffee? I can heat it."

Grace brushed the crumbs off a chair and sat down. Kirby was going to be real surprised if he came home and she wasn't there.

Tulip poured a lukewarm cup of morning coffee in a chipped white restaurant mug. Had it been damaged before or after she brought it home? And how many germs did it house?

Tulip paced the length of the kitchen. "Marshall's been harassing me since he broke up with his girlfriend, sneaks over when I'm not here. He bribes the kids with candy, tells them I'm a bad mother, a *whore*!" She laughed, whipped her mug at Grace. "They don't even know what a whore is. He threatens me that he'll take them." Holding her arms tight against her chest, as if to keep from breaking apart, she sagged onto a chair.

What had Grace gotten into? The only other conversation she had had with Tulip, she had been yelled at. Now the woman was baring her soul. What should Grace say? That's too bad? I'm sorry? What she wanted to say: You're talking to the wrong person. I'm all used up. Call the police. Come home and take care of these kids. At least you have children who need you!

But it seemed Tulip did not want Grace to speak. She just kept talking, on and on. "I can't afford a sitter. They went to D's after school until that rat Joe changed her schedule." I know they're too young to be alone, but it's only a half hour."

She was deceiving herself. It was at least an hour, and she'd left her children alone even longer in the summer. Those children needed a caretaker. Grace pictured Rickey as a child, hollering for a snack, news of the playground bubbling from his mouth. Was Tulip expecting Grace to volunteer?

"I don't know what he'll do next. I can't get off any earlier. I'm pushing it already."

Tucker came into the kitchen and stood next to Grace, his arm against her arm, too close. "M-M-Miss G-Grace, what did you call that?" He pointed toward the pan.

"Lasagna."

"L-l-lasagna," he repeated. "It s-s-smells good!"

His mother's voice was steely. "Tucker, go out and play."

Grace did not know if Tulip was irritated with the interruption or if she didn't want her son to see her upset. Regardless, a ripple of indignation rolled up Grace's back. "I hope you'll like it, Tucker," she said.

He left the kitchen, banging the door behind him. Tulip was quiet, spent. Still, she remembered her manners and forced a crooked smile, a bit like Ernest's. That was what reminded Grace! Their smiles were lopsided like Rickey's.

"Thanks, thanks for dinner. I don't feel much like cooking tonight."

And what would it be if you did, boxed macaroni and cheese? Tulip's child-care problem was her responsibility. Grace had no intention of volunteering. "Thanks for the coffee. I'd better get home." Face vacant, Tulip remained at the table. Pathetic! Outside, Tucker leaned against a porch post, eyes closed, his dirty shirt missing a button. Poor, neglected child.

Encroaching on Grace's property line, Hunter and Ernest tossed a softball back and forth. Hunter called, "Miss Grace, Tucker said you brought us lasagna!" She pointed to her younger brother. "Ernest loves lasagna."

Blue eyes shining, the boy smiled his lopsided smile.

"Catch." Hunter tossed the ball.

Grace raised her hand and felt a hard thud in her palm.

"You're good, Miss Grace!" Hunter hollered.

Grace laughed, a genuine laugh. The first since… She threw the ball to Ernest and started down the walk.

"Thanks, thanks for supper!" Hunter called.

"You're welcome." The little stinker *could* conjure up some manners. Grace massaged her stinging hand. She was amazed that she had caught the ball, more so that she enjoyed it. She stood for a moment watching the children. Hunter's hair, released from its cap, flew wild. Ernest's pants were too short, his tennis shoes soiled. Innocent children. What was to become of them?

She turned back up the walk to the porch and into the kitchen. Tulip still sat at the table. Grace cleared her throat. "I was thinking. I'm home anyway. Maybe I could…?"

Tulip looked at Grace as if seeing her for the first time.

"I'll watch them."

"You'd do that?" Tulip shook her head. "But I told you I can't afford a sitter. I can hardly pay my bills."

"I don't need the money. We could try it, see how it works out."

When Grace entered her kitchen, Kirby stood at the counter with a fork heaped with lasagna. "Where were you? I was worried."

"Not too worried to eat."

He kissed her forehead. "My absolute favorite! It's been a while." He held out his arms and she snuggled into them.

"Too long," Grace murmured. "And I have another surprise for you. I've gotten myself into something—something you'll worry about, something I'm not certain I can do."

Even before Rickey died, Grace would wake thinking that he was still asleep in the next room. In some distorted way, she thought if she could stay in bed and keep her eyes closed, she could change the story. Now she was determined to change the next-door urchins' story. The one way she knew to care for them was to feed them, and on those still-warm autumn days, Grace's oven blasted away, baking cookies and bread.

Tucker crammed an entire cookie into his mouth, hiccupped crumbs, and held up a chocolate-covered hand.

Grace chuckled. "Chocolate-chip boy. Go wash."

"Humph," Hunter said. "He has the manners of a pig."

Pipsqueak, how about you? "Hunter, Ernest, when you're finished eating, put your glasses in the sink, then *you* both wash up." Grace sprayed Spic and Span on the counter and scrubbed.

"Tucker won't get out of the bathroom," Hunter said.

When Grace checked, Tucker was happily splashing warm water on his face. Water pooled on the counter and dripped onto the floor. She wanted to snap him with the tea towel but instead thrust it into his hand. "Turn off the water! Wipe it up!"

Tucker looked at the towel and then at Grace. She pointed to the counter. His mouth opened in an O of understanding. He sopped up the water. Putting her hands on his shoulders, she escorted him from the bathroom.

Tucker was slow, retarded even, but splashing in the sink was something toddlers did. "Does he do this at home?"

"We don't got hot water," Hunter replied.

"What?"

"It broke. Black, nasty stuff came out the bottom. Mom shut it off."

"How do you take baths?"

"Heat water on the stove and take turns. It's too hot when you're the first one, cold and yucky when you're last. Don't want to be first and don't want to be last." She dismissed Grace with a nod and opened her *Weekly Reader*.

Grace's face flushed. She remembered her mother complaining about their poor neighbors years ago. "They could at least keep themselves clean," she'd said. Even then Grace knew that was hard to do if you didn't have soap and hot water.

Tucker slumped into a chair and stared at his workbook. Grace opened it and handed him a pencil. What else wasn't working in that house? Grace picked up the cookie sheet, one cookie remaining, and inhaled the buttery flavor. Food would not make things right. She bit into the still-warm chocolaty goo.

That night Grace asked Kirby if he remembered being poor. He just chuckled and asked, "What have you got up your sleeve now?"

Kirby had left for work. Grace stood at the kitchen window in a narrow beam of sunlight, allowing herself the pleasure of coffee, rich with cream and sugar. The sun shone. The children would come. She would bake cookies, but she would not eat any—not even one.

Wearing slacks, her hair loose, Prudence stepped onto her porch and hurried toward Grace's house. Uh-oh! Prudence up and about this early spelled trouble. The bell jangled, but before Grace could answer, Prudence was in. Without makeup, her face was lined and shallow, her eyes sunken.

Grace motioned to a chair. "Coffee?"

Raising herself to her full Amazon height, Prudence spoke in her operatic voice. "What did you do *that* for?"

"What?"

"The water heater. You gave that woman a water heater! Next you'll have Kirby and Dennis shingling her roof."

"You're acting like we committed a federal offense."

Prudence shook her fist. "Those kids get in my yard and trample my flowers. That old pickup is a junker. The house is a disaster. They're bringing down home values. And Dennis, you're involving Dennis in it."

"What are you talking about?"

"He helped Kirby with the heater. He went over there. It could get him into more trouble!" As though to take back her words, she put her hand over her mouth.

Grace set the coffee on the table and again motioned toward a chair.

Prudence stood her ground. "The way he looks at her—disgusting!"

"He's a grown man. What do you expect?"

"She's too old for him. And he can't get mixed up with those kids!"

"So he's got a crush on an older woman. So what?" Grace's voice rose. "And I won't have you maligning those children!"

"You don't understand!"

"What don't I understand? What *is* the big secret?"

Prudence flinched. "Nothing, nothing. I've got to go. I—I have something in the oven." She whirled to leave.

"Wait!" Grace took a breath, calmed herself, and spoke with what she hoped was a soothing voice. "This is not about Dennis helping Kirby install a water heater."

Prudence's body sagged against the counter. She fixed her gaze on the cupboard directly above Grace. Her voice was a whisper. "A lot has happened since Dr. Goodwin died. They questioned if it was really an accident! All the debt I didn't know about..." Her voice rose. "Then Dennis!" She glared at Grace. "You can't imagine what I've been through!"

The coffin of Grace's anger sprang open. "You have the nerve to tell me that *I* can't imagine? It's been three years since your husband died!"

Prudence gasped. "Oh! I didn't mean."

"No, of course you didn't mean. You never mean!"

Prudence's eyes clouded. "You don't know. I never told you."

"What didn't you tell me?"

"About the other woman. The—the gambling."

"Don't act so naive. Did you really think that I didn't know? "

"I was devastated. And Dennis...well, he's sensitive. I worry that—"

Grace's hand flew up, accenting each word. "Safe in bed every night!"

"But Dennis's number didn't come up. Your son wanted to go!" Again Prudence clamped her hand over her mouth.

A storm exploded from the part of Grace that she'd thought dead. "How dare you! Dennis has his whole life ahead of him. Rickey will never date, never marry, and never have children!"

Prudence gaped at Grace. "I-I'm sorry. I didn't mean to hurt you. You're such a good neighbor. Kirby helping Dennis—the broken step, the leaky toilet…" She waved her hand. "It's just…it's just, Dennis can't get mixed up with those kids." Her eyes moistened.

Crocodile tears. "I think you'd best leave."

"But—"

"Go, just go!"

Prudence pursed her lips, turned, and strode out of the kitchen, slamming the door.

Grace's inclination was to fling the coffee, but she would have to clean up the mess. As she tossed the murky contents down the drain, the mug slipped from her hand and banged against the porcelain, dismembering the handle. She gasped. Years ago she had purchased three pottery mugs at the Ann Arbor Art Fair, Rickey claiming the largest for himself. After football games, attentive to their son's excitement about the win or disappointment at the loss, they drank hot chocolate from those cups.

She fitted the handle onto the cup. Broken and empty. She had to lie down. Grasping the handrail, she pulled herself up the stairs into the hall where, as a third grader on a rainy afternoon, Rickey had run back and forth practicing for field day. Head aching from the pounding of his feet, she had ordered him to take off his shoes.

"Can't. They're my running shoes."

"And running is for outside!"

"Oh, Mom!" He bolted down the stairs and out into a downpour.

Grace peered into Rickey's room. The shades were down, the light dim. Trophies lined the shelves, a model BMW on the nightstand. She sank onto his bed and held the football pillow, the pillow he had made in a six-week home-ec class. The mechanics of the sewing machine were a quick learn for him, but hand sewing was a different matter. He took the needle in his overgrown hand and held it between thumb and forefinger, jabbing awkwardly at the fabric. He and Dennis had thought it would be a way to get to know girls but had been disappointed to learn it was a boys' class. At least he'd learned to thread a needle, he had said, and he thought he could sew a button on a shirt.

Why Rickey? She had told herself stories, changing the outcome each time, but always Rickey lived. He made his way through the dense forest, trodding undetected over the enemy's tunnel. Or, in her most vicious moments, he came upon the Vietcong napping under a canopy of trees. He and his buddies raised their rifles and fired. The enemy lay in pools of blood—boys with frightened eyes. In the best story, he was cramped with his unit in the belly of a jet, flying over the ocean toward home. Imagining the welcome-home hug, she crushed the football to her chest.

Grace ached all over as though she had been encased in wet leather, the slowly drying strips tightening around her body. She lifted her legs, trying to stretch, but had no strength to break the bonds. Defeated, she curled into a ball and closed her eyes. In her dream, Rickey pulled up to the house in a red BMW and honked the horn. Laughing, she ran to him, but when she tried to open the door, it stuck. Next, Dennis was driving away in the car, Prudence waving from her porch.

She woke from the dream, head throbbing. Pure and simple—Dennis lived. Rickey died. Consumed with pain and envy, she had no empathy for Prudence as she had none for Tulip. Grace snorted. Prudence and she were more alike than Grace cared to acknowledge. Tab leapt onto the bed and snuggled up to Grace, her paws padding a rhythm on Grace's chest. As Tucker said, Tab's motor hummed.

11

~◌

Tulip dumped kids' bubble bath into the tub and flipped on the faucet full blast, filling the tub with scalding water till it was like one of those Jacuzzis everyone talked about. She stuck a foot in and yanked it out. Ouch! She marched in place—one foot up, relief; one down, pain. When she could bear it, she sank into the bubbles, luxuriating. Fancy word.

She sang, "H-h-hot water, h-h-hot water!" Then the country song, "Skip a rope, skip a rope, oh listen to the children while they play. Now ain't it kinda funny what the children say? Skip a rope, Daddy hates Mommy and Mommy hates Dad…" True, but she had gotten her kids out of the hate.

The O'Shays had bought a new water heater. Her good luck. Grace said their old one was big for a family of two, wasted too much gas, so Tulip could have the reject. Tulip said she couldn't take it, but Grace said that was silly. "Why let a perfectly good heater go to waste? Besides, I'm tired of Tucker splashing water all over my bathroom."

Tulip hadn't wanted Grace to know that she had a broken-down heater. A girl had some pride. But standing in Grace's spotless kitchen, with the rich smell of roasting chicken, Tulip looked into her wrinkly face and smiling eyes and it seemed like the right thing to do—accept a gift, freely given, no prickles or thorns. And it was even nicer that it was Grace's. The same heater that had warmed her would warm Tulip. She caught herself wishing that Grace was her mom. Better not wish for too much.

Tulip should have known that there was too much goodness in her life, that she'd fall off God's list again. Marshall had broken up with his girlfriend and showed up at Tulip's house, intending to exercise his parental rights. Against her better judgment, Tulip let him take the kids for ice cream. As though she had any power to stop him. In a lousy half hour the Thunderbird squealed back into the drive. Hunter scrambled out and hightailed it into the house, Ernest hot on her heels. Tucker stumbled out of the car, shirt smeared with ice cream, blood trickling down his paper-white face.

Marshall rolled down his window and threw a lit cigarette into the dry grass. "Say goodbye," he shouted to their backs.

"What happened?" Tulip called from the porch.

Marshall shrugged. "Fell, smacked his face." He rolled up the window and peeled out, scattering gravel.

Tulip caught the children in the hallway—three limp scarecrows. Hunter did the talking, her brothers nodding. "Daddy yelled at Tucker. He spilled his malt, just a little, but some got on the seat. Daddy slapped him and called him a dumb-shit bastard. Tucker cried and Daddy hit him again."

The imprint of Marshall's serpent ring glowed evil on Tucker's cheek. She knew that ring too well, the glaring ruby eyes and pin-sharp tail. *The better to cut you with, my dear!* Tulip's face flushed red. "Bastard! He's the dumb-shit bastard! He's got no right to hit you!"

Tucker's eyes bulged with terror.

He thought *she* was going to hit him! "Not your fault," Tulip muttered.

Tulip gently sponged the blood from Tucker's face. When she dabbed iodine on the cut, he flinched but did not whimper. She smoothed a Band-Aid over the cut and patted his back. "You'll live." But would he always have this picture stuck in his mind?

At supper the kids were quiet. Tucker ate a couple bites then put down his fork, but it was Ernest who complained of a tummy ache. Tulip nursed a cup of cold coffee.

She was not her mother. She would protect her children. "Are you guys scared of your dad?" Tulip blurted.

Dead silence. Dumb question. If she was scared, they must be terrified. "Well?"

As though Hunter had the answer, the boys looked toward her. She said nothing. Tulip lost patience. "Do you want to go with him or not?" she asked, louder than she meant.

Hunter shook her head.

"Then you don't have to. Eat your goulash."

When Marshall was on a rampage, he could do great bodily harm, and from the beginning he'd had it in for Tucker. That night in bed, when Tulip closed her eyes, a scene played over and over. The baby cried. Marshall seized him, shook him, like one of those carnival rides jolting up and down. Even then she knew that shaking a baby, his little brain bumping against his skull, could cause damage. She screamed and grabbed Tucker's leg, horrified that he would be ripped apart like a chicken. Thankfully Marshall's crazy eye went dead and he dropped the wailing baby into her arms. She shivered in terror. If only there were a mind eraser that could rid her of these horrible pictures.

The next Sunday, when Marshall came for the kids, she locked the front door and ran out to the drive. It would be safer in the open. Marshall rolled his window down.

Tulip clutched the door handle to steady herself. Long-simmering molten lava spurted from her. "I could report you to the welfare! You called Tucker names, hit him, cut him! They don't want to go with you!" She stopped herself and spoke with what she hoped was authority. "They are *not* going with you. You are *not* hurting them anymore."

Marshall took a drag on his cigarette, blew smoke in her face. His voice was slow and deep. "Yes, they are. They're *my* kids. You can't keep them from me."

"Your kids! You dead-beat dad. You don't even pay child support most of the time."

Crazy Eye danced. The door flew open.

She ran. He caught her by the arm. Daggers shot up her shoulder. She saw herself thrown into the grass, Marshall on top, his fist pummeling her, the serpent's tail digging into her forehead, blood spurting from the cut. "Help! Oh God, somebody help me!"

"Let her go," said a steely voice.

She opened her eyes. She was not lying in the grass but standing, Marshall clutching her arm. Her free hand went to her face—no blood.

"Let her go!" Kirby repeated.

Marshall dropped her arm. Like a pricked balloon, he seemed to shrink. Although Kirby was older, he was broad and strong from handling all that heavy stuff at his store. Marshall acted tough, but it was a big deal for him to get a beer out of the fridge, and he had a wicked smoker's cough. If it came to blows, Kirby could more than hold his own.

"Bitch, you'll pay for this!" Marshall jumped in his car, revved the motor, and peeled out, the dice on the mirror dancing wildly.

"I saw out the window. Did he hurt you?" Kirby asked.

Again Tulip's hand went to her face. No blood, not this time. But she could not speak.

"Did he hurt you?" Kirby asked again.

Say something, idiot. "Nah. I'm used to it."

"Used to it? That man is not right in the head! You get a restraining order, young lady!"

His face bloated with anger. She saw her father threatening her. She stumbled backward.

Strong arms steadied her. "Sorry, didn't mean to bark at you. Are you OK?"

She nodded dumbly. He backed away and hurried across the grass and into his kitchen, slamming the door behind him.

Kirby? It was Kirby angry at her—angry like her father.

Tulip glimpsed Prudence gawking out her window. Snoop! Would she call the cops if Tulip were in trouble? No. She'd just stand there and watch Marshall kill her. Tulip stuck a thumb in her ear and wiggled her fingers.

When Tulip came downstairs the next morning, the curtain flapped in the wind. A brick—orange, the color of Marshall's walkway—lay in the middle of the living room. Glass blanketed the floor. "Shit!"

Ernest lay shivering on the couch. "Did Daddy do it?"

Although it was not his fault, Tulip turned on him. "Your bare feet! You walked in here with bare feet! You could have been cut."

He rubbed his tummy." I don't feel so good."

"Sick?"

"Stomachache. Hot, hot all over."

Caught between cleaning up glass and tending to her son, Tulip wondered how he'd heard the window breaking and she hadn't. Perhaps because she'd tossed and turned but finally fell into a sleep of the dead. She'd overslept and it was late. She felt Ernest's forehead. "You're cool as a cucumber. Get dressed. I gotta get this glass up and get to work."

"Can I go with you?" His watery eyes pleaded.

She tapped him on the bottom and told him to get cracking. He puckered his lips and puffed his cheeks—a full balloon ready to explode. He did that sometimes when he was upset. "Why do you want to go to work with me?" He looked at her in the same vacant way that Tucker sometimes did. "Ernest, you feel your scare in your tummy. You know you're not sick." He nodded. "I'll clean up this mess and close up the hole; you get breakfast. You'll feel better." She clapped her hands to get him moving.

Ernest rolled off the couch but took his sweet time getting ready. When he left with the others, his bowl of cereal sat on the table. Tulip felt bad that she'd hollered at him. He was such a timid soul. What if he were really sick? The thought nagged her all the way to Joe's. However, when she got busy at the diner, it went out of her head. The only way she survived, one worry at a time.

As he did most days, Ken stopped in. Black coffee and apple pie. Tulip didn't know where the beanpole put it. Maybe in his prick. He was screwing her and his wife. Who else? Maybe she was jealous.

"What you looking so down about?" Ken asked.

"Asshole ex. Broke a window."

"We can patrol your block."

"Once a night while Marshall's at work. Lot of good that would do."

"Tomorrow's my day off. You off too?" She nodded. "Good. I'll come over and fix your window."

"Yeah, sure, like you always do."

"Tulip, sweet one, believe me, I'll be over."

With a wife and kids, Tulip knew she was far down on his list. She might have to wrestle the window herself. Maybe she could get D to hold the glass while she puttied.

Just after the kids left for school, Ken strolled up the walk, looking sharp in a milk-white T-shirt and jeans with an ironed-in-crease. "Geez, your wife's got nothing better to do than iron your pants?" Tulip asked.

Ken grasped her waist, twirled her around, and kissed her cheek. "I'm hungry. Feed me."

"No way. First the window."

Tulip held the pane while he slopped on putty, dropping globs on the porch and cussing when he got some on his prissy jeans. To make matters worse, eagle-eyed Prudence was hiding behind her curtains, watching their every move. Tulip gave her the finger. She disappeared. After the window was in, Tulip made grilled cheese sandwiches, then led the way to bed. Fair payment—lunch and a screw.

That night, after the kids were asleep, Tulip wandered onto the front porch. The weather had warmed again and the mosquitoes were after blood. If she smoked as D did, it would keep them away, and she'd have something to do with her hands. A cigarette seemed reassuring, its smoke nodding in agreement. When one was gone, if she wanted she could light up another. Comforting— inhaling its warmth, exhaling, watching smoke curl and float away.

With Marshall after her, she had to admit she was relieved to have a cop in her life. But she'd been seeing Ken for over a year and this idea of no attachments wasn't working so good. At first she'd been afraid, afraid of sex, afraid he would hurt her. But she was the one on the muscle. When she got mad—and she frequently did—he simply called her stubborn, sweet Tulip and kissed her nose. No, he hadn't punched her, hurt her physically, but she had this inside ache. She seemed always to be waiting. She waited for him to come to the restaurant, spent an hour with him, then waited some more. She thought of him with his wife. What pet name did he call her? Worse, Tulip pictured him going home to his kids every night, picking up Timmy and whirling him around— something he could never do with her kids.

Next door the porch light came on and Prudence pranced out of the house. Heels clicking on cement, she hurried to her baby-blue Cadillac. Probably going to church. That's what she was—a spy for the Lord. Tulip dismissed her and gazed at the stars, searching for the Little Dipper. She was tired but needed a minute to just be. She hugged herself tight, leaned against the post, and closed her eyes.

"Sitting in the dark." Dennis stood on the walk. "How's it going?"

"How does it look like it's going?"

He planted his foot on her step and pointed to the window. "That ex of yours giving you a hard time?"

"Yeah."

Dennis sat down. His leg touching hers felt warm and strangely comforting. He said nothing, seemed to be waiting for her to talk.

She spoke into the darkness, her words slow at first, then a river of worries pouring out. "He's crazy mean. I never know what he'll do." She did not tell him that Marshall wouldn't stop until he killed her.

Dennis ran his hand over her hair gentle-like, as if she were a kitten or a puppy. "That's tough."

They sat silently, looking at the stars in the night sky and listening to the crickets, the cars on the next street, occasionally a honking horn.

He rubbed her neck. "Want me to beat him up?"

Tulip chuckled. "You're just a wiry kid." Dennis was about the same size as Marshall but not muscular and certainly not mean. In a temper, Marshall might stomp him.

"How old do you think I am?

Tulip touched his baby face. "Seventeen?"

He roared with laughter. He was laughing at her. She wanted to stamp him out like a lit cigarette. "Why'd you come over? You know your stuck-up momma doesn't want you near me."

"Ooh, that's below the belt." He stood.

"Well, she *is* stuck-up."

"Didn't she bring you brownies when you moved in?"

"You could have used those brownies to patch the porch floor."

He chuckled. "She meant well. She doesn't cook much. She's having a hard time."

"Why? Rich, nice house, expensive clothes, great son."

"Thank you." He gave a little bow and sat back down.

Tulip swatted a mosquito on her arm and wiped the blood with her hand. "A frost. We need a frost to get the little devils."

"About Mom." He paused, then continued, his voice hesitant. "Dad left us in a mess. Other than playing the church organ, Mom doesn't have a job. And I, the prodigal son, don't make much checking at Kroger. She works hard to keep up pretenses."

Prudence's Cad wheeled around the corner. Dennis leapt up. "Got to go." He jumped off the porch.

"Got to get home to Momma?"

He waved and jogged toward his house.

He met his mother as she stepped out of the car. "What have you been doing?" she demanded. Putting his arm around her shoulder, he ushered her into the house.

Tulip had wanted a minute to herself to breathe, not to think. Too much was happening. Her life was on the fast track and not uphill. Now questions about this mama's boy were taking up space in her head. She'd never seen him drive. Each morning, he wore a backpack to the bus stop. Was he going to Kroger or to school? He looked young, almost elfin, with his pointy ears and sparkling dark eyes. But he acted older, more sure of himself, and he was easy to talk to.

Enough. She swatted a blood-filled mosquito on her cheek, walked into the house, and locked the door.

12

As Tulip wheeled Old Ruby into the drive, Ernest bolted out of the house. "Mom, we don't have lights! No TV!"

"Shit!"

"Shoot, Mom, shoot. Miss Grace says not to say that word."

"Can Grace get the electricity back on?"

Bills were the extent of Tulip's mail, with a big red delinquent stamped on them. Like she was a teenage law-breaker. She tossed those babies in a shoebox and watched them multiply. D had urged her to go after Marshall for child support. "I know what kind of support I'd get," Tulip had said. Now she'd have to ask D for help.

D was not pleased. "Yeah, I'm good for it, but you can't manage on your piddling salary. You *have* to make Marshall pay."

Tulip filled out the paperwork.

Surprise: a few weeks later she got a check. No surprise: shithead started his shenanigans. He snuck in the night and flipped on the outside faucet, flooding the lawn, which ran up the water bill. He murdered her hose, cutting it into tiny pieces, and, as if it were a sign advertising her, arranged it on the grass to spell "bitch."

There were phone calls and hang-ups. Tulip and D worked out a code: one ring, hang up, call again. When Tulip refused to answer Marshall's persistent ringing, Ernest went to his room and curled up on the bed. Always the quiet one, he became even more so, scarcely speaking. He picked at his food and developed a rash. He said he was sick—stomachache, headache, sore throat—different complaints each day. Tulip bribed and threatened to get him off to school.

In desperation Tulip took Ernest to a doctor. The six-foot-four man towered over Tulip and dwarfed Ernest. The giant prescribed medicine for acid indigestion and salve for rash. "Come back in a couple of weeks and we'll see how he's doing."

Another visit? Money Tulip did not have. Still Ernest claimed he was too sick for school. He begged to go to work with Tulip, just for a couple of days till he got better.

Under Joe's watchful eye, Tulip ushered Ernest into the diner and installed him in a back booth. "What's the kid doing here?" Joe asked. She told him that Ernest had a few days off from school and nowhere else to go. She wasn't about to tell Joe Ernest was sick. It was a slow day and her boy did real good, reading and doing homework. Tulip made certain that Joe saw her pay for Ernest's chicken noodle soup. Maybe he would have been OK at school, but she felt better keeping an eye on him.

At the end of Tulip's shift, Joe took her aside. "This is a restaurant. We don't provide babysitting service."

"What do you want me to do, flush him down the toilet?"

Tulip could not quit. Hell, she couldn't even afford a day off. Ernest would just have to stay home. Then D broke it to her. It was against the law for nine-year-old kids to stay home alone. No way was Tulip inviting the welfare to take her kids. So she pried Ernest out of bed and sent him to school. He cried, pleaded, and refused to eat breakfast, but when she did not give in, he dressed and shuffled after the others.

The letter came with the bills. Ernest had skipped a week of school. When Tulip confronted him, he confessed that although he walked to school with Hunter and Tucker, after they went inside he doubled back. He didn't know why. School wasn't so bad. He just felt like he had to be home. Then he shut up. Tulip wasn't going to beat him; that would only make him hate her. He was too spindly to send to bed without supper, and she hadn't the heart to do it.

Again she took Ernest to the giant doctor, where she could at least get an excuse for the teacher. Tears peeking from his eyes, Ernest sat on a white table, swinging his skinny legs, nodding or shaking his head in answer to the doctor's questions. The doctor examined him, then sent him out of the room.

The giant tried to talk low, like he knew a secret, but his voice matched his size. "Is school hard for the boy? Is something frightening him?"

"You're the doctor. You tell me."

He shook his head. "There is nothing physically wrong with your son."

"Good! So how do I get him to school?"

"Has anything been going on at home?"

"You mean other than that he's got a dick for a dad?" Too late she caught herself and remembered a word she'd heard on TV. "I mean his father's abusive. He's mean. He makes threatening calls."

The doctor stroked his smooth, plump chin. "Yes, that would be distressing. Perhaps the boy should talk with someone."

"He don't talk."

"Therapy, psychotherapy…counseling."

"How much?"

"Oh." He took off his glasses and wiped his forehead. "Maybe sixty. But Family Services and Catholic Social Service have reduced fees."

Tulip took a deep breath. "So if I can scrape up sixty bucks, a *counselor* can fix him?"

The doctor checked his fancy watch. "No, sixty per session. But remember, they do have a sliding scale." Sweat beads forming on his fat face, he looked down on her and tried to explain emotional problems, the benefits of psychotherapy. "Rome wasn't built in a day. These things take a while."

Tulip's kid needed counseling. That's what the giant sweat-hound doctor had said. Personally she didn't put much store in it. A counselor's job was to sit and listen. They didn't help with the rent or the heat, or get the bad guy. They didn't come to the house, haul your kid out of bed, and march him off to school. But if she didn't do something, she was going to have a nine-year-old dropout or lose him to the welfare.

Tulip knocked on Ernest's door. No answer. "I'm coming in." Ernest was curled on the bed. Leaning against the door, she tried to make her voice soft. "What are you doing?"

Ernest buried his head further in the pillow. His voice muffled as he answered, "Nothing."

Ask a dumb question, get a dumb answer. Tulip sat and ran her fingers through his tousled hair. "Ernest, you're smart, a good student. What's bothering you about school?"

"Nothing."

Heat rose in Tulip's chest. She wanted to shake him. She told herself to calm down but her voice came out harsh. "Something's wrong. Why won't you go to school?"

He bounced up, screaming, "I don't know, Mom! I just can't! Leave me alone!" He plunked back on the bed.

Tulip's inclination was to swat him. She checked herself. She was mad, mad at herself because she couldn't make it better. She rubbed his neck, his stiff little back. Somehow she had to get the money. She whispered, "Do you want to talk to someone?"

His face buried in the pillow, he asked, "You mean a counselor?"

"Yes, someone who can help you with your…feelings." She waited.

She felt his shudder, his back going slack. He mumbled, "OK."

"Good." Tulip patted the cover. He looked at her, dark eyes hopeful. "Wash up for supper. And you need a bath before bed."

Mission: get her child a counselor. Tulip called Family Services. There was a wait list. "A wait list?" Tulip asked.

"Just a month or so," the woman replied. Tulip called Catholic Social Service—same answer. She pleaded, "My kid won't go to school. I need help now! Not next summer!"

"Sorry."

Tulip slammed down the phone.

D suggested that welfare might pay for a private counselor. "They do stuff for needy children."

Tulip was offended by D's calling her kids needy, but she held her peace. Tulip went to the poor-folks building and waited on a folding chair in a cold, gray room with a bunch of other deadbeats. After an hour, just as she was walking toward the restroom, someone hollered, "Tulip Burns, Tulip Burns." The loudmouth pointed toward a door marked protective services. Tulip walked down a puke-green hall and into a maze of open cubicles.

The social worker was a kid, one of those cheerleader types, with bleached-blonde hair and a fake smile. Her gaze darted around the tiny space as if she was looking for a way out. A woman sniffled in the next booth. Typewriters clacked.

"Real private," Tulip said. She sat on another folding chair, put her hands over her ears to drown out the sound, and tried to explain about Ernest.

The cheerleader nodded, clicked her tongue, tapped her pencil, and waited for Tulip to finish. The cheerleader shook her head. "I'm not sure we can help. We do have funds for counseling, but only if the child is in an abusive or neglectful home. Those are the rules." She paused, clicked her tongue again. "You look like a good mother. But if you sign a form stating that you're a neglectful mother, I might be able to get it past my supervisor."

"What?"

"We only serve abused and neglected children."

Tulip jumped up, the chair slamming against the wall. "I may be poor, but it'll be a cold day in hell before I sign a paper saying I'm a bad mother." She grabbed her purse and got the hell out of there.

At home the mail was lying on the kitchen counter, two bills and a letter from the principal. Tulip dumped the bills in a basket and tore open the letter. The words *legal action* leapt out at her.

The next day she put her pride in her pocket, went back to the welfare, and waited on the cold steel chair. She signed the damn paper. She was officially a neglectful mother.

Each week, Ernest spent exactly fifty minutes with a social worker—a listening one, not a by-the-book welfare one. Contrary to what Tulip believed about counselors, Ms. Parin did talk. She told Tulip that Ernest was school phobic—fancy word. Ernest was afraid his dad would hurt his mom. Big news. Tulip could have told her that for free.

"He wants to protect you," the counselor said.

"But he's just a kid. And I'm at work and he's at home. How can he protect me?"

"Home is symbolic."

Although Ms. Parin had strange ideas, she didn't judge and seemed to understand. Ernest didn't give Tulip grief about counseling. Through the waiting room door Tulip could hear the murmur of their voices, Ernest's sometimes breaking. Ms. Parin talked to Tulip sometimes too— "checking in," she called it. She didn't give the answers Tulip needed, but she didn't judge. After a while, sitting with Ms. Parin in the cozy, carpeted room, listening to her soothing voice, Tulip felt calmer.

Tulip didn't know what Ernest told Ms. Parin or what she said to him. But like magic, Ernest stopped skipping school.

13

The children were due home from school. Grace had baked cookies and saved the beaters and bowl for the kids to lick. With great effort she managed not to test the dough and resisted the buttery aroma of warm cookies. As she scraped the last one from the pan, she heard a scream. Out the window, a big kid whirled Hunter in circles, her feet dragging on the grass. Laughing maliciously, he hurled her to the ground.

Grace raced out of the house. "Stop! Stop!" She grabbed the boy by the shirt. "Leave her alone!" The bully wrenched away and loped down the sidewalk. "Don't you *ever* bother her again! Don't you *ever* come in my yard!" Useless, empty words to a disappearing back.

Grace reached for Hunter. The girl lurched away.

"Sh-sh-she's mad." Tucker slouched toward the house.

Inside, Hunter ran to the bathroom and locked the door. Tucker, as always comforted by food, sniffed his way to the pan and grabbed one.

"No!" Grace opened Tucker's fingers and took the cookie. He flinched. Grace was angry, but not with him. She rubbed his shoulder and spoke softly. "You wash up first. Use the kitchen sink. Then you can eat on the porch."

While waiting for Hunter, Grace watched the boys: Tucker stuffing his mouth, crumbs flying, Ernest holding a napkin under his cookie, catching the crumbs. When she could stand it no longer, she called through the bathroom door, "Hunter, come out. We can talk about this."

Water stopped. The lock clicked. Hunter emerged, red eyed. Grace motioned to a chair at the table. Hunter sat, head down, her little pointer finger smearing circles over a melted chocolate chip on a warm cookie.

Grace poured herself a cup of stale coffee and sat next to her. "Well?"

"Nothin'."

"Nothing! A kid twice your size was tossing you around like a sack of potatoes!"

Hunter bit her lip.

"You don't want to talk about it?"

"Talking don't change things."

"Maybe I could help."

Hunter pulled a letter from her pocket addressed to Mrs. Marshall Burns and handed it to Grace. "Don't tell Mom!"

Grace opened it. "Hunter has been caught fighting on the playground several times. Please make an appointment with me at your earliest convenience. Bill Dickerson, Principal."

Grace held out her arms. "Oh, Hunter, what happened?"

The girl leapt from the table and ran out the door, across the lawn, and into her house. Grace was inclined to give chase, but she couldn't catch that imp. Hunter would talk when she was ready. Grace picked up a cookie, a cookie she had had no intention of eating, and took a huge bite.

Ernest stood in the doorway, last year's T-shirt tight over his slender chest, baseball cap holding unruly hair close to his head. Words tumbled out. "It's Tucker. They, they tease him, call him a stupid retard. They—they make him do things. Like they drop a candy wrapper on the ground and tell him pick it up." He gulped for air. "Hunter and me, we warn him to stay out of their way. But they find him. At first they're nice, then they do something like trip him or push him down. Hunter tells them to leave him alone, but they laugh at her. Yesterday on the playground she punched the big one. You know how mad she gets. Teacher saw her and she got in trouble." Again he gulped for air. "Those boys, they call her the bloody Hunter!"

Grace opened her arms. He hesitated and then came to her. She held him, aware of his stick-thin ribs. He hiccupped. "They're real mean!"

"Yes, yes. I'll talk to your mom. We'll work something out."

Grace waited till after nine, when the children would be in bed, and then reluctantly walked across the lawn. Tulip was sitting on the porch, a blanket around her shoulders, eyes closed.

"Tired?" Grace asked.

"Yeah, long day. It's getting cold. Winter's coming. I hate it."

"Mind if I join you?"

Tulip pointed to the step. "Sit. Well?"

"What?"

"Kids did something, right?"

Tulip was on edge, ready to fight. But even in the dim light, Grace could make out dark circles around her eyes. She was exhausted. This was the last bit of news she needed. "It's Hunter. A bully was picking on her in front of the house today. He knocked her down."

"What'd she do to him?"

"What do you mean, what did she do?"

"She fights."

Like mother, like daughter. "The kids at school have been picking on Tucker. They're older, bigger than Hunter, but she's still trying to protect her brother. Yesterday she hit the ringleader on the playground. Wouldn't that be something to see, tough little Hunter pummeling a loudmouth bully?" Grace forced a giggle. "But a teacher saw it, got the wrong idea." Grace handed Tulip the note. "From the principal."

Tulip sighed, read it, and reread it. "Good for her. It ain't right, them picking on Tucker like that."

"No."

"So one's in therapy, one's retarded, and now one's in trouble. I'm a lousy mother."

Trying to think of something helpful, Grace patted her hand. "You're doing the best you can. You've fine children. Ernest is sensitive and kind. Tucker has a childlike love of the world, and Hunter's protective of him. So she's a little feisty."

"She don't stand a chance. I'm afraid she'll turn out mean like her dad. But I sure don't want her to be a chickenshit like me."

"You? You're gutsy, raising three kids by yourself, their father harassing you every step of the way...and the school—did a counselor talk to Ernest about his absences? Did anyone ask Hunter why she's fighting?"

Tulip's eyes flew open. "Do they have counselors at school?"

"Yes, and a social worker too. Now that I think of it, they should have already been involved."

"Really?"

"I thought you knew."

Tulip whipped the blanket tighter. "So the school should have been helping? I *should* talk to that principal!"

Grace imagined Tulip late for the appointment, flying into the principal's office, eyes blazing, incoherent and cursing. Tulip needed someone to take her side and keep her calm. "Maybe I could go with you to see the principal."

"You?"

"Why not? I saw what happened today. Hunter shouldn't be punished for defending her brother. It's the bullies who need discipline." Grace felt a shiver run the length of her spine. What had she gotten herself into? "But when we go, there will be no cursing!"

14

No cussing—no, no cursing was what Grace had said. And she shook her finger at Tulip. Bossy! Tulip said damn and hell, but she didn't say those other words. Well, not often. She was swimming up a shit stream, working till four or five or whatever damn time Joe said, and she had to be at school before three because that's what the principal said. She was sick of everybody telling her what to do.

Tulip had to get out of work early, and to get out of work early she had to butter up Joe. She thanked him for pouring coffee when the diner was slammed, told him she liked his awful blue fish tie, and generally made a fool of herself. The diner cleared late. No time to change her uniform, but at least that principal would know she was not one of those lazy welfare moms.

It had rained and the air was steamy wet, her hair a mass of frizzy curls. She went into the restroom and clamped it up in a knot. In the mirror a bedraggled, freckle-faced woman with wild red hair stared out at her.

When Tulip saw Grace by the school, dressed in a navy suit, she breathed a sigh of relief. Even with gray hair, Grace could pass for a teacher, or better yet, the principal. Heels clicking on cement, Grace guided Tulip down a dark, windowless hall. She marched into a room marked office and greeted a grim woman behind a counter. The woman pointed to straight-backed chairs against the wall. A sign above another door read principal.

Wiping sweaty palms on her uniform, Tulip sat. The door popped open and a kid charged out, a suited man following. "Now remember what I said," he hollered after the kid. The suit walked to the two women and extended his hand, not to Tulip, but to Grace. "Bill Dickerson."

Grace beamed. "Why, Billy, I didn't know you were the principal."

His eyes popped open. "Mrs. O'Shay?"

"You remembered." Then to Tulip, Grace said, "Billy delivered the *Ypsilanti Press* when he was a boy not much older than Tucker." She laughed. "He was always throwing the paper in the bushes."

Billy blushed. "But you straightened me out. And you gave big Christmas tips." He must have remembered then that he was all grown up and a principal; he smiled sort of sheepish like, stepped back, and sounded professional. "What brings you here?"

"I'm with Tulip."

Tulip forced the corners of her mouth up in what she hoped looked like a smile and gripped his hand a might too firm. "I'm Mrs. Burns, Hunter's mother. Grace is my neighbor."

Inside Mr. Dickerson's office, he motioned the women toward two chairs. Standing behind his desk, he picked up a paper. "Fighting on the playground."

"They were picking on Tucker, and they're bigger too," Tulip blurted before she could stop herself. "They're always picking on Tucker, and you're not teaching him anything, just shuffling him along. And Hunter's a good kid. Those others are bullies!"

Grace squeezed Tulip's leg. Tulip closed her mouth. Grace explained that when she was watching the kids after school, a bigger boy had followed them home. "He was taunting Hunter and threw her on the ground."

Mr. Dickerson nodded. "That must be Danny Thompson. We've had some trouble with him. His parents just divorced. An angry child." He looked at the paper again. "Hmm, it doesn't say who she hit on the playground."

Tulip rose in her chair. "You send a note home and you don't even know what happened?" This time Grace clamped her hand on Tulip's leg.

The two of them talked. After Tulip's heart stopped pounding, she was lulled by the sound of their voices, hers soft, his deep—a melody. Tulip was a kid listening to adults trying to figure things out. If she were honest, really honest, it felt like having a mom, a good mom go to bat for her.

In the end Grace had him. Tulip's head was whirling with all Billy Dickerson said he'd do for her children. Danny Thompson would be disciplined. The school social worker would talk to Hunter. Tucker would get extra help. They'd keep an eye on Ernest and let her know if he missed school. Billy Dickerson would keep in touch.

With his gaze fixed on the nametag just above Tulip's breast, the principal shook her hand. "Is there anything else I can do for you, Mrs. Burns?"

He was sounding awful friendly, and she was tempted to ask *Billy* what the hell he wanted from her. Instead she put her purse between them. "I'll let you know."

On the way to the car, Grace raved about how well things had gone and what a nice person Billy—no, Mr. Dickerson—was. Tulip didn't mention that he'd been gawking at her boobs. She did tell Grace that she'd wait and see.

Grace grinned. "Oh, Tulip, you get more bees with honey than vinegar."

Tulip knew that. But bees sting.

Hunter came home from school the next day with a smile as big as Texas. The principal had called her to the office and listened to her side of the story. "And Mom, he's making Danny stay in from recess for a week."

"Billy" did not call, no more bad reports from school. Tulip had to admit he was not an ogre.

Angel Grace continued to care for the kids after school. Marshall had dropped out of sight. Maybe he'd found a girlfriend or, better yet, was in jail. No one was trying to use Tulip for a punching bag or even screaming at her. The tightness in her chest eased, leaving space to take in air. She felt lighter. She could think. She could plan.

Sitting in her kitchen drinking coffee, Tulip noticed the walls were almost as dark as her coffee. Cereal bowls were on the table, dishes in the sink. The place was a mess. It would be a relief to come home to a clean kitchen. She jumped up and did the dishes lickety-split. The kitchen was desperately in need of work—a new fridge, linoleum, a light that didn't flicker. The list went on. Twenty bucks stuck in her sock drawer for emergencies was not even a start. But it would buy paint. She should get off her lazy duff. She'd love to have a cheery kitchen, maybe yellow, sunshine yellow, with a jar of red flowers on the table. Wouldn't that be pretty?

Tulip bought the paint on her way to work. Clearance. Sam, Kirby's hippie, ponytailed clerk, assured her that it was decent paint. Emergency money usually ended up on the grocery counter, and the kids were sick of macaroni. But for once she was going to have something that she wanted!

When Tulip pulled into the drive, Tucker raced out of the house as a pigeon-toed kid could go. He walloped into her. "M-M-Mom, I d-d-didn't mean to d-d-do it!" he sobbed.

It had been a long time since she'd held Tucker. His arms were firming, more like a man's. He was taller than she was. She lifted tangled hair from his face. "Hey, hey, big boys don't cry. What happened?"

His arms pumping up and down, he tried to speak. Finally he pointed toward Prudence's house, where she peered from behind the drape.

Hunter stomped down the porch steps. "It's that witch next door. Our ball went into her yard and Tucker tried to find it. She caught him in her bushes. She screamed at him! She said we were unruly, had no respect, and never *ever* to come on her property! She said she wouldn't let us make any more trouble for her son. Then she grabbed the ball and took it inside."

"She said all that?"

The children bobbed their heads.

Hunter trailing behind, Tulip headed down the sidewalk to Prudence's. Tulip laid on the doorbell. She would damn well ring that bell until Prudence came out. Finally Prudence cracked the door.

"I've come for the ball." Tulip's voice was gas vapor ready to blow.

Prudence smiled and spoke ever so sweetly. "No, I don't think so."

"What?"

"It will teach them to stay out of my yard."

"That's stealing!"

Prudence's eyes flickered. "Your children are loud, undisciplined, and—and sneaky! If you can't keep them out of my yard, I will!" She tucked in her chin and talked slowly like Tulip's sixth-grade teacher. "It is a natural consequence of their behavior. Any ball that comes onto my property is mine. It will teach them a lesson." Prudence pushed the door to close it.

No longer a sixth-grader, Tulip blocked the door with her shoulder. "What is the matter with you? You've been spying on us since we moved in! I bought the house. I'm fixing it up. We've a right to be here!"

"Your house is a disaster. You've got the whole neighborhood helping you. Even roped in my son."

"What?"

"I'm done with you. You and your children stay off my property!" She slammed the door.

As though on cue, Prudence's son came up the walk. "Hi. What's going on?"

"Your mother, that's what's going on! Come on, Hunter. I got painting to do."

Dennis just stood there gaping. Tulip seized Hunter's hand. In the house, snot running down his chin, Tucker waited on the couch. Tulip pulled a Kleenex from her pocket and wiped his face. "Tucker, she's nuts. I'll buy you another ball."

"P-promise?"

Tulip had failed to retrieve Tucker's ball and he doubted she would buy another. "Yes, son, we can afford a ball. Just stay out of her yard." She tweaked his nose with the Kleenex. "Blow."

"I'm going to trash that witch's yard," Hunter muttered.

Tulip spoke sternly. "No, you won't. We won't stoop to her tricks." Her lips curled in a half smile. "And you shouldn't call her a witch."

The witch was not going to ruin Tulip's day. Tulip was painting the kitchen. She shooed Hunter and Tucker off to play and hauled paint, rollers, and brushes out of Old Ruby. But when Tucker saw the paint, he oohed and awed and dogged her steps. She pointed him toward the living room. "Go watch TV. Paint's messy."

Hunter's glare could have fried an egg. "You never let us do anything fun!"

Tulip hadn't thought the kids would want to paint. But why wouldn't they? Tucker had loved painting at summer camp, but this was different. It was hard work and messy, but it was their house too. She could paint over any mistakes after they were in bed. "OK, but you need to be careful and do exactly as I say."

While Tulip stirred the paint, Hunter covered the counter and floor with newspaper. Tucker rolled and Hunter brushed woodwork. Tulip painted the high parts.

Amazingly, after the first few spills, Tucker's roller met the wall. "Th-this is fun!" He began to hum, then sang out, "Old MacDonald had a farm..." Hunter joined in, then Tulip. When Tucker sang the oinks and the quacks at full volume, Hunter doubled over with laughter. They sang and they painted and painted until, incredibly, the first coat was nearly on. Paint had oozed from Tucker's roller onto his hands, and his hands had wandered—face, hair, shirt, pants.

Tulip surveyed the work. Her children had stuck with it. There were missed spots but it didn't look too bad. She grinned her lopsided grin. "You kids did a good job."

"G-good job!" echoed Tucker, raising his roller in the air.

Tulip wiped paint off Hunter's nose. "You deserve a reward. First paycheck we'll go to McDonald's. Tonight we'll have to settle for peanut butter and jelly. Now, you yellow-bellied kids, get washed up. I'll make sandwiches." She shook her finger. "And please don't get paint on anything!"

Ernest walked in holding *Tom Sawyer*. "Wow! You guys did this?"

"Yep!" Tucker replied.

A knock. Ernest went to answer.

"Better not be that witch from next door," Tulip mumbled.

Hunter put her hands on her hips. "Mom, you said not to call—oh, Miss Grace!"

Grace stood in the doorway holding a steaming pan, sweet tomato aroma filling the kitchen. She laughed. "So now I'm a witch? I saw you painting and thought you might need some supper. But if you don't want it…" As if to go, she turned.

"No! Not you!"

Grace set the lasagna on the counter. "Tulip, it's lovely. So bright." Grace caressed Tucker's paint-spattered hair. "I see you helped. Your mother must be proud of you!"

Tulip nodded. "I am."

Although Tulip usually read the children a bedtime story, they did not complain when she said she was too pooped to read. She was determined to finish painting. If she took a break, she could, she would. She went out into the cool night air and sat on the porch. Putting up the hood of her sweatshirt, she pillowed her head against the post. Through half-closed eyes she watched the witch's house—dark. Light in Grace and Kirby's bedroom. The lasagna had been a godsend. Grace always showed up at the right time. Tulip lived between a witch and a fairy godmother. All she needed was a prince. She laughed out loud.

A voice spoke from the dark. "What's so funny?"

Tulip's eyes flew open. That kid Dennis stood in the shadows. "Where'd you come from?"

He pulled the hood of an Ypsilanti High sweatshirt over his head. "Sorry, didn't mean to scare you. A bit chilly to be sitting out."

"So what's it to you?"

He held up a ball, tossed it to Tulip. "I found it when I was picking up your trash."

"Our trash?"

"In our front yard. Didn't think you'd miss it, but figured the kids would want their ball."

Tulip wanted to smack that smartass guy in his too-tight sweatshirt. "We do not go on your property!"

"Of course not. A gremlin delivered it."

"What makes you think it's ours?" *Please Hunter, don't have thrown trash in their yard.*

The little snot laughed. "You can tell a lot about a person by his garbage: Cheerios, macaroni and cheese, No-Brand peanut butter."

Caught. "So what else did you learn?"

"I like the yellow paint."

He was smooth for a kid. "How old are you anyway?"

"Twenty-two."

"No!"

"You thought I was seventeen?"

"But you act thirty."

"Mom has a short fuse. Sometimes she does things she regrets. She'll get used to you." He pointed toward the kitchen. "Maybe I can make it up—help. Can I have a look? "

Tulip remembered eighth-grade grammar. "If you're able." She hurled the ball at him. He caught it and gently tossed it back.

Dennis scrubbed the dripping roller handle until it looked as if it had just come out of the package. His hands were small for a man, almost dainty but with long fingers. He held the roller as if it were a delicate instrument and eased it back and forth in the paint tray. Then, as though it were leading him, the roller glided up and down the wall.

Dennis rolled. Tulip painted trim. He did not try to make small talk. Other than the clock ticking, the swish of Tulip's brush, the tiny plop of the roller hitting the wall, it was quiet, a sort of comfortable quiet. Tulip was curious about him and his crazy mother, but she was not going to pick a fight.

When they were cleaning up, Tulip broke the silence. "What's this your mother says about me staying away from you? Does she think I'm going to seduce you?"

He squeezed the roller, foamy paint trickling down his hand. "Would you like to?"

Tulip slapped him on the butt with her brush, making a yellow print on otherwise clean jeans. "I don't seduce kids."

He smiled a sad smile, took the soap, and scrubbed his hands one finger at a time, up and down, till they were pink. Finally he spoke. "Legally I've been an adult since I was eighteen."

"Your mother doesn't think so."

"Mom married Dad young, in college. Dad was older, did everything for her. She never had a chance to grow up. They had problems." He sighed as though he didn't want to say more. "They fought—a lot. Then there was the wreck. I'm all she's got…and I've given her a hard time."

"You, the good son, giving her a hard time?" Tulip didn't say, *Shit, your mother doesn't know what a hard time is.* And she didn't ask, like a civilized person would have, about his dad's death or how it was for Dennis.

He reached his hand toward Tulip's shoulder, let it drop, and took a step back. "Got to go. I've got an early class…oh, heck." He hugged her, his clean T-shirt pressed against her painted one.

Tulip stiffened, then relaxed into his lean, firm chest. He smelled sweaty, but in a woodsy sort of way. Sort of like it must smell in a forest after a spring rain. She stepped back and tried to brush the yellow from his chest. "When your mom sees your clothes, you'll really be in trouble."

"Maybe not. I'll wash them when I get home. It was fun." He gave her a playful shove. "The kitchen looks great."

As he came, he was gone, and she had not thanked him.

She picked up the last of the newspapers and threw the kids' clothes in the tub to soak. She would deal with them in the morning. She couldn't get Dennis out of her mind. He was twenty-two, not quite a kid, but he didn't act like any man she had ever known. It wasn't that she was attracted to him—too young. What could he have done that was so terrible? He seemed decent, the kind of guy she wished she'd had for a brother.

Tulip thought about goodness, Grace bringing supper, how she treated the kids respectfully—like grownups, but not like grownups. It was hard to put her finger on it. Grace was firm, told them what to do, but asked for their opinions. She noticed when they did something right and praised them for it. She watched out for the good. Not like her, always ready to fight, not noticing when things went right.

Enough thinking. Tulip was exhausted, but they had done it, Hunter and Tucker and her, and she mustn't forget to thank Dennis. They'd painted the kitchen sunlight yellow. And *that* was good!

15

Grace chose the flowered muu'muu that Kirby had bought her years ago on vacation in Hawaii. She wanted to look festive for this afternoon tea. As she picked up the phone to remind Kirby that she wouldn't be home, he walked in.

"You're early. Something the matter?" she asked.

Sighing, he slumped onto the couch. "Just tired."

"Maybe you should have a nap. I'll get you some water. I hate to leave, but I have to go to Prudence's for tea."

"You're abandoning me to have tea with Prudence? I thought the two of you weren't speaking." He eased himself onto the couch, his hair fanning the pillow.

"You need a haircut…Tulip's invited too. "

"How'd you orchestrate that? I thought Prudence didn't like Tulip and her brood."

After Grace's confrontation in the kitchen, Prudence had not come near her for a week. When Grace found the tea invitation in her mailbox, she wondered if it was Prudence's way of apologizing. Grace was amazed when Tulip ran across the lawn with *her* invitation. Had Dennis talked some sense into his mother? Still, it was hard to imagine Prudence making amends, especially to Tulip. "It will be interesting."

Kirby caressed Grace's leg. "You could stay home with me."

Grace sat on the edge of the couch and smoothed dark hair sprinkled with gray from his forehead. His musky scent drew her to him. When they kissed, she felt the pineapple-prickle of his beard. "You're not good for anything right now. You had no business unloading deliveries. And a bunch of snow blowers! You're not twenty anymore."

"Or forty, or even sixty." He drew her into his once rock-hard arms, just beginning to succumb to the pull of gravity. She snuggled against his chest.

Through the open window Grace heard Tulip call, "You kids be good now, ya hear? I'll be back in a while." The couple watched as Tulip strode down the walk, her bottom taut, bell-bottom jeans flapping against her ankles.

"Isn't she pretty?" Grace asked.

Kirby kissed her, a warm kiss filled with desire. "But skinny and wound too tight. You are voluptuous, something to hold onto."

"Sure, size sixteen and starting to grow again. Plenty to hang onto."

"The more to love." He patted her buttocks, then slid his hands up the small of her back. "Couldn't you let Prudence and Tulip figure this out themselves?"

Recently Kirby had become affectionate, more the way he used to be. Grace attributed this to a change in him. But he said that after Rickey died she had pushed him away, that she recoiled each time he touched her. Now she felt a warmth in her breasts that she had not felt for a long while. She took his hand from that sensitive spot and tucked it by his side. Later, she thought, and pulled away. "I've got to go. Can't leave Tulip and Prudence alone for long."

The sun's rays cut through a dull sky. The last errant autumn leaves swirled and danced in the breeze. Swishing leaves out of the way, hoping Kirby was noting the sway of her "voluptuous" bottom, Grace swaggered to Prudence's, sauntered onto the porch, and pressed the bell. Remembering the war zone she was about to enter, she braced herself.

Breathless, as though she had run across the room, Prudence flung open the door. "Come in, come in, come in!" Her rich soprano voice chased the wind.

Tulip sat, straight-backed and diminutive, at the ornate dining table with its eight chairs.

"She sings," Grace said to Tulip.

Prudence pecked the air near Grace's face.

"So, am I late?"

"No, Tulip was early." Prudence enunciated every word as though it were an accusation. Tulip flushed, looked imploringly toward Grace.

So this was the way it was going to be, tea with the ice queen. Grace whispered, "Be nice." Breathing in dusty, stale air, she suppressed the suggestion of opening a window. Her feet sank into rose carpet, the blossoms tired and worn with footprints tracing a path to the kitchen. The Victorian sofa was faded, a small tear on the arm. Sheers, muting slivers of sun, covered the windows. The gold chandelier with its candelabras was smudged and unlit. Grace had not realized Prudence had let her cleaning lady go, or how shabby the house had become.

In the midst of this decay, wearing a low-cut dress suitable for a cocktail party, hair arranged in a drunken mass of curls, Prudence stood tall. Had she been so distressed by her little gathering that she had fortified herself with a glass or two of wine? With her portraying a prudish Emily Post and Tulip frozen in her chair, Grace was the elected go-between. The outcome of this "party" depended on her.

Grace forced a smile. "My, aren't you dressed up! Ooh, look at this!" She pointed to the table set with china, roses on white. She picked up a delicate cup, light shining through it. "Prudence, I've never seen your china. It picks up the colors of the room, or did you decorate around it?"

Prudence managed a tight smile. "Mother's. The sterling was my grand-mother's. I'll get the tea."

Grace touched Tulip's rigid shoulder. "How're you doing?"

"I didn't wear the right clothes." She pointed to her faded T-shirt, with the words Hot Momma barely visible. "It's all I had clean. I didn't think—"

Grace patted her back. "If I had your figure, I'd have worn a T-shirt and jeans too."

The kettle whistled in the kitchen. Shortly, Prudence swept in with a silver tray containing a plate of tiny sandwiches and another with three miniature scones. Placing them on the table, she spoke in a strained voice. "We're having English high tea." She hurried back to the kitchen. Water swooshed into the teapot.

Tulip whispered again, "What's high tea?"

Holding the tray as though bearing jewels, Prudence returned. Teapot, milk, sugar, and lemon were arranged on the tray. She sat at the head of the table with Tulip and Grace across from each other—a mismatched threesome with five empty chairs.

"The tea needs to brew a bit, but help yourself to a sandwich." Prudence gestured to the serving plate that dwarfed eight crustless triangles, arranged on lettuce with tips pointed inward. Grace took one and passed the platter to Tulip, who lifted the bread and looked at the filling.

"Cucumber," Prudence said.

"Cucumber?" Tulip asked.

"Yes, that's what the English serve."

"They cut off the crust?"

"Yes, that's how it's supposed to be."

"What a waste."

Prudence took in air and let it out. "Tea?" She picked up the pot and carefully poured each cup.

"I think they may use the crust for breading and such. Don't you think so, Prudence?" Grace asked.

"I never thought about it. Milk, lemon?"

Tulip poured milk into her tea and then squeezed a slice of lemon into the cup; she sipped, grimaced, and set it down. She took a tiny bite of sandwich, chewed, and tried to swallow. Setting the remainder on her plate, she looked miserably at her cottage-cheese tea.

Her voice strained, as if she couldn't reach the high note, Prudence sang out, "You don't like the sandwich."

"No, no. It's…cucumbers give me gas."

"Do you like scones?"

Tulip nodded blankly.

Prudence carefully set the plate next to Tulip. "They should be fine even for delicate stomachs."

Tulip took a bite of the dry scone, chewed, and struggled to swallow, her face turning scarlet, her freckles more prominent.

"Prudence, would you bring water?" Grace asked. "Somehow I'm really thirsty today."

Prudence grimaced. Obviously water was not on the menu.

While Prudence was in the kitchen, Grace touched Tulip's hand and whispered, "She puts on airs. Would you like another cup of tea?"

Tulip shook her head.

Pretenses stripped away, Prudence entered with two glasses of tap water and set them on the table with a thud. Tulip gulped water and cleared her throat. "Grace said you sing."

Prudence cocked her regal head and began the sing-song speech that Grace had heard more than once. "It comes naturally. I just open my mouth and it comes out. I never had to work at it. I could have been trained, made it a career. But I met Dr. Goodwin in college. He was just setting up his practice." She drew the words out. "*Very* handsome—eligible—physician! He swept me off my feet."

Her smile faded. Her voice softened. "I was so young and inexperienced." She sighed and gestured at the darkened living room. "So here I am."

Grace was struck by Prudence's sadness, her attempt to be real, and her admission of disappointments, all in Tulip's presence. Again Grace wondered if Prudence had been drinking. "But you're a local celebrity. You sing at church, for weddings, all sorts of occasions."

Prudence's gaze met Grace's. "I wonder what would have happened if I hadn't married, if I'd finished college."

"I know what you mean. I was saving money for nursing school when I met Kirby."

Prudence nodded. "That's what we did back then. We didn't think about what we wanted. We just thought we should get married and have babies."

"Even that wasn't so easy for some of us. I was forty when I had Rickey."

Tulip's mouth fell open. "You have a son?"

"Had a son. He was killed in Vietnam—just last year."

Tulip's glass struck the table, water sloshing onto the rose tablecloth. "I'm so sorry. I didn't know."

Prudence mopped at the spill with her napkin.

No, you wouldn't notice that I was half dead from grief. You're too focused on fighting your own demons. "Yes, he was quite a boy—outgoing, full of energy, not fond of school but an amazing athlete, handsome too." Her voice caught. "Ernest smiles a lot like him."

"But he was killed?"

A light in Grace's mind switched on. She had been mired in self-pity. But even before Rickey died, all was not right. She had already lost a part of herself. After months of feeling anesthetized, her brain seemed clear. "I should have been a nurse, that's what I wanted!"

Prudence continued to dab at the cloth. Tulip leaned forward, her head on her hands.

To calm herself, Grace stirred her tea, the leaves forming a whirlpool in the cup. "I grew up on a farm, seven of us. Mom worked all the time, even in the field—old before her time. There was no money for school. When I married, I tried to be this spectacular homemaker—cleaning, cooking, baking—but I had this vague feeling of discontent. When Kirby finally wanted a child, I couldn't get pregnant. I thought there must be something wrong with me. I felt like I'd failed. When I did get pregnant, I was redeemed."

"So you were happy then?" Tulip asked.

"I loved being a mother, but I still wasn't quite satisfied."

"You could go to school now," Tulip offered.

Grace chuckled. "Interesting thought, an old lady in nursing class. But the world is different now. Young women are more assertive. They recognize that they have choices, options, and they exercise them."

"I wish I felt that way," Tulip said. "I just tried to keep from getting beat up. Life just happened."

"I know what you mean," Prudence said.

"You? The queen bee!" *I said that?* Grace was stunned into silence.

"What!" Prudence's blue eyes blazed. "I gave up my career. You think because my husband was a doctor I had it so good? You don't know what he was really like! And now I have to worry about paying the mortgage, the taxes, servicing the furnace!" She struggled to breathe. "You, you have a husband who adores you, takes care of you!"

As though she had been punched, Grace exhaled. "I am *not* a kept woman!"

Prudence blinked. "Oh, oh, no, I didn't mean that. It's just harder when you don't have a man, a husband to help out, fix things…and Dr. Goodwin didn't leave his financial affairs in the best shape."

What about Rickey? What about losing a son? Could anything be worse? Grace gripped the table and kept her words even. "If something happened to Kirby, I *would* take care of myself!"

"You don't know. You can't know till it happens." She nodded to Tulip. "You and I know what it's like to be on our own."

That night, sleepless in bed, Grace tried to understand what had transpired. Surely Prudence had been drinking and it had loosened her tongue. What a threesome they were. Perhaps Grace had not been empathic with Prudence about her aborted career, because of her own unarticulated desires. In spite of her declaration of solidarity, Grace knew Prudence had no sympathy for Tulip. At times Grace felt like Tulip's mother superior, advising, helping her out. But it was Tulip who was taking initiative for her life in a way that neither Prudence nor Grace had done.

16

After the fancy tea, Prudence would greet Tulip across the yard, nothing more. Tulip often spotted her peeking out from behind her drapes, spying. She knew Prudence thought she was white trash and didn't want her precious son having anything to do with Tulip or her kids. But if Dennis wanted to drop by Tulip's, it was his business. After she put the kids to bed, Tulip unwound on the porch, listening to the crickets chirp and cars humming on the next street. When the lights went off at the Goodwins', sometimes Dennis walked out of the shadows, casual like, leaned against her railing, and talked. Tulip didn't have many friends, certainly none of the male variety, and she didn't know quite what to make of Dennis.

"Your mom told me she had to do everything when your dad died, that she and I are alike—alone," Tulip said.

Dennis laughed.

"What's so funny?"

He shook his head. "Mom fell apart. She was crazed, up all night drinking and crying, sleeping all day, not cooking, not paying the bills."

"You never said that before."

"Her not giving me credit makes me mad. I took care of her for months. But when I got into trouble, she straightened up."

"You, in trouble?"

"That's what woke her up. Now she's having a hard time letting me go."

"You *do* live with her."

"We used my college fund to pay off the house. I'll finish my associate's in the spring, get a scholarship. Then I'm out of here."

"Oh, the backpack. In the morning I see you walk to the bus. I thought maybe you were still in high school," Tulip taunted.

He smirked, but he wasn't touching that with a ten foot pole. "Mom wants me to be a doctor like Dad, but I'm not sure. I think it would be fun to teach. I like kids a lot."

The screen door opened and slammed shut. "M-Mom, I p-peed the bed." Tucker stood in the doorway, hand covering his pecker as if he could turn off the faucet.

Dennis stood up. "Got to go." He loped down the walk.

Tulip stared after him. He disappeared fast for a guy who liked kids.

In November the weather turned cold. One Saturday when the kids were acting up, Tulip shooed them off to the park. Hoping Dennis would drop by, she made a fresh pot of coffee, bundled up, and sat on the porch. As if Dennis knew she was waiting, he strolled up the walk.

"Whatcha doing out here in the cold?" Dennis asked.

"Want some coffee?"

"Maybe." He looked toward his house.

"She drove off a while ago."

He nodded, leaned against the post.

Tulip motioned toward her door. "I shouldn't be sitting. Got to caulk around the bathtub. Water's leaking through the kitchen ceiling."

"So what's stopping you?"

Tulip shrugged. She was certainly not going to tell him she was waiting to see him.

"It's easy," he said.

"Maybe for you, Mr. Know-It-All."

He laughed. "Maybe I should take a look."

Perhaps Dennis would offer to help. Tulip led the way into the house. In the hall he slipped on a Lego. He laughed again. "Kids' booby-trap."

"Tucker's been building, didn't pick up last night. They're nasty on bare feet."

"I played with Legos. What's he making?"

"Not much. Mostly puts them together in blocks."

"Someone should help him."

"Are you volunteering?"

Dennis clicked his tongue. "Guess you can't ask his dad." His gazed flitted over the living room, cluttered with books and toys. "And you're swamped... how about Ernest?"

"How about you?"

He grimaced, shook his head.

Uh-oh, he knew she was after his help. "For someone who likes kids, you act like mine've got a contagious disease."

Dennis continued up the stairs, speaking slowly, as if she might be daft. "I don't mean any harm. I like your kids. It's just…not right now."

"Huh?"

"I'll explain later. Let's check the tiles."

At the sight of caulk gunked around the tub, Dennis screwed up his face. "Somebody's been messing with this."

For once, Tulip remained silent.

"It was that cop. Wasn't it?"

"So?" Now she was really pissed—him judging her for seeing Bigfoot.

Dennis shrugged. "So he does lousy work." Mr. Goody-Two-Shoes peeled off a piece of caulk. "What it really needs is a grout job."

"And what I really need is a tub and shower that the kids can use without flooding the house."

Dennis was right. On his way to work, Ken had stopped by and done a hurry-up job of caulking. Dennis, on the other hand, was very—what was it called? Meticulous? Loosening the caulk, he pulled it out in taffy streams. "You have to prep it. Get all the cracked grout out." His driver slithered between the tiles, easing out yuck. He grimaced. "Your boyfriend made a mess."

"We're just friends. He helps me out."

"He's an inferior caulker."

Tulip bristled. "Maybe there was something wrong with the caulk. Maybe it was old, too dry."

Dennis shook his head. "Too big a hurry. Didn't prep. You need a steady hand, take your time, get the old stuff out…" His voice matched his words, rhythmic, hypnotic.

Tulip leaned against the wall, watching. When Dennis finished, he turned to her. In the small bathroom they were nose to nose, his piney aftershave smelling of outdoors.

Dennis stepped back. "I need a bucket and bleach. It'll clean the mildew."

Relieved to be out of the close space, Tulip clattered downstairs to find a pail.

Dipping the rag into the warm mixture, Dennis rubbed the tiles, then dried them, pressing the cloth firmly into the damp cracks. "We have to give it time to dry or the caulk won't stick. I'll bet that guy couldn't wait."

Tulip's cheeks were burning.

"Don't use the shower. I'll be back tomorrow." He handed her the bucket and skipped down the stairs.

The next day, Dennis returned with his caulk gun. Dark eyes teasing, he held it out for inspection. "Got to have the proper tool."

Muscles flexing under his T-shirt, he pumped the white stuff into the cracks, smoothing it with his finger. Up and down, in and out of the tub, with deliberate, artful strokes. When he finished, sweat trickled down his elfin face. Leaning against the wall, he touched Tulip's cheek. "How's that?"

Tulip felt the cool goo on his fingers, whiffed his piney aftershave. Her breath caught.

"Don't shower for a couple of days. Give it time to set." He smoothed her face, then—embarrassed?—stumbled back. "Got to go. Late for class." He bounded down the stairs.

In the mirror, a not-so-bad-looking redhead with gunk on her face grinned out at Tulip. Strange, she didn't feel dirty. She felt cleansed, relieved, almost happy. Her battery was charged and she was operating on all cylinders.

When the kids came home, Tulip stood in the doorway waiting for them to notice the spick-and-span house. The boys barreled off to the kitchen for a snack. Hunter looked at Tulip and wrinkled her nose. "What's the white stuff on your face?"

17

❦

"**I** gotta make more money." Tulip stood by the counter, trying to get Joe's attention as he sorted the noon receipts. As though she were a gnat to be rid of, he flicked his hand. Tulip leaned over the counter, her face in front of his. "Listen, Joe. I got a leaky roof. My kids have outgrown their clothes. I need a raise."

Joe harrumphed, "Not bad. We did OK today."

"Joe, you're not listening."

"You need more money. We all need more money. I got a car and house payment, utilities, salaries, venders, insurance. The list goes on."

"I can't live on what I make."

He winked. He actually winked. "Get yourself a husband."

Tulip snorted. "You met my ex."

"Tips, work the supper shift. Tips are better."

"I got kids."

"Get a sitter." He stacked the receipts and put them in the register.

Tulip thumped the counter. "I can't afford a sitter! I can't afford to feed my kids!"

Joe raised himself to his full five-foot-seven. "Don't shout at me! You want more money? Wiggle your ass. Flirt with the guys."

Tulip felt smacked, but she was determined. "I should get paid for the work I do."

Joe clicked his shiny loafers together and headed for the kitchen. He wasn't having a hard time—driving a new Impala, wearing dress pants and Ivy League shirts. He didn't get his clothes from the Salvation Army, worry about paying thirty-five cents for school lunch, or rob his kids' piggybanks to pay the electric bill. Tulip was a good manager. She'd been able to save money when she lived with D and didn't pay rent or utilities or have Old Ruby. Now, on her measly paycheck, even with tips, she was short, and had nothing for emergencies. What if Old Ruby needed new brakes?

"Asshole," D whispered as she walked by with a tray of dirty dishes.

After the restaurant cleared, D and Tulip sat down for burgers and coffee. It was good that Joe was out because D was raving about what she called women's rights. "It's not fair what they do to women. I could be a damn good shift manager. Think Joe would give me the job? No way." She jabbed a fry in a pool of ketchup and stuck it in her mouth. "He's never had a woman manager. I'll walk my legs off until I can't, then they'll put me out to pasture with nothing—no retirement. I don't have medical, no benefits. If I get sick, I've had it." She swiped her hand across her throat in a cutting motion. "And you're worse off. You got kids to think of."

Tulip had taken men being up and women down as a fact of life. She was plenty mad about it but had no idea how to change it. D managing Joe's—a *woman* in charge? Tulip pictured her in high heels and a suit, sauntering around asking the customers how they liked their food. D would hate being dressed up every day.

Tulip first heard D's tirade a few days after Tulip had moved into Old Grouchy. Boxes were still piled in the living room. The kids were ramming through the house, hunting their toys. Tucker couldn't find Mr. Knight. He was crying and refused to go to bed without that rabbit.

D barged in, stepped around the clutter, and flipped on the TV. "You got to see this."

Tulip's mouth fell open. "Is this what you came over for, to watch TV? Why didn't you stay home? Your TV's a hell of a lot better than mine!"

"You need to know what's going on in the world!"

When D got something in her head, you did not mess with her, and Tulip was out of gas. So they sat there in the middle of the chaos watching the news, a protest in New York City. A sea of women marched down Fifth Avenue carrying banners: equal pay for equal work.

"Sounds good to me," Tulip said.

Snot running down his face, Tucker tapped her shoulder. "Mommy, h-h-help me find Mr. Knight."

D shook her head. "I'm serious. Women have to work together. There is power in numbers. We should join NOW."

"Join what now?"

"The National Organization for Women, egghead. They're for equal pay for equal work, twenty-four-hour child care, and abortions on demand. That's why they're marching." D pointed to the TV. "That's her. That's Betty Friedan."

"You mean the ugly one?"

"Gloria Steinem's younger and prettier, but Betty started it all." D shouted at the screen, "Go, Betty!" Then to Tulip, "She wrote *The Feminine Mystique*."

"The what?"

D looked at Tulip as if she were an idiot.

There was a shot of the Statue of Liberty with huge banners flying from the top: WOMEN OF THE WORLD UNITE.

Tucker tugged at Tulip's arm. "M-Mommy! I can't find Mr. Knight!"

"Tucker, go look in the…the…" Tulip motioned to the bedroom. "D, there's no way the women of the world could unite in time to pay my bills."

D read about it in the *Ann Arbor News* while taking a coffee break at Joe's. "Aha!" D cried, and waved the newspaper in front of Tulip. "You can do *this*."

Tulip read the headline: "Adult Foster Homes Needed." "You mean old people—take care of old people?"

D nodded in her all-knowing way. "They dress themselves, feed themselves. It's not like you're running a nursing home. You just give them three squares a day and make sure they take their meds."

"You've lost your mind. I can hardly take care of the kids and work. How could I manage a bunch of old codgers?"

"Not a bunch. Just one or two. You think about it."

At her kitchen table, while shuffling through past due bills, Tulip noticed D's crumpled newspaper article. Would it be so bad having an old person in the house? Tulip thought of her grandma with the roly-poly arms and wrinkledy skin. She remembered being little and sitting in her grandmother's Kentucky kitchen, similar to Tulip's, with cupboards floor to ceiling, except Grandma's kitchen had smelled like fresh-baked bread. Her bunions bothered her, and she sat at the table to work. The first day Tulip helped, her grandmother handed her a dull knife. "Hold the underside of the potato," she said. "Peel away from you so's you don't cut yourself." She sliced a sliver, salted it, and handed it to Tulip. When Tulip crunched down, earthy flavors exploded in her mouth. Better than an apple.

Tulip's happiest memories, few and far between, were of her grandmother. Tulip's children had no memory of their grandparents—zip. Thank God!

They'd moved south after Tulip married—gone, kaput, out of her life. Not all grandparents were created equal. Still, it might be good having a grandmotherly woman around. She probably couldn't do much, but she'd be there when the kids got home from school. Maybe they wouldn't have to go to Grace's. Counting the little room at the back of the hall, the one she used for storage, there were four bedrooms. It was big enough for a twin bed, dresser, and chair. If one person worked out, they could get another. Hunter could move into the little room and the old folks could bunk together in hers.

Tulip stopped at the welfare office and picked up an application. At supper she told the kids about getting an adult foster care license, that they could have an old person live with them. "It'd be nice having a grandma-type person around," she said.

Hunter's green eyes were gigantic. She puffed her cheeks. Macaroni spewed across the table, hitting Ernest. Wide-eyed, Ernest wiped his face.

Tulip inhaled. "This is the way it is! I can't pay the bills and your no-account dad doesn't pay child support half the time. I'm in charge here, and we gotta have more money!" She pointed to the stairs. "Hunter, go to your room!"

Ernest helped Tulip with dishes, then hightailed it out of the kitchen. She felt bad about her anger with Hunter, probably should apologize. But she'd had it with her daughter's snottiness. Hunter would get used to having someone around. You could get used to anything. But what if Prudence made a stink, found some ordinance, called in the law? Well, it was Tulip's property. She made a cup of tea and sat at the table. Shoving the bills to one side, she filled out the application. The next morning she took it to work for D to check.

That evening, when Dennis walked by, she asked what he thought.

"Mom doesn't have to know. I'm twenty-two. If neighbors have to sign off, I can do it."

Tulip put the application in the mail. Then she waited. It took forever for the government to do anything for the little people, but do something wrong like park in a no-parking zone and the next thing you knew your car was towed.

One Saturday weeks later, Tulip sorting through Friday's mail, found an official-looking envelope, the return address Social Services. Finally! She took a knife and slit it open. Words jumped at her. *Denied…negligent mother.* What the hell? The paper! She had signed that paper. In getting her son help, she had signed her reputation away! She tore the letter to shreds and stomped around the kitchen, cursing. She could think of only one profession she qualified for that would bring in the kind of money she needed. And she'd be damned if she'd do that.

She totaled the bills. Six hundred dollars. Twenty bucks in her billfold. If she didn't pay the electricity, they'd turn it off. And how long would they let you stay in a house without paying taxes? There was no way to cut back. She shopped for clothes at Salvation Army. She was sick of peanut-butter-and-jelly sandwiches for supper. She mixed powdered milk with whole milk. OK, so they could drink straight powdered milk, but that would not put a dent in the bills.

December tenth. Tulip's next check would pay the gas and electric, but there'd be nothing—zip for groceries. She checked the cupboards: a box of dried milk, two cans of tomato soup, one box of macaroni and cheese, and three cans of green beans. Her kids hated green beans. She would have to smuggle food home from Joe's—a thief *and* a negligent mother. And there sure as hell wouldn't be a Christmas.

Trapped, caged, she had to get out of the house. She threw on her coat and headed out the door. Snowing, the flakes wet and clean. Her postman Frank came up the walk. He nodded, handed her the mail, and hurried off. A couple of fliers and a letter from the county. She was steaming. *Did they want to take her kids because she was a negligent mother?* She ripped the envelope in two and flung it in the snow. Wait! She did not want her business buried in the snow. Whatever it was, she needed to know. She picked up the pieces and pulled out part of a—check? Five? Five what—dollars? She looked at the other half—hundred. *Five hundred dollars!* Marshall had paid some back child support. She held the two pieces together and laughed, delicious wet flakes settling on her tongue.

Tulip danced into the house, blocked the TV, and waved the check at her children. "Get dressed. Clean your rooms. We're going to McDonald's for lunch!"

Hood tight around his head, Dennis sat next to Tulip on the frigid stoop. After the kids were in bed, except for Old Grouchy creaking as Tulip walked the floor, the house was silent, lonely. She bundled up in her winter coat and sat shivering on the porch, watching the clouds float across the dark sky, waiting for Dennis. She didn't even have the excuse of smoking. Sitting next to him, hips touching, listening to the melody of his voice soothed her.

Rubbing her hands to warm them, Tulip watched their breath steam into the porch light. "It's too cold. Want some cocoa?"

As if she'd asked him to rob a bank, he seemed to be checking the lay of the land. "Are the kids in bed?"

"What's with you and the kids? You don't even know them. Is it Tucker?"

He held up his hands. "Wait a minute. Have I ever indicated that I don't like your kids?" He grinned. "Didn't I pick up their trash and return their ball from the Wicked Witch of the West?"

No way was he putting her off with a joke. "You avoid them like the plague. You come over after they're in bed, and if one peeks in, you scram."

He stuck his legs out as if to leave. Pulling them back, he cleared his throat. "Maybe I don't want to confuse your kids with a male presence."

"Shit, you're just a kid. Don't compliment yourself by imagining my children think you're my lover." She thought of the meanest thing she could say. "You don't even drive!"

Dennis jumped up. "My not driving has nothing to do with my age! I do what I have to do. I'm going home before I say something I'll regret."

That little jackass just took off. What was his problem? He was kind and thoughtful and seemed so sure of himself. But ask him a question and off he'd run. There was something he didn't want her to know.

18

"What's wrong with this toast?" Kirby asked, sopping the last bit of egg from his plate.

Grace and Kirby had overslept and were eating a hurried breakfast before he went to work. Grace shrugged and picked up the newspaper.

"Grace, whole wheat bread is bad enough, but you've done something to this."

She sighed. "It's got strawberry jam on it." She did not tell him that she'd not buttered it. The doctor had told Kirby that he must cut down on fats, lose thirty pounds, and exercise. Grace was monitoring his every bite.

"And where's the bacon?" Kirby asked.

"You're not supposed to eat it."

"I'm not eating this crap." He pushed his plate back, leaving the second piece of toast slathered with diet jam untouched. "What are you feeding me for dinner?"

"A nice chicken breast with a new sauce I'm trying."

"Chicken breast again! How about fried chicken with mashed potatoes and gravy, something to stick to your ribs?"

Grace picked up his cholesterol medication from the counter. "You've got to change your way of eating." She spoke in her most commanding voice. "And when you get home from work, we're taking a walk."

"It's too cold to walk!" He stood up and put on his coat. "Not that it matters to you, but what I'm really craving is barbecued ribs."

She swallowed her anger. "We'll splurge for your birthday."

"Six months. You're a hard woman." He walked out, slamming the door behind him.

Grace touched her lips where his kiss should have been. In a fury, she pawed through the freezer's icy white wrappers. Meat for two: sirloin, T-bone, rump roast, and hamburger. The O'Shays bought beef by the quarter. No more! She pulled out a package of chicken breasts that bore a Kroger label.

Kirby liked legs, thighs, even wings and backs. "Chicken breasts, ugh. Like eating salted leather," he said.

The kitchen door bounced open. Grace laughed. "Couldn't leave without—"

Hands on her hips, Tulip stood glaring in the doorway.

"Oh." Tulip in a snit was the last thing Grace needed. She tore open the package. "We *do* have a doorbell."

"I came to ask you about that asshole!" Tulip blurted.

"Watch yourself!" Grace yanked out two anemic, stuck-together chicken breasts and cracked them on the counter.

"The kids ain't around."

"I don't want to listen to your potty mouth!"

"Did Dennis Goodwin kill his dad?"

Stunned, Grace dropped the chicken into the sink, and looked at Tulip. She was trembling, her face flushed. "What are you talking about?" asked Grace.

"The night of the accident, was Dennis driving?"

Grace's anger dissipated. She placed her hand on Tulip's shoulder. "Sit down." She poured coffee into Tulip's favorite Lassie mug. "I'll tell you what I know."

As if to keep herself from springing up, Tulip clutched the table with both hands. Grace stood between her and the door. "Dennis was with his father the night of the accident. He remembers a black car, maybe a Lincoln, speeding down Highway 12. His dad swerved to miss it."

"That highway's full of curves. It's not safe," Tulip said.

"Precisely. Dr. Goodwin lost control, hit a telephone pole. The driver's side crumpled. If Dennis had been driving, he would have been killed."

Tulip pursed her lips. "So how'd he lose his license?"

"Prudence claims that after the accident, Dennis gave up driving, but it was later that I'd see him walking to the bus stop."

"Yeah, he takes the bus."

"Dennis started drinking, partying, out all hours. One morning, when I got up early, I saw him skid into his driveway. He was not in control." Grace paused. "Why are you asking me this?"

As if Grace knew the answers, Tulip gazed at her with child's pleading eyes. "OK," Tulip said. "He lost his license; that makes sense. But it doesn't explain why he's super nice to me but vamooses when he sees my kids."

"Doesn't sound like Dennis. He likes children. When he was an Eagle Scout, he helped out with the Cub Scouts, took them camping."

"He's weird."

"You seem awfully interested in him. Are you attracted to him?"

Tulip leapt to her feet. "Nah. Got to go."

"Wait a minute!" Grace pressed Tulip back into the chair. "Dennis is a fine young man, a good friend to have. If you think he avoids your children, you should ask him about it. It helps to talk about things, communicate. Fight-or-flight does not solve problems."

"Fight-or-flight?"

"Isn't that what you've been doing? Isn't that how you live your life?"

"Shit! Who are you to tell me how to live my life?" Tulip flounced out of the kitchen.

Grace hollered at her back, "You need to clean up your language!" *Damn her anyway. And damn Kirby!* Grace dumped the untouched coffee and set the Lassie cup in the sink. She had enough on her mind without worrying about Tulip. That woman always had her back up, ready to fight at the slightest provocation. She was impulsive—fists or flight. Her running out proved Grace's theory.

She thumped the frozen chicken breasts on the counter.

19

The kids were dead to the world. It was snowing, and Old Grouchy's arthritic bones had absorbed the cold. Tulip was determined to set one thing right before she fell into bed and piled on covers. Squeezing no-brand soap in the sink, she blasted it with hot water, dumped in plates, and scrubbed off rivers of cheese. The steaming water stung her hands. Her feet were icicles.

All day she had thought about what Grace said, "Fight or flight." Did she think Tulip went around picking fights? And flight! Wouldn't she love that! She slogged from home to work and back, stuck like a pig in a wallow. Grace thought Tulip should *communicate*. She didn't know the half of it. Tulip's family never talked. If her mom opened her mouth, she was liable to end up with a black eye. And that was the way it was with her mom's mom too. Don't talk, don't think.

Tulip put the last plate in the drainer and threw the silverware in the sink. Bubbles sloshed onto the counter. Marshall had been her way out. She never told him about the beatings, and certainly not about Calvin. Thankfully, when Tucker was born early, Marshall didn't say pip squeak and her mouth was zipped shut. But Marshall got nasty mean. The house was burning with hate. When he was at work, Tulip had thrown clothes in garbage bags and set them by the door, but she had no place to go, not until D. Then she grabbed the kids and ran—flight? But what should she have done instead? Tell Marshall it was against the law to beat his wife? She rinsed the silver and stuck it in the drainer.

Till D and Grace, Tulip had never confided in anyone. Some things were too painful, shameful. Tulip was attracted to Dennis. He was too young, but maybe they could be friends. If she were honest, they were friends. With Dennis she felt like she had in middle school before—before she shriveled up and died. That's how she thought of it. A part of her dead. Soul murder, that was it! Before it happened, no matter how bad things were, the sun had shone through. She would grow up and get out of there. She popped the stopper. The plugged drain gurgled as water trickled out of the sink.

There was a boy she had liked, Jackie. They sent each other Valentines, nothing special, but he put a candy heart in hers that said, "Be Mine." When the other boys picked on her, he smacked 'em. It was after, when she felt so filthy with that dark shadow following her, and people looking through her, that she told him to buzz off. "What'd I do? What'd I do?" he asked. But she'd turned around and run. Flight?

Tulip put the last dish in the cupboard and watched wet flakes of snow settle on the trees and cover the yellowed grass, the dirt, the pavement. Everything looked white and clean.

Dennis, bundled up, backpack swinging, jogged by. Tulip flipped soap off her hands and ran out into the snow.

Dennis stopped. "Where you going in such a rush?"

"Where the hell do you think I'm going? I'm trying to catch you."

"So you caught me." He looked at her soapy hands.

She flicked suds at him. "I was doing dishes. Do you want to come to supper?"

"Supper?"

"You eat supper, don't you?"

He grinned. "What are you having?"

"What do you want?"

"Pork chops are my favorite."

"Can't do. How about hamburgers?"

He grinned again, a dimple showing in his cheek. "I like burgers...oh, but will the kids be there?"

"They live with me."

He shifted his weight from one foot to the other and shook his head. "I should take a rain check. Maybe in a couple of weeks."

"What the hell are you talking about?"

"It'll be OK in a couple of weeks."

"Your mother going on vacation?"

"No, nothing to do with her. Can we stand on your porch for a minute?"

"Pretty damn cold. You can tell me anything you want to right here."

"Maybe we should go inside where it's warm. This may take a while."

"What for?"

"Um..." He swiveled his foot in the wet snow. "I'm on probation."

"Probation?"

"I can't be around kids."

"What's the matter with my kids?"

"It's not your kids. It's the probation."

"You can't see my kids because of… probation?"

"Yeah. But it's not as bad as it sounds."

Tulip sucked in air. *Not him!* "You son of a bitch! Get out of my yard! Don't you ever let me catch you around my kids!"

"Wait, wait! It's not what you think!"

"I know about that stuff and there is no way I'm letting it happen to my children! You get the hell out of my life!" Tulip grabbed a clot of ice and threw it, hitting him on the cheek. She wanted to pound him, pound him, pound him until she could feel no pain.

Dennis whirled and headed for home. Tulip ran after him, punching his back.

On the porch he turned, blood beginning to show on his cheek. He put up his hands. "Tulip, let me explain."

"I don't want to know about your shit!" Tulip ran across the yard, crusted snow working its way through her tennis shoes. In the house, she sank down at the kitchen table. Her luck, living next door to a—pervert? Fight? Kick him out of the neighborhood? Fat chance of that. Every penny she had was tied up in Old Grouchy. She couldn't take flight. She sat there thinking, trying not to think, snow puddling around her feet.

*Ping…ping…ping…*It was too early to get up. Tulip rolled over and covered her head. *Ping…ping…Who left the water on?* She cracked an eye open. A trickle of water dripped from the ceiling and plunked onto the tin cigar box where she kept her earrings. She didn't wear jewelry much but she'd taken a liking to dangly earrings, not gaudy, just cheap. Her only splurge. God was raining on her parade. She should have put the two bucks into a roof jar, not wasted it on baubles. She eased her feet onto the icy floor and hurried to find a bucket.

Back in bed, Tulip burrowed under the quilt. She had hoped, even prayed, that the roof would hold till spring. Snow had piled on the rotting shingles, and during the night the temperature had shot up—a midwinter thaw. Old Grouchy was wounded and leaking. Sailors on a capsizing ship, they'd be wading through a foot of water. *I, Tulip Burns—height: five-two, weight: one-fifteen—must climb up on the old gal and stitch her together. So be it!* She threw on clothes and ran downstairs. Outside the air was thick, eerie, a scene in an English novel when Jack the

Ripper was on the prowl. She'd rather the O'Shays not know about the roof, but she needed Kirby's ladder.

Grace's kitchen was bright and welcoming, the smell of coffee filling it with goodness. Beautiful in a red flowered robe, hair brushed to a silver sheen, Grace gestured toward a chair. "Have some coffee."

"Can't. Need to borrow your extension ladder." What Tulip really wanted was to plop down, pig out on eggs and hash browns, and pretend that she lived in this put-together, leak-proof home, with Grace and Kirby as her parents.

Kirby took a bite of pale scrambled eggs, grimaced, and waved his fork at Grace. "These are tasteless!" Then, pointing his fork at Tulip, he asked, "What do you need the ladder for?"

"Got a leak. Need to check it out." Tasteless eggs did not sound like Grace's cooking.

Kirby grabbed his coat. "Not surprised, that roof was bound to go. Let's have a look." In the garage, Kirby pulled out the ladder. Tulip carried the lighter end.

When Kirby was partway up the ladder, Dennis opened his door and hollered, "Kirby, what are you doing?"

"She's got a leak."

"You get down. I'll go up." Dennis started for Tulip's house.

"Get a coat!" Kirby yelled.

Dennis disappeared into the house and moments later, coat unzipped, raced across the snow. Grabbing Tulip's arm, he whispered, "Why'd you let him go up there?"

"Get your hand off me!"

Dennis dropped her arm. "It's icy, and he's not young!" Then to Kirby he said, "Come on down. I'll check it out."

Kirby waved him away, crawled onto the roof, and cautiously got to his feet. He took a step, slipped, and fell to his knees.

"Get off the roof!" Dennis yelled.

"OK, OK. I've seen enough."

"Be careful." Dennis shoved Tulip out of the way and steadied the ladder.

Kirby put one foot on the rung, then the next. Slowly he made his way down. Panting, he leaned against the house. "It's bad. Shingles are curled, some gone." He shook his head. "You need a new roof."

Tulip felt a pain in her stomach. "Can't I just…tar it or something? Get through the winter?"

Kirby looked at Dennis. "Well, maybe we could secure some shingles, replace the worst ones. It *might* get you through the winter."

"I can do that," Dennis said.

"I don't want *you* on my roof."

Kirby shook his head. "Patching isn't such a big job. Dennis could do it."

"No! I'll get a roofer."

They stood there in an awkward silence, snow soaking their shoes. Kirby must have thought Tulip had lost her senses. She could hear him thinking, *Beggars can't be choosers.* But he must not know about Dennis, and she wasn't going to tell him.

Dennis reeled in the ladder. "Come on, Kirby. I'll carry this home."

They crossed the slush, Kirby's labored steps leaving deep, watery prints. But even under the weight of the ladder, Dennis seemed to glide. Tulip pulled herself up short. She would not be beholden to that pervert. And no way in hell would she let him near her children.

"Thanks, Kirby," Tulip called. His door slammed shut.

That day, winter rains began. When she went upstairs, she found water had dripped from the light socket onto her bed. She turned off the light, moved the bed, and put towels over the sheets to sop up the dampness. Thank God the roof wasn't leaking in the kids' rooms, and the leak in the bathroom was over the tub.

For the next few days, Tulip emptied containers first thing in the morning, when she got home from work, and before bed. Sometimes they overflowed. Finally the rain stopped. She moved the bed back.

When Kirby and Dennis fixed the roof, Tulip was at work. If she had known, she would have lied, told them she had a handyman coming. So she was glad she didn't know.

The same night, a screeching siren woke Tulip. When she looked out, an ambulance was parked in Grace's yard. Tulip fumbled for her jeans, but before she could dress, she saw medics carrying Kirby to the ambulance on a stretcher. Siren blaring, they sped away.

As Tulip reached the door, Grace zoomed past in the Lincoln.

20

Kirby's arteries were full of fat. Too many burgers, too much barbeque. He'd been a heart attack waiting to happen. Climbing on Tulip's roof had not caused it. At least that was what Grace told her. The doctors did emergency surgery, put something in to unplug the artery. But he still couldn't breathe right and his skin was gray from lack of oxygen. Two weeks later they did a quadruple bypass. Grace slept in a chair next to his bed, only left the hospital to shower and change. Her eyes were almost as sunken as his. She wasn't eating and the skin began to hang on her face. She had always talked about dieting, but this was one hell of a way to lose weight.

After Kirby and Grace came home, Tulip tried to help. She dropped off groceries but she wanted to set the bags on the porch, ring the bell, and run. She didn't know what to say. Should she say, "Sorry I almost killed you"? Or, "I told you not to get on my roof, numbskull"? Grace invited her in, but Tulip always gave an excuse: "Supper's on the stove." "Tucker needs help with homework."

Sunday morning the kids were planted in front of the TV, chomping on Rice Krispies: snap, crackle, and pop. One thing Tulip was doing right, not rotting out their teeth with sugar cereal. They would be comatose watching cartoons. She wouldn't be gone that long and she'd be right next door.

Fight or flight. Not this time, Grace.

Outside, the freezing air smelled of pine. Tulip high-stepped across the powdered-sugar snow, which fluffed over the top of her loafers and clung to her socks. The spaghetti sauce in the cottage cheese container warmed her bare hands. It was Valentine's, and Grace still had her red-bowed wreath of real pine hanging outside the window. Grace's holiday clock had stopped.

Before Tulip could knock, Grace flung open the door. She wore a floor-length, bright blue kimono, what the Japanese wore, elegant with her silver hair. Tulip liked that word, elegant. But instead of telling Grace that she looked elegant, Tulip shoved the container at her. "Spaghetti sauce, like you make but no meat, just oil. Didn't have any Tupperware, but at least you can throw out the box when you're done."

Grace swept a finger across the dripping sauce and licked it. "Hmm—good. We'll have it for supper. I've not been cooking much. Kirby can't eat like he used to." She studied Tulip. "Are you all right? You look sick. Are you taking care of yourself? And the children?"

Tulip flushed. "No lipstick. The kids miss you, but that they're doing just fine." What she really wanted to say was, "With Kirby so sick, how can you even think of us?" Grace waved her in. Tulip kept her coat on but left her shoes at the door. The house was warm, too warm.

Grace pointed to a stack of get-well cards on the counter. "Look what came in the mail! And these for Valentine's Day!" She motioned toward a bouquet of white roses filling the air with a honey-sweet scent good enough to eat. She grinned. "Kirby. He phoned and had them delivered."

"That's right," Kirby called. "Don't count me out yet."

Grace led Tulip into the living room, where Kirby was watching TV. On his lap was a piece of wheat toast on one of those pink, see-through, old-fashioned plates. The toast was cut on the diagonal with a bit of red jelly by the side. Pretty.

"It's raining in Florida," he said. "It's got to stop so they can have the Daytona 500. Pete Hamilton won last year. Should have been Richard Petty. But Petty is sure to win this year." Kirby watched all the races. He loved cars and had models all over the living room—on the coffee table, end tables, and on shelves he'd built for them.

Kirby took Tulip's hand in his great white one. His silky black pin-striped pajamas and Grace's kimono looked formal. Tulip felt as though she had crashed a private party. Still, all was not as it should be. Kirby's usually short hair was shaggy and curled above his collar. Tulip thought she might offer to cut it. She cut the boys' hair, trimmed Hunter's. She could see herself flipping black and gray strands of hair on the plate-clean kitchen floor. "For a guy who nearly kicked the bucket, you look pretty good!" Tulip's hand flew to her mouth. She had come to make amends. Instead she'd insulted him.

A slow smile spread across Kirby's broad face. "Tulip." His eyes sparkled. "*You* look really good!"

Tulip was forgiven. She twirled around, a little girl whose daddy had just said she was pretty.

Kirby took a bite of toast, grimaced, and dropped it. "I can't eat this."

"I'll fix it," Grace said.

"Gracie, I want your biscuits and gravy, fried chicken, steak."

Grace sighed, then tried to make light. "Maybe we could go to a health spa. I could learn how to cook delicious, healthy food."

Kirby shoved the tray away. "That's an oxymoron. Cardboard and paper, that's what I'm allowed to eat, maybe with a sheet and pillowcase."

Grace laughed. "What about tablecloths and napkins?"

"Nope! I'm on a restricted diet."

They all laughed. Grace smoothed jelly on the toast and handed it to Kirby. He took a bite, made a face, and flung it. It slid from the plate and bounced onto the floor.

Grace's face tightened. Her voice was strained. "Kirby, you've got to eat something!"

"I am not eating this crap!" His plate clattered onto the side table.

Tulip's breath caught. "I should go." She headed for the kitchen.

Grace caught her at the door. "He's frustrated. We weren't really fighting. He'll apologize in a minute." She hugged Tulip's rigid body. "Thanks for the sauce."

Kirby called from the living room, "Tulip, you get back in here and say goodbye. Didn't mean to scare you off." He took Tulip's hand, and with amazing strength pulled her to him and kissed her right smack-dab on the lips.

Outside, Tulip waved to Grace. Tulip's mind was aflutter. Kirby had thrown his toast and yelled at Grace. Next thing Kirby had kissed Tulip as if nothing had happened. He did not blame her for his heart attack. Still, it had happened the night after he had worked on her roof. It wasn't fair. She had just found them, and Kirby might die! She was relieved for the cold wind biting her hot cheeks, icing her tears.

As she stepped onto the porch, Tucker's howls greeted her. Inside, cereal bowls were still on the counter, the kitchen floor slushy from Tucker's spills. She lived in chaos, from one crisis to the next. Grace had a really sick husband and her house was…immaculate. Tulip thought that was the word. But all was not perfect there. For a moment it had seemed they were going to have a real fight.

Tucker cried, "H-H-Hunter hit me."

Tulip turned off the TV, made her voice soft but firm. "No more fighting. I'll have no more fighting today. Life's too short."

Tucker stopped howling. Tulip stroked his hair. "Now all of you get dressed and pick up your rooms. We're going to clean this house and get ready for the week."

Hunter's eyebrows shot up. Tulip motioned toward the stairs. "Go on, now. After, we'll have a treat."

Tulip had no idea of what the treat would be. As always, money was short, but maybe they could play Monopoly, have popcorn. She did the dishes and tore into the kitchen, even mopped the floor. When done, she poured a cup of coffee, got out the dictionary, and looked up oxymoron.

Careful not to disturb the children, Tulip tiptoed up the stairs and into the boys' room. The bed was made, the floor clear of toys. Tucker sat next to a box piled high with cars and trucks, spinning the wheels of a dump truck. Ernest put the last of his Matchbox cars on the shelf. Blue eyes shining, he grinned at his mom. "Pretty good?"

Hunter ran in holding her old Raggedy Ann doll. "I found her under the bed!"

For the second time that day, Tulip felt her eyes tear. This was a good thing. Why would she be teary?

That evening, Grace called. "He won!"

"What?"

"The Daytona 500. Richard Petty won. Kirby wanted me to call."

21

⌒つ

Kirby reclined in his overstuffed chair watching John Wayne in *The Alamo*, medicine and ice water on a tray next to him. His burly chest had caved in on itself. Jeans bagged around his waist, reminding Grace of Rickey in clothes one size too large, needing to grow into them. Her heart went out to him. She explained that she had decided not to babysit for Tulip's children after school. While he was in the hospital, the children had managed, and she would not have them tiring him.

Kirby reached for Grace's hand. "No, they're good kids. You love them and they need you. They'll bring a little life into the house."

Words from years past rang in Grace's head: "Kids are noisy, keep you up at night. They're expensive. Then they get sick. What happens if they get sick?"

"What happens? You take them to the doctor." Grace knew he was remembering his little brother gasping for air. Kirby had run for the doctor—too late. When Lance died, six-year-old Kirby stood in the doorway. Kirby had been adamant about not having children, not because he didn't want them but because he couldn't risk it. Rickey had been a late-life surprise, a much-loved surprise. Grace feared that the children would remind Kirby of all that he had lost.

The children came back, quiet and timid, staying in the kitchen, eating snacks and doing homework. It was Tucker who inched his way into the living room and sat on the couch next to Kirby, watching Western reruns with him. Soon they were all there, on the couch, on the floor, at the dining room table.

Tucker was stretched out on the floor next to Kirby's chair, building a Lego pyramid. "G-g-got to pee," he announced. Stumbling to his feet, he kicked Kirby's foot, which flew out and hit the structure. Legos scattered across the floor.

"You're sitting too close!" Kirby scolded.

"S-s-sorry." Tucker attempted to gather the Legos.

"Didn't mean to holler," Kirby said. Then to Grace, "Don't they have kits you can make that will stick together? Car kits?"

After the kids went home, Grace explained that Tucker wouldn't be able to build anything by himself. "He can't read the directions, and when Ernest or Hunter try to help, they take over and Tucker gets upset."

Kirby's eyes opened wide; his brows arched.

What now? Grace took care of him, the house, the children, even checked on the store. She did those tasks that he had always done that she had never thought about: trash to the road, clean the litter box, change light bulbs. Now she should be Tucker's teacher too? She wanted to rail at him. Instead she asked, "You think I should help him?"

Her demanding husband chuckled and held out his hand. "Come here. You have a bit much on your plate. Buy a couple of Lego kits. I'll teach him."

After forty-plus years of marriage, they could read each other's moods. Grace sat on the edge of Kirby's chair, touched his soft lips with her own, and inhaled the pungent scent of garlic, one food he could eat. Relieved that she had held her temper, she snuggled against him, only to be interrupted by the ringing phone.

"Do you need anything from the store?" Prudence asked.

That evening Prudence delivered the kits. When Grace offered to pay, Prudence waved her off. "After all you did for me when Dr. Goodwin died, it's the least I can do." Her eyes twinkled. "I'd bring you food, but cooking is not one of my talents."

Grace was touched by Prudence's generosity and especially her honesty. How well Grace remembered the dinner invitation—the smell of burned potatoes, leathery roast beef that required the recommended twenty chews before she could choke it down. The eminent doctor added little to the conversation, his food growing cold on the plate. In spite of his rude behavior, Prudence had presided queen-like, pretending they were enjoying the meal and the company. Her voice high and strained, she talked about singing in church and asked about Grace's flowers. Before dessert the phone rang and Dr. Goodwin excused himself for an "emergency" at the hospital. Prudence followed her husband to the entryway. The door slammed as he left.

Kirby sorted through Lego kits and ranked them in order of complexity. Shortly after lunch, he began asking Grace the time. Finally she set a clock on his side table. When the kids tumbled in, Kirby called them to the living room.

Legos did not impress Hunter; Ernest commented that he liked to build model planes. Kirby nodded. Grace noted that Prudence would need to make another trip to the hobby store.

Kirby tousled Tucker's hair. "Guess it's you and me."

Grinning, Tucker ripped open the package. Heads bent in concentration, the two went to work, Kirby pointing out where each piece belonged and explaining why. Tucker began to anticipate the next step. Holding up a curved Lego, he exclaimed, "N-n-now this one! It's the h-h-hood!"

Shortly before Tulip was due, they finished the car. Kirby closed the box and patted Tucker's back. "Well done, fellow!"

Glowing with satisfaction, Tucker brought the boxy car out for Grace to admire.

Kirby stretched his legs and dozed. He was awakened by Tucker's hollering, "S-s-see, Mommy! S-see what I did!"

Tulip beamed. "Wow, Tucker. You made that car?"

"W-well, me and M-Mr. Kirby."

Prudence called Grace that evening. "What do you need?" she asked. Grace asked if she would pick up something more for the kids, and said that of course Grace would pay. "You're thinking I won't want to because of Tulip, right? Well, you're wrong. This is something I can do for you."

The following day, Ernest sat at the kitchen table gluing a model together while Tucker and Kirby whooped and hollered in the living room. Tucker raced his slow-moving car against Kirby's 1960 model Corvette. After a few races, in which Kirby had held his car's speed to the minimum, Tucker played with Kirby's models, zooming them on the kitchen linoleum making his *zzzmmm*, *zzzmmm* sound. Miraculously Kirby did not seem worried about the fate of his precious cars.

It was bittersweet. When Grace had invited the children back, she worried that Kirby would be standoffish, afraid to get too close, or that he would not tolerate the disruption of his schedule, the commotion, and the demands on her time. But she had underestimated her husband. He could not do enough for those urchins. If Grace were the jealous type, she would be feeling left out.

By the third week, Grace was stir-crazy. The weather had warmed, snow was melting, and daffodils were pushing out of the crusted earth. She needed to get out, take a long walk, and clear her head. She gazed longingly out the window at a car sloshing up the street and imagined it on the way to Kroger. She would enjoy pushing a cart down those wide aisles. Never before had she wanted to go grocery shopping. She sighed and turned away. "I sure could use a fresh head of lettuce for salad, and some peppers too. Guess I'll have to ask Prudence."

Hunter looked up from her homework. "Go get 'em. Mom will be here in half an hour and we can all stay till you get back."

22

Old Ruby coughed, sputtered, and finally started. Spring had taunted and then gone underground. It was freezing cold, but Tulip wasn't saying that word, at least not out loud. She and the children were headed to the new Borders Bookstore in downtown Ann Arbor, where they'd been begging to go since Grace had given them gift certificates for Christmas.

Tulip had never been to downtown Ann Arbor and had not looked forward to driving there. The streets were one-way this way and one-way that way. They didn't know which way they were supposed to go. When she married Marshall, they'd lived in Ypsilanti, and the biggest trip she took was to Farmer Jack's for groceries. But the kids were excited and she *would* make this an adventure for them.

No place to park and the parking structure was a forbidding fortress with a yellow-and-white beam across the entry. Punch a button, take a ticket, and the arm went up. You had to know the password. The place was full, cars leaving, cars coming. Tulip cranked the wheel and spun in circles up the ramp. Tucker squealed with excitement. Hunter told him to shut up. Slowing for some old fogey to pull out, Tulip shifted from second to first. They wound their way to the roof—level six, icy. The kids asked to ride the elevator down. Snow blanketing their bare heads, they waited so long that Tulip thought maybe the elevator was broken.

Borders, a lit-up department store for books, was just across the street. A man in a camouflage hunting jacket—a man Marshall's size—rounded the corner in front of the store. Tulip gripped Tucker's hand. Marshall hadn't bothered them for months and he wouldn't be prowling around a bookstore. Still, Tulip couldn't get her feet to move right.

"Come on, Mom." Hunter ran past her and into the store.

The lights were blinding. Tables and shelves overflowed with books. Tucker stopped dead in his tracks. "W-w-wow!"

Hunter rushed past tables and row after row of books. She led the family to a corner filled with children's books. "My class came here on a field trip. You don't remember, do you, Mom?" She made a beeline for *The Boxcar Children*. No, Tulip didn't remember. Had Hunter told her? Had it been one of those times when she was too busy to listen?

The space was downright pretty—bright yellow, red, and blue, with pint-sized tables and chairs. Lots of books. Tulip herded Tucker to the picture books. Ernest wandered past shelves, leafing through books and carefully putting them back. Tulip scrunched into a chair. A woman sat on the floor with a scrubbed-clean toddler, stroking her daughter's perfectly brushed blonde hair. Hunter, Tulip's matted-red-haired Orphan Annie, sorted through the *Boxcar* books. She and Ernest whispered, comparing prices. Tulip felt in her pocket and touched Tucker's gift certificate.

Tulip longed to buy a mystery or maybe a classic to learn something. Grace would have known what she should buy. It would be a luxury to have lots of time, to wander past all these books, touch them, read a beginning or an ending, like having your own library. But this was for the kids, their first trip to a bookstore—well, Ernest and Tucker's, anyway. It was comforting, sitting in a warm place and watching her children do something a regular family would do. And how could she pick just one book? As long as she kept the certificate, she could always come back. Like saving your Halloween candy until you were really hungry.

The camouflage guy—Marshall?— darted behind a bookcase. Spying! Tulip leapt out of the chair. "Come on, kids. We gotta go!" She was afraid that rounding them up would be like starting Old Ruby in the cold. But they heard her voice, saw her eyes, and they came.

Loaded down with coats, her head on a swivel on the lookout for Marshall, she rushed them toward checkout. She didn't have a chance if he followed them to that tomb of a parking structure.

Hunter tugged at her arm. "Mom, I got *The Boxcar Children*—four books, and they come in a *box*." Tulip nodded dumbly. She tried to concentrate on the titles of the books. Ernest had *Little Lord Fauntleroy* tucked under his arm, Tucker *Horton Hatches the Egg* and a couple of other Dr. Seuss books. "Do you have your certificates?" she asked.

Hunter did her you-stupid-mom shake of the head. Ernest held his certificate up. Instead of asking for his, Tucker pumped her hand up and down. Tulip fished in one pocket, then the other.

Tucker tugged on her sleeve. "G-g-give it to me!"

She felt in both pockets. "It—it's gone."

"You had it! I saw it," Hunter said.

Tucker wailed. "S-s-somebody stole it!"

"No, no, I must have dropped it."

"I w-w-want my ticket!" Tucker's chest heaved. A howl was surfacing. He opened his mouth. Tulip clapped her hand over it.

He tapped Tulip on the shoulder. A hand reached out of a musty hunting jacket and thrust a crumbled paper toward Tucker. "Is this what you dropped?" His voice was deep and musical.

Tucker took the certificate. "T-t-thanks, m-mister."

The man grinned at Tucker, his brown eyes warm. "You're welcome." Then to Tulip, "Nice kids. Love books, huh?"

Tulip managed a nod. She had been scared to come to Ann Arbor and park in the structure. In the bookstore, she thought everyone was judging her and her raggedy kids. And she had almost lost it when she thought the guy was Marshall. Turned out he was a Good Samaritan. D would get a kick out of this.

The elevator spilled them out on the dark, deserted roof. Giggling, Hunter slid across the icy concrete, Ernest skating behind. Tucker grabbed Tulip's hand and they were in pursuit. Surprise, Old Ruby started right up, and Tulip didn't meet any cars circling the maze. By the time she got to the booth, she was feeling pretty good. She paid. The gate arm went up. No traffic. Old Ruby chucked onto Thompson Street.

A siren! Flashing lights! Tulip pumped the brake and pulled over. Not wanting the cop see the kids all crammed in the pickup, she hopped out.

A kid in a police uniform swaggered over. "Lady, get back in your vehicle. Did you know you were going the wrong way on a one-way street?"

"Do you think if I'd known I'd-a done it?" Tulip got back in the pickup.

"Driver's license, registration, and proof of insurance, please."

Thank God she'd been able to pay the insurance. She fumbled in her pocket for her billfold. "Ernest, get the envelope out of the glove box."

The guy stuck his smirky face in the window. "Lady, you got a full load— one too many."

"Did ya want me to leave one home?"

"It's against the law to have four in a seat. I could give you a ticket for that, too."

The jackass was threatening her. He took her license and insurance paper back to the patrol car. Tulip glued her hands to the wheel. How the hell was she going to pay a fine? Bribe him with a Borders gift certificate? Fat chance of that.

"Is he g-g-g-going to put us in jail?" Tucker asked.

"The bastard's just going to give me a ticket."

"A t-t-ticket?" Tucker might have thought it was a ticket to a movie or the zoo. That was how innocent he was, how he could turn bad into good.

The guy thumped on the window. Tulip rolled it down.

"Tulip. Unusual name. You work at Joe's?"

She nodded.

He licked his lips. "Know a friend of mine, Ken Gordon?"

She nodded again.

"Thought so." He was playing a game and it was his turn to nod. As if he were tasting something real sweet, honey or ice cream, he licked his lips again.

Tulip clutched the wheel tighter, felt the blood drain from her fingers.

The jackass nodded, looked from her to the kids and back at her. He chuckled. "You'd better watch for one-ways. They're tricky." He pulled his cap back on his head, put his arm on the window seal. "Ken and I work different shifts. Maybe I'll see you at Joe's." He winked, sauntered back to the patrol car, and turned off the spotlight.

Tulip gunned Old Ruby and made a right onto East Williams off the one-way.

Tulip sat in a booth with Ken, his policeman's cap on the table. She had finished her shift and had a right to sit, be a customer, and eat apple pie. The closest she ever got to a date, pie and coffee. She was mad, real mad. That smart-aleck cop had leered at her as if she were naked, ripe for the picking.

"What are you saying about me to those jackasses down at the station?"

"What?"

"The cop, the cop who stopped me on the wrong way! You told him!"

Ken shrugged.

"He's been in here nosing around. Sleazy. He thinks I owe him 'cause he didn't slap a ticket on me."

Ken grinned, patted her leg. "No harm in trying."

It was his grin that did it. He thought a cop making a pass at her was funny. "You son of a bitch!" She shoved him. He tightened his hold on her leg. "Let go of me!"

"Hang on, Tulip. It just sort of came up."

"Well, maybe it will just sort of come up in a phone call to your wife."

"You wouldn't!"

"Wouldn't I?" She kicked him in the shin, grabbed her purse, and walked out.

She had wanted a fling, no strings attached. But she had gotten more than she'd bargained for. She had looked forward to seeing him, counted on it. For the first time in her life, she liked sex. After, her head on his shoulder her talker would start, not about anything important, just day-to-day stuff. Not that the giant scarecrow said much himself, but he lay there stroking her hair and she pretended he cared. But he had a wife he went home to at night. And then to tell his buddies about her?

Men were scum—Marshall, Ken. And that cocky Dennis had squirmed his way in by being helpful—a pervert on parole! He'd tried to talk to her, called, and knocked on the door; when she wouldn't answer, he tried to stop her on the sidewalk.

She was done with men. End of story.

23

Walking from bed to bathroom left Kirby panting. This man who loved food now found eating a chore to be endured. It exhausted him to read. He dozed while watching TV. Making love was out of the question. When the doctors said that there was nothing more to do, Grace insisted that they go to the Cleveland Clinic for a consultation. There Kirby was told to rest as needed and not to stress himself. Grace pleaded with him to go to the Mayo Clinic but he refused. Her strong husband, who had promised to always care for her, had given up. She wanted to scream at him, *Try, Kirby. Try!*

Slamming the door as she left the bedroom, Grace saw the day's dirty dishes piled on the kitchen counter and she seized them to vent her anger. Scrubbing off bits of tasteless, hardened scrambled egg white, she pictured the plaque plugging Kirby's arteries and pressed harder as though her scouring could dislodge it. The plate snapped, a clean surgical cut. She shrieked, a shriek that had been building since Kirby's heart attack, one she'd tamped down again and again. She had broken one of her favorite dishes, white with a rim of yellow daisies, passed down from her grandmother—irreplaceable.

"Grace! Grace!" Kirby called from the bedroom.

Holding the two halves, which would never again make a whole, tears streaming down her face, Grace stood before Kirby's bed. He held out his trembling, hospital-white hands, hands that had renovated their bathroom and kitchen. Grace sank onto the bed. "I pressed too hard."

"You can buy another."

"They don't make them anymore."

The tiniest glint shown in Kirby's sunken eyes. "Look on the good side. You have six plates left, an even number." He took the pieces, laid them on the bed, and eased her toward him.

Supporting her weight with her elbows, Grace leaned into him. "Oh Kirby, what am I going to do without you?"

He brushed the tears from her face. "How about hitting all the yard sales and finding another plate?"

"Kirby!" How could he be so cavalier?

"I'm the one who's dying. You have to be nice to me."

If she could stay angry, distance herself from him, it wouldn't hurt so much. But Grace could not resist his banter. She reared back in mock horror. "I haven't been nice? Fetching and carrying, fixing you delicious meals that you don't even eat?"

"Nothing tastes as good as those bacon-and-tomato sandwiches with the pickle and chips that you made when we met."

Grace laughed. "Silly! You were smitten."

"You made them just for me."

"And every other guy who ate at Woolworth's counter."

"But I knew you liked me best when you forgot the bacon."

"I did not!"

Grace picked up the two pieces of porcelain and fit them together, the crack almost down the center. "You promised you'd always take care of me, always be there for me. I know I shouldn't be, but...but I'm so mad at you!"

He ran his finger along the edge of the plate that Grace so desperately wanted to make whole. Exaggerating seriousness he said, "I lied."

She cupped her hand over her lips to suppress a giggle. But this was real. "I mean it, Kirby. How am I going to get along without you?"

"Sell the store. You'll have enough money to travel. You've always wanted to. You could take classes, go to college, get that nursing degree."

"I'm sixty!"

"Rickey should have lived. I wouldn't be leaving you so alone." He sighed, stroked her face. "I'm sorry, Grace. I just can't go on like this, hardly alive, burdening you."

"Remember, I wanted to be a nurse."

"Grace. I need to be in control."

"You are *not* talking about suicide."

Again he reached for her hand. "I'm talking about a little nudge."

Grace reared up. "You can't leave me! Not like that!"

"Everybody dies, some sooner than others. You're strong. You can do it."

Grace kissed Kirby's eyes, nose, and lips. Pressing her body close to his, she felt his labored breathing ease into sleep. She pulled the spread around him and went in search of superglue.

Grace had been eighteen, working the lunch counter at Woolworth's and saving money for nursing school, when Kirby O'Shay sauntered in. His dark hair was slicked behind his ears, a wayward strand drooping over twinkling dark eyes. Even under his flannel shirt, she could see the ripple of his muscles. As though he were in a hurry, his words were rushed. "I'll have a bacon-and-tomato sandwich and a chocolate—" His gaze met hers. "A—what's your name?"

"Grace."

"Yeah, you sure are."

Goose bumps rose on her arms.

That was it. Every day the same time, same order. Hanging over the counter, gliding salt and pepper shakers back and forth, Grace fell in love.

When Grace came to bed, Kirby woke and beckoned her. He kissed her cheek. "I love you, Gracie."

Two nights later Kirby did it. He must have taken the pills while Grace was in the bathroom brushing her teeth. They had watched Johnny Carson on the bedroom TV. She rubbed his feet. They drifted to sleep holding hands. When she woke before light, Grace felt his hand, cold and waxy. She listened for his breathing. There was none.

He had been emphatic that he was not going to linger, to be a vegetable. He was going to be in charge. She had argued, shouted even. When he was steadfast in his decision, she told him she would not help. She would not murder her husband! Still, she refused to believe he would do it. And not to say goodbye, to deprive her of that! But if he had told her when he planned to do it, she would have tried to prevent it. They would have fought. That would have been her last memory of him. Instead he had said goodbye with a kiss and a declaration of love.

She covered him, put on her robe, and stumbled to the kitchen. The coffee sat on the counter. Wasn't that what she did each morning? The sun came up and she made coffee? She filled the pot with water, pried open the Folgers can, and dumped in the coffee. She stood by the stove and watched as the water began to bubble, then perk. It would be days before Grace would realize that she no longer needed a full pot. She poured the steaming liquid into a cup, wrapped her hands around it, and held it to her chest. Kirby would never share this with her again—never. "Get used to it," she said. Through the window she watched the sun peek over the horizon, its rays unable to brighten the dismal day.

The coffee had cooled. Grace's bare feet shivered on the icy linoleum. She went to the thermostat to turn it up, but her mind could not connect to her hand and she stood immobile, staring at it. *Brr-ring, brr-ring, brr-ring.* Placing her hand on the wall, she felt her way to the phone.

"Hello? Oh, Prudence...we're fine...no, he's still sleeping...no, please don't bring cinnamon rolls. He shouldn't eat them." Grace clicked the receiver in place. She wasn't ready to tell anyone, especially not Prudence. She needed to be alone with him, to say goodbye.

In the bedroom Kirby's silk bathrobe was furled on the floor next to his side of the bed. Why did he always throw clothes on the floor? Grace lifted the sheet from his face. He looked peaceful, as though asleep. Was she mistaken? *Wishful thinking.* Slowly she folded the covers into a neat rectangular pile. He wanted to be cremated. Would they incinerate him in his clothes or strip him, send him out as he had come? Tears streaked her cheeks. How could she live without him?

In the old days, the living performed their last act of caring by cleansing the dead. Grace unbuttoned Kirby's shirt. Pulling, pushing, and lifting, she removed pajamas from his unyielding body. Then, as though he would wear them again, she folded the pajamas and put them in his drawer. In the bathroom she warmed a washrag. She wiped his face and then gently kissed his eyes and cool lips. She worked her way down an arm to his workman's hands. His nails, which in life had always trapped a bit of dirt, were pristine. Touching her nose to his underarm, she caught the slightest whiff of woodsy Old Spice. After cleansing his chest, Grace went back to the bathroom and warmed the cloth again.

As she held his small, rubbery penis in her hand, she thought of all the pleasure they had had exploring each other, of how amazed she had been that this sleeping part of him could, with little enticement, grow firm. When he was inside her, she had felt as though he were a part of her. When her heart was smashed by Rickey's senseless death, Kirby had patiently picked up the jagged pieces and fitted her together like a puzzle. Now she was split apart, shattered, with no one to pick up the pieces.

Grace washed each leg, taking special care with his feet, easing bits of lint from between wide toes. Last she combed his hair, slicked the long strands back as he used to wear it. She pulled the spread up over his arms and kissed him on the forehead.

Then she made the call.

24

Grace had been living a storybook life. Then slam-bang, Kirby had had a heart attack and died, right in bed with her. Tulip told the kids not to bother her. "The last thing she needs is three snot-nosed kids over there asking questions and making noise," The words were hardly out of her mouth when she spied Tucker, big as a fuel tank, sneaking next door. Tulip hollered, but he kept going. She ran out and got in his face. "Tucker, you know you ain't supposed to go to Grace's."

"Sh-sh-she's all alone. Sh-she's sad. I could f-f-feed Tabby." His puppy eyes spurted tears.

Tulip's heart squeezed up but she couldn't let Tucker pester Grace, not right now. "It's only been a few days. Grace needs to be alone. She's in mourning."

"B-but it's afternoon."

Tulip wrapped her arms around him. "That's not what I meant. Mourning is when you're sad because someone died and you miss them."

"M-me too."

Later Tucker came up missing. When Tulip went to Grace's to retrieve him, he and Grace were sitting on her porch, her arm around Tucker, her head on his.

"Tucker bothering you?"

"Does it look like it?" Grace lifted her head. Her eyes were black-circled potholes, her skin flour-white. Silvery hair swirled every which way as if she'd been in a windstorm.

Tucker was braver than Tulip. She wanted to run, get away from all that pain, but following his example, holding the railing to steady herself, she asked, "Is there anything I can do?"

Grace's veined hand stroked Tucker's unruly hair. "The nights are the worst. I'm so tired, but I can't bear to go to bed. Kirby's side is cold and I'm tempted to put the heating pad and pillow there to hang on to."

"Why don't you?"

Grace smiled the thinnest smile. "When I took care of him, I functioned on adrenalin. I always wanted to be a nurse...my patient died...the house is dark."

"Open the curtains."

"I have this empty feeling in my stomach but I can't eat. When I hear a noise, a car horn, a dog bark, I jump. I've been with Kirby most of my life. I don't know how to be alone."

Wanting to comfort her, Tulip sat next to Grace. They sat for a long time. Traffic rumbled on the next street. The sun came out from behind a cloud. Finally Tulip was able put her jumbled thoughts into words. "Marshall and me weren't anything like you and Kirby. Most of the time it was rough, real rough. But when I finally got away, when I realized I had to do it alone, I was scared. He was mean, but he paid the bills, kept food on the table. And I was used to him." Tulip touched Grace's knee. "I thought women were supposed to be married, not get divorced. I was so ashamed that I'd gotten myself in such a mess."

"It's hard raising children by yourself."

"Better than being dead." Uh-oh. Kirby was gone. Grace had lost her son. She had no one, and Tulip was rattling on about her problems.

"I feel like there's nothing to live for. Yesterday about five o'clock, I caught myself waiting for Kirby to come home." Grace looked out in the street as if he might come pulling in.

"Yeah, everybody needs someone. How about a dog?"

Grace tossed back her head and chortled. "A dog?"

Tulip was downright ashamed of herself for hiding from Grace. Tucker knew better how to comfort her than she did. Then Tulip had offered dumb suggestions like open the curtains or get a dog. She wanted Grace to get up and start moving. But for what? She was a caretaker with no one to care for. But she *had* come to life when Tulip mentioned a dog. Maybe it wasn't such a bad idea. A puppy, that was it. A puppy would take Grace's mind off herself.

The following Saturday, Tulip loaded up the kids and tooled off to the Humane Society. She told them they could help pick out a puppy, a surprise for Grace. The Burns were not getting a pet. End of discussion.

The kennels smelled of Clorox and animal piss. Mutts of every size and shape sniffed and stared, whined and barked—discards looking for a home. A bone-thin racer jumped up on the gate. A foxlike dog studied them. Cats mewed from their end of the building.

"Th-th-that one!" Tucker yelled, pointing to a jumbo-size dog drooling at them.

"Nah, he'll eat too much," Tulip replied.

"Soft," Tucker said, touching the furry coat through the bars.

"This one!" Hunter stuck her hand through a cage and petted a puppy with big floppy ears and a yellow patch around his eye. The half-grown pup licked her hand. Huge brown eyes begged them to take him home. "Could *we* have this one, Mom?"

"You can have visiting rights to Grace's. We can't afford a dog!"

"Wait!" Ernest called. "Over there with the big dogs—the little one, sleeping."

Several overgrown dogs were crowded in a kennel. In the corner was a lump of matted hair, a ball of yarn. "How'd he get in there?" Tulip asked.

"They forgot him," Ernest answered.

Tucker jammed his nose against the wire mesh. "Where?"

Hunter stuffed her hands in her pockets. "He's not nearly as cute as Yellow Patch."

"You can't see him. You don't know." Ernest beckoned to the little one. "Here, puppy, puppy. Wake up, puppy."

The runt opened its crusty eyes.

"He's ugly," Hunter said.

The pup stumbled up, only to be knocked down by Tucker's jumbo dog.

Hunter shook her head. "There's pee on the floor. He's been laying in pee, and he looks half dead."

Ernest glared daggers at her. "That's just it. No one wants him. He'll die if we don't take him. Those big dogs'll kill him!"

Hunter nodded. It was unusual for Ernest to go up against Hunter, but she knew Ernest was right. The runt needed out of that kennel. Still, Hunter wasn't giving up. "Patches wouldn't eat much. Maybe *we* could take him home."

"Someone will want Patches. He'll live."

Hunter stomped her foot. "But I want Patches!"

"Hunter!"

"I want him!"

"You know what I said. Come on!"

Hunter wound her fingers through the fence wire.

Tulip gritted her teeth. "Now!"

"No!"

Tulip's hand flew up. A door slammed. Her heart pounding, Tulip lowered her arm. If the volunteer hadn't come just then, she might have smacked Hunter, not because she was being bad but because Tulip couldn't give her child a dog.

It took some time to sort out the paperwork. Although the dog was for Grace, it was less complicated to put it in Tulip's name. She put her arm around Hunter and said they could be like parents and Grace could be the foster mom. Hunter gave her the evil eye.

Ernest took the peppery ball of stinking yarn and held him to his chest.

"Don't hold him so close. He's muddy," Tulip said. Ernest didn't have many clothes and what he did have needed washing—another job to do when she got home.

The pup nudged its head into Ernest's shirt. "He's scared, Mom. Feel his heart thumping."

Tulip concentrated on the paperwork. "Where's Tucker?" she asked absently.

"Looking," Hunter said, pointing toward a sign that read cats.

"You let him go in the cat room? You know he'll want a kitten!"

Hunter had Marshall's smug look.

They found Tucker cradling a half-grown yellow kitten, the kitty's eyes closed, its little white paws padding back and forth on Tucker's arm. "She's mine! Th-th-the nice lady said I could have her."

A plain-faced young woman in spanking-clean plaid shirt and jeans was feeding the cats. How did she manage to be untouched by all that piss and shit? The woman pushed her baseball cap back on her head. "I said the kitten was available for adoption."

"I 'dopted it." Carefully Tucker handed Tulip the ball of yarn. "Sh-sh-she's got a white spot on her head."

The kitten blinked its crystal eyes and purred—a sun-bleached kitten decked out in white Sunday boots.

Plain Face smiled. "Great choice. She's affectionate, not too young."

"We came for a dog." Tulip pointed to Ernest, holding the poor excuse of a puppy.

"The boy said he wanted a kitten."

Tucker's head bobbed up and down. "Grace has a cat. Sh-she t-t-taught me how to pet it. I feed it sometimes. I know about cats!"

"We're not getting another pet." Tulip made it sound like they had a zoo at home.

Plain Face shifted on her feet. "I'm afraid I misunderstood."

"I'll keep her in my room. Sh-sh-she can sleep with me."

"We don't have money for shots right now." Tulip did not say that they would never have money for shots, not while she was a waitress and her shit-ass ex didn't pay child support.

Plain Face lit up. "No problem. This kitten's had her shots."

"We didn't come for a cat!"

"That happens a lot. People come for a cat and end up with a dog, or vice versa. Sometimes you just fall in love."

Tulip spoke through gritted teeth. "We can't afford a pet."

"Cats aren't nearly as expensive as dogs. I'm a cat woman myself, have three of them. They're independent, make great pets. Besides, like I said, this kitten has had her shots."

The kitty opened her eyes and stretched, her tail whipping Tulip's face.

Hunter's testy look was gone. She shrugged. "It's only a cat, Mom. It's not going to send us to the poorhouse."

No, it wouldn't send them to the poorhouse. They were already there. Tulip shook her head. Tucker's eyes pleaded. Tulip nodded once, only once, not meaning it as yes but as recognition of how much the kitty meant to Tucker. But her son took it as yes and grabbed her in a bear hug.

Well, maybe she did mean yes.

25

⁓

When the doorbell rang, Grace was asleep on the couch, a rerun of *I Love Lucy* blaring on the TV, its noise filling the empty house. Dazed, she took her cup, which had been perched precariously between the cushions, set it on the floor, and stood. Coffee trickled onto newspaper. Messy. Kirby did not like newspapers or anything else scattered on the floor. "You'll trip and hurt yourself," he'd say.

Hunter burst through the door screaming, "We got you something!" Tucker crowded ahead, but his sister shoved him aside, bowed, and made a sweeping gesture with her hand. "Ta-dum!"

Ernest stepped forward holding a wadded-up sweater in his arms. The scent of wet wool and strong urine wafted through the room. Grinning, he thrust the wad at Grace. She recoiled.

"It's for you, so you won't be so sad," Ernest said. "We named it Pepper."

The stinking wet wool whimpered. "A puppy?" Grace asked.

"Yeah, and I got a k-k-kitty," Tucker said, holding up a ball of yellow yarn. Grace felt for the chair. "A dog? A cat?"

"You said you didn't have anyone to take care of," Tulip declared.

Tucker pressed the ball of yellow fluff toward Grace. Hunter yanked him back. "Not now, stupid!"

"Hunter!" Tulip's voice pelted Grace's ears. "Don't call your brother stupid!"

The room spun. Tucker swayed back and forth. *Twins?* Again Ernest offered the sodden mass. When Grace refused, he set it on the newspaper—a tiny, mangy puppy. Standing on trembling legs, it emitted a golden stream of urine. *So there, Kirby, newspapers on the floor* are *good for something.* Grace stared at the beaming little group, looking as though they were posed for a family portrait.

"He's for you," Tulip said. "Something to take care of."

"Something to take care of?"

"Yeah!"

"No. I can hardly take care of myself."

"You need something to love. We'll get you set up. You got a box for him? I think it's a he."

"I know where there's a box and some old towels," Hunter said.

Grace could not accept this…gift, but she had no will to protest further. She must stop taking valium. Ernest and Hunter scurried around, making a bed for the pathetic thing. Tucker stood uncertainly, holding his yellow fur ball. All were strangely quiet. They left quickly.

Grace sank onto the couch. The pitiful thing huddled in the box. Its tangled, wiry fur was salt-and-pepper gray—aging before its time. It whimpered. Bones creaking, Grace rose and warmed some milk. Its ears dragged in the dish as it lapped listlessly. It was just like Tulip to gift her with a malnourished puppy. It would probably die. Everybody she loved died. Her parents, but that was only natural. But it was not right to lose a child. It should have been her. And then, after what seemed forever, when she could finally lock the pain away for a few minutes, an hour, even a day, when she could enjoy her flowers, dig in the garden, then her husband…

The puppy whimpered, the weakest whimper. Film-covered eyes peered up at Grace. Just like her, nobody wanted him. She forced herself off the coach and made her way upstairs to the bedroom, where she found old slacks and a shirt crumpled in the closet. Downstairs she filled the sink with warm water. When she dunked the pup in the sink, wiry fur clung to his bony body. She washed him and wrapped him in a towel. Although he had barely moved, she was exhausted. Holding him to her chest, she lay on the couch and drifted into a deep sleep. She was awakened by a sandpaper tongue scraping her face. She batted the mutt away. He thudded onto the carpet, stuffed-animal still. She grabbed him a might roughly. He opened his eyes. She stood him on his wobbly legs; he collapsed. Surely that little trip to the floor had not done him in. The little guy was sick. He had to see a vet. She was reluctant to leave her four walls and was incapable of going alone. Nestling the little fellow in her arms, she settled into Kirby's chair. He licked her hand and then was still.

After a while Grace called the vet, then Tulip. "I'm taking this—this mongrel to the vet," Grace said.

"Pepper. We named him Pepper."

"Something's wrong with him. Would Ernest go to the vet with me?"

Hunter and Ernest had walked to the store for bread, but Tucker was excited at the prospect of a trip to the vet. "B-but I can't leave y-yellow Fluff." That's what he'd named her, Fluff.

Tucker held the writhing, mewling kitten and Grace drove as quickly and carefully as possible. The kitten's mewling escalated to screeches. "You must be hurting him," she said.

Tucker loosened his hold. Fluff leapt into the backseat. Kicking Grace in the shoulder, Tucker wriggled over the seat. "You sh-sh-shouldn't have told me…" Bumping his head on the door, he squirmed onto the floor. The desperate kitten crawled under the seat to the front and latched onto Grace's foot.

"Damn!" Grace flipped him off and handed him to Tucker. All the while, the mutt just lay there.

At the vet's, Grace instructed Tucker to wait in the car. As she opened the door, a blur of yellow flashed by. Tucker tumbled out hollering, "F-f-fluff, F-fluff, come back!"

After the kitten was captured, Grace went in and bought a pet carrier. Ignoring Tucker's protests, she shoved Fluff into it. What was she thinking allowing Tucker to bring that cat? She sat on a vinyl chair holding the mutt, with Tucker clutching the cage beside her. The kitten mewed. A golden retriever and black Lab, both on leashes, lay obediently by their masters' chairs.

Grace touched Tucker's scratched hand. "Does it hurt?"

He shook his head. "F-fluff. W-we hurt her."

She put her arm around the boy. "No, it's just all new to her. She's scared. She misses her mother."

"Like I m-m-miss Mom when sh-sh-she's at work? Like you m-m-miss M-Mister Kirby?"

"Mrs. O'Shay, we're ready for you now." In the examining room, the seasoned vet gently turned the puppy over. "She's a girl." The vet shook her head. "She's weak, full of worms. I'll give her shots and deworm her. You feed her all she will eat. But I want to warn you, she may not make it." The vet drew out a needle and vaccinated the pup, who merely twitched. Grace took the little bundle from her and held it against her chest, listening to the faint heartbeat.

"Cute kitten. Might as well have a look at her too." The vet lifted the kitten from its cage. She examined the cat and declared her healthy, just small. "Didn't get enough nourishment when she was born."

Grace bought deworming pills for both animals, a big bag of kitten food, a smaller one of puppy chow, and four cans of high-nutrition dog food. Being told the pup might die reminded her of Kirby's kind doctor bearing bad news. Grace could not save her husband. But with medicine and the right food, she might save this puppy.

26

With the kitten in a carrier, the cat food, and litter, Tucker headed up the stairs. Tulip hollered after him, "You're not going to let that kitten shit in your bedroom!"

"M-M-Miss G-Grace says! Sh-she needs a s-small space." He disappeared into his room and slammed the door.

Damn, damn Grace! Damn me for letting Tucker bring that fur ball home. Did cats cause diseases? Tulip shouldn't go flying off the handle at Grace. She tried to calm herself by whispering Dr. Seuss's words—left foot, right foot, this foot, that foot—over and over as she hurried to Grace's house. In the kitchen, the refrigerator and freezer doors were wide open, and Grace was hurling jars and packages into a giant wastebasket.

"You still don't ring the doorbell?"

"What are you doing?"

"Cleaning."

"Nobody sees the fridge."

"I do! And every time I open the door it reminds me." Grace waved a package of meatless burgers that she'd purchased at the Seventh Day Adventist bazaar and hurled them into the basket. "He hated those! Why did I feed him this crap? Cardboard, he called it. I thought if I did everything the doctor said, I could keep him alive."

Tears rolled down Grace's cheeks. She clung to Tulip—too tight, the way Tucker squeezed. Tulip went board stiff, then pulled away. She should have said something comforting like "You took good care of him" or "You didn't know." Instead she said, "Why'd you tell Tucker to keep the cat and litter in his bedroom?"

"Go to hell, Tulip!"

Tulip gasped. Grace talking to her like that! She wheeled to leave, then turned back. "OK, I get it. The mutt...I'm sorry. Maybe it wasn't such a great idea."

Pepper brought Grace back to life, but not entirely in a good way. She turned on Grace's energy button, and Grace got off the couch and just kept going. She washed the stacked-up dishes, dusted, and vacuumed. In one week she washed walls, woodwork, windows. She tossed out newspapers stacked by her door. "That was a mistake," she said. "I should have kept them for Pepper to pee on." Twice in the first month, Tulip saw the Ann Arbor Carpet Cleaning van in front of Grace's house.

Grace took better care of that mongrel than Tulip did of her children. Pepper's ribs filled out and her ears perked up. As soon as she had strength to waddle, before any sane person was awake, that mutt was on a leash, zigzagging down the sidewalk, Grace reeling her in like a fish. The woman was in overdrive. One night, when Tulip got up to pee, she saw Grace in her living room—vacuuming!

Tulip dialed the phone. "What do you think you're doing? You should be sleeping."

"Isn't it obvious?"

"What?"

"I can't sleep."

"You're working like a crazy woman and you're not eating, all skin and bones. And you shouldn't be walking that mongrel in the dark!"

"Don't tell me what to do. And don't call Pepper a mongrel!"

"'Don't cuss, be polite!' That's what you tell me. And now I'm not supposed to tell the truth! She *is* a mongrel!"

"You got the damn mutt for me!"

Tulip felt the hair rise on the back of my neck. "You're the one who's cussing now!"

"Tulip, I am not having this conversation!" Grace slammed down the phone.

27

Grace glared at her empty bed. "It's all your fault! That snit Tulip is giving *me* advice! She has no idea. Four decades, most of my life sitting across the table from you, sharing your bed. I washed your clothes, bleached your underwear. I knew what foods made you pass gas *and* I didn't mind hearing when you did.

"Why didn't I go to nurse's school after we were married? I've got nothing. I crawl into cold sheets at night, lie on my back, and stare at the dark, empty ceiling. In the morning I stagger out of bed, perk a pot of coffee, and drink your half as well as mine. My stomach's a mess. When we first married, I didn't even like coffee! When I crack an egg, I feel like I'm depriving you. I catch myself eating dry toast dabbed with jelly...and the house is getting like Tulip's! The kitchen faucet leaks and the furnace fan makes funny noises...Call a repairman?"

"I'm turning into a crazy old woman talking to a dead man. Enough!"

After Rickey died, Kirby had implored Grace to brace up, get on with life. You're not dead, he'd said. He was right. Even now she could feel knife-stabbing pain. Her body pulsated with the energy of life's injustice. But how to channel it? Grace gazed at Pepper dreaming on the carpet, pawing the soft fibers. The puppy opened her eyes and rubbed against Grace, bristly fur tickling her legs. Grace picked her up. "I do care about you, those children, even their ditzy mother." Holding the pup to her chest, she crawled into the cold bed.

Grace rose early and boiled water for tea. Dunking the bag, she inhaled the crisp, earthy smell. She threw on Kirby's old pants and a sweatshirt. Careful to avoid Tulip's house, she took Pepper for a walk. After, while Pepper lapped up kibbles, Grace made toast and slathered it with butter. She showered, applied her first makeup in weeks, and drove to Kirby's Hardware.

Sam was unlocking the door.

"Hi, Sam."

He jerked, his braid flipping over his shoulder. "Grace, great to see you!" He hugged her. His slim chest and sinewy shoulders felt so different from Kirby's, but Old Spice, Kirby's scent, made her head spin.

"I don't know if I can do this, Sammy."

He clasped her shoulders and gazed into her dark eyes. "Yes, you can. You have to go on. The books are a mess. We need you."

"You need me?" Grace sighed. Yes, this is what she needed to do.

Sam had worked for Kirby for more years than Grace could remember. In cowboy boots and hat, an unselfconscious grin displaying the gaping hole where his front top tooth used to be, he could have stepped out of a Western. In his youth Sam had been on the circuit and a bull had gotten the best of him. He said he should get a new tooth, but having a dentist poke around in his mouth would be worse than being thrown.

Sam flicked on the lights, the worn pine floor looming ahead. Grace's breath caught. She imagined Kirby walking down the aisle toward her. She turned her attention to the shelves loaded with adhesive, paint, tools, and objects unknown. If no one else had it, Kirby did. Grace tugged open the office door and confronted Kirby's desk—neat, a few pencils, pen, paper, and the dad cup Rickey had given him. Sam stepped behind the desk and pulled out Kirby's chair, the leather streaked with wear. They stood awkwardly.

Grace willed her legs to bend and sat. Kirby would have been relaxed in his chair, slouched even. But Kirby was a man and commanded respect. She was a woman, a housewife. If the store were to survive, she had much to learn. "Well—"

Sam pulled a couple of folders out of the file cabinet and dropped them on her desk. True to his rugged image, Sam was a man of few words. "Books aren't my strong suit. The new kid, Mitch, he's not going to set the world on fire. There's plenty of traffic, but sales are down. Maybe people are buying at discount from Ace Hardware."

Grace's heart pinched. Kirby had loyal customers who came in just to chat, and always they would leave with something—men with a new drill, women with picture hangers or a mop. Customers must be missing him too.

Sam offered Grace coffee. She said she'd switched to tea. "Can do," he said, walking toward the door. "Let me know if you need anything."

Let him know if she needed anything. Ordinary, thoughtful words. *Well, Sam, what I really need is Kirby to help me with the mess. And while you're at it, how about Rickey? What, no can do, cowboy?* Grace brought herself up short. Sam was her loyal employee. He had kept the store afloat all those months when Kirby was ill. The store was her livelihood. She had to take charge.

Sam returned with tea in a Styrofoam cup. Leaving, he quietly closed the door. Grace set Kirby's mug in the drawer and opened the ledger. Working steadily, she deciphered Sam's figures and began to pay bills, some past due. When her stomach growled, she realized it was lunchtime. Her shoulders ached but her mind was amazingly clear.

At the register, Sam was ringing up a sale.

"See you tomorrow," Grace said.

Smiling, he gave a thumbs-up.

Near the door, Mitch was sweeping, his long, skinny arms an extension of the broom, a Detroit Tigers cap pulled tight over shaggy dark hair. Grace extended her hand. "Hello, I'm Grace O'Shay, Kirby's wife."

His gaze fixed on the broom, he muttered, "Sorry about Kirby." He turned and with long, hard strokes swept his way toward the back of the store. She had not looked forward to meeting Mitch, or anyone, for that matter. She had not wanted to engage in trivial conversation, but it was strange that Mitch did not shake her hand. What was it Sam said? Not going to set the world on fire? She'd have to ask him what he meant.

At home Pepper ran to greet Grace, her nails clicking across the waxed floor. Tab, stretched out on the kitchen table in a strip of sunlight, opened an eye. "Naughty kitty!" In slow motion, as though to taunt her, Tabby arched her back and leapt to the floor. The Formica counter was nearly bare. Only the mixer remained, reminding her of the children devouring cookies. Grace missed them. It had been nearly a week since her little tiff with Tulip. Perhaps Grace could bake something and offer it to the children as they passed by. No chocolate chips, but she had peanut butter.

With cookies in the oven, she licked the beaters, washed the mixer and bowl. She stood by the window listening to the clock tick, drinking tea, nervously eating cookies, one after the other until she lost count.

At 3:45 they rounded the corner: Hunter, hair ratty under a baseball cap, swinging her backpack. Next Tucker, in worn, holey jeans, dragging his pack. Ernest bringing up the rear, shirt too tight. If they were hers, they wouldn't go to school looking like ragamuffins!

"Hi there," Grace called. Tucker grinned and started toward her.

"No, Tucker!" Hunter yelled.

"Come in, have some cookies," Grace said.

Hunter shook her head. "Can't. Mom says not to bother you."

"She did?" Grace held up the platter. "Did she say you couldn't eat my cookies?"

"Nope." So a little later, they entered their empty house with bellies stuffed full of cookies.

Sinking into Kirby's overstuffed chair, Grace smiled ruefully. This was the second time today she had sat in his place. Pepper plopped down by her feet. Grace broke off a bit of the last cookie and offered it to her. The pup gulped it, then nuzzled Grace's foot. "Begging, are you?" Dogs could die from eating chocolate; what about peanut butter? She reached for the brush on the side table and worked it through Pepper's tangled bristles, the pup whining and squirming.

"I know it hurts, but we don't want you uncared for like those ragamuffins next door."

28

⌒〇

Like taffy stretched too thin, her muscles crying out with each step, Tulip climbed the stairs to bed. Get the kids off to school, work, supper, homework, laundry. And although Marshall was otherwise occupied at the moment, he could show up drunk and fearsome at any time. She had to be on alert. It was less than two weeks since Tulip had seen Grace, but it seemed much longer. She hadn't realized how much Grace had done for her and the kids. Although she saw D at work, she missed their late-night talks, and she missed Dennis too. She was so alone.

The door to Tucker's room flew open. He ran past her and down the stairs. The porch door banged. "K-k-kitty, k-k-kitty, k-k-kitty!"

Tulip followed Tucker to the porch. "It's after bedtime. You're in your PJs."

"Sh-she's gone!"

"That cat will come home when she's ready."

"W-w-what if she gets cold?"

"It's spring."

"She'll be s-scared in the dark."

"Silly, cats can see in the dark."

"B-b-but I c-can't sleep without her!"

She rubbed his neck. "You'll be fine. Fluff'll be back in the morning. Go on to bed!"

"P-p-promise?"

"Promise." That cat had better not make a liar out of her.

Tulip splashed water on her face, pulled the covers off the floor, and fell into bed. How long since she changed the sheets—two weeks, three? Better to wash the kids' clothes. She tried to stretch, but her taffy body had grown brittle.

The sound of creaking stairs woke her. *Marshall!* More creaking. Heart racing, she felt for the hammer and crept to the pitch black hall. The front door snapped shut. That bastard wasn't getting away this time! She raced downstairs and flung the door open.

Barefoot, Tucker paced the porch hollering, "K-k-kitty, k-k-kitty!"

Tulip latched onto him, her face next to his. Although the scream was in her throat, she kept her voice down. "You scared me half to death. Fluff will be fine. Cats love to prowl at night, hunt. Stop this nonsense and come to bed."

"C-c-can I s-s-sleep in your bed?"

Although Tucker slept like a whirling dervish, Tulip guided him upstairs to her bedroom. The next day she dragged herself to work, a picture of Marshall creeping up the stairs playing in her head.

Tucker and Dennis ran directly in front of Old Ruby. Tulip slammed on the brakes. The pickup swerved to a stop. Trembling, Tulip rolled down the window. "Get out of the street!"

Fluff jumped out of Tucker's arms and sped toward Grace's house, Tucker howling and trotting after her. By the time Tulip got to Grace's, Dennis had caught the cat.

Tulip grabbed Fluff by the nape of the neck and handed her to Tucker. "Take her home, *now!*" She glowered at Dennis. "I told you to stay away from my kids!"

Dennis clamped his hand on her shoulder. "Tulip, he was chasing the cat and nearly hit by a car. You should thank me."

She shoved him. "*I* could have hit Tucker!"

"But you didn't. I've done nothing wrong. You've been avoiding me for weeks. You need to hear me out."

Tulip's inclination was to walk away. No, run. But Grace's words rang in her head—fight or flight. It was better to talk things out. You might learn something. What did she have to lose?

"Come over after the kids are in bed."

Just the butcher knife, its edge dull with use, remained on the table. Tulip covered it with newspaper. Silly, but reassuring. She felt a twinge of excitement, or was it fear? They sat on opposite sides of the table, the clock's tick ungodly loud. A car squealed around the corner. "Well?" Tulip asked.

Dennis breathed deeply. He spoke real slow but did not turn the volume up. Tulip had to concentrate hard. "After Dad died, Mom was, well, lost. I couldn't stand her clinging and crying. I started skipping school, but I couldn't go home. I hung out with the burnouts. No hard stuff, though. One night I met this hot chick. Her dad was real strict, so she snuck over to my buddy's apartment." He held up his hands. "I'd never been with a girl before. Next thing two policemen showed up at my house."

"Police?"

"Her dad had followed me the night before. She'd told him everything, except that she'd lied about her age. It was crazy." He snickered. "If you'd seen us together—her fifteen going on twenty-one, and me eighteen, a snot-nosed kid—she'd have been the one going to court."

"You were arrested?"

"I got drunk, ran a red light, and smashed into a car. Totaled both cars. Could have killed the driver. Could have gone to jail, prison even, but the judge had known my dad. They took my license for the DUI. I got probation for molesting a minor." He laughed. "Even though I was the virgin."

"Did you tell them?"

He snorted. "I was on my way to prison. I stopped drinking, went back to school. Probation was tough."

"Tough?"

"Part of probation was to stay clear of children. That's why I couldn't be around yours. You were so touchy, I couldn't tell you. I felt bad. I like you. I like your kids."

He was quiet then. Tulip wanted to touch him, take a wet, warm rag and wash away his pain. She didn't have the words to comfort him, to say she was sorry these terrible things had happened. Instead she said, "You wouldn't hurt my kids?"

His eyes shot open. "Tulip, do you think I would?"

"No, not this instant, but when you leave, I'll doubt you. I'm deficient in the trust department. Never trusted anyone till D and now Grace. Never a man. You don't know what's happened to me."

"Tell me."

This trust stuff was new to her. But he'd come clean. This must be how you did it. You tell me something, I tell you something. Her hands went sweaty. He was not going to hurt her, not with words, not with fists. She picked up the knife, put it in the drawer, and turned to face him.

The words popped out. "I was twelve. My brother raped me."

When Tulip finished, she was crying, a stream of tears cleansing her wounds. She did not know that she would have to wash them again and again, that having exposed them to the light, she would be red and raw and need soothing. Dennis reached for a napkin and gently wiped her face.

"That's why I can't trust."

"But you do trust me or you wouldn't have told me."

But she had not told him all. Some things were unspeakable.

Dennis was coming over to collect on the dinner invitation. Tulip couldn't buy steak, but she wanted to make something nice. Lasagna! She'd been missing Grace's. For that matter, she missed Grace too.

Shopping for the fixings, she was shocked at the price. It had cost Grace a pretty penny to feed Tulip's crew. A box of mac and cheese was a far cry from lasagna but easier on the budget. Grace used red and green peppers, onions and garlic, maybe fresh tomatoes. But canned Farmer Jack's sauce was on sale and it had all that stuff in it. Mozzarella cheese, hamburger, and noodles, that was all she needed. Dennis was due in an hour and a half.

When she came out of Farmer Jack's, Ken was sitting in his patrol car. Long legs slid out the door. Giant shoes thudded on the pavement. "How you doing, Tulip?"

Tulip pointed to the no-parking sign where she had parked Old Ruby. "Goin' to give me a ticket?"

He snickered. "That depends."

"Taking bribes now, are you?"

He winked. "From you, always."

"I'm in a hurry. Write me the damn ticket!"

"Tulip, how are you? I've been worried about you."

"I'm busy, Ken. I'm a single mom. I don't have time for this."

"I'm not trying to start anything." He looked up and down the street as if he'd lost something. "I'm...I'm sorry."

"Your big mouth helped me do what I needed to do."

He studied the ground, searching for that lost item. "I...I want you to know I've got your back. If you need anything..."

"Are you going to write me a ticket or not?"

He shook his head, curled his lanky body into the patrol car, and zoomed off.

Had he really meant it, that he had her back?

At home the kids were at the kitchen table, Hunter and Ernest doing homework, Tucker coloring. "Hi, Mom," Ernest called.

Seeing her children contented and busy in their own home, Tulip felt a surge of pride. "Got a surprise. Dennis is coming for supper."

Tucker lit up like a neon sign. "D-D-Dennis?"

"What are we having?" asked Hunter.

"Lasagna. But you got to let me get at it."

Hunter leaned against the counter watching Tulip unload the bag. "Miss Grace makes her sauce."

"So does the store."

"Won't be as good as hers."

"Then go eat with her!"

"You bet!" She started toward the door.

"Don't you dare go over there!"

"Make up your damn mind!"

"Hunter, don't say that!"

"You do."

"I'm a grownup. You're a kid."

"Miss Grace says you're setting a bad example."

"D—dang Miss Grace! Clear off that table and set it."

Hunter grinned and gathered up the books and papers. "You miss her too. You know you do." Hunter got out the plates. "She's all upset 'cause Mr. Kirby died." She pawed through the cupboard. "We don't have no napkins."

"Any. We don't have any. Use paper towels."

"Remember when we went to Miss Grace's house for supper? She had a red tablecloth and white, see-through dishes and glasses with stems."

Tulip tore the wrapper off the meat. "Tucker broke one of those fancy glasses."

"She didn't cuss him out. She wasn't even mad."

"No! She's perfect! You want her for a mother?" Tulip tossed the beef into the sizzling skillet. Grease splattered onto her hand. "Damn!"

Hunter laughed.

Marshall's vindictive laugh! Tulip smacked Hunter's face. "Get out!"

Hunter's cheek showed red. "I hate you!" She ran from the kitchen.

Tulip held the spatula, grease popping from the skillet. She'd slapped Hunter. That was what Marshall or her dad would have done. No wonder Hunter loved Grace, wanted her for a mom. Tulip's fingers traced the scar on her forehead. Her mind went blank. *Stabbing pain.* Marshall pressed a dishrag against the gash, blood oozing onto his serpent ring. "You made me do it! You made me do it!" he screamed.

Tulip's mind cleared. No, Hunter had not made her do it. In spite of Hunter behaving like her father—that malicious cackle—Tulip should not have slapped her. As D said, hitting just made a person angrier. Tulip knew that well.

She turned down the gas and dumped the sauce into the pan. Dennis would be here in less than an hour. The kitchen was a disaster—last night's dishes still in the sink, breakfast bowls on the table. No time to boil noodles. She lit a match and turned on the oven. No blaze. She lit another, then another. Sickly sweet fumes stung her nose. *Mother killed in gas explosion on Hamilton. Three children orphaned.* One more match. The oven flared. She set the temp at 450, layered rock-hard noodles, meat, cheese, and sauce, added a cup of water, and stuck the concoction in the oven.

Tunnels of rot had burrowed through the lettuce. She cut out the brown, tore the rest into hunks, and wiped gunk off the rim of the French dressing. Lasagna bubbled in the oven, sauce dripping over the edges of the pan. She opened the window and tried to wave away the scorched odor seeping from the oven. At least the Wonder Bread was fresh.

Mr. Punctuality started across the lawn wearing a button-down shirt, his hair slicked back. Tulip ran upstairs to the bathroom and looked full in the mirror. Splotchy freckles, untamed hair, and a grease-stained shirt. No time to change. She splashed water on her face and ran a comb through her hair.

Downstairs, Tucker clutched a cardboard box. "S-smells good." He pulled at the lid.

Dennis took the box and set it on the counter. "Not now, a surprise for after dinner."

She hadn't thought about dessert. Depend on Mr. Perfect. "You didn't think I'd have dessert." Her voice was accusatory.

Honeyed sarcasm dripped from his mouth. "It was nice of you to invite me."

"My pleasure," she responded in a falsetto voice. "You kids go wash up."

Tulip jerked open the oven. Heat blasted her. She snatched a dish towel, pulled out the blackened dish, and plunked it on another dish towel on the table.

"Th-th-that's lasagna?" Tucker asked.

"Just because it isn't Grace's doesn't mean it's not good." She grabbed a knife and stabbed the crust. A burnt-rubber smell filled the kitchen.

"Let me," said Dennis. He took the knife and sawed grainy, red-brown shingles. "Pass the plates. I'll serve."

Dennis pierced a piece, blew on it, put it in his mouth, and chewed and chewed. Tulip watched the lump work its way down his throat. He gulped a drink of water. "Interesting," he whispered.

"You can eat this stuff? Your mom must be a lousy cook," Hunter declared.

"D-d-doesn't smell like M-Miss Grace's."

"I'm not eating it." Hunter shoved her plate away.

Dennis put his hands on the table and looked directly into Hunter's eyes. "It's not so bad. Your mom went to a lot of trouble."

"I can't cut it."

Dennis snipped her shingle into several pieces. He passed the wilted lettuce. Tucker opened the bottle of dressing and poured a river of orange on his salad.

"You're spilling, Tucker," Tulip said, her voice an octave too high.

"How's school?" Dennis asked. No response.

"Favorite subject?" he asked Ernest.

"Recess," Tucker blurted.

Cheeks aflame, Tulip toyed with her fork. Finally Tucker's words penetrated. "W-w-well, can I, Mom?"

"Good idea," Dennis said. He picked up his lasagna and bit into it.

"It's like pizza," Ernest said.

Tulip picked up her piece and bit, the outside burnt leather, inside rubbery. Hunter poked at her salad. Tulip did not insist that they clean their plates.

All eyes were on the mystery box. Dennis asked Tucker to help him clear the table. Beaming, Tucker brought each plate to Dennis, who scraped the uneatable mess onto a plate, a pyramid of shingles.

"Do you have more milk?" Dennis asked.

Thank heaven she'd bought milk. Ernest popped up and got it. With Dennis helping him steady the gallon jug, he poured, not spilling a drop. Then, as though Dennis were offering the family jewels, he opened the box: five perfect brownies, heaped with snow-white frosting, each on its own doily.

"Not very big," Hunter said.

"They're rich, one bite is enough. But for you, four bites, perhaps more if they're dainty. Gifted dwarf chefs come in each night and bake these incredibly delicious morsels. They're made to savor."

"What's s-s-savor?" Tucker asked.

"To look at, inhale, and see how slowly you can eat them. Let the frosting melt in your mouth." Dennis pulled lacy napkins from the box and asked Ernest to serve. As though waiting for prayer, they sat staring reverently at the miniature brownies.

"Look how the frosting swirls," Dennis commented.

"Like waves," Ernest said.

Hunter sniffed hers. "Smells like one of those fancy chocolate bars."

"C-can we eat it?" Tucker asked.

Dennis grinned and took the tiniest bite. Tucker grabbed for his, paused, then carefully picked it up. His tongue swirled around the frosting. He licked his lips and set the brownie on its doily. Dennis nodded.

"Wow! Even Grace doesn't make brownies this good!" Ernest exclaimed.

Hunter's green eyes sparkled. "It's like chocolate from *Charlie and the Chocolate Factory*."

Later Ernest found the book for Dennis to read. Hunter begged him to bring brownies again. Grinning, he promised he would, providing they went to bed without complaint.

Up to her elbows in humiliation, Tulip tried to scrub burnt lasagna off the pan. "Next time I'll boil the noodles."

"And you might turn the oven down a bit more. Three-fifty, I think that's the temperature."

"How do you know so much about cooking?"

He laughed. "Like Hunter said, my mom's a bad cook." He paused. "Tulip, we could have waited supper, maybe eaten the salad first. You should try lasagna again, just allow more time."

Him telling her how to cook! She scrubbed vigorously, soap splattering her eye. "Ooh!"

"Rinse it," Dennis commanded. He nudged her out of the way. "I'll scrub that."

Tulip cupped water in her hand and held it to her eye. "You do dishes too?"

"I do everything."

Tulip grinned. "You are one girly man."

Laughing, Dennis whirled her around and sponged her eye with a paper towel. "Given your experience with men, I'm going to take that as a compliment." He held her chin, his long surgeon's fingers circling an ear.

Tulip's skin tingled. Uncertain if she was excited or frightened, she scooted away. Like a fool she turned in a circle and ended facing the refrigerator. "Want some Boone's Farm?"

"Sweet drink for the girly-man," he said, pouring wine into juice glasses. "Let's have a toast—a toast to neighbors and friendship." He clinked his glass to hers. "And how about a toast to Grace, the neighborhood Good Samaritan?"

"We're not on the best of terms."

"What happened?"

"I don't remember."

He shook his head. "Yes, you do."

"She hung up on me—cussed."

He snorted.

"What's so funny about that?"

"She cursed you! What did you do?"

"The mutt! I gave her the damn mutt!"

Dennis collapsed on a chair laughing. "After all she's done for you. Tulip, you should get your butt over there and apologize."

Later, Tulip crawled into bed thinking about what Dennis had said. Apologize. Grace *was* the best friend ever. It was stupid, Tulip reacting so badly to Grace cussing. Even when she tried not to, Tulip cussed. Why had she been so offended? She could not make sense of it, but this she did know: she must apologize to Grace, and soon.

As if he'd had all the time in the world, Dennis had been calm and patient with the kids. He'd made a celebration out of eating baby brownies. He'd helped Tucker clear the table, Tucker not spilling or dropping. Dennis expected the kids to do what he said. They were marshmallow good when he was around. Respect, that was it. He treated them with respect. She talked to her children like they were stupid. She yelled, and she had slapped her daughter! She was no better than her parents or Marshall. She couldn't take it back, but she could tell Hunter she was sorry and that she would never do it again.

29

⤳

Grace established a pattern: an early morning walk for Pepper, and then she drove to Kirby's, the pup curled on the seat beside her. The store's strong man-smell, oil, dust, and out-of-doors, reminded her of Kirby. When she touched an item, she pictured it in his competent hands. For moments, the pain receded.

Attacking months of accumulated dust and grime, a mindless sort of thing that she was good at, she came across a bulging envelope marked Grace. Cards spilled onto the desk, dated and in order. She picked up a pressed red maple leaf mounted on yellow construction paper, the handwriting her own: "Since you came to me, I am alive. Without you, life would be empty. Happy birthday! I love you, Grace."

She had waited anxiously as Kirby read the card. "The best ever," he had said.

Every year, using fabric, wrapping paper, even paper bags, she had made him a birthday card. The last was dated June 2, 1968, the year Rickey died. Grace stacked them in order and shut them in the drawer. Pepper padded over from her blanket and rubbed against Grace's ankles. She picked up the pup, tears wetting her fur.

Sam cracked open the door. "Are you all right?"

Grace sobbed. "Memorabilia."

"Oh, the cards. He was banty-rooster proud of those."

"He showed them to you?"

Sam fished in his pocket, pulled out a crumpled hanky, and handed it to Grace. "Guess he figured you and he would reminisce in your old age." He shifted awkwardly. "It'll get easier. How about I get you some coffee?"

Grace wiped her tears. "Tea. Bring me tea."

Sam brought tea and quickly excused himself for lunch. Grace idly dunked the Lipton bag up and down, steam rising from the cup. Soon, like life, the heat would be gone, wasted. Without Kirby, her life had no purpose. Sell the store, travel, he'd said. Did he think her incapable of taking over the business? Humph.

She stuffed Sam's hanky in her pocket. Sweet, him giving it to her. She'd take it home and wash it. Now she'd best go and see what Mitch was up to.

Hands in his pockets, Mitch paced the aisle.

"Is something wrong?" Grace asked.

He ran his fingers through greasy hair. "No, nothing. Mind if I go out and have a smoke?"

"You seem worried."

Mitch's attempt to laugh reminded her of a tiny Fourth of July fire cracker fizzling out. "I'm fine." He pulled a crushed pack of Lucky Strikes out of his pocket and started toward the door.

Grace stepped in front of him. "Something is wrong."

"You're my employer, not my parent." He pivoted past her.

Grace followed him up front and peered out the window. Leaning against the light post, Mitch blew a stream of smoke rings. A broad-chested man in a leather jacket strode up. Standing too close, he spoke and then punched Mitch in the stomach. Grace gasped. Did Mitch owe him money? Was it drugs? Mitch's work had suffered. He was disrespectful. She was not his parent, but she was his employer. Kirby would have confronted Mitch head on. She was just a housewife and had no experience with employees. But her husband was not here to deal with Mitch. Somehow she would do it, but later. She had to get out of the store.

Grace stood on her porch, holding a plate of cookies. Hunter ran up the walk, grinning. "Hi, Miss Grace. I've got an idea. Mom didn't say nothing about you being at our house."

"Hunter, you have the best ideas. It's a nice spring day. We'll have a sort of picnic on your porch."

Ernest squinted. "Should you be there?"

Hunter attempted a wink. "Mom didn't say."

Ernest nodded. "Whyn't you make up with Mom?"

"Your mom doesn't want to."

"You're both so stubborn!" Hunter ran into the house and slammed the door.

After, Grace walked home, Hunter's words playing on her mind. She had never thought of herself as stubborn. She was the caretaker. Although she hated to admit it, she saw herself as wise, Tulip's superior. But when Tulip gave her Pepper, Grace had been mired in a bottomless pit of despair. Flighty, thoughtless Tulip had known what Grace needed—someone, something to take care of.

Thump, thump. Grace pulled the blanket over her head but the thumping grew more insistent. Knocking at the door? She peeked at the clock. Eight. She felt for her robe.

It was Tulip, hand poised to pound. Grace flung open the door.

Tulip clutched the doorjamb. "It's Tucker. He's sick."

Grace's tone was icy. "Why tell *me?*"

"Can't miss work."

"So?"

"Can—can you come over?" Tulip's words were barely audible.

"Well...I *was* going to the hardware store this morning..."

"Oh...I forgot. I'm sorry to bother you. I'm sorry for *everything.*" She whirled to leave.

"Tulip, you stop it! Of course I'll be over—as soon as I'm dressed."

Tulip nodded and fled.

Hadn't she known Tulip needed her? Alive with purpose, Grace tossed on her only pair of jeans, a long-sleeved shirt of Kirby's, and ran a brush through her hair. Hesitating in the kitchen, she thought about making tea, but today she wanted coffee. Tulip's filthy pot seemed to brew mud, or perhaps it was the coffee she used. That mystery could be solved today.

Dressed in her polyester uniform, Tulip waited at the door. She cleared her throat.

"Yes?" Grace was not going to make it easy.

"Sorry about what happened."

"Indeed." Grace said it as a matronly teacher would to a disobedient student. "You go to work. We'll talk later."

Tulip grimaced. "Call if you need me." The door slammed shut.

Upstairs, Tucker was curled in a blanket, his face damp with sweat.

"You are sure tucked in, Tucker," Grace joked. "How're you doing?"

"M-m-my throat hurts."

Grace tossed Fluff off the bed and felt Tucker's forehead. He needed cooling. She made a path through dirty clothes to the bathroom, found a wet rag in the sink, and rinsed it. Back in the bedroom, she wiped Tucker's face and arms with the cool cloth, unbuttoned his top, and sponged his developing chest.

"Do you have a thermometer?"

"B-broke."

When Grace returned from her house with the thermometer, Fluff was lying across Tucker's neck. "Cats do not belong in a sick room."

Tucker's glassy blue eyes met hers. Grace relented, simply moving Fluff to the side of the bed. Tucker's temperature was a hundred and three, his face pale, freckles glistening with perspiration. "You are one sick puppy."

Too weak to speak, he nodded.

Grace panicked. Children who ran high fevers could die in hours. Tulip should have stayed home. After her previous experience trying to reach Tulip at work, Grace did not call. Instead she phoned the doctor. Pulling out of the drive, she remembered the permission-to-treat slip that Tulip had signed when Grace cared for the children. She had been determined not to end up in the same predicament she'd been in on that first day.

After the doctor's, they stopped at Rexall to fill the prescription, and Grace purchased juice and a Superman comic. At home, Tucker crawled back into bed. Grace gave him aspirin and the liquid medicine. He sipped orange juice and sank into the pillow. Fluff jumped onto the bed and curled up next to him.

Dr. Malone had said that Tucker would be feeling better in a day and that Grace had done what she could. But she was uneasy, as she had been when Rickey was Tucker's age and came down with measles. During Rickey's convalescence, she had cleaned until her home was spotless. Tulip's house was just the ticket. Grace flitted through rooms, picking up Legos, books, shoes, discarded winter coats, and pillows from the floor. In the kitchen, cereal and dirty bowls were still on the table, dishes in the sink, cupboards and counters grimy. With great satisfaction, Grace gave the coffeepot a good scrubbing and made herself a decent cup. Mystery solved.

By the time Tulip came home, the kitchen was sparkling. Tucker was drinking orange juice and engrossed in his comic.

"He's better?" Tulip asked.

"He will be. The doctor thinks it's strep throat."

"You took him to the doctor?"

"Put him on antibiotics."

Tulip pursed her lips. "I—don't—have—money for that."

That was how Tulip treated her! Grace's voice rose. "He was ill. You went to work. You didn't even phone to see how he was!"

Defeated, Tulip sank into a chair. Dark circles ringed her eyes. Her uniform was wrinkled, her apron stained. She gazed at the floor. "I—I'm sorry. We were slammed. Sometimes there's just too much to think about, too much to do." Why, she was acting like a little girl disciplined by her mother. "Besides, I knew you would take care of him. You've been so good to us. I'm so sorry." Her head sank lower. "You're right. I shouldn't have gotten you that puppy. I should have asked." She raised her head and gave the slightest hint of a smile. "But I'm not sorry for calling her a mongrel!"

Grace curtailed her laugh. "*That's* what you're apologizing for?"

Tulip shook her head. "I didn't like being cussed at."

"So you didn't like being cussed at?" This was one point Grace intended to drive home. "No one does, young lady."

Tears formed in Tulip's eyes. "When I woke up this morning and Tucker was so sick, I didn't know what to do. Joe hates it when I miss work. I thought of you."

Grace opened her arms and Tulip swooped into them, her back slight and brittle as though the slightest blow could snap it. Grace was shamed for making her squirm. "It felt good to be needed." Still, there was a score to settle. Grace looked her in the eye. "You forbade your children to come to my house. You know I love those kids."

Tears running down her cheeks, Tulip nodded.

"But I was stubborn too. I should have called," Grace said, digging in her pocket for a Kleenex.

Tulip blew her nose. A corner of her mouth twitched up. "Yeah, you're the communication expert."

Grace laughed, but Tulip did not. Her gaze met Grace's. "I'm damaged—broken—irreparable."

"What? What do you mean? You're a good mother. You take care of the kids and work. You've made a home out of a wreck of a house. What is so bad about you?"

Gaze fixed on the floor, Tulip mumbled, "Some…some things are best forgotten."

Grace had an image of Tulip being held together by Band-Aids, of ripping them off one by one, blood spurting. Perhaps it would be better not to open old wounds, but Tulip needed to talk. "If you keep horrible things inside, they twist and grow. Talk about them with someone you trust and they don't seem as horrific."

Tulip clenched her fists. Was she going to strike Grace? Instead Tulip thumped her chest. "Trust! You want *me* to trust? Why am I damaged goods? My shit-faced brother, that's why!"

"He raped you?" Grace should have known. Perhaps she did.

"He was drunk—I didn't cook the fucking roast! Mom was mad about the smell, the mess. She blamed me."

"Blamed you?"

"Maybe she knew, but she couldn't stick up for me. She had to live there."

"Oh my! You ran away?"

"Run away? Where could I go? I was twelve. They'd catch me and put me in juvie. My own mother didn't believe me. It was war, with Pop exploding and Mom tiptoeing around pretending it wasn't happening. And Calvin—Calvin leering at me, waiting to pounce."

"Twelve? When you were twelve your brother raped you?"

"I was smart. School was my haven. But I closed up. It was like I was shut in one of those metal school lockers, fists banging on the door, voice echoing through the vents. I couldn't speak, couldn't think. When I tried to read, words blurred on the page. And if I managed to make them out, I couldn't remember what they meant."

Tulip paused for breath. "I watched the popular girls, how they dressed, how they acted. I imitated them. I tried to dress like them, wore my bobby socks rolled down, scuffed my saddle shoes. I made gored skirts in home-ec. But no matter how hard I tried, I could not be one of them. I was an empty shell."

Grace reached for the trembling girl. "You were an abused, confused child."

Tulip screamed, "But they thought I did it! Good girls didn't do it. And I did it!"

Grace took Tulip's face in her hands and spoke slowly. "You were raped. It was done to you. *It was not your fault.*"

"They thought I was fast. The guys made bets about who could make me. They lied. There was this one guy I liked. At a drive-in movie he got me down on the seat, said he loved me. But I knew better. I couldn't get a 180-pound football player off me, so I hollered no as loud as I could. He bolted up and threw the window speaker on the ground. Shortest date ever. The next week there was this rumor at school that we did it. Calvin heard it—or maybe he started it."

Enough. Bandage it, bandage it. "He tried to rape you. You couldn't stop your brother, but you stopped this brute the only way you could. You screamed."

Tulip sank onto the sofa. "I never thought of it that way. I felt so alone, like it only happened to me, that it was my fault."

Grace's words had found their mark. She was reminded of the boy who tamed the lion by plucking the thorn from his foot. "Rape is not your fault. Nothing to be ashamed of."

"Were you ever raped?" Tulip's eyes were large, her face open.

Grace laughed in relief. "You grew up in the fifties. I was young in the late twenties. But yes, there was rape, even back then. It wasn't acknowledged, even worse than it is now. But my parents hardly let me talk to a boy. Kirby was my first real boyfriend."

Sun streamed through the kitchen window, wrapping its warmth around Grace. Was it a day like this, the day Tulip's brother raped her? No, she had said it was fall. Strangers did horrible things, not your family. To be so betrayed was beyond Grace's imagination. When Kirby died, she had felt betrayed. Hearing what Tulip had been subjected too, Grace was ashamed of indulging her pain. She had good memories. Life was lonely, but unlike Tulip, she had been loved. Life went on.

She needed to tidy the kitchen and wash the dishes before the children came home from school. She tossed the beaters and spatula into the bowl and set them in the sink. In her mind's eye she saw Rickey, the age of Ernest, with the same crooked smile. His face streaked with chocolate, he scooped the last bit out of the bowl. "Licking the bowl's the best part, Mom." Grace wiped tears with her apron. *No time for this now.* She set the bowl aside for one, beaters for two. The buzzer dinged. She opened the oven door and stood back from the rush of heat. The cookies were perfectly round, each with a chocolate kiss melted in the middle.

A scream. Out the window, she saw the children running from three boys, Ernest's hand on Tucker's back, propelling him toward her house.

"Retard, retard! Tucker is a retard!" hollered the boys.

Hunter skidded to a stop, turned, and raised her fists to the largest boy, a head taller than she. "His name's Tucker! Call him retard again and I'll beat you up."

As Grace rushed toward the door, she caught a succulent whiff. Cookies— her weapon of choice. She grabbed a hot pad, picked up the tray, marched onto the porch and down the walk. Controlling her rage, she made her voice friendly. "Why, children, I see you've brought friends with you."

The bullies turned on their heels. She called out, "Wait, I made cookies. Would you like one? Peanut butter, just out of the oven."

The strapping bully in the red baseball cap turned. "Cookies?"

"Do you like them?"

No response.

"I bake something for Hunter, Ernest, and *Tucker* every day. Their friends are always welcome to join them."

No response.

Comprehending, Ernest's eyes lit up. He walked to Grace, scooped three cookies off the tray, and held them out. "Try them! Miss Grace makes the best cookies ever."

The little one looked at the ring leader for permission. None given. He looked toward Grace. She nodded. He stepped forward and took one. "Thanks," he mumbled.

"Have a cookie!" Hunter taunted.

"They're really good." Ernest extended his hand tentatively, as though afraid a dog might jump up and bite him. The ringleader grabbed one and stuffed it in his mouth.

"Have another," Grace offered.

The littlest took one off the tray. The other two followed suit.

"What do you say?" Grace asked.

"Thanks," they mumbled.

"We should introduce ourselves. I'm Mrs. O'Shay. You may call me Miss Grace. I believe you know Hunter, Ernest, and of course *your friend* Tucker. What are your names?"

"I'm Henry," the little one said.

"Tom," the ringleader said. Grace would make it a point to call him Tommy.

After stuffing a couple more cookies in their mouths, they started toward the corner. Henry turned and hollered, "Thanks for the cookies, Miss Grace!"

"Come back anytime. It's a pleasure to meet Tucker's friends."

"I'll be d—darned," Hunter said.

Grace had tamed Tucker's tormenters, Tommy, Henry, and Johnny. Every few days they followed her brood home. Sitting on Grace's front porch, they restrained themselves from gobbling cookies in two bites and minded their manners with "thank you" and "please." Tough Tommy said little and stayed on the fringe of the group. Grace learned he had difficulty in school, that he was in Tucker's slow reading class.

As they came up the walk one Tuesday, Tommy and Tucker were bent with laughter. "What's so funny?" Grace asked.

Tommy grinned. "Just something in reading class."

"J-just something in class," Tucker mimicked.

Grace noticed Henry stealing glances at Hunter. Why not? She was a cutie with freckles and red hair. Her hair had grown long and she often popped in before school to have Grace braid it or put it in a ponytail. Grace would urge Tucker to tuck in his shirt and gel down his hair. Ernest did not seem to need any extra grooming. The youngsters were flourishing and Grace was not above taking some credit.

Marshall was in jail for not paying child support. Now, although Tulip was short of money, her persecutor was contained, and she was less frenzied and less abrupt with her children. Still, Grace was distressed by Tulip's revelation and the glimpse of what Tulip called her broken self.

"Oh, Kirby. You wanted me to get on with life. So here I am with this little family—the caretaker, the fixer. And I don't know how to help her."

30

Tulip checked the Texaco for Marshall's car or pickup. He was out of jail, and D had spotted him drunk at the bar. When Tulip saw it was clear, she pulled into the station. She had to have gas; Old Ruby was running on fumes. She stood on sizzling pavement, working the nozzle, feeling like an overdone burger. No rain for two weeks. Her yard was tufts of withered grass strangled by a mass of healthy weeds. No hose, but, even if she could water, she couldn't pay the bill. College students were gone for the summer, business was slow, and she was short on tips.

Thankfully Tulip didn't have to worry about her children. Safe and busy with Grace, they went to the park, the library, and Grace registered them for swim lessons and arts and crafts. She said everything was free, a public service. Grace was Tulip's public service. The children spent more time with her than with their mother.

A black pickup roared to a stop at the pump next to Tulip—Marshall? She jammed her fingers on the trigger. It wasn't a gun, but she could spray him. The door popped open and a cowboy slid out. Gas had gushed onto her legs and shoes. *Shit!* She pictured herself in flames. *Divorced mother of three sets fire to self and burns down gas station.* She snatched an old T-shirt of Ernest's out of Old Ruby and rubbed the hell out of her legs. There was nothing she could do about her shoes. Five-ninety-nine on the pump, more than she'd intended to pay. She dug in her pockets for tips. Five-fifty. She looked in the ashtray, on the floor, under the seat. Three nickels and a dime. *Damn!*

Tulip squared her shoulders, marched into the station, and slammed the coins on the counter. "D—darn thing overflowed! I'm short twenty-four cents."

The bald attendant smiled through a face of wrinkles. "Sorry about that. Can't take it off the register, but I think I've got a quarter." He fumbled in his grubby pocket and added two dimes and a nickel to her pile. Opening the register, he pulled out a penny.

Tulip's mouth flew open. The old man's shirt was faded, his cuffs frayed.

"Oh…I'll pay you back next time."

He shrugged.

"Well…well, thanks. Thank you very much. But I *will* pay you back." She walked past a couple of customers who had witnessed her humiliation.

Tulip would stop tomorrow and pay the Good Samaritan. He needed that quarter more than she did. At least it was one bill she could pay. No child support. The heat was off for the summer but the electric bill was sky high. She didn't know how the h—heck, heck; she had to learn to not think cuss, because when she did, it came out of her mouth—how the heck she would pay the gas when winter came. The wind sucked the heat right out of Old Grouchy.

At home, the TV blasted in the empty living room. *Past due on the electric bill and the kids leave the TV on.* The screen went blank. Out the window, Tulip saw a guy in a khaki uniform hightailing it out of the yard. Flinging open the door she hollered, "Did you turn off our electricity?"

Hair in his eyes, zits on his face, he looked more like a teenager caught in a prank than a grown man. "Sorry, ma'am. Past due."

"I'll pay first thing in the morning. Can't you leave it on till then?"

"Sorry. Office opens at eight-thirty. We can turn it on right after you pay." He trotted toward the truck.

"Yeah, hurry! See how many lights you can turn off before five!" Tulip sighed. It wasn't personal. He was just a guy trying to do his job.

The stove was gas, and it didn't get dark until almost bedtime. It wouldn't kill the kids to do without TV. But when Hunter tried to turn it on, she turned on her mother. "At least with Dad we had electricity."

Tulip called D and asked for a loan.

31

Too warm. Grace opened the kitchen window; faded yellow curtains billowed in the crisp fall breeze. She'd made the curtains when Rickey was a child and it seemed disloyal to replace them. The children had left and Grace rested at the kitchen table with a cup of tea, three remaining cookies beckoning her. She bit into one and felt the crunch of oatmeal and tasted the sweet, buttery flavor. Not without guilt she reached for the second, but was saved by the ringing of the phone.

Sam, nearly incoherent. Last week he had taken Grace aside and said that his wife had discovered a lump in her breast, that they had an appointment with a specialist. On the phone now, his voice was clipped. "We just came from the doctor. The biopsy was conclusive. It's malignant." He did not use the word cancer.

"So they're taking out the lump?"

"The breast." His voice caught. "They're cutting off her breast."

Grace's hand went protectively to her chest. "Oh, Sam. I'm so sorry."

Maggie was tiny, feminine. She often joked that in a T-shirt and jeans she could pass for a boy. Although her breasts were small, they were a defining part of her, of any woman. Breast cancer was not discussed. It was as though the disease was shameful, as though a woman without breasts was deformed, less than. Grace did not know how to tell Sam that even without breasts, Maggie would still be whole inside, still the loving woman he had married.

Sam focused on the business at hand. He would be away for a week or so after the surgery; he'd have to be with Maggie for chemo and radiation. Grace would have to fill in, might want to hire someone part time.

"No problem. I'll take care of it. Your place is with Maggie." Grace said it over and over again. After she hung up, she sat in the chair a long time, the cookie untouched. First Kirby, now Maggie. But surely Maggie would survive.

Sam could take as much time as he needed, but he was the backbone of Kirby's. She could not keep up with his schedule, nor could she depend on Mitch. Although it would be costly, she had to hire someone. But who? Just today Tulip had borrowed money for gas. Grace had wanted to reach in her wallet and pull out a ten, but Tulip's scarlet face betrayed her humiliation. She needed money and Grace needed an employee. Tulip had been trying to curb her crude ways, but clerking at Kirby's would require more tact than joshing with patrons at Joe's. She would have to be professional, and she would have to be trained. But Tulip was bright and a hard worker. Perhaps it was a workable solution.

Grace waited until the children would be in bed and then crossed the yellowed lawn. Tulip's kitchen was warm. She was up to her elbows in suds, washing a huge stack of dishes, her hair a frizzy mop which she kept pushing off her perspiring face. Grace picked up a towel. How could she ask Tulip to take on something else?

"Kind of late for you to be visiting," Tulip said.

Grace dried a plate and put it in the cupboard. "Sam's wife has breast cancer."

"Cancer? Oh, no."

"Yes. She's having a mastectomy."

"Will she be all right?"

Grace shrugged. "Sam will need to be with her; he'll need time off. I'll need to hire a part-timer." Grace paused, then in a tentative voice, "Would you be interested in filling in a few evenings?"

Tulip's blue eyes shot open. "Me? Why me?"

"Why not? You deal with the public all the time."

As though this were new information, Tulip grinned. "You really think so?"

"Do you think that I'd ask you to work at Kirby's if I didn't think you would be an asset?"

Tulip laughed. Then she frowned, shook her head. "But I can't. Can't leave the kids."

Grace nodded. "I could stay with them. I'd come over after supper. It wouldn't disrupt their schedule, and it's not the quantity but the quality of the time you spend with your children that's important."

"But that's more work for you and I can't pay you."

"You gave me Pepper to have something to take care of, to live for. I love your children. They take my mind off Kirby. They are not work. You'd be doing me a favor by letting me watch them."

"Oh, Grace!" Tulip flung soapy arms around her.

When it was settled, Grace said, "By the way, some of the workmen curse, but my employees do not."

32

"You be good, you hear? Don't tire Grace out," Tulip called as she closed the door behind her. She rushed back in and kissed each child's cheek. "You'll be asleep when I get home. Won't see you till morning. Good night."

She had hurried the children through supper. Tucker cleared the table, Hunter and Ernest washed dishes. She had promised each fifty cents a week for these chores and they had not complained, had even seemed pleased.

Although Tulip had been to Kirby's many times, she had never paid attention to the workings of the store and she was plenty nervous. Kirby's was just a few blocks away, but with Marshall on the loose, it would be foolhardy to walk home in the dark. She parked Old Ruby in the lot and ran to the front of the brick building. The sign, Kirby's Hardware, was crimson red. Display windows held a hodgepodge of products and an air conditioner not yet put to bed for the winter. The heavy door swung open easily. Inside, Tulip blinked in the harsh fluorescent light. Tall shelves with boxes, plastic and metal parts, bottles and cans crowded the narrow aisles. The bright light glowed on the dark, worn pine floor, which smelled of oil and dust.

Sam stepped forward, tall, with gray-streaked dark hair pulled back in a ponytail. He held out his hand. "Tulip?"

She wiped a sweaty palm on her jeans. "Reporting for duty."

Sam took her hand in both of his. "You're prettier than I remember. It's a pleasure to meet you formally. I'll show you around. Then I've got to get home to Maggie. Mitch will be working evenings with you."

A shaggy haired, thin-faced young guy knelt on the floor by a bunch of cardboard boxes, a pack of Lucky Strikes rolled up in his T-shirt sleeve, a tattoo peeking out from under. His wide leather belt was studded with silver.

Tulip inhaled and stuck her hand out. "Hi, pleased to meet you."

The kid sliced through a box with his giant pocket knife. Sneaky eyes traveled up and rested on her breasts. A shiver worked its way up Tulip's back.

Leaving the knife open, he jumped to his feet. "Trash—dumping." He gathered up the broken boxes and limped to the back door.

Tulip gaped at Sam. "He works here?"

Sam nodded. "Motorcycle accident messed up his leg. He's having a hard time adjusting."

"Why hire him?"

"His dad's a contractor, was a friend of Kirby's. Asked Kirby to give him a chance. Grace has kept him on. You know how she is." Sam ushered Tulip through the store, pointing out the different areas: tools, hardware, paint, cleaning supplies, the list went on. "It's pretty straightforward. You shouldn't have any trouble. Mitch will show you how to work the cash register and answer any questions."

Tulip nodded, but daddy's little boy did not look like a fountain of information.

After Sam left, Tulip wandered through the store studying the unfamiliar tools, mostly labeled and priced. The cash register was similar to Joe's. That should be a snap. The biker kid kept busy stocking rakes and wheelbarrows.

The bell jingled. "Someone's up front," the kid hollered.

He could talk, but he had no intention of helping her. Tulip hurried to the front, where a bubble-blowing teenybopper asked for thumbtacks for a school project. Tulip looked down the long aisle. The girl pointed to the rack behind the register. Relieved, Tulip rang up her first sale.

Those first evenings, Mitch grudgingly answered Tulip's questions, usually a word or two, never a complete sentence, never hi or goodbye. Leaving her to wait on customers, he took long breaks out back. She was pretty sure it wasn't cigarettes he was smoking out there. Studded belt, dagger tattoo—daddy's little boy did not like Tulip.

It was Sam who trained her. In spite of his worries about a sick wife, he was patient and thorough. Tulip learned the difference between wood and metal screws, and semi-gloss, flat, satin, latex and oil paint. When she had painted the kitchen, she'd picked the paint from the clearance bin; she'd not thought about kind or quality. There was much to learn and she was determined to learn it.

On payday Tulip stopped by the hardware to pick up her check. "Your pay, my lady. Well earned," Sam said.

Tulip's cheeks flushed. "You really mean it?"

He smiled. "Nah, I just say that to all the pretty girls."

She giggled and slapped his wrist with the envelope. It was good to see that he could still joke with his wife so ill.

Tulip made a beeline for Farmer Jack's. The first time ever that she skipped down the aisles of a grocery store, not calculating the bill in her head. Still, she limited herself to three splurges—ice cream, doughnuts, and a red pepper. She was due at Kirby's in a couple of hours. That morning Tucker had worn jeans and a shirt out of the dirty clothesbasket. She must do a load of laundry. She'd have Hunter help with supper—grilled cheese and canned peas, ice cream for dessert.

Breathless, Tucker met Tulip at the door. "M-M-Mom, you got t-t-o see!" He grabbed her hand and pulled her up the stairs to his bedroom. "Th-th-three! There's three!"

Fluff was sprawled on the bedspread in the middle of a tomato-soup-colored stain with three tiny kittens. Two nursed, their mini paws padding up and down on her belly. Licking a third ball of fur, Fluff worked her tongue over its face and head. She finished the clean-up and nudged the baby toward dinner. When the kitten had difficulty, Tucker gently guided it to a teat.

Tulip closed her eyes. Her breathing slowed. She was six; Snoopy had birthed kittens in Tulip's closet. Three, soft and tiny. She had to hide them, keep them safe. She made a bed in a box and hid them under the porch. She cared for them, watched them grow. Their eyes opened. They tried their legs. She dunked their little heads in milk that she'd snuck from the kitchen. At first they gulped, sputtered, shook their wet fur. They wobbled through the bowl, lifting and shaking their paws. Finally they got the hang of lapping. Holding them close, their sandpapery tongues tickled her cheeks. And then one day they were gone.

Tucker tugged at her arm. "I-I-I saw the last one b-born. Sh-sh-she had to push and push."

"Yeah, it's hard to give birth."

"W-w-was I?"

"A little, but you were worth it."

"C-c-can we keep 'em?"

"Till they get big enough to give away. We'll find good homes for them."

"J-just one?"

Tulip shook her head.

"M-maybe Miss Grace would want one."

"She has Tabby and Pepper." Tulip propelled him toward the door. "Go to the basement and get that empty box. We'll make them a bed."

173

"C-can I keep them in my room?"

When Tulip had asked her dad what happened to her kittens, he had shrugged. "We can't afford no kittens," he'd said. Now her son beamed with pleasure, as though he had performed this small miracle that took place on his bed. She would do right by these kittens.

The diner was slow. Tulip left Joe's early. She and the children had cleaned the previous evening and she was looking forward to a neat house all to herself. She loved the oily scent of Pledge, the lemon of Mr. Clean, and a living room she could walk through without stepping on Legos. She would check on the kittens, turn on the TV, put her legs up, and have a Coke before the kids got home.

Tulip opened the door and inhaled—beer? Smoke? A six-pack of Old Milwaukee sat on the coffee table; an empty bottle on the floor, an open one stuffed in the crack of the couch. *Marshall!* She grabbed Ernest's bat by the front door and tip-toed toward the kitchen. Upstairs, the toilet flushed. She crept up the stairs. Again the toilet flushed. The door opened. Pants unzipped, belt buckle hanging, *he* weaved in the doorway.

"Hello, little sis." Calvin lunged for her.

She sidestepped him. "You're in prison!"

Drool dribbled from his mouth onto his scruffy beard. He stuck his fingers in his belt loops and tried to swagger. "I was a good boy. I am on probation!"

"Get out!" Heart thumping, she rammed the bat into his chest and pushed him toward the stairs.

"You wouldn't turn your favorite brother away, would you? You need me. You got three kids and your old man left."

"*I* was the one who left. And I don't need *you!*"

He teetered on the landing. "So you're doing good. Nice house, plenty of room."

"You are scum! Get out!" She lifted the bat to swing.

Calvin backed down the stairs, tripped, and crumpled onto the step. He reached for her hand. "Help me."

She poked him in the ribs. "I'd as soon kill you!"

"Why, you little slut!"

She rammed the bat harder.

He stumbled to his feet and swayed toward the door, halting in front of Tucker's picture. "Is this the retarded one?"

She swung the bat. "Get out before I do something I may regret!"

"Remember how close we were?" He cackled.

"*Never* set foot in this house again! *Never* try to contact me, or my kids!"

He staggered to the couch, picked up his beer, and teetered toward the door. Pointing his finger at her he hissed, "I'm not finished with you, little sister."

The slam of the door thudded in Tulip's ears. A slow-motion picture reeled through her head. Calvin stood over her, hitting her with the raw roast, again and again, bloody hunks filling her nose. She gasped for air.

The door flew open. Tulip raised the bat. "Out, you shit-ass!"

"Whoa!" Grace raised her hands. "I saw that guy leaving. Are you all right?"

The rancid odor vanished. Tulip could breathe. "I thought he was in prison."

"Who?"

"Calvin."

"Your brother, the one…?"

"He wanted to stay."

"How dare that *bastard*!"

Sobbing, Tulip fell into Grace's arms.

Grace rubbed her back. "It's OK, Tulip. He's gone."

"Do you count *bastard* as swearing?"

Grace chortled. "In this case it's merely descriptive. How'd he get out?"

"Said he was on probation."

Grace held her shoulders. "Tulip, you must call the police."

After the police left, Grace made a pot of coffee. They sat at the kitchen table, Grace's lips moving intently. Hand trembling, Tulip managed a sip. Same coffee, pot, and water, but it was better than when she made it. How did Grace do it? The kids would be home soon. Tulip should be starting supper.

Grace touched her arm. "Tulip, you're not listening. You've got to do what the police said. Call the probation officer. You have to tell him what Calvin did to you! He needs to know. Tulip, you must!"

Tulip put sugar in her coffee and sipped. "I'll dial, but you have to talk." Grace must use four heaping scoops of coffee to a pot.

Grace picked up the phone and twirled the dial. Tulip heard a faint ring, the murmur of Grace's voice. "Yes, the police asked her to call…gone for the day?" She hung up and took Tulip's hand. "Mr. Thomas, that's his name. You are to call first thing tomorrow."

Grace was expecting Tulip to tell a strange man that her brother had raped her. Did she have to go on the radio and broadcast it? She wouldn't, couldn't think about it now. "The kids can't see this mess. I've got to fumigate, get the bottles out of here."

Grace nodded. "Yes. I'll take the empties home. But tomorrow you *must call.*"

Tulip shook her head. Grace reached for her. Nuzzled against Grace's soft breasts, comforted by her vanilla scent, Tulip felt protected, childlike. Grace took Tulip's face in her hands, gazed into her eyes. "I'll be over in the morning and sit with you while you call. Do you understand?"

Tulip slept on the couch. She needed to be close to the door. If Calvin came back, she had to protect her children. They must never know of his existence.

The next morning, dazed, she stumbled around getting the kids off to school. As they left, Grace came up the walk. Tulip followed Grace into the kitchen where Grace poured herself a cup of coffee, took a sip, and grimaced.

"Lousy?" Tulip asked.

Not to be sidetracked by small talk, Grace handed her the phone. "Once it's done you'll feel better."

Tulip had difficulty finding the right numbers. It took several tries before the phone buzzed in her ear. No answer. Finally a receptionist piped, "Probation Department." It took a long time for her to sort out that Tulip should talk to Mr. Thomas. The receiver was clammy, Tulip's face dripping sweat. When the receptionist finally rang this Mr. Thomas, he didn't answer. Tulip sighed in relief. Grace wagged her finger at Tulip. She took a deep breath. "It's important! Please call him on the intercom."

The probation officer had a low, calm voice and did not seem perturbed that Tulip had interrupted him. With Grace's hand on her knee, Tulip croaked out her story. Mr. Thomas was silent. "Are you there?" Tulip asked.

"I had no idea. I'll call him in today. He won't be harassing you again. If he so much as calls you, let me know. He will be on his way back to prison."

The phone clunked into its cradle. Grace patted Tulip's shoulder. "You did it, Tulip."

Grace's hand felt heavy, her words distant.

Tulip was stuck in a fog. One foot in front of the other, zombie-like, she took orders and delivered meals. Returning home, she switched to hyperalert, checking her street for strange cars. All clear. Gulping air, she realized she'd been holding her breath.

Eating a Hershey bar, chocolate smeared on his face, Tucker met her at the door. He pushed an envelope at her. "D-D-Daddy told me to give this to you."

Tulip took the envelope and the bar. "He gave you candy?" Tucker nodded. "Did he ask you to get in the car?" He nodded. "Did you?" He shook his head. "Good boy!" Tucker reached for the candy. "You've had enough! Tucker, listen to me." Tulip held his chin. "Don't ever get in the car with him! And don't ever get in a car with someone you don't know! It isn't safe!"

Tulip read the note: *No job! No money! Your fault! You'll pay!*

Her heart clenched. What was the worst he could do? Kill her—the mother of his children? First Calvin, now Marshall! She had to go to the police.

"Go wash up, Tucker. I have to go out. Make sure all the doors are locked and don't let anyone in."

Tulip ran out and climbed into Old Ruby. Turning the key, she noticed chocolate melting in her hand. She stuffed it in her mouth, then snorted. She was eating candy that she'd forbidden Tucker and getting every bit as messy. Gunning the motor, she headed for the police station, where she parked in the one open space, "Police Only." She took the steps two at a time.

A jowly sergeant sat at a desk, devouring a Big Papa ham sandwich, mustard dripping onto the wrapper. Tulip plopped the note down in front of him. "I'm being threatened, my children harassed. I want you to arrest my husband!"

He caught a drip of mustard with his finger. "Your husband? You got a restraining order?"

"We're divorced."

"What'd he do?"

"Bribed my kid with candy. And this note." She waved it in front of him.

Reluctantly he put the sandwich down and took the paper. "He bought his kid candy? Not a criminal offense." He grinned and pointed to Tulip's face. "Looks like you got some."

"Read the note!"

"Lady, there isn't anything we can do until he tries something. Call when he hits you. Then we can intervene."

"I won't be alive to call!"

Fat Slob Mustard Face shook his head. "Sorry, lady. Wish we could do more." He picked up his sandwich.

Tulip pulled herself up to her full five-two. "I'm reporting this now! If you had more interest in your work than feeding your fat face, you might think of something! You make a copy and put it in the record. If he kills me, I want it documented."

Tulip flounced out of the station as a meter maid slapped a ticket on Old Ruby's windshield. "You can't give me a ticket! I was reporting a crime!" Tulip cried. The meter maid flipped the wiper over the ticket.

She wasn't going down easy. She wanted a gun but D said the kids might find it or Tulip might accidently shoot her own child. Tulip kept the hammer under her pillow, the bat by the front door. Grace gave her sliding bolt locks for the outside doors and Dennis installed them. They'd have to smash a window to get in, but Marshall had that down pat. If Marshall or Calvin did break in, she'd call the police. If she couldn't call, she would flash the lights. At night she fell into bed dog-tired, sleeping evading her. The littlest creak and she'd bolt up, checking for Calvin or Marshall lurking in the dark corners of her room.

The kids knew the drill. They were never to go anywhere alone. If they saw Marshall, they were to keep walking. If he got out of the car, run. If he caught them, scream. This also applied to strangers. And as far as her children knew, Tulip's brother was in the stranger department. She wrote a note and taped it to the fridge.

1. *Keep doors locked.*
2. *Know who is at the door before you open it.*
3. *If I'm gone and something scares you, call Grace.*
4. *If she doesn't answer, call Dennis.*
5. *If your dad comes, call police.*

She wrote the number in black crayon.

When Tulip stopped at Grace's to pick up the kids, they were at the kitchen table, gobbling pie, Tucker with a rim of cherry-red around his mouth. "You'll ruin your supper!" Tulip blurted.

Hunter glared at her. "What's for supper? Grilled cheese or mac and cheese?" She had her.

Grace was apologetic. "It was hot and smelled so good that we just couldn't resist. I'll wrap a piece for you to have *after* you've eaten." She grinned. "We wouldn't want to ruin your supper."

Constantly on alert for the bad guys, with kids and two jobs, Tulip was in overdrive. One day became the next, with her hustling at Joe's, then home to throw a meal together, then off to Kirby's. After, it was chores that were never finished. Grace was more of a mother to her children then she was. And now pie! Tulip couldn't even bake a pie.

At supper, the kids picked at their grilled cheese, and Tulip noticed Ernest's T-shirt was inside out. "Dirty," he explained.

When Tulip came dragging home, Grace had the kids in bed. She left quickly and Tulip headed to the basement. Between laundry loads, she went up to the kitchen, and, after eating Grace's damn good cherry pie, she pulled off her tennis shoes and rested her head on the table. At midnight she finished the laundry, pulled the light chain, and felt her way up the unlit stairs into the kitchen. A sliver of moonlight shone through the window. Calvin or Marshall, maybe both of them, could be outside watching her every move. She checked the bolts on the doors and went upstairs. Too tired to wash her face or brush her teeth, she peed, crawled into bed, then felt for the cold steel head of the hammer under her pillow.

In her dream the kids and Tulip were playing hide-and-seek at the park. She was It. Resting her head on a tree, she counted one, two, three, four, five, on and on. Footsteps! Hot breath on her neck.

Tulip grabbed the hammer.

"Mom, Mom! It's me!" Mouth open, eyes wide, Ernest gripped Tulip's wrist.

"Oh, my God. I'm so sorry. I was having a nightmare." She peeled his hand away and hoisted him into bed. "Sorry."

"Daddy. It was Daddy, wasn't it?"

She held him close, kissed his forehead. Gradually his breathing became heavy with little boy snorts. Stretching her legs, she tried without success to relax her body. Watching shadows in the room, she lay until sun peeked through the window.

In the morning, Ernest went from door to door checking the locks. He'd been doing so much better, going to school, getting good grades, and now *this*. Tulip wanted to reassure him, tell him that there was nothing to fear. But when she was so frightened that she'd nearly done him in with a hammer, what could she say?

Ever vigilant, Tulip kept Old Ruby locked. Before stepping out, she checked for Marshall's pickup or any other suspicious vehicle. She noted each customer entering Kirby's. Even if it was only Mitch at the store, it was a relief to know that she was never alone.

D, a grin plastered from ear to ear, sauntered across the restaurant and thumped Tulip's arm. "I know something you don't know," she sang.

"Joe promoted you to night manager?" Tulip asked wryly.

D roared with laughter. "The guy from Ford who just left, he knows Marshall. Said Marshall has a girlfriend. He's living with her. *And* he's working construction. No time for you, baby."

Tulip felt a weight, a rock—no, a mountain—crumble and topple from her shoulders. Tears flooded her eyes.

"What! I thought you'd be relieved."

"I—I am. I felt like a windup toy, wound too tight, waiting, waiting to spring. Now it's like the spring broke and I'm unraveling."

"That scum, flying under the radar, not paying child support. Now he'll have to pay."

"Maybe. And the kids won't be so damned scared."

"What about your brother?"

Why in the hell did D have to remind her of Calvin? Tulip loaded a tray with dirty dishes. "Mr. Thomas told me Calvin wouldn't bother me anymore, but I don't know where he is."

"You'd better call that probation guy."

With Marshall out of her life, Tulip could breathe, but Calvin on the loose gave her chills. D was right. Tulip needed to know where he was. She called Mr. Thomas.

"He's washing dishes at a restaurant, the Roadhouse, in Lansing, over an hour away. He knows the consequences of harassing you. I'm confident you will not hear from him."

"Thanks, thanks. You'll let me know if there's any change?" Tulip put down the phone and sank into a chair. She could not remember a time when she was not frightened, when she was not looking over her shoulder, not checking who was in the room. Gradually she became aware of the ticking clock, time passing. The kids would be home for supper. She dried her eyes, got up, and took ground beef out of the fridge. She could fry a decent hamburger. Maybe she could invite Dennis for supper.

33

It was quiet at Kirby's, almost relaxed. Customers talked in normal tones and did not talk down to Tulip. She was learning the hardware business: toilet replacement parts, how to clean oil-based paint off brushes, the list went on. She practiced what Grace called "social skills," greeting people with a genuine smile, not a Joe's pasted-on one. She tried to use proper English and above all *not to cuss*. Grace said if Tulip cursed, she was out the door. She made a game of selling something to every customer, even if it was just a roll of masking tape. After all, people didn't come to a hardware store to browse.

Tulip's only complaint was working with no-account Mitch. Just her luck to get hooked up with a lazy jerk who avoided customers and scuttled out to the parking lot to smoke. And sometimes when he came back, she caught the sweet smell of weed.

While tallying receipts one busy evening, Tulip noticed Pothead had only rung up two sales. "What happened, Mitch?" she asked.

"Guess they were just price comparing," he mumbled.

It didn't ring true. Customers didn't come to Kirby's to check prices on things they needed. They were in a hurry to get home and fix the toilet or rake the yard, whatever it was they were doing. And Mitch looked so guilty staring at the floor.

On her way to her day job the next morning, Tulip ran into Grace's house. "Mitch is not ringing up sales."

Grace's eyes opened wide. "Pocketing the cash? That can't be."

"Only two sales last night. And that's not all. He takes a lot of breaks, smokes pot. I can smell it."

"Oh, Tulip! Surely you're mistaken."

"No. You're too trusting."

"Well…" Grace tapped her coffee spoon on the table. "Of course we'll keep an eye on him, but let's not jump to conclusions."

Grace's "good" boy from a "fine" family was shit, and Grace was not going to acknowledge it.

Mitch was agitated, pacing the store, checking the door. He'd not even gone out back for a smoke. A couple of tough guys Tulip had not seen before sauntered in, their paunch bellies leading the way. Mitch slunk behind some shelves. Stalking their prey, the men weaved their way through the aisles. Black Coat grabbed Mitch by his shirt and backed him into a corner. Tulip could see his snarling face. Scar Cheek made a cutting motion across his neck. Mitch nodded. Black Coat released him.

As they left, Scar Cheek sneered at her. "Take care of our boy."

Tulip ran back to Mitch. "Are you all right?"

His face beaded with sweat, he had difficulty speaking. "Yeah…yeah. It's… it's nothin'.'"

"I saw! Those guys were out for blood. You owe them money?"

He opened his mouth as though to fess up, but instead shook his head. "You've been on my case since you got here. I ain't talking to you."

Tulip thumped his chest. "Listen, buddy. I know you're in deep shit. You'll be a hell of a lot better off if you come clean. I know Grace would help you."

"I'll handle it!" He shoved her away and limped to the back of the store.

For the rest of the shift, Mitch kept his distance. Working the register, his hands trembled—not a good sign that he was handling anything. Just before closing, he showed a young couple garbage disposals. Tulip dusted nearby, eavesdropping. "I think I want this one," the girl said.

A woman stood hesitantly in the doorway. Tulip approached her. "Good evening. May I help you?"

As Tulip locked up for the night, she asked Mitch which disposal he sold. He shrugged. "She thought it cost too much."

The next evening Tulip checked the shelf—three disposals. Hadn't there been four?

Again, Tulip told Grace that Mitch was ripping her off.

34

As Grace walked around the corner to Kirby's, she heard Sam's deep baritone. "Broad at the shoulder and narrow at the hip. Everybody knew you didn't give no lip to Big John, Big Ba-a-ad John." Ponytail swaying to the rhythm of the song, Sam swept the sidewalk. He grinned at Grace. "Caught me. What are you doing here so early?"

"You seem pretty chipper. Maggie's better?"

He smiled, a full smile, showing the gap where his tooth should have been. "Yep. Almost frisky. Just a couple more treatments." He resumed sweeping.

"Oh, Sam, I'm so glad." Wanting to ask more, she lingered, but Sam did not have the answers and she needed to focus on work. "When Mitch comes, please send him back to the office. I have to talk with him about that matter."

Grace made a cup of tea and sat at Kirby's desk. She dreaded confronting Mitch. Kirby would have known what to do. Sam was preoccupied with Maggie and didn't seem to have an opinion. Tulip was certain Mitch was on drugs, even stealing. But she was excitable and jumped to conclusions. She had no proof. Grace would see what Mitch had to say but would also check the inventory.

There was a loud knock. Grace clasped her hands tightly in her lap. "Come in, Mitch."

Prudence flew into the room. Her hair hung limp, her face pale.

"What's the matter?" Grace asked.

"I couldn't sleep last night. I have to talk to you about Dennis and that—that woman."

"Tulip?"

"She's too old for him, and the children…I don't want him hurt."

"What do you mean?"

"He won't listen to me."

Prudence, tracking her to work to lament about Dennis—it was too much. Grace's inclination was to tell her that she was a meddling mother and dismiss her from the office. Grace barely managed to be civil. "You don't want to get into a power struggle that will drive him closer to Tulip. He has to sort it out."

"He has no idea of what he's getting into. She's a redneck, no manners." Prudence paced the length of the office. "I do have to give her credit—earning a living and raising those kids." She shook her head. "But not with *my* son. Not a ready-made family!"

Grace bristled. "I have no knowledge of any proposal. They are friends, good for each other. Call it what you like—attraction, infatuation. They are *both* responsible adults."

After Grace pried Prudence out of the office, she slumped into Kirby's chair. It felt like she'd witnessed a soap opera, with Prudence playing the neurotic, conniving mother coming between son and lover. True, Prudence was concerned for all the right reasons. Tulip was damaged, scarred. But people grow.

Grace remembered Tulip rushing over on a Sunday, her sunshine hair washed and fluffed. "Dennis is coming," she blurted. "I made lasagna before and it was awful. I want to do this right. I've got everything I need. Tell me step by step."

Grace laughed. "It's four-thirty. You can't make the sauce and bake lasagna by supper."

Tulip's eyes flew open. "I've got an hour and a half."

"No, silly, the sauce should simmer for at least that long."

"Ohhh."

"I have sauce in the freezer."

"You'd give it to me?"

Grace pawed through the frozen food. "Thaw it in hot water. Bake the casserole at 350 for an hour and it should be delicious." She took out a notepad and wrote directions.

Tulip studied the recipe. She grimaced. "But…do you have some extra parmesan cheese?"

At six Grace stood at the kitchen window and watched Dennis lope to Tulip's. Tucker charged out of the house and banged into him. Laughing, Dennis hugged him. As Grace boiled water for her bedtime herbal tea, she just happened to see Dennis leaving Tulip's.

Late the next morning, Grace answered her work phone. "The lasagna was the best!" Tulip exclaimed. "'Course, not as good as yours. But I redeemed myself. Thanks, Grace." The phone clicked.

Tulip was blossoming, even trying out a new word—redeemed. Grace shivered. She remembered the aftermath of Calvin's visit, beer bottles strewn about the living room, Tulip's face drained white.

Interrupting her thoughts, the office door swung open. Mitch limped in, his greasy hair leaking out from under a Tigers baseball cap. Grace's gaze was drawn to the dagger tattoo just below his sleeve. Unable to stop herself, she pointed to the tattoo. "I told you to keep that dagger covered when you're at work."

"You wanted to see me?"

"Sit down." She had not meant to be so confrontational. "Mitch, we need to talk. Are you not feeling well?"

"What do you mean?"

"You've slacked off. You're often late. You haven't shaved, your hair…is something wrong?"

He stroked his chin. "Nothing, nothing. She's been complaining, hasn't she?"

"She?"

His knees jiggled. "She don't like me. And you should be looking at what she does."

"You've been taking a lot of cigarette breaks. Sales are down."

He clamped his hands on his knees. "Down after she came. It's her word against mine."

"Something's bothering you." Grace waited. "Those men who came to the store…you're not on drugs, are you?"

He shook his head. "She's saying that, too?"

Grace leaned forward. "You don't have to talk to me, but I am your employer. You must clean up and take fewer breaks. Sam was sweeping this morning. That's your job."

"So I'll get my act together." He rose. "You done?"

Dragging his right leg, Mitch left the office. Grace felt like a mean old woman. She'd known Mitch since he was a boy, when he tagged along with his dad. He'd started as a decent employee but had slowly gone downhill, getting in later and withdrawing. She'd been too filled with sorrow to intervene or to even notice. Now, rather than taking responsibility for his slovenly behavior, he was blaming Tulip.

Grace's tendency would have been to bury herself in guilt. But this time she felt a certain distance, a sardonic sort of humor. It was as if she were watching a soap opera: Tulip threatened by her ex-husband and her crazy brother; her romance with Dennis; Prudence's hysteria; Mitch possibly stealing and abusing drugs, being threatened by gangsters; even Maggie's illness. Who was she in this drama—a spent old lady, the narrator, the one with no life of her own?

35

As Tulip poured her first cup of coffee, Grace rapped on the door. "It's me. Let me in." Still in her housecoat, Grace breezed into the kitchen. "We need to talk." She poured herself a cup of coffee and parked herself at the table. "Sit down, Tulip."

Tulip's heart skipped a beat. "What...what have I done?"

Grace smoothed her hair. "I must be a sight, but I just figured it out—a way to solve both our problems." She beamed at Tulip. "How would you like to work full time at Kirby's?"

Tulip's mouth fell open.

Grace sighed. "You were right. Mitch has been stealing. Sam caught him selling a toilet and pocketing the cash."

"He stole a toilet?"

"He's on drugs. He admitted it, seemed relieved to be caught. We estimated what he owes and he signed a statement. His dad checked him into the hospital's new psychiatric unit. I told him we wouldn't press charges, providing he gets clean and starts to reimburse us."

"Fat chance of that."

"Tulip, everybody deserves a chance."

The moment Grace left, Tulip dialed D. "I got news!" she hollered.

"It's a little early."

"It's after eight."

"I'm not working today. I don't have kids. We're still in bed."

Tulip felt heat rise to her face. "Oh! I'll call back later."

"What is it?"

"I'm quitting Joe's. I'm going to work for Grace."

D heehawed into the phone. "Kathy! Wake up! She's leaving Joe's." D's laughter came in short bursts.

Tulip had expected D would be a might upset about her leaving. Some friend she was. "I don't know what's so funny!" Tulip slammed down the phone.

B-r-r-ring. If she thought Tulip was talking to her—! *B-r-r-ring, b-r-r-ring, b-r-r-ring.* Tulip picked up. "What?"

"I quit yesterday."

"You quit? And you didn't tell me?"

"After you left, Joe saw me peck Kathy on the cheek. He called me queer. I told him I wouldn't work for a homophobic, male chauvinist pig and walked out. I was trying to figure out how to tell you. I didn't want you mad at me."

"You were worrying about leaving me?" Tulip heard Kathy chortle in the background. "Tulip, this is too good! We do the work of four. We're leaving him high and dry."

"What are you going to do?"

"Kathy and I have some money. And she has your monthly house payments. We're going to open a little sandwich shop—call it D and Kathy's." Tulip heard a thud like maybe Kathy had punched her in the arm. D laughed. "Or maybe Kathy and D's. Customers from Joe's will follow me. I'll make cinnamon rolls, great desserts."

Tulip was not abandoning D. They were both moving on to better things. Tulip shivered with delight—working full time at Kirby's, a great employer, dependable pay, and a chance to learn. Maybe Grace could teach her how to do the books.

Walking into the restaurant, Tulip felt a chill. Joe, wearing an apron, was scrubbing tables. "Late!" he muttered.

"I'm not late! You're in a lousy mood."

"The dyke quit, and I'm sick of you being late."

"She doesn't have a name? Just a shit-ass label?"

"Smartmouth, do you want to keep your job?"

"Actually…" Tulip tapped her fingers on the counter. "I'm giving notice."

"Notice?"

"Yeah, I'm quitting."

"*You're* quitting?"

"Yeah…I'm quitting."

"No!"

"If you behave yourself, I'll stay a week till you can train someone."

"You little cunt!"

Tulip rose to her full height and spoke very slowly. "I believe that calling someone *that* name is nasty and *that* says nothing about four years of butt-patting."

He took a step back and looked at her, *really* looked at her. "You never complained before."

"You never heard me."

"Is it a raise you're after?"

"I got a good job, one where I'll be treated like a human being."

"Ten cents?"

Tulip shook her head.

Wordless, Joe watched as she slipped the apron over her head and tied a perfect bow. I'll give you a quarter, tops."

Grinning, Tulip curtsied. "I am so pleased you appreciate me. I'll expect it on my check, but I am out of here in a week." She headed for the kitchen.

"You fucking bitch! Demanding a raise the week you check out!"

Tulip turned and stuck her finger in his face. "Yeah, Joe, watch your language! You're losing two of the best waitresses in Ypsilanti." She spoke slow and loud like she did to Tucker when he did not understand. "You *will* give me a raise. I will stay one week and help train a couple of girls. And you *will* put it in writing."

Joe's face swelled, a red balloon ready to pop. He smashed his fist on the counter.

Tulip chortled. "Don't hurt yourself."

Reaching for his Camels, Joe stormed out the door. Smoking cigarette after cigarette, he paced back and forth in front of the restaurant. Finally he came in and huddled by the register, shuffling through old applications.

Ignoring his tantrum, Tulip waited on late-breakfast customers. D's stingy old couple, Herman and Mary, came in and ordered the he-man breakfast with an extra plate. "Who gets the third egg?" Tulip asked.

Her smile fitting into smile lines, Mary nodded toward Herman.

"Look at his belly, and you're such a skinny little thing! You should have the extra egg. You want the cook to put it on separate plates so you don't have to split it up?"

"I didn't know you could do that."

"It's my last week. I can make it happen."

"Where's D?" Herman asked. "She usually waits on us."

"Quit."

"Both of you? What'll we do without you? You're always having such a good time."

Remembering D's complaints about stingy Herman, Tulip laughed. "You'll get used to the new waitresses. And you can eat at D's new sandwich shop."

Though there was too much work for one, Tulip flitted around in a happy haze, doing what she'd done for years, the trays light and her smile real. She served the old folks each a plate, one egg for Mary, two for Herman. "Your pheasant under glass."

When they shuffled out, Herman leaning heavily on his cane, Mary holding his other arm, they paused. "Goodbye," Mary said. "We won't be in again before you leave. We're flying out to visit our daughter in Boston."

"Not goodbye. I'll help you when you come into Kirby's. Have a good time at your daughter's." They were so frail. Would she see them again, and at Kirby's?

Clearing the table, Tulip noted that Mary had not eaten her whole egg, and when she picked up Herman's plate, she found five ones stacked in a neat pile. She couldn't wait to give it to D. The money seemed like a final goodbye, made it real. She had worked with D for four years. They had laughed and bitched together, an intimacy Tulip would miss.

Later that day, still in uniform, Ken came in and hunkered down in a booth.

"You haven't been in for a while," Tulip said.

"Didn't think I was welcome."

"I've noticed the patrol cars on my street."

"High-crime area."

"Guess it was. Thanks. Marshall and Calvin are sort of out of commission. It's better now. And I have good news." She did a pirouette. "I'm quitting! I'm working full time for Grace."

His smile filled his face. "Good! You need to get out of here. You deserve better. And Tulip…I'm sorry." He reached for her hand. "Forgiven?"

Tulip shook his hand, a firm shake. The thrill was gone, but his hand felt warm and reassuring. Ken had tried to protect her from Marshall, helped her feel again. "Truce. But I've got to bus these tables before quitting time."

As Tulip left work, Joe slammed down the phone. "Those damn girls, sound like they're ten."

"The paper," Tulip said.

"What?"

"No raise, no waitress."

He gaped at her. "You're not serious?"

She nodded. "Not that I don't trust you, but I want the raise in writing."

He picked up a notepad, scribbled on it, tore the paper out, and clapped it in her hand.

"Thank you, Joe." Outside, she burst into laughter. *So there, Grace, I didn't fight. I didn't run.* Tulip was not leaving the guys in the kitchen in the lurch, and she had a raise to boot. She would have to go home and call D.

For Tulip the week passed in a hectic blur. Nothing Joe did riled her. She almost felt sorry for him. Her regulars expressed disappointment at her leaving but seemed pleased at her opportunity. Several traded at Kirby's and said they'd stop in. They were seeing her in a different light. Or maybe she was seeing herself differently.

Joe hired a shy blonde who barely uttered a word. At lunch she dropped a tray. Soup splattered. Bowls broke. Joe hollered. She did not finish the day. Finally, on Thursday Martha started work. Experienced and efficient, five-foot-eight and two hundred pounds, she could take care of herself. Joe sure as hell daren't pat her ass.

36

⌒⊙

Flaunting a fur coat that was too warm for the day, Mrs. Patel, wife of St. Joe's noted cardiac surgeon, breezed into Kirby's. Tulip closed the register and hurried to the imperious woman. "Hi, can I help you with something?"

Mrs. Patel peered down at her. "I don't know. *Can* you?"

Tulip's brows shot up. Grace, having heard the interaction, stepped forward. But Tulip spoke calmly. "What do you need?"

"Shelves, picture wire."

"Sounds like you've got a project going. I have a house that needs a lot. What'd you do to yours?"

Too familiar—Tulip's being too familiar, thought Grace.

As though she smelled a bad odor, Mrs. Patel sniffed. "Renovated the kitchen—tile floor and custom cupboards with decorative tile for the counter."

"Real nice," Tulip replied.

A customer tapped Grace's shoulder. "Where are your light switches?" When Grace returned from the back, Tulip was ringing up Mrs. Patel's sale.

"I'm not so sure I can do this myself," the woman said.

Tulip grinned her lopsided grin. "It's easy. But you said your husband was a surgeon. This would be a snap for him."

"I don't know. I'm all thumbs and Robert is seldom home. He hates to be bothered with this sort of thing. I need to hire someone. You wouldn't want to moonlight?"

"Can't. Busy, divorced, three kids."

"Really?" Mrs. King's voice went icy. "Must be hard being a *single* mother and working."

Tulip looked her in the eye. "And it must be hard living with a guy whose good with his hands but won't hang a picture."

Grace clasped her hand over her own mouth, and prayed Tulip would not get into an altercation on your first full day.

Mrs. Patel laughed. "How right you are. Robert doesn't do much around the house."

"Yeah. I was married to a jerk. But I know a college student, real handy; he might do it for you."

Grace grimaced. *Tulip, enough. Leave it alone.*

"You're sure he's capable?"

"Fixed my porch, my roof, caulked the bathroom. No complaint. Dennis Goodwin."

"Oh, Dr. Goodwin's son! Of course." She put the change in her purse and snapped it shut. Eyebrows raised, she questioned Tulip. "But wasn't he in some kind of trouble?"

"He's capable, responsible. You'll like him."

Mrs. Patel nodded. "If you say so."

Tulip wrote down the Goodwins' number and handed it to her. Mrs. Patel left the store, placing one foot exactly in front of the other.

"How does she walk like that, and in high heels?" Tulip asked.

"What I want to know is how you warmed her up."

Tulip's blue eyes twinkled. "Got her off her high horse. And what's so damn special about *custom* cupboards and *decorative* tile? The price?"

"No cursing, Tulip."

"You're not a customer."

"You might as well get used to it. And you really shouldn't be so outspoken with customers."

"What are you talking about?

"You implied her husband was less than helpful."

"He's a jerk."

"Not your business. You could have offended her."

"She was talking down to me."

"This isn't Joe's, Tulip. You have to always be courteous."

"I know that."

"Then act like it!" Grace hurried to the office and closed the door to muffle her laughter. Tulip was bullheaded, and Grace could not have her chasing customers away. Still, Tulip had been working evenings and Sam had not complained about her behavior. Mrs. Patel had not been offended. And she *had* been condescending. That remark about being a single mother, the way she stressed "single." Tulip had called her on it, and the woman accepted it.

The store wasn't doing the business it had when Kirby was alive. Grace hoped she was doing the right thing, hiring Tulip full time. She needed help and Tulip was reliable, honest, even personable. Yet she was crude and coarse. "Damn" might explode out of her as though lying in wait for her to open her mouth. Still, she saved it for Sam or Grace. The regulars—contractors, electricians, plumbers, carpenters—enjoyed Tulip, teased her. On occasion she was offended and bristled at them but they took it in stride.

Stamping her feet and rubbing her hands, Tulip barged in from sweeping the sidewalk. "Snow's too wet. It sticks to the broom. Besides, November's too early for snow."

"You should have worn gloves," Grace said.

"Hunter lost hers; I loaned her mine." Tulip pirouetted around the broom. "I'm a good mother."

Grace smiled. Occasionally Tulip displayed a childlike pleasure that warmed her heart. What would Tulip be like if she'd not been abused? What if Grace had been her mother?

Saved from her futile musings, the door opened and Bill Swartz shuffled in, a hulk of a man sprinkled with white.

"You're dragging in snow," Tulip complained.

"Sorry." With his head down and stocking cap pulled nearly to his eyes, it was impossible to see his expression. "Roofing, ran out of nails," he mumbled.

"You shouldn't be doing that on a day like this. The wind'll blow you off the roof."

"Wouldn't be such a loss."

"What do you mean?"

Bill walked to the nails and looked in the bins. "Should have known. Not the right kind."

"We're hardware, not a roofing factory." Tulip turned away.

Uh-oh. Tulip, you don't know what you're dealing with. Grace intervened. "Bill, how is Cynthia?"

He took off his cap, revealing empty gray eyes. "Bad, real bad. We don't know how much longer."

"I'm so sorry, Bill."

"She doesn't complain, just lies there getting skinnier. Some days she's lucid, some days not. She's so gentle even her ramblings are sweet. I can't do a damn thing to help her." His pleading eyes meant Grace's.

As though he thought she could help. Grace touched his arm. "I'm sure your being there is what she needs."

He shook his head, snowflakes sprinkling the floor. "It's hard to bear." He straightened. "Sorry...I forgot about Kirby. Does it get better?"

And Rickey, don't forget Rickey. Grace nodded. She could not, would not tell him that the ache in her heart lived on and, like an infant, cried out when she least expected. Bill enveloped her in his workman's arms. Her face buried in his damp coat, she inhaled the snowy out-of-doors. She patted his back, more of a thump through his mackinaw. "Your strong, you'll get through this."

"I know. I know." He dropped his arms and stumbled from the store, leaving a trail of water.

Tulip was at Grace's side, her voice tense. "His wife's dying?"

Grace shook her head. "Maggie and now Cynthia. Sometimes life is too hard. They caught Cynthia's cancer too late. They just married a couple of years ago. Bill's in his late thirties. Shy. When he roofed Cynthia's house, she saw past his gruff demeanor. He reminds me of Kirby." Tears pooled in Grace's eyes. "He knew we didn't have those nails. He just needed an excuse to talk."

37

〜◯

S un streaming through the window woke Tulip. Humming, she dressed
hurriedly and made coffee. At seven she called the children. "Go away!
Too early!" Hunter growled. Ernest, her good boy, rolled out and dressed.

Over juice and cereal, Tulip hyped the day. "We'll see these beautiful gardens. Take a hike, have a snack, and maybe see a cowboy show at Stage Coach
Stop." Their ears perked up at that. She hurried on. "But I'm not sure how
much it costs. We can go to Adrian, eat at a Mexican restaurant. There's a
bookshop, Booknook, across the street. They have used books too. I'll buy you
all a book. Reward for doing good in school."

Tucker's head bobbed up and down. *Two on board.*

"I don't like to hike, and we can check out books at the library," Hunter
lamented.

"We've never been to a Mexican restaurant," Ernest said.

"The Grasshopper. Burritos are good, sort of like rolled-up pizza with rice
and beans."

"I hate rice and beans. I want to go to McDonald's," Hunter whined.

"It's ethnic food. We're going to get some culture."

It was summer, almost three years since Tulip had escaped Marshall. She
could not afford a real vacation, but she could take her children on a day trip.
The Irish Hills were less than two hours away. Hidden Lake Gardens was beautiful, with rolling hills and deep-green evergreens, petunias and geraniums in
full bloom. Tulip had borrowed Grace's Lincoln. She had considered asking
Dennis, but it seemed important that her family have good memories just their
own. Besides, she didn't know how much longer Dennis would be around.

With a paycheck she could count on, even without child support, Tulip was
holding house and home together. Her mothering skills had risen from a D to
a C. She hollered less and listened more. Grace and Dennis helped with that.
Nothing they said, she just watched how they treated the children. Children
were people too, just littler and more sensitive. Twelve, eleven, and ten, her
children were maturing. The school had not called Tulip about Hunter fighting

or Ernest skipping. Except for Ernest's C in English, he and Hunter had finished the year with As and Bs. Ernest loved to read but was shit-scared—oops, scared—to give an oral report. The school didn't grade Tucker, but he deserved an A for effort. And Tucker was in love. The last day of school he helped himself to a bouquet of late tulips from Grace's yard and presented it to his special-ed teacher, Ms. Gardner.

The best thing: Tulip had not seen hide nor hair of Marshall or Calvin. Maybe she could quit looking over her shoulder. Maybe not.

Hunter sat in the front seat so she wouldn't start something with the boys. As soon as they hit Highway 12, Hunter and Tucker nodded off. Tulip could see Ernest in the mirror. "How come you didn't give your oral report in English?" she asked.

"Forgot."

"Nope, not buying it. You're too responsible to pull a trick like that."

Ernest played with his unbuckled seat belt, pulling it back and forth. "Didn't want to."

"Were you scared?"

"They all look at you, and they laugh if you make a mistake."

Tulip nodded. "I had that problem. When I had to give a report in class, I could scarcely breathe, let alone speak." But Ernest hadn't been through what she went through. "Sometimes you need to tough it out." Silence. "So something's bothering you. What?"

"You wouldn't understand."

"Try me."

Ernest grimaced. "I can do stuff on my own, read and write essays. It's when people stare at me that I get all nervous."

"What's to be nervous about?"

"Counselor says I worry a lot."

"What about?" Through the mirror Tulip could see him staring out the window. "Yes?"

His voice a whisper, "Dad. That he'll hurt you."

"Oh, no, Ernest. I can take care of myself."

"Yeah." But he shook his head from side to side.

"Maybe you should talk to Ms. Parin about it."

Ernest laid his head on the seat and closed his eyes. Silence the rest of the way.

Tulip paid the admission to the Gardens. When the kids saw the pond with the swans and their babies, they came to life. Tulip handed each child a couple of pieces of bread. Remembering what Ken had told her, she instructed them not to get too close. Tucker flung both pieces in the shallow water.

"Dumbhead!" Hunter called.

Tulip tapped her bottom. Hunter and Ernest tore bread into hunks and flung it as far as they could. The swan parents swam closer, three little ones trailing behind. Tucker ran toward them.

"Stop! They'll chase you!" Tulip screamed.

Too late. The papa raced onto the shore, flapping his wings. Tucker ran toward the car. Hunter doubled over with laughter. The papa started for her. They all dashed to the safety of the car.

When Hunter refused to hike, Tulip threatened her with dishes for a week. Hunter relented. Sunlight shining through the trees, they started down the grassy path. Tucker stumbled on a broken limb, picked it up. Pretending it was a horse, he trotted down the hill. Hunter watched with contempt. Tulip's heart ached. Hunter would have loved this when younger. Too little, too late.

Tucker galloped up. "Can't catch me!" To Tulip's surprise, both Ernest and Hunter ran after him. When she entered the meadow, which was aglow in yellow wildflowers, she saw they each had a stick.

"Take that!" yelled Hunter as she whipped Ernest's stick from his hand. He tackled her and they fell to the ground laughing. Tucker galloped through the meadow whinnying.

Tulip, mesmerized by her carefree children, sat watching in the still-damp grass. Oh, for a movie camera! Brilliant flowers swayed in the gentle breeze, stretching for the sun, which played hide-and-seek with the clouds. Tucker joined the fray. The three lay laughing in the grass, trees framing the meadow— a perfect picture. *Click!* Tulip snapped it in her mind. When Hunter complained that they never did anything, Tulip could describe this moment.

The birds had made good use of the picnic table. Ernest took a tree branch and brushed it off. Tulip unwrapped peanut-butter-and-jelly crackers and waited for Hunter's complaints. Instead she spied the chips. "You got potato chips!"

Stage Coach Stop, with its rough wooden fence, imitated a Western fort. The kids hopped with excitement. A tall man wearing a cowboy hat, boots, and chaps met them at the gate.

"A c-c-cowboy!" Tucker squealed.

"Howdy, folks. Want to buy tickets?"

Tulip stopped short. "Tickets, what for?"

"Come in, see the show—a real holdup and shootout." He tipped his hat to Tucker. "I'm one of the good guys."

Ernest pointed to a woman in an old-fashioned dress boarding a stagecoach. Tucker shifted his weight from foot to foot, barely containing his excitement.

Tulip had not planned on paying just to get in. Hunter gave her a what-are-you-going-to-do-now? look. Wondering if it would have been enough to buy a camera, Tulip dug money out of her pocket. They walked into the fake Western town and down a wide dusty road lined with a general store, saloon, post office, and doctor's office, with a corral at the end of the street.

Entering the general store, Tulip cautioned the children, "We can't buy anything. It's not in our budget." It sounded better than saying they were poor or didn't have money. "Remember, we're getting books at that Booknook in Adrian."

Tucker eyed the cap guns. "I-I'd rather have a g-g-gun!"

"Guns are violent. And your teacher says you're supposed to read every day so you don't forget everything."

"Mom's right," Ernest said, putting a long-nosed gun back on the shelf. "Books last. Guns break."

In the saloon, Tulip bought one sarsaparilla. "Just to have a taste," she said.

Hunter sipped and coughed. "Tickles your nose. Don't see why they drink it."

Tucker sputtered and spit his out. Only Ernest seemed to like it. But in the end Tulip was pleased to drink it, the tangy fizz clearing her nose.

"The stagecoach is coming!" Hunter shouted.

It lumbered down the street, outlaws galloping by, shooting into the air. The outlaws closed in. Guns blazing, the sheriff darted out of the jail. Women in the coach screamed. An outlaw fell, then another. More shooting. When the outlaws were defeated, the sheriff tipped his hat to the cheering audience clustered on the wooden sidewalk.

Hunter beamed at Tulip. *Click!*

"Hungry?" Tulip asked as they rolled into Adrian on 52. After zigzagging through one-way streets, not Tulip's forte, she was relieved to see the Grasshopper sign. Luckily there were two parallel parking spaces in front, plenty of room.

It was late afternoon and the crowd had cleared. Tulip took the kids to the café part, away from the bar. Tired, hot, thirsty, and hungry, she was tempted to order a beer—certainly not a margarita—but thought better of it. They guzzled Cokes and gobbled tortilla chips, Tulip dunking hers in salsa. Memories of the restaurant were less than great, and she wondered why she'd brought the children there. Perhaps because she knew the way, or maybe she wanted a different experience. She ordered a couple of quesadillas to share and a beef burrito each. Tucker stuffed his mouth, sauce dribbling down his chin. Hunter reached over and wiped it with a napkin. Memories to store.

Loud voices from the bar disrupted Tulip's reverie. A man Marshall's size, his back to her, was arguing. He shouted, punched the air above his head. Ruby eyes flashed in the silver skull ring. Tulip gasped and frantically waved to the waitress. "The bill! Now!"

"Something wrong?"

"That guy in there." She pointed.

The fellow stood abruptly. Tulip could see him clearly. Red-faced, he stumbled drunkenly toward the exit.

"I thought it was someone I knew," Tulip said to the waitress.

"Yeah, and from the look of you, someone you'd rather not know. I'll bring your bill." She hurried to the register.

"Wh-wh-who, Mom?" Tucker asked.

"Dad, you idiot. She thought it was Dad," Hunter said.

"Don't call your brother an idiot." Tulip stood. "I'm paying, then we're going to the bookstore."

Holding Tucker's hand, Tulip jaywalked across the street to Booknook. Heedless of traffic, Hunter rushed ahead and flung open the door. A bell clanged. The huge room smelled musty sweet. Shelves lined the walls from floor almost to ceiling. Hardcovers and paperbacks were displayed on long wooden tables. A couple of stuffed chairs sat in a corner with a floor lamp. Captain's chairs circled an ancient oak table. Inviting. Tulip whiffed coffee and tracked it to a metal percolator on the counter. "Smells good."

"Would you like a cup?" A slender woman about Tulip's age, dark hair in a ponytail, stood from where she was adjusting books on a lower shelf. She poured coffee into a mug and pointed to a creamer and sugar bowl. "How about a cookie? Finch made them." She held out a china plate with miniature peanut butter cookies. Tucker reached for one.

"Say thank you," Tulip said.

"Th-th-thank you."

Smiling, the woman held out the plate to the other children.

"Who's Finch?" Hunter asked.

"My daughter. She's about your age. Are you ten?"

"Eleven. She makes cookies?"

"Sure does. Are you a cookie maker?"

"I-I-I help Miss Grace," Tucker said.

A girl clattered down the stairs. "Hey, Mom, can I go over to Angie's?"

"Don't holler, Finch. Come here." She put her arm on the girl's shoulder and spoke softly. "It's nearly suppertime. Maybe tomorrow, *after* you've cleaned your room."

"Aw, Mom."

"You heard me, Finch." The mother spoke with authority but did not raise her voice. Turning to Tulip, she asked, "May I help you with something?"

"How do you get books off the top shelves?"

"Ladder," a gruff-voiced man said. An old guy with shaggy white hair sat at the table doing paperwork.

"Your store?" Tulip asked.

"Supposed to be." He pointed to the clerk and spoke just loud enough for her to hear. "She's the real boss."

"It's a great store. I've never seen anything like it."

"Where you from?"

"Ypsilanti."

"You don't have bookstores in Ypsilanti?"

Tulip thought of the trip to Ann Arbor and the unused gift certificate in her wallet. "Borders in Ann Arbor. Brand-new."

"Damn store!" The gruff old goat glared at her, as though she'd been the one who cussed. "You liked it?"

"Yeah. But they didn't offer me cookies or coffee when I walked in."

"Humph. Look all you want." He bent over the invoices.

The pretty woman shook her head. "He thinks Borders will hurt our business. I tell him we're different, hands-on. And we stock used books."

"That's all I can afford. We've been to Stage Coach Stop. They held me up."

"We've never been." She sounded wistful.

"You live this close and never gone?"

She shook her head. "Finch, show the children the used books we just got in."

Finch was spindly, pixyish. She too had dark hair, straight, shoulder-length with bangs hanging past her eyebrows. She looked into Tucker's broad, vacant face and seemed to know he wasn't quite right. "Over here. Do you like animals?"

Tucker nodded. "I g-got a c-cat. Sh-she had k-kittens."

Finch rose on her tiptoes and looked Tucker in the eye. "I have a favorite book. Mom reads it for story hour. She's going to let me do it one of these Saturdays when there aren't too many kids. *The Velveteen Rabbit*. It's about a stuffed rabbit that turns into a real rabbit. Love makes it real." Eyes sparkling, she flipped through a few pages.

"What are you interested in?" The woman pointed to Tulip's T-shirt. "Women Power. Perhaps you'd like some feminist literature, Betty Friedan?"

Tulip touched the faded words on her shirt, the same she'd worn when she came to Adrian with Ken. "A friend gave it to me. I don't read much. I'm a single mom, no time for all that feminist stuff."

The woman continued, "I couldn't live without books. A used copy of *A Tree Grows in Brooklyn* just came in, the first book I read when I came to Booknook. Everybody likes it. It's about a poor but very bright girl making her way in the world. There's an old movie of it."

They left with seven books, Tulip's last twenty bucks. Grace wouldn't mind her waiting till payday to fill up the Lincoln. In the car Tulip started singing. "I'm a man of means, by no means king of the road." As they passed McDonald's on the north side of Adrian, they were all singing, Hunter's soprano and Ernest's alto ringing true, Tucker with off-key gusto. By the time they reached Clinton, the children were sleeping, Tucker snoring softly.

Tulip was intrigued by Booknook, so unlike Borders. Hands-on, the woman had said. Sort of like Kirby's was different from Ace's. The Booknook woman, Sparrow, called Tulip by name and chatted a bit. She was gentle yet firm with her daughter, expecting Finch to help out. Sparrow had never been to Stagecouch Stop. That seemed odd. Would that old guy not give her time off? Did she not have the money? Not Tulip's business. Sparrow's influence was obvious throughout the store. Coffee and cookies were a welcoming touch. Maybe Kirby's should offer coffee to customers.

As Hunter headed up for bed she asked, "Mom, can you make burritos?"

Tulip grinned. "Maybe. They shouldn't be too hard. Maybe we could do it together."

Tulip was exhausted, but in a good way. She sat on the porch in the cool night air, cherishing the day's memories. Dennis strode out of his house and up the walk, his snug T-shirt showing his sinewy arms.

Resting his foot on the porch, he handed Tulip a bottle of Boone's Farm. "Ernest told me you had a great time in the Irish Hills."

Tulip waved the bottle at him. "Trying to seduce me?"

He sighed. "You didn't ask me."

"You're mad? I thought about it, but it didn't seem right."

"Why? The kids like me. It would have been fun."

"I wanted to, but it's not that simple. The kids need good family memories. You're not a member of this family, Dennis."

"So what are you saying?"

If she'd been honest, she would have told him that she missed him, that his being there would have made the day complete. "You're a good friend—the best of the male variety. You help me out, make me laugh. My kids adore you. But you'll be going away soon—gone, kaput. You're going to be a doctor, worlds apart from us."

He held her face in his hands. "I don't need to go anywhere. I *will* finish school, but I don't have to be a doctor." He kissed her, his lips gentle on hers. "Oh, Tulip, you are as skittish as an alley cat." He tenderly smoothed her face, then worked his hands up and down her back.

Standing on her toes, their bodies fit perfectly. Tulip nuzzled her face into his neck. He kissed her, his tongue finding hers. A tingling in her breasts, between her legs. She urged him toward the door and into the living room where they fell onto the couch. He worked her bra loose, unzipped her jeans. Her breath came in spurts.

"Mom, Mom, I got a stomachache." Ernest stood at the landing.

Tulip unwrapped herself from Dennis, pulled her shirt over her jeans, stood on shaky legs, and walked up the stairs. "Let's get some Pepto-Bismol."

Ernest waved to Dennis, then followed his mother into the bathroom. Tulip measured out the medicine, settled him back into bed, and kissed his forehead. "You'll be all right. Go to sleep now."

Aching with desire, Tulip crept downstairs. Dennis was in the kitchen pouring wine into fruit jars. He shook his head. "A close call. It wouldn't be good if one of your kids found you making love with a nonfamily person."

"I do have a lock on my door."

Dennis put his arms on Tulip's shoulders. "Do you really think Ernest had a stomachache? Maybe he heard us and was frightened. What if we're in your bedroom and Tucker tries to get in and your door's locked? He might think it's Marshall hurting you." He stroked her cheek. "You're right. I'm not a part of this family...at least not yet."

He sat and pulled her into his lap. Her face nestled in his neck, he stroked her back. The clock ticked. The faucet dripped. Tulip's body ached for him. "Marshall beat me in front of the kids. Hit them. Do you think they're going to be scared seeing us kissing?"

"Tulip, we were pretty intense. Some things need to be private. We'll figure out a way."

She scooted off his lap and onto a chair. He lifted his glass. "To the future!"

Alone in bed, she couldn't get Dennis out of her mind. She imagined them, just the two of them, at Hidden Lake Gardens, walking hand in hand in the woods. In the meadow he spread out a blanket, opened a picnic basket, and laid out cheese and wine. He folded her into his arms, his kiss deep but gentle. But she could not hold onto the dream. Tossing and turning, she tangled herself in the sheet. If this was love, she could do with plain old sex. She rose and crept down to the kitchen. She mimicked Dennis. "Gotta be quiet. Don't want to scare those kids." Her jar was on the table. Mr. Perfect had set his in the sink. She poured the last of the wine into her lone glass.

Tulip asked Sam if she could take a couple of hours for lunch. "I've got something I need to do."

"Sure, it's slow. Take all the time you need." He glanced up from the receipts he was sorting. "Geez, Tulip, you look great. Got a date?"

She snorted. "Me? No luck with men."

"You're a gutsy girl, Tulip, cute and funny. Some guy would be lucky to get you."

"Do you think so?"

His eyes crinkled. "Sure do. Don't sell yourself short."

"Too bad you're old and taken, Sam." Basking in his laughter, Tulip walked to the back of the store.

In the restroom she studied herself in the mirror. She did look different from two years ago. She'd had dark circles under her eyes then, bags even, looked forty and unkempt. Now she preened in the mirror, tossing her glossy hair, the waves softening her face. Fitted jeans emphasized her flat tummy and slim hips; a new blue shirt brought out the cloud-blue of her eyes. Although her teeth were not toothpaste white like Dennis's, they were even. She smiled at the attractive woman in the mirror. *Click.* Respectable women had boyfriends and lovers. Dennis *was* over twenty-one, single, cared about her, and had the best interests of her children at heart.

Tulip swept past Sam and practically skipped the few blocks home, where Dennis waited on the sidewalk. She took his hand and led him up the porch steps and into Old Grouchy.

"You sure it's safe?" he asked.

She pecked him on the lips. "I told you this morning. They're at swimming lessons—two hours."

38

◦⌒◦

G race sat in the living room drinking coffee. She no longer lingered in the kitchen mornings, her favorite time of the day with Kirby. There was a mewing at the door. Fluff pranced in, rubbed against her legs, and sniffed Tabby's empty dish. "Smart kitty. You know where the good stuff is." Stroking Fluff from head to tail, Grace felt her backbone in spite of all that soft fur. "You are a skinny thing. Those kitties took a lot out of you." She smiled at the thought of how Tucker loved those kittens. He had named them, and when they'd been given away, he informed both children and their parents what each kitten liked. "P-pet Boots under his chin," he'd said. After Tulip hustled the last kitten out the door, Tucker stalked upstairs and did not speak to his mother the remainder of the day.

"Let's see if we can fatten you up." Grace retrieved an open can of tuna from the fridge and spooned it into a cracked yellow bowl. Fluff lapped greedily, then licked her paws, stretched, and walked toward the door. "Eat and run. That's the sort of guest you are." As she passed Pepper napping in the sunlight, Fluff batted the pup with her paw. Pepper's eyes sprang open. Fluff batted her again. Pepper leapt up, skidded on the rug, and hurtled after her. Pepper caught Fluff under the kitchen table, the two toppling head over heels, and they were off again. Grace burst into laughter. She couldn't wait to see the expression on Tucker's face when she told him.

Leaving the two in their tumble, Grace poured a second cup of coffee. Avoiding the kitchen table, she sat in a chair across from Kirby's overstuffed arm chair. There was a single knock. The door burst open. Grace wagged her finger at Tulip. "Still don't wait till I answer?"

Tulip grimaced. "Sorry. I'm in a hurry. Could you sit the kids tonight?"

"What's going on?"

"I'm…going out."

"Dennis?"

"Yes, but just as friends."

"Are you sure it's wise?"

"Well! I didn't expect an interrogation. Forget it!" She turned on her heel.

"Tulip, stop! Of course I'll sit."

Face flushed, Tulip picked at a string on her shirt. "You think I'm too old for him?"

"Do you?"

"No! Well…maybe. But he's more grown up than Marshall ever was. And he likes my kids. He's good with Tucker."

Grace nodded. "Well, he *is* mature. And he cares about you, and the children too."

"You think?" Tulip sat down. "You got more coffee?"

Grace led her into the kitchen and poured a cup. When someone was with her, Grace didn't mind relaxing in the kitchen, but this would not be a relaxing encounter.

Tulip drummed her fingers on the table. "You tell me I need to talk about things, so here goes." She breathed deeply. "I'm almost ten years older than Dennis, uneducated, and have three kids. One's retarded. I had an abusive husband who'd like to kill me, and a pervert brother who'd do the same. I am not a good catch." She paused for breath. "Dennis is normal, smart, and wants to be a doctor. He has umpteen years of college ahead of him. Oh, and I forgot his mother. Prudence hates me. I know Dennis can't marry me." She sighed, flattened her hands on the table. "Does that sum it up?"

"Oh, Tulip! You and Dennis *are* at different stages in your life, but you are a diamond in the rough, a determined, caring person. If you and Dennis have something real, you can work it out. Prudence would come around. Just don't rush into anything."

As though to leave, Tulip jumped up.

"Wait a minute! I thought you wanted to talk about this."

"I just did! Will you babysit or not?

Grace nodded.

"Good. Can't be late to work. Don't want my boss mad at me."

"Wait." Grace pointed to Fluff lying in the sun on the floor. "Take your cat with you."

Tulip snatched the cat and rushed out the door.

Grace could not countenance Tulip demeaning herself and had countered, more optimistic than she felt. Perhaps Tulip had sensed it and taken flight.

Was she too damaged to trust and love? She was young, too vital to be alone. Feeling a headache coming on, Grace went to the living room and took refuge in Kirby's chair, resting her head against the back. As though to comfort her, Pepper curled up at her feet. Tabby padded out of the bedroom and mewed by her empty bowl.

That evening Tucker met Grace at his door. "C-c-can we p-pop corn?"

"Sounds like fun. Where's your mom?"

"G-getting dressed."

In the bathroom, Tulip rubbed rouge onto her flushed cheeks, freckles soaking up the red. Dime-store makeup—lipstick, eyeliner, mascara, and powder—was clustered on the sink.

"D—d—drats, I just can't get this right. I look like a circus clown."

"Drats, a new word?" Grace picked up the eyeliner, still sealed in its packet. "Did you buy out the store? She pointed to the toilet seat. "Sit down. Let me do it. "

Tulip sat and stared at the floor.

"You have to look at me." Grace sponged Tulip's face with a warm washrag, then carefully applied lotion and blush. "A little goes a long way."

Tulip gazed at her glowing reflection and grinned. "I don't look half bad."

"You look lovely. The blue in the dress matches your eyes."

"Do you like it?"

"As I said, you look lovely!"

Tulip turned back to the mirror. "Click."

"What's that about?"

"Memory picture. I'm collecting good memories." She hugged Grace. "Thanks."

The doorbell rang. Tulip ran down the stairs.

Passing Tulip's bedroom, Grace noted clothes strewn across the bed and imagined Tulip's frenzied selection of something to wear. From the landing, she watched as Dennis handed Tulip a bouquet—marigolds and zinnias. From Grace's yard? He glanced up and winked. Hunter ran to get a jar of water for the flowers. Dennis and Tulip stood awkwardly by the door.

Grace walked downstairs to the kitchen for scissors and snipped the tag hanging from Tulip's cardigan. "The two of you go on. Have a good time. The kids and I have corn to pop."

The children followed their mother onto the porch. Clearly they would have liked to have gone too. "Now you kids behave yourself," Tulip called as she led the way to the car.

Grace glimpsed Prudence peeking out from behind her drape. Well, at least she had loaned Dennis her Cadillac.

39

⤳

D ennis opened Tulip's door and skipped around the car. She scooted to his side, unlatched his lock, and slid back.

Dennis's onyx eyes sparkled. "I've never seen you in a dress before."

Heat rose in Tulip's cheeks. "Sears, sale rack. It's a sundress, but with the sweater, I can wear it when it's colder."

Dennis reached for Tulip's sweaty hand. She leaned back on the plush upholstery and squeezed his warm hand. "No one ever gave me flowers."

He grinned. "Stolen. Next time roses, or better yet, tulips."

Driving on Washtenaw toward Ann Arbor, Dennis raved about the RFD Boys, the band they were going to see. "They're college students, regulars at the Pretzel Bell, but tonight they're playing at the Ark. You'll like them. You're a bluegrass sort of girl."

Tulip did not say she was country.

The Ark was in an old house, not too different from Old Grouchy, but hopefully the roof was intact. People were crowded into a living room and dining area. Dennis weaved through the mass to a small table with mismatched wooden chairs. Four young guys in jeans and boots, three wearing cowboy hats, walked onto the stage. When God had passed out instruments, he'd tossed the banjo to the big guy and the bass to the runt. They tuned up. Music exploded. The crowd clapped. Tulip cringed. *Too loud, too close.*

Dennis stroked her arm. "Are you all right?" With his thumb, he gently tapped out the music on Tulip's hand. She inhaled deeply and banished the squinty-eyed fat guy at the next table out of her mind. Giving herself over to the music, she tapped her foot. The guitar player sang "Are you missing me?," his voice clear and sweet. What the little guy, Paul, lacked in size he made up in energy, beating on the bass. His song "I'm My Own Grandpa" had her in spasms.

After, Dennis asked, "Are you hungry?"

"Starved." She did not tell him that she'd been too nervous to eat.

"Me too. I'd like to take you to Weber's, but I spent most of my money on tickets and beer. How about the Dag-Wood—no, I mean the Fleetwood Diner?"

"Dag-Wood, Fleetwood?"

"They just changed the name. It's in a trailer. The Dag-Wood Company in Toledo manufactured a bunch of diners. Don't know where Fleetwood comes from."

The Fleetwood was a dirty trailer with a griddle, counter, and tables along the side—a smaller, sleazier version of Joe's. The place was hopping: a group of kids in faded jeans and pierced ears, the boys' hair long and shaggy; an older, nicely dressed couple eating burgers; a bum drinking coffee and mumbling to himself. One empty table in the corner.

"The food's cheap and good. See the guy in the suit? He's a professor. Those are students," Dennis said, pointing to the kids. "The guy with the coffee is homeless. It's a cultural melting pot."

"Cultural melting pot?"

"Diverse. All sorts of people come here. No pretensions."

"No pretensions?"

"Airs. Unlike my mother, no one puts on airs here."

"Got it. But wouldn't Burger King have been as cheap?"

"Wait till you taste the food."

Steaming eggs arrived with crisp bacon and hash browns. Dennis watched as Tulip dumped on ketchup and dug in. "Good! But who could screw up eggs?" she asked.

Dennis took a huge bite of burger. "Joe."

Tulip hiccupped with laughter. Embarrassed, she looked around. She gasped. *Marshall!* He was paying his bill, the chain dangling from his pocket.

"What?" asked Dennis.

The man turned. Tulip let out her breath. "I thought it was Marshall."

Dennis reached for her hand.

"Geez, we were having a good time, then I have to freak out. I hate it when I do that."

"You're safe with me."

Dennis did not know what Marshall was capable of. There was no way Dennis could protect her.

In the car, he kissed her lightly on the lips. "I hope you're not disappointed. For now it's diners. But when I have money, I'll take you to fine restaurants."

Tulip pulled away. "I wouldn't know how to act in a fancy restaurant. I wouldn't fit in. I got baggage."

"Baggage? You mean the kids?"

"No. It's me. I'm always on the lookout for danger. Scared." Her voice was harsh. "You saw me in Fleetwood. I see Marshall everywhere I go."

Dennis held her face to his chest and caressed her hair. "So you were frightened. That's one of the things I like about you. You're real. You show your feelings. You told me about it."

"Some things are better not said."

"We can talk about anything."

"No! Talking can't solve everything. There are things about me that you don't want to know." Tulip slid to her side of the car. "Maybe we could just have sex."

He reached across and took her hand. "We can't *just* have sex. I care about you and you care about me. Like it or not, we have a relationship. But you're afraid of intimacy, afraid of being hurt."

Something snapped. "Right! You'll go to college, leave, forget me soon enough."

"I'm not going anywhere. We have two universities right here."

"Your mom hates me."

"She's worries."

"And why wouldn't she? You're dating an older woman with a passel of kids. What do you know of life? You're just a kid yourself!"

Dennis's eyes sparked. "Damn it, Tulip! Age does not insure maturity!" He jammed the car into gear. He did not speed or run lights. He did not look at Tulip, nor did he speak or walk her to the door.

Grace sat on the couch with a book. "I didn't hear you drive up. Did you have a good time?"

Tulip glared at her. "Don't start, Grace!"

"I just asked you if you had fun!"

"I don't want to talk about it!"

"Oh." Grace took a long time fluffing the couch pillows. "The kids went to bed about nine thirty. Tucker popped the corn himself. I helped him clean up the mess." She closed the book and walked toward the door. "Good night."

"Thanks," Tulip mumbled to Grace's back. When the door closed, Tulip shut off the lights and felt her way upstairs. She was ashamed. She had unjustly taken her anger out on Grace. In the bathroom, Tulip studied herself in the mirror. Her eyes were dull, cheeks one huge freckle, hair a mass of frizz. She looked like she felt—damaged goods.

Tulip had fought with Dennis, but unlike any other fight she'd had, he had not struck her. He had accused her of fearing intimacy. True, she had never been close to anyone. Marshall thought he owned her, and when they fought, they cursed and called names. Dennis's words were—well, loving.

Tulip tossed and turned. In her dream, dogs chased her to a cliff over a deep ravine. Dennis stood on the other side, holding out his hand. She teetered on the edge, unable to reach it.

Next morning Tulip's head throbbed. Although she ached to pull the covers over her head, she stumbled out. When Tucker spilled his milk, she screamed at him and then felt like shit. At work, footsteps hammered on the pine floor and customers seemed to shout. She was nauseated and feared she might vomit. Finally she asked Sam if she could leave work early, saying she wasn't feeling well and needed a couple of hours to rest before the kids came home from swimming.

When she drove in, Dennis was waiting on the porch. Her heart leapt. "What are you doing here?"

"I called Kirby's and Sam said you were on your way home."

"Aren't you afraid your mom will see you?"

"Remember, she loaned me the car. She knows I had a date."

"With me?"

He grinned. "No, with Tucker."

"We just had a fight!"

"Yep! That's part of a relationship. I'm giving you a chance to apologize."

"Apologize!"

"On second thought…" He took her in his arms and kissed her right there in front of God and everybody—everybody being Grace, who was walking out to her car. She waved. They waved.

"We've got some unfinished business, Tulip." He took her hand and led her into the foyer. He lifted her chin. "Well?"

Her breath caught. "I—I'm sorry. I get so scared."

"Me too." He held out his arms.

Some things are private. Not always secrets that tear you apart, but sometimes intimate memories that linger and rise up to comfort you when you need them: the smile on the porch; the kiss; his holding her hand and leading her up the stairs. Tulip felt like a budding flower, unfurling in warm sun.

Click.

40

〜9

G race stepped out of Tulip's house into the dark night, dark as her mood. Tulip had no right to take her anger out on her. In her home, there was no one to greet her. Even her animals were asleep. She made a cup of herbal tea and sat across from Kirby's chair, where she imagined him looking up from the newspaper.

Well? he asked.

"I'm so angry! After all I do for that ungrateful woman and she treats me like I'm the enemy."

You shouldn't take it personally. You know she's a loose cannon.

"A lot of help you are!" She waved her arm at the empty chair and took her cup to the kitchen. The children's peanut butter cookies were still on the counter, their rich, nutty smell inviting. One bite. Instead, standing there fuming, she ate one and then another and another.

"Fatso! Go to bed," she said.

Bereft, she covered the cookies, put them in a drawer where she could not see them, and went upstairs.

The phone rang, waking Grace from a restless sleep.

Tulip's voice was tense. "Grace, thanks for taking care of the kids." Silence. "And I'm sorry I sniped at you last night." The phone clicked. Seven, too early to be calling. Now Tulip should apologize for waking her.

At nine sharp, Prudence knocked at the door. Unlike Tulip, she was a woman who knew proper manners. She held up a bag. "Got some coffee? I brought cinnamon rolls. You look tired. Having trouble sleeping? I did after James died. Sometimes I took a little nip before bed. That helped. Finally it got better. Now I just fall asleep when my head hits the pillow." She paused for breath. "Except when I'm worried about something. I…"

Grace rubbed her aching head. "Are you worried about something, Prudence?"

Prudence sighed. "It's bad enough, them dating. But like you told me, I'm staying out of it. It's not like I have anything against her. But a while ago at the bakery, *he* walked in. And he *threatened* me! I was so scared. I didn't know what to do."

"Dennis?"

Prudence threw out her arms. "No! Tulip's husband!"

"You mean her ex?"

"He smelled like a brewery!"

"What did he say?"

"'Tell your kid to stay away from my wife, or else I'll…!' Then he shook his fist at me."

"Did you tell Dennis?"

"Class. He's at class. Grace, that guy was appalling, foul. He had this bushy beard with food stuck in it, a thick chain on his belt loop connected to something in his pocket—probably one of those ninja things." Prudence voice reached a crescendo. "What if he goes after Dennis?"

Grace tapped the counter. "Calm down. Marshall's a spineless bully who limits his abuse to women and children. Call the police. And as a precaution, we should all lock our doors." She did not tell Prudence that Tulip and Dennis had had a fight so he might be falling off Marshall's hit list. "Sit down, have some coffee."

Prudence sat. "You're so wise. Just telling you helps. I'll call the police." She jumped up. "Oh, I forgot. I've a practice with the organist. I sing a solo Sunday." She flourished the bag. "Hot out of the oven." She tossed it to Grace and tripped toward the door, her heels clicking on the linoleum.

Cinnamon sugar wafted through the kitchen. Depend on Prudence to bring her exactly what she did not need. Tulip's nastiness last night, waking her this morning, and now Marshall on the warpath. Grace was trembling with exhaustion, or maybe she was frightened. In an effort to calm herself she walked outside to the picnic table, coffee sloshing from her cup.

It was a lovely day, the sun bright but not yet hot, a brilliant red cardinal perched on the feeder, her obese squirrel scavenging on the ground. When Grace went back inside to fetch bread for the squirrel, the tantalizing sweet smell lingered in the kitchen. After last night's cookies, she should not be indulging in a sweet roll.

Grace tossed the bread. The squirrel scampered away. She brushed off the picnic table and made herself comfortable. The roll was soft, a bit doughy, the glaze just right. The greedy squirrel skittered back and grabbed a hunk of bread. Standing on his haunches, he took little mincing bites. "Nice of you to join me. I hate to eat alone." He picked up the last bit of bread and scooted up the oak tree. She laughed. "So even you disregard me."

Working off calories, Grace busied herself sweeping the porch. Other than birds chirping, it was quiet, but she felt uneasy, as if she were being watched. Across the street at the end of the block, a car, black, the color of Marshall's, parked. The driver remained inside. Strange. Grace locked her door, put Pepper on a leash, and walked down her side of the street. The man in the car appeared to be asleep. A beard all but hid his face.

Marshall?

The dice on the mirror were gone, the car muddy, the license plate unreadable. Pepper pulled on the leash, taking Grace farther down the street. It would be too obvious if she turned back right then, but she didn't want the man leaving before she called the police. She hurried around the block.

Pepper stopped short. Grace tugged on the leash. Pepper squatted. "Hurry up with your business." Grace hadn't thought to bring a plastic sack. She looked to make certain that no one was watching and left Pepper's offering to fertilize the grass. The car was still there. She hurried into the house, locking the door behind her. Maybe it wasn't Marshall, but it was suspicious. She called the police.

In what seemed an eternity but was less than ten minutes, a patrol car pulled into her drive. Grace opened the door. Tulip's policeman tipped his cap. "Ken Gordon, ma'am. Something about a strange car in the neighborhood?"

"Yes, it was parked at the end of the block. The driver seemed to be sleeping. I couldn't tell for certain. I thought it might be Tulip's ex-husband. You know he's threatened her. Today he menaced Prudence." The words tumbled out and Grace hoped she was making sense.

Policeman Gordon nodded. "I checked the surrounding area, no cars on the street. What was the make?"

"I—I don't know.

"You didn't get the make?"

"I was trying to read the license plate. It was covered in mud."

"Big, little, new, old?"

He was using kindergarten words for a daft old woman. Grace answered curtly, "Newer. Marshall has a Fairlane. I was worried about Tulip...sorry for the bother."

"No bother, Grace." His reassuring smile covered most of his thin face. "You can't be too careful. And Mrs. Goodwin alerted us to the threat. You did the right thing. Marshall has a short fuse. All three of you should lock up, be on alert. Don't hesitate to call." He tipped his hat and backed away.

He'd seemed concerned, his words staccato, and he'd been almost familiar with her, more like a concerned friend, calling her Grace. How much had Tulip told him? Maybe the cop did care for Tulip. Perhaps Grace should talk with Tulip and Prudence about the car, but she didn't want to alarm them needlessly.

Grace was frightened, needing the comfort of her husband. She took the last bottle of Miller beer from the fridge, opened the kids' chips, and eased into Kirby's chair. Tabby leapt onto her lap and licked her salty hands. Pepper curled at her feet waiting for crumbs. Grace held up the can. "Kirby, you'd never guess what happened." She took a sip, then another, then set it down. "How could you drink this? And why am I stuffing myself?" She pushed the recliner back, closed her eyes, and breathed deeply.

She woke to the rustling of the chip bag. Tab batted it to the floor and leapt from her lap. Pepper grabbed it, shook it, chips scattering onto the carpet. Tab nibbled. Pepper crunched. She should have put an end to it, but she watched as the two of them cleaned up the floor.

The next day, when Grace walked Pepper, she spied a mud-splattered black car turning the corner. But what would she say if she called the police? "Someone in a dirty black car just drove down our street?"

41

❧

B-r-r-ring. Tulip rolled over, buried her head under the pillow. *B-r-r-ing—b-r-r-ing.* Sunday was the one day she could sleep in. *B-r-r-ing—b-r-r-ing—b-r-r-ing.* She grabbed the damn—no, darn phone. "Who?"

"Tulip, I'm coming over, making breakfast for you guys."

"Dennis! You woke me up!"

"The sun's shining, a great day."

She pried her eyes open and looked at the clock. "It's just 7:30."

"Don't the kids get up early?"

"Did you get glazed raised doughnuts?"

"Better."

"Custard-filled long-johns?"

"I'm cooking, and I want to get over there before the kids fill up on Cheerios."

Tulip was pissed Dennis had called so early, but she held her peace. After all, he was going to make breakfast, but he'd better bring groceries or there'd be slim pickings. She yawned, fumbled for some shorts, washed her face, pulled her hair back in a ponytail, and checked the kids. Hunter lay on her back, arms and legs extended, her little body attempting to claim the entire bed. In the boys' room, Ernest stirred, sat up, and plopped back down. Tucker, wrapped in his blanket, snored softly. Tulip crept downstairs. Outside it was pleasant, cool even, but the sun was promising a hot day. Grace's saucer-sized red, yellow, and orange zinnias called to her. She popped over and picked one of each.

Carrying a Kroger bag, Dennis met her on the walk. "Flowers for the table, perfect. And so are you."

Tulip giggled and pecked his lips. "You're the one who's perfect."

Dennis tossed the sack on the counter. "I have your favorite—eggs, bacon, potatoes for hash browns, and for the kids, squishy white bread to toast." He held up a bottle. "Want a cocktail?"

"*Real* orange juice! And you remembered what I ate at Fleetwood."

He kissed her, his tongue finding hers.

"Hmm!" She curled her arms around his neck.

He patted her bottom. "Don't distract me. I've got a meal to prepare."

"I'll set the table."

"Nope." He guided her to a chair. "The kids will do it when they come down."

Tulip watched in amazement as Dennis skimmed the potatoes with the ancient peeler and chopped them effortlessly with a dull knife. He tossed the pieces into the sizzling grease, held up the spatula, and grinned.

She formed a box with her left hand and pressed a button with her right pointer finger. "Click."

"What are you doing?"

"Memory pictures."

"Memory pictures?"

"Moments I want to remember."

He smiled. "Get your camera and we'll take some of the kids."

"My ex has ours. D took pictures when we lived with her. Haven't got around to getting one." *Liar, liar pants on fire.* As though she had a dollar to spare.

Footsteps on the stairs. Three sleepy-eyed kids stood in the doorway. Dennis popped an egg in the skillet. "Hungry?" He rested his hand on Tucker's shoulder. "How do you like your eggs?"

Tucker screwed up his face. "O-o-over easy, s-s-sunny side up."

Dennis's gaze met Tulip's. "Sure, Scout, anything you order."

Tucker beamed. "C-c-can I help?"

"Sure." Dennis handed him a spatula. "Turn the potatoes."

With both hands on the spatula, Tucker carefully turned the hash browns. Hunter sidled over to Tulip's chair and climbed onto her lap, her head against her mother's chest. Tulip laid her cheek on Hunter's hair and whiffed a combination of Breck shampoo and salty, sizzling bacon—the best smell ever.

42

⌒⊙

Dressed in faded pedal pushers and Kirby's denim shirt, Grace retrieved kneepads and tools from the garage shelf. Occupied with the children and store, she had allowed weeds to engulf her neglected flowers. Planting seeds and watching them push through the loose earth, grow, and bloom had been important before. Now that she was beginning to feel the warmth of the sun, the cool dirt on her fingers, she ached to get on her knees and dig. And after an hour when she rose to her feet, her body would have a different kind of ache, but a lightness, a sense of accomplishment.

Outside, Dennis, Tulip, and the children were playing ball. Dennis pitched to Tucker, who swung wildly. "Watch the ball, Tucker." Dennis moved closer and tossed the ball gently. The bat made contact. The ball bounced to the ground and rolled a few feet. "Great, Tucker, you're getting the hang of it."

Dennis hollered to Grace, "Come play! We need a third baseman."

Grace laughed. "When we played ball at school, I was the last chosen." She thought for a moment. "Fifty years. It's been fifty years."

"Then you're overdue."

She pointed to her kneepads and shook her head.

"C-c-come on, Miss Grace. We need you."

"No way, Tucker. I'm too old."

"P-p-please!"

It was a lamebrain thing for her to do, but Grace could not tell Tucker no. Dennis pointed to third base. "We have a pitcher, catcher, basemen, and a batter. I'll start as pitcher, Tulip as catcher, and three of you will be basemen. That leaves one person to bat and run. We'll rotate."

Hunter pulled her baseball cap over her eyes. "It's dumb. We don't even have enough people for a team."

"You go first, Hunter," Dennis commanded.

Grinning sheepishly, Hunter picked up the bat. Dennis threw a slow ball across home plate.

"Strike!" Tulip called.

Hunter stomped her foot. "Was not!"

"Concentrate. You can do it," Dennis called. He pitched a bit slower, again over the plate.

Whack! The ball flew toward second base. Tucker lurched after it, fumbled, scooped it up, and tossed it toward Grace on third. Hunter cleared third. Grace walked to the ball and tossed it wildly toward Tulip. Hunter started for home.

Tulip stood on her toes and caught the ball. "Out!"

Hunter glared at her mother. "Why'd you have to catch it?" She slouched out to relieve Ernest, who was up next.

Ernest missed the first pitch. Dennis threw the ball again and Ernest swung.

"Strike two!" Tulip hollered.

Ernest planted his feet and took a couple of practice swings. Dennis wound up and threw a ball over the mound. *Thwack!* The ball hurtled into the outfield. Ernest cleared first, second, and third. Too late, Hunter retrieved the ball and tossed it to Tulip.

"Home run!" Dennis shouted.

Tucker jogged up to bat. His bat thumped the first ball. It flopped to the ground near his feet. Yelping, he trotted toward first. Dennis strolled toward the ball, waited until Tucker cleared the base, and tossed it to Grace, who threw it to second. The ball followed Tucker home.

"I-I-I d-d-did it!" Tucker flung his arms around Tulip.

Hunter shook her head and muttered to herself. Grace knew her mantra: "Not fair, not fair."

Dennis motioned to Grace. "You're up."

"Me? I can't."

Tulip picked up the bat. "I'll go. Grace, you catch." Tulip took a wide stance and swung the bat wildly. "Watch the expert!"

Dennis threw his leg up and swung the ball in circles. "Strike one! Strike two! Come on, Tulip. You can do it." He hurled a fast high ball. Tulip tilted her bat up and swung hard. *Whack!* The ball flew into Prudence's yard, bounced against the house, and landed in dense ivy.

Tulip whooped and did a victory lap.

When Prudence pulled into the drive, Ernest was pawing through her ivy. She scooted out of the car, her broad-rimmed pink hat catching on the door jamb. Pink heels clicked on the pavement. Everyone stilled.

As if conducting a ragtag orchestra, Prudence waved her arms down to stop discordant music. "Dennis Goodwin, this is where you were!" She pointed at Ernest and yelled as Grace's high school chorus director would have. "You are tromping my ivy!"

Dennis spoke soothingly. "Ball, Mom. We're playing softball. Grace is playing. And we need an outfielder."

"Humph! I have better things to do on a *Sunday* morning!" Prudence wheeled and stormed into her house, the door slamming behind her.

"Who does she think she is? The fun police?" Tulip asked.

Dennis shook his head. "Could be she thought we'd had our fun quota." He turned to Grace. "You're up!"

"You bet!" Grace was not going to let the prude spoil her fun. She clamped her hands around the bat.

Dennis moved her hands apart. "You'll have more leverage."

Grace swung the bat as she had seen Tulip do. Tulip moved back out of her way. The first pitch was slow and easy. Grace's wild swing did not connect. The same with the second. She wiped perspiration from her face, planted her feet, and took some practice swings.

Tucker called, "C-come on, M-Miss Grace, you c-can do it!"

The pitch was slow, waist-high. Grace tapped the ball. It flopped to the ground six feet in front of her. After she cleared first, Dennis moseyed over and tossed the ball toward Tucker.

"Go, Grace! Go, Grace! Go, go, go!" they chanted.

Grace hustled around the field, the ball always behind her. As she reached home base, arms raised in victory, her foot slipped—twisted. She slammed to the ground, pain shooting up her leg. Stupid, stupid! An old woman acting like a kid.

"Safe!" The words came from a tunnel.

Dennis bent over her. "You're bleeding."

Grace touched her cheek, felt warm blood on her hand.

Ernest picked up a piece of clear, jagged glass that had been hidden in the grass. Grace remembered her concern that the children would be roughhousing, that someone would get cut, but she had not thought it would be her. She lifted her throbbing ankle. "I think I sprained it."

"Guess you had your fun quota," Hunter said.

Still dressed for church, Prudence rushed out and pushed through the circle. Bending down, she applied a wet cloth to the gash on Grace's cheek. "I don't think you'll need stitches." She sighed, in what Grace hoped was relief. Still, Prudence glared at Grace. "You should know better than to be running bases at your age!" She turned to the team. "This game is over!"

Pain subsiding, Grace lay on the dewy carpet, looking up at the clouds, the sun peeking through. She had not lounged in the grass for decades. It felt decadent, naughty. She giggled. "I made a home run!"

No one laughed. No one applauded.

Prudence took charge. "Dennis, you help Grace onto her porch. Tulip, you cleanse the wound, stop the bleeding. I've got Epsom salts at home. Ernest, you go find a pail or pan big enough for her to soak her foot. Hunter, you and Tucker put the bat and ball away, pick up the bases. And check for more glass while you're at it. This yard is not safe!" High heels digging into the grass, she tried to hurry home.

"Geez," Tulip said. "Now she's the emergency room director."

"You never know." Dennis hooked his hands under Grace's arms and gently hoisted her to a standing position.

It felt good being cared for, Dennis and Tulip supporting her weight, the warmth of their tight bodies, the male and female scent of their sweat. Between them Grace hopped along, one foot skimming the grass. In an earlier time, when she was young and vain, she had worn spike heels and twisted her ankle on a crack in the sidewalk. Kirby had swooped her up and carried her into the house, her arms tight around his neck, inhaling his pungent man-smell. Inside the bedroom, he had unhooked her nylon and tenderly worked it down her leg and over her foot. He stroked her ankle. She moaned, not in pain, but in the pleasure of his touch.

Dennis eased Grace onto the porch swing. While Tulip went for medical supplies, he untied Grace's oxford, gently prodded and turned her ankle.

"Ooh! Don't twist!"

"Sorry. I don't think it's broken. You've survived sliding into base."

"I did not slide. I slipped."

He grinned. "Was it worth it?"

Tulip appeared with a warm soapy rag and dabbed Grace's cheek. "This is all I could find," Tulip said, holding up a three-by-three gauze patch that would dwarf the wound. She slathered on iodine and taped the patch in place.

Still in pink but minus her heels, Prudence returned holding a tray with lemonade, cookies, and a box of Epsom salts. "I thought you'd be thirsty."

"Oreos!" Hunter made a beeline for them.

Prudence lifted the tray. "Go wash up!"

Chastened, the children traipsed into the house. Grace wiped her hands on the washcloth and handed it to Tulip. "Trying to make up, are you, Prudence?"

Prudence wagged her finger. "At your age, Grace! You should know better than to play ball with a bunch of hooligans."

"I beg your pardon!"

"How was church, Mom?"

"How was *church*? Your mother sang a solo while you organized the neighborhood death squad!"

Dennis slapped his head. "I forgot. That's why you're so mad."

"I am not! If I were angry, would I do this?" She flourished her hand at the kids, who were now intent on consuming the entire package of Oreos. "When I got up this morning you were gone." Eyes piercing, she puckered her lips. "Did you come home last night?"

"You *know* I was home last night."

Prudence's voice rose. "You were gone this morning!"

"I was making breakfast!"

Her face scarlet, Prudence screamed, "Breakfast! So you slept in your bed all night, got up, and went to Tulip's to make breakfast?"

The children's heads pivoted from mother to son. In their experience, angry voices led to blows.

Hunter screwed up her face. "Dennis did make breakfast!" She slammed down her cookies. "And you can keep your damn Oreos. They're probably poison anyway."

"Hunter!" Tulip yelled. "Don't talk to Mrs. Goodwin that way!"

"She was being mean to Dennis!"

"That's between her and Dennis. You apologize."

Hunter looked to Grace for help but Grace nodded.

"Sorry," Hunter mumbled. "But you were being mean." She ran into the house.

"Well!" Prudence exclaimed.

"Sorry," Tulip said.

After they left, Grace remained on the porch. What a wreck the morning had been. She was too old to be playing softball. She must have been a sight, hobbling around the bases. And the drama with Prudence—that woman tried so hard, but she couldn't contain her jealousy. She did not understand that when children were grown, mothers became peripheral; they were the cheering section, encouraging and admiring from a distance. Grace visualized Dennis walking out the door, his mother latched onto his legs.

Hunter came out of her house, checked to see that no one had seen her, and walked pensively to Grace's porch. "Are you all right?" she asked.

Grace nodded and motioned for Hunter to sit. She sidled in beside Grace and they swung slowly, listening to the creak of the swing. Finally Grace asked, "Something on your mind?"

"It's not right her shouting at Dennis like that."

Grace put her arm around Hunter. "No, it's not."

"I thought she was going to hit him."

"People can get real mad and still not use their fists."

"When Dad got mad, he hit Mom and sometimes Tucker. Tucker shoulda hid."

"It must have been frightening."

"I shoulda stuck up for Mom."

"You were little; he was big. You couldn't."

"When I stand up to bullies I get in trouble. Like with Tucker and that big kid. I know Dennis is a grownup, but I just get so mad."

Grace pulled her close. "You're a loyal friend. It's hard to know when to intervene or let people work it out. It's something you learn from experience."

"Like you?"

"Hunter, *you* put an end to the yelling."

"Then how come Mom was so mad at me? She's always mad at me."

"Sometimes when you speak out, even if it's the truth, people don't want to hear it. But you can learn to do it without making people mad."

"What do you mean?"

Grace chuckled. "Do you really think Prudence would poison us?"

Hunter puckered her lips. "It's not fair."

"What's not fair?"

"Mom loves Tucker more."

Grace stroked her face. "No, she doesn't. But you're right, life isn't fair. It's not fair that Tucker is not as smart as you that everything is harder for him."

"But Mom *is* nicer to him."

"He needs her help more than you. A parent has to give to each child according to the child's needs."

"She does more for him."

"Oh, Hunter! How do I help you understand? Each day, he meets failure. He stutters, is uncoordinated, can barely read the comics. You are smart, athletic—also very pretty." Grace kissed the top of Hunter's head. "Believe it or not, life will get easier. You will be successful. Tucker will always need extra help. Today we helped him make a home run—one home run. He'll remember it all his life."

Hunter jerked away. "But I know she loves him more!"

"He asks for it. He accepts love and gives it. It's hard to show love to a prickly cactus."

"I'm not a cactus!" Hiding tears, Hunter looked toward the floor.

"Come here."

Hunter hesitated, then snuggled into Grace's arms. Grace removed Hunter's cap and smoothed her snarled hair. Cushioning Hunter between her breasts, Grace willed love into the stringy little girl. After a while Grace felt her relax, Hunter's body molding to hers. Sun's rays spread across the porch, birds chirped, traffic hummed on the next street.

A black car snaked to a stop on the next block. Headlight-eyes watched her watching them. Hunter stirred; Grace pulled her closer. A man walked out of the house and down the sidewalk to the car. The motor revved. The car sped around the corner and out of sight.

43

At seven a.m., Tulip crawled out of bed to say goodbye to her children, then back for more shut-eye. It didn't take a minute and she was dreaming: she sat under a tree, listening to Dennis play a guitar.

D and Kathy had taken the kids to Cedar Point. Kathy's idea; she loved the Blue Diamond. D hated roller coasters but would risk an upset stomach for Tulip's children. Although Tulip mentioned going, D had winked and said, "You could use a day to yourself." Then, when Tulip told Dennis the kids would be gone, he had mumbled something about working. She'd been disappointed, even hurt, but she would make the best of it. Had she ever had a whole day just to herself to do whatever she wanted? She would begin by sleeping in. Curled around her pillow, she did just that.

There was a soft knock at the back door, another. It creaked opened. Footsteps on the stairs, in the hall, in her room. "Good morning, Tulip."

Tulip sprang up, hammer in hand. "How the hell did you get in?"

"I knocked. You didn't answer. The door was unlocked...you sleep with a hammer?"

Tulip had not seen hide nor hair of Marshall or Calvin for weeks, but they had a habit of lying low and then striking. Although she always had to be prepared, she made light of it. Tapping Dennis with the hammer, she laughed. "I have my weapon. And you'd better be careful, sneaking up on me!"

"Oh, Tulip, I would never ever hurt you." He kissed her lightly on the lips, then cheeks. Brushing hair from her eyes, he smoothed her forehead. "We have a whole day, just you and me."

"I thought you had to work"

"Wanted to surprise you."

"You scared me."

"Sorry. I don't want you to be frightened, ever." His hands wandered down her arms.

Too much goodness. "Are we in kindergarten? Are you tracing my body?"

Dennis laughed. "Great idea!" He opened his hands and inched his way up under her arms then slowly down her body. His tongue swirled around her belly button. His face on her stomach, his hands continued their journey down hips, thighs, calves, and ankles until he reached her feet. One by one he kissed her toes. His hands circled her ankles, worked themselves up inside her legs.

Tulip gasped. "Thank you, D, for taking the kids!"

He cradled her head, his dark eyes burning into hers. "This is not just sex."

"What are you saying?"

"I think I'm in love with you."

Tulip froze. Love! Her voice faltered. "You can't be. I'm older…got three kids…"

"They need a father, and I love them too."

"You have two more years of college."

"I could go to Eastern, work at Kroger. After I graduate, I'll find a good job."

"What about med school?"

"What about it?"

Tulip pulled away. "I thought you wanted to be a doctor like your dad."

"The doctor business is Mom's idea."

"You'd be a great one." Damn, why was she taking Prudence's side?

"I'm not so sure. There are other things I want more." He nuzzled her hair.

No matter how she tried not to, she'd imagined waking up with Dennis, his coming home to her, the five of them sitting down to supper. If only she were younger, smarter, hadn't made so many mistakes. If only—she went limp in his arms. He held her, rubbed her back.

Dennis whispered, "Let's make love."

"I haven't even brushed my teeth."

"I love your smells: dish soap, burnt lasagna, paint. Any smell you conjure up is perfume to my nostrils."

He jumped up and flipped off his belt. Tulip gasped, then blinked away the picture of her dad whipping out his belt.

Dennis took her in his arms. "You're trembling. What's wrong?"

"Bad memory."

"I'm here now," he murmured. Her breathing slowed and she curled kitten-like around him. Soothed, she floated in the warmth of his caresses. "Oh, Tulip, I do love you." His touch became insistent, tingling, electrifying. Her hands greedily grasping his body, her hips moving in rhythm, she rose to meet his passion. She gave herself over to the most indiscernible, delicious sensation. She felt him melt into her, become a part of her.

Cocooned together, they slept.

Tulip woke to Dennis staring down at her. "Wake up, sleepyhead. Get dressed. I have more surprises. I'm making breakfast." He pecked her cheek. At the door he blew a kiss. "Hurry up now."

Totally satisfied, feeling safe and cared for, Tulip stretched, waved her legs in the air, and crossed them back and forth, scissor-like. Nice legs. Maybe it wasn't a pipe dream, her and Dennis.

Salty, smoky bacon called to her. She hauled herself up, started to make the bed, then simply pulled up the covers. She looked in her closet for something pretty: a couple pair of jeans, shorts, and several stained T-shirts. She pulled out a pair of shorts that in a former life had been jeans and scrounged up a shirt, blue like her eyes. She splashed water on her face, brushed her teeth, and stuck her hair in a ponytail. He would just have to take her as she was. Leaving the bathroom, she glanced in the mirror. Radiant! No other word for it—a radiant woman stared out at her. *Click.*

Dennis kissed her nose and pointed to a box wrapped in newspaper on the kitchen table. "Sorry about the wrapping. I didn't want to ask Mom where the gift paper was."

"Looks like Tucker's wrapping." Terrific. Insulting the only guy who ever gave her anything.

Dennis grinned. "I like your appreciation."

"Sorry." She picked up the box and tore off the paper. Her eyes flew open. "A Polaroid! You bought me a camera?"

Again he kissed her nose. "I knew you wanted one."

"I—I don't know what to say."

"Thank you would work."

Tulip threw her arms around him. "Thank you! Thank you!" The words came easily.

"Film's in it. Aim, push the button, wait a minute, and you have a picture."

Tulip's hands trembled as she pulled the Polaroid from the box. She pointed it at Dennis and clicked the lever. Slick, smelly paper rolled out of the camera. She counted off the seconds. Dennis tore off the covering and there he was, grinning from ear to ear in front of a skillet of eggs.

44

The garage-sale fan died—a good death; it had not taken Fluff with it. Thinking the whirling blades were skittering mice, the cat had stalked it. Night after night, Tulip had tossed Fluff out of her bedroom and shut the door. Now, although the door was open, the room was pressure-cooker-hot, and without the whirring of the fan, the house seemed eerily silent.

She harrumphed. She, who had been so independent, not needing a man, needed Dennis. She felt safe with him—whole. When he was not with her, a part of herself was missing. He was her goodness. He'd bought her the Polaroid, no strings attached. He knew she wanted a camera and just went out and bought it. She remembered their day together, a whole day, sitting with him in the grass at Riverside Park sharing a hot fudge sundae, his kissing the chocolate from her lips. Being with Dennis was like walking out of storm clouds into a sunny spring day. She sighed. Must get to sleep. Pretending it was him, she hugged her pillow and drifted off.

The floor creaked. Warily she opened her eyes. In the moonlight she could just make out a shape. "Tucker?" Silence. Then another creak. "Tucker, is that you?"

A grimy hand slapped across her nose and mouth. "Don't make a sound!"

Yanked out of bed, arms twisted behind her back, she was shoved out of the room and propelled down the stairs, her feet barely touching. In the kitchen she fell against the counter, her arm knocking the money jar. It teetered precariously.

His face next to hers, she gulped in foul smoky breath. "Lansing! You're supposed to be in Lansing!"

The dim light of the street lamp outlined his rotten teeth and beady eyes. He panted into her ear. "Shhh, little sister. I've come back for a *visit*. Did you miss me?"

"You son of a bitch!" She elbowed him and struggled from his grip.

He punched her, his ring digging into her chin. She stifled a scream. *Calm, stay calm, don't, can't wake the kids.*

"Miss High-and-Mighty in her big house! Siccing the proby on me! Think you could get away with it? I've been watching you."

The stench—whiskey—drunk. He couldn't last long. She wasn't that kid. She could talk him down. "You're out of prison. You're working, a chance for a decent life. You don't want to mess it up."

He snarled, "Shit job. Fired! What's this?" He grabbed Hunter's jump rope from the counter and slung it around Tulip's neck. He spat, putrid phlegm pelting her face. "I could kill you!"

The rope tightened. Tulip twisted, fighting for air. She managed a whisper. "You're drunk. Don't do something that will make it worse…sleep it off…on the couch. We can figure it out in the morning."

The rope loosened. Calvin's eyes focused. He looked toward the living room. "Sleep?"

"Yeah, I'll get you a blanket." *Yes, pass out on the couch.*

"Slut!" He punched her in the stomach, hurled her into the counter. His brick-hard prick dug into her. The rope cut into her neck. A weapon, she needed a weapon. The damn bat was in the hallway. The knife—the paring knife. Had she left it out? Her fingers scooted across the counter, touched the blade. He wrenched her forward. The dull knife thudded to the floor—useless. *Talk—talk—try to talk!* She croaked, "Why? Why? You know…?"

"What?" The rope went slack.

"About Tucker."

He snarled. The rope tightened.

"It's true, Calvin!" She gasped. "You know it's true."

He jerked the rope. Tulip kneed him in the balls. He threw her onto the floor, leapt on her. Other than his panting, silence. Her head spun. The world darkened. *R-r-r-rip.* Her pajamas! No! Not this time!

The blade glinted in the moonlight. Tulip wrenched her arm free and stretched her fingers toward it. She felt the rough handle. Gripped it. Growling, she plunged the knife into his side.

"Bitch!" He reeled backward and slumped to the floor.

Horrific pictures flooded her head: all the times he'd hit her, hurt her, all the terror and hate. She staggered to her feet and kicked him in the gut.

He grabbed her leg. "Stop! Stop! You're killing me!"

"You shit-bastard! You deserve to die!" She wrenched her leg away to kick him again but slipped—blood? Her fucking brother's blood! The knife dropped from her hand and slithered across the floor. Her legs buckled and she grabbed the counter. Calvin pulled himself up and lurched toward the door.

Sirens pierced the air. Light flooded the room. Grace stood in the doorway clutching the baseball bat, her white nightgown billowing around her. "Are you hurt?"

"M-M-Mom—?" Tucker cried out. His hundred fifty pounds plummeted into her.

Tulip held him tightly, as much to support herself as to comfort him. "It's OK, Tucker. It's OK. Grace called the police."

"Tucker did! Tucker called the police!" Ernest whispered from the hallway, holding Hunter's hand.

Sirens blared. Cars skidded into the drive. "Stop! Stop! Or I'll shoot." A shot rang out. Muffled voices. A car door slammed. Then silence.

Tulip motioned to Hunter and Ernest. They ran to her. She held them close, willed her gasping to still.

Two policemen, guns drawn, stormed in the door. "Tulip, Tulip, are you all right?" Ken demanded.

"Yes! Yes!" She laughed hysterically.

Grace spoke soothingly to the children. "There was an intruder, but your mom handled it. See, she's fine. Now she has to talk with the police. Let's go upstairs. She'll be up in a while and explain." She stroked each child's head.

As she herded them toward the stairs, Hunter asked, "Why was that man hurting Mom?"

Ken guided Tulip into the living room. "What happened? You're trembling. I'll get the afghan." He tucked it around her and gently raised her chin. "You're going to have a bruise."

"Did you shoot him?" Tulip asked.

"Shot in the air. Tackled him. The guy's crazed. Who?"

"My brother…" Tulip nodded to the rookie. "You might as well both sit down. This is a long story."

After they left, Grace came downstairs. "They're asleep in your bed. You sit. I'll clean."

Trussed up mummy-like, Tulip sat on a chair and watched Grace scrub blood from the kitchen floor, the floor she had just mopped. Depend on Calvin to make a mess.

Her barefoot angel rubbed Tulip's neck. Teeth chattering, Tulip leaned into her. "You know what I was thinking? That he would steal my roof money and that I'd die before I let him do that. Isn't that silly? If I was dead, it wouldn't matter, now would it? I'm so cold…thanks, Grace. You're always here when I need you. So strong."

Grace enfolded Tulip in her arms. "You've been to hell and back. You're the strong one, and watching you grow has been a sort of gift. You and the children have enriched my life."

Pointing toward the bucket, the water red with Calvin's blood, Tulip chortled. "This?"

Grace laughed. "I know what will help. It'll settle us both down. I'll be back in a minute." She wrapped the blanket more tightly around Tulip and led her into the living room where she sank onto the couch.

Shortly, Grace returned waving a bottle of Jim Beam. "On such a night, Kirby'd be pleased to have us finish this off." She raised her juice glass. "To a gutsy woman, who," she giggled, "has saved me from a boring old age."

Although Tulip hated whiskey, she tossed it down. Heat jolted her throat. She sputtered, coughed, took another swig. Her head felt light. When she could finally talk, she asked, "How'd you know Calvin was here?"

"Couldn't sleep. I was making a cup of herbal tea. I thought it was Marshall's car in the drive. I didn't think. I just ran over. Your bat was in the entry. Good thing the police came or I might have done him some real harm."

45

B-r-r-ring, *b-r-r-ring, b-r-r-ring.* Seven a.m. Tulip fumbled for the phone. "Dennis, it's too early to be calling."

"Not your boyfriend."

Her heart thumped. "Marshall?"

"I need to talk to you."

"And I need child support. Where have you been the last six months?" She could hear him breathing. "Marshall, you can't scare me anymore. I've faced worse than you. I got a good job and the kids are doing fine." No answer. She screamed into the phone, "What the hell do you want?"

"I hit bottom."

"What?"

"Yeah, Tulip. I'm an alcoholic."

"So?" Hell, she knew that.

"I'm in a twelve-step program. I got to apologize. Can you meet me at Joe's?"

Tulip could not imagine Marshall participating in AA meetings, taking responsibility for his threats and violence. She did not remember a time when he'd ever apologized. Well, maybe once or twice when they were first married. It was so long since she'd had a conversation with him that she'd forgotten how his normal voice sounded. She groped for words. "How do I know that this is on the up-and-up?"

"Damn it, Tulip, why do you think we're meeting in a public place? I'm supposed to apologize, not scare you."

Somehow his tone when he said "damn it" was Marshall, the one before Tucker was born, angry but not yet mean. She *had* been married to him. The children were his, and Grace said no one was all bad. She must have forgotten about Calvin.

After Tulip hung up, she wanted to call Dennis, but if Marshall made trouble, what could he do? She dialed Ken's number.

Shivering, she dressed and brushed her teeth. Splashing water on her face, some sloshed on the mirror. She wiped it and gazed at the woman peering out at her. Clear blue eyes, shiny hair curled around a tanned face. This was not the beat-down woman of three years ago. She forced a lopsided grin. "You can do this." She stepped out of the jeans, thumbed through her closet, and pulled out a navy skirt and blue sweater. She would be home before the kids were up, but just in case, she left a note.

By the time she reached the restaurant, Ken, camouflaged in civvies, sat in a back booth, his nose in the *Ypsilanti Press*. She nodded, he nodded. Tulip hurried to a booth on the other side of the restaurant. She was relieved that Joe wasn't working. Last thing she wanted was him snooping around. Workmen and businessmen who had no wives to cook for them were chowing down on eggs and pancakes. Or just maybe they let their wives sleep in. She should be safe... that is, if Marshall didn't bring a gun. *Don't be a scaredy-cat! Remember the woman in the mirror.*

The door swung open. Marshall stood in the entrance, plaid shirt wrinkled but clean, new jeans and a Band-Aid on his smooth cheek. "Hello, Tulip."

"Cut yourself shaving?"

"Still at it, Tulip?" He sat. Picked up the menu and stuck his face in it.

"Well? Did you call me for breakfast or do you intend to apologize?" Her voice was icy.

The menu fell from his hand. "Damn, Tulip, this is hard!" He smacked his hands together and twisted them. His fingers were bare, the wedding band long gone. White skin marked the spot where the serpent ring had lived. "I hit bottom. Lost my job. Got picked up for DUI. But that's not why I'm here." His voice shook. "I—I'm...sorry."

"That's it? You're sorry? You beat the shit out of me, scared the hell out of the kids, don't pay child support, and you're sorry? That's it?"

Crazy Eye twitched, then shut. He slumped back against the seat. In the past what she said would have cost her a trip across the room.

"I *am* sorry. I've been out of work a lot. I apologize for hitting you, for scaring the kids. I never treated you right. I can't remember a time I wasn't angry, aching for a fight." He chortled. "My dad taught me good." He clasped his hands, opened them, and then, as though he'd been deprived of oxygen, took a deep breath. "When I met you, you were so pretty. I was crazy about you. I couldn't believe my good luck when you married me. I thought you could make me better. But you were sort of off in la-la land...cold even. I couldn't make you love me. I tried to beat it into you."

"You didn't think I loved you?"

Crazy Eye flickered, then stilled. "I'm not stupid. I know why you married me."

Tulip's breath caught. "Is that why you hate Tucker?"

"I don't hate Tucker. It's just that…well…"

Tulip leaned forward. "Why didn't you say something?"

He shrugged. "Wouldn't have changed anything."

Best to let sleeping dogs lie. Tucker must never know the truth. Tulip sank back into the booth. "This is an apology?"

"It's the truth. I was angry and a drunk even before I met you. I took it out on you."

"So?"

"I'm going through the program. Anger management. And I got me a job at Tecumseh Products. Don't make as much as I did at Ford. They'll take child support out of my check. After a while, after I prove I'm not the devil, I want to see the kids. I'd like to be a different kind of dad to them than my dad was to me." He clapped his hands on the table. "That's all I wanted to say." He stood and pointed toward Ken. "Tell your cop friend I won't be bothering you." He walked to the door, thumbs in a narrow brown belt the same color as his loafers.

Ken stepped up to the booth. "You did it?"

She nodded.

"Good girl! Call me if you need something." He saluted and hurried out the door.

All those years she had thought of Marshall as the enemy. But, like her, he had been broken. If she had been honest with him, could it have been different?

"Sorry to be so long," a harried waitress said. "What would you like?"

To relive my life. Tulip smiled. "Nothing." She corrected herself. "I don't need anything." She laid a dime on the table and went home to her children.

Tulip rinsed her hands under cooling spray arcing from the hose. The grass was greening, tuffs from seeds she'd sown in the spring. Like her, it had been scorched, half dead, and now revived. Amazing what the right mix of water and sunlight could do. Calvin was in prison. True to his word, Marshall was paying child support and she could pay her bills.

Marshall had stunned her. He knew. He had kept her secret, a secret that could only hurt and confuse Tucker. Tulip basked in a feeling of feathery lightness, as if she had been caked with dried mud and now stood in a shower, warm water washing over her, dirt melting away, disappearing down the drain.

Tulip was in love. She needed Dennis like flowers needed sun and water. She imagined him living with her. She'd wake to the smell of coffee and bacon. He'd go to school, she'd go to work. They'd fix up Old Grouchy. They'd all paint. Dennis would put up new shutters. At the best part of her dream, Prudence came out on her porch, stood for a moment eyeing Tulip, and then marched toward her—a mother bear protecting her cub. Tulip geared up for the attack. Some mother-in-law she would be!

Prudence was dressed normally in pedal pushers, T-shirt, and sandals, hair slicked back in a ponytail. "You're looking good, Prudence," Tulip said, meaning she didn't have on her war paint.

Caught off guard, Prudence smoothed her T-shirt. Her voice was hesitant. "May I talk with you?" She motioned toward her house.

Tulip hung onto the hose and braced herself. "Here's fine." No way was she moving into enemy territory. If worse came to worst, she'd hose Prudence down.

Prudence smiled, more of a grimace, and thrust an envelope addressed to Dennis Goodwin toward Tulip. It was from Bowling Green University.

Tulip waved it away. "I'm not reading Dennis's mail."

Prudence pocketed the letter. "I didn't know if you'd believe me. Bowling Green is offering Dennis a full scholarship. We knew he was an alternate." Her pleading eyes locked onto Tulip's. "He says he won't go."

"He's going to Eastern."

Prudence sighed. "His father graduated from Bowling Green, and they're offering Dennis a full scholarship." She lifted her chin. "*You* may not understand what that means."

"A full scholarship? I may be poor but I'm not stupid."

Prudence sighed. "Of course not."

"You want *me* to tell him to go to Bowling Green?"

Prudence's voice was nearly a whisper. "He's passing up a great opportunity. You're the only one who can convince him."

Tulip jerked back. "Why should I?"

Prudence opened her hands, pleaded, "He'll just be a few hours away. And it's not forever. If you truly love each other, you can work it out." She shrugged. "I thought you should know. You're more mature than he is."

Tulip's blue eyes widened. "You think so?"

Prudence nodded. "I was younger than Dennis when I married, crazy in love. I didn't finish college. I didn't know who I was or what I wanted. Dennis's dad molded me into what he thought a wife should be. It didn't work out well, not for me or for him." She touched Tulip's arm. "Please, just think about it." Walking slowly, she returned to her house.

Prudence had not been arrogant or condescending—a word that Tulip had just learned. She wanted the best for her son. Tulip would have felt a whole lot better if Prudence had picked a fight. Dennis was smart and would make a terrific doctor. He should go to the best school. But how could Tulip compete with lily-white, sophisticated coeds? Even if she and Dennis did get married, what would it be like in twenty years? Tulip pictured her mother, all used up at fifty, graying and bent—a picture she did not want in her memory file. Dennis would be a doctor, maybe a surgeon, and he'd have this wrinkled, hillbilly wife.

Tulip put her thumb over the nozzle and battered the marigolds until they flopped onto the ground, yellow heads driven into the dirt, some severed from their stems.

Dennis had splurged on a bottle of merlot. He raised his glass. "To our future." Tulip hesitated, then clinked her glass to his. A celebration of sorts. They sat by a window at Haab's, having just ordered dinner, juicy London broil.

For this occasion Tulip had sprung for a new tailored dress, navy blue, slim in the hips, with a Peter Pan collar. She'd brushed her hair behind her ears to show off the silver hoop earrings Dennis had given her.

"Nice dress," he said. "But different from what you usually wear."

"Too conservative?" she asked, her cheeks burning. "Maybe I'm trying to compete with those sophisticated rich girls you'll be in class with."

"Nah. The clothes, the hair, their impeccable manners—they look like my mom. You can't tell what's under their veneer. *You* are real, honest, down to earth." He chuckled. "I know exactly what I'm getting with you."

"A hillbilly?"

"I love your humor."

That stopped her dead. Compliments didn't come her way too often. Still, she had to ask, "Humor?"

"Funny with a bit of a bite."

"You think I'm sarcastic."

"Well?" He put his elbows on the table, held up his knife and fork, and waited for her reaction.

A few months earlier Tulip would have been offended, and maybe she still was, but he had a point. She giggled. "Put down your weapons. I'm not going to fight."

Dennis made chitchat. Tulip listened and waited. He ran his finger over the knife to check its sharpness, sliced the meat, then used his left hand to fork it into his mouth. With the dull knife he expertly buttered his roll and Tulip's. She pictured him mincing tomatoes, pointy edge first, a swift cut, then more until small pieces covered the platter. He would scoop them up and lay them on the lettuce, then dip his hands into the salad, gently rolling carrots, onions, and tomatoes through the lettuce until all was blended. Tulip couldn't keep her gaze from those knowing, expert hands.

Then, although the restaurant was not cold, Tulip shivered. A different picture—Dennis wearing rubber gloves, a patient on the operating table. He picks up a scalpel.

Prudence's words haunted Tulip: "I was young. I didn't know what I wanted...you're more mature than he is." More mature than Dennis? Not her. But what if he did come to regret tying himself to a ready-made family, missing opportunities? She could not bear to see him unhappy, and worse, for him to grow to hate her.

He had to tell her. They had to talk. She shook her head.

"Something wrong?"

"The way you take care of people...you'll make a great doctor."

"Maybe." He spooned the last of the melt-in-your-mouth chocolate mousse from the bowl. "For you." He brushed crumbs from the table, took her hand in his. This was it. He was going to break it to her. He reached into his pocket and brought out a small velvet box. His dimpled smile and pointy ears reminded her of a festive Christmas elf, totally out of place.

"What?"

"Hope you like it." He flipped open the lid. A sparkling opal, pink and green, circled by tiny diamond chips—the prettiest ring she'd ever seen.

"Put it on. See if it's the right size."

She wanted to grab it before he took it back. Instead she placed her hands in her lap. "What exactly does this mean?"

He blinked. "I wanted to get you something nice, pretty."

Tulip's mouth fell open. Sweet, sweet Dennis. But how could she take this ring that they both knew meant more than just something pretty? Her voice was a whisper. "Don't you have something to tell me?"

Onyx eyes twinkling, he leaned toward her. "Like what?"

"Your mom talked to me."

He reared back. "What do you mean?"

"The scholarship."

He stiffened. "She told you about Bowling Green? You didn't need to know about that. I've made up my mind. I want to be with you. I'm going to Eastern."

"You should have told me. We should have talked about it. You can't begin a relationship with a lie."

"I didn't lie."

Tulip's voice rose. "You kept it secret!"

His perfect hand banged the table. "It's my business. She had no right to tell you!"

46

Tulip burst into the office. "I've got to talk to you."

Grace looked up from the card she was reading.

"I've been thinking and thinking about it. He lied to me. I trusted him and he lied."

"What?"

Tulip plopped into the chair across from the desk. "We went to dinner. He knew, and he didn't tell me that he got the scholarship!"

Grace opened her hands. "That's an omission."

"Isn't that the same?"

Drumming her fingers on the desk, Grace spoke thoughtfully. "He invited you for a nice dinner. Perhaps he didn't want to spoil it. You don't know that he would have kept it from you. Hadn't he just received the letter? He may have needed time to think it through."

"Oh…I never thought of that."

Grace cocked her head. "And when you confronted him, did he deny it?"

"No."

"Not a lie, Tulip. Why do you think he didn't want to tell you?"

"Said he wasn't going to Bowling Green."

"Figures. Dennis acts suave, older than his years. Probably learned it from watching his dad—one smooth man. But Dennis is inexperienced. You're his first love. He's afraid of losing you."

Tulip inhaled, puckered her lips, and blew. "If he stayed here, he'd have to work full time. He'd have me and the kids hanging on his shirt. He might drop out."

Grace's mouth twitched in a slight smile. "Or he might be motivated to do well."

"You think?"

Grace shrugged. "I wish I knew. This is something you and Dennis will have to figure out."

I got it. Me and Dennis need to talk. This is so d—darn complicated. I thought you could tell me what to do." Frowning, Tulip left the office, quietly closing the door behind her.

Grace shook her head. "Oh, Kirby, if only you were here. She thinks I'm a wise old woman, that I have answers." She folded the card, the one with the construction-paper heart, and worked it into the bulging folder. When had she given it to Kirby? Perhaps she'd been Tulip's age. She smoothed the file and put it in the drawer.

When Rickey died, Grace had been half dead with grief. Tulip's brood had wakened her, given her purpose. In spite of their problems, they brought sunshine and laughter into Grace's dreary house. After Kirby died, Tulip nudged, pushed, and finally forced her back into the world of the living. Now Grace was busy with the store, her garden, Tulip and her children, even that mutt Pepper. And still it was not enough. No matter how tired she was, how exhausted, when she slipped between cold sheets at night, her thoughts were of Kirby, and her body ached for him.

Tulip had been misused, abused. Finally she had found love. Yet Tulip could entertain the thought that, for his sake, she might have to give Dennis up. If she could persevere, surely Grace, who had known love and been cared for, could give up her endless grieving.

She lifted Kirby's "dad" mug and held the cool porcelain to her cheek. He had laughed with delight when Rickey presented it to him. It was a memory she would cherish. Comforted, she tucked the cup in her desk drawer. Next week she should check out the senior center. Perhaps she could make some friends closer to her age, maybe learn to play bridge.

Tulip had fallen into Grace's life as a prickly cactus unable to give, unable to receive. Now Tulip was more like her name, bright petals unfurling in the sun, easily scorched but rising each spring. The young lovers would work it out. Together or not they would be OK.

They had to be. And so would she.

47

⌒᠊ᢒ

Late August, fickle weather was beginning to flirt with fall and lanky zinnias reached in vain for the sun's warmth. Although rain had greened tuffs of grass, weeds still towered above. Fingers tracing the dusty window ledge, Tulip gazed at the scene before her.

Dennis was loading his secondhand green Ford: suitcases, hanging clothes, bedding, record player. Nervous-bird Prudence fluttered from house to car and back again. "Got it covered, Mom," he hollered. When the car was packed, Prudence ran into the house and back with Dennis's roller-skates. As he took them, he looked toward Tulip, his gaze meeting hers. She pictured him with a skinny blonde coed, skating through Bowling Green's campus.

As though to draw him to her, she placed her palm on the cool windowpane. The night before, after dinner, after dishes, after the children had said tearful goodbyes and gone to bed, she and Dennis had finally been alone. They clung to each other, Dennis making promises that Tulip was not certain he could keep. But she knew he meant them. When he left, it felt as though a part of her had been ripped away. She was wounded, with a sort of raw openness that would heal but leave a scar, a love scar, memories she would want to keep.

With heavy feet, Tulip climbed the stairs to the bathroom. Lifting the money jar from the counter, she jingled the coins, distracting herself from her pain. Yes, the roof, she thought. She gazed ruefully at the woman in the mirror. If not for those blasted freckles, not bad. Attractive even, with curly red hair and sky-blue eyes—someone she would like to know. She ran a comb through her hair and dabbed on lipstick. Squaring her shoulders, she walked down the stairs and out the door.

Dennis stood on the porch. Holding her, his face nuzzling her hair, he whispered, "I love you. I—I don't want to let you go."

"It's only a few hours away." Tulip's mouth twitched up in an attempt to smile. "It'd be worse if you'd been drafted, if you had to go to Vietnam."

He groaned and pulled her tighter. In spite of her resolve, tears streamed down Tulip's cheeks and onto his T-shirt. Taking the tail of the shirt, he wiped her face.

"I'll call, write, come home first chance." He kissed her lips, his tongue finding hers.

He wrenched away and walked to the Ford, where he embraced his tearful mother. Then, waving, he drove past Tulip.

Prudence gazed at Tulip and mouthed, "Thank you!"

Tulip nodded, turned, and entered her home.

In the bathroom, huddled on the toilet, desperate for something to hang onto, Tulip picked up the roof jar, heavy with coins. They'd made a game of it, clinking every spare bit of change into the jar, guessing how much was in it. Even Hunter had added pennies. It was time. Tonight they would break it open, sit at the kitchen table, and count their treasure.

Tulip thumped down the jar. She would call that sad-sack Bill guy, the one who roofed in winter.

Yes, by then she would have enough.

30361374R00154

Made in the USA
Charleston, SC
13 June 2014